Even a Pandemic Can't Stop Love and Murder

Even a Pandemic Can't Stop Love and Murder

VOL. I

Break the Bank

A.E.S. O'NEILL

ISBN 979-8-9851224-0-4

*To my wife, Nadine Caputo, for freeing my
writer's soul from the bondage of fear and
doubt. She allowed me to reclaim my true
Creator who first spoke to me at age twelve.
She lives on in Ginger.*

Contents

Friday 7 p.m., the story begins—and in seven days, at 11 a.m. Saturday, it is done.

Acknowledgements

In 1994, over lunch in Manhattan, my father told me the story of a crime at a mob bank that is the core part of this story. He was there. Why? Because he worked for the mob.

My incomparably beautiful wife, Nadine Caputo, upon hearing this tale and how much I had been thinking about it, said as if it were the most obvious thing in the world: "So just write it." She freed my creative heart. I was married when I began this book and a widower as I write this.

My friend, Beth Goehring, an editor in New York, who encouraged me: "Ninety-nine percent of people have a book in them. One percent write it. You've done that." She put wind in my sails.

My spiritual guide and friend, Jesse Frechette, who led me to a place where I was able to channel these lives through me into words. He taught me "soul."

To my big sister, Kate O'Neill, for being loving, patient, kindly blunt and supportive in ways that make me stronger every day; I am blessed beyond words to have her in my life. (Always listen to your big sister!)

Rosie Pearson, who edited the book with uncommon skill and wisdom. In her open-hearted, spiritual professionalism, she has given me a great gift. Meeting her confirms that there are no coincidences. In Rosie, I trust.

Last, my dearest and lifelong friend Douglas Greenfield, who came to visit me after my mother died, having known her since he was five. As he was leaving, I asked him, "What should I do with my life?" Gruff and loving, he did not hesitate: "I don't know, but I do know Nadine and I want you to finish that damn book!" We lost Doug a few weeks later, but his love let me understand what being a vulnerable male was about.

So, thank you everyone, I love you all—and because of all of you it *is* done.

Always have the reader feel like the main character has a knife at their throat.

—Lee Child

The greatest thing you'll ever learn is just to love and be loved in return.

—"Nature Boy" by Eden Ahbez

No illusions, lots of hope.

—Ida Mae Egan, my grandmother

Prologue: Away-Time

…then to sum it all up, there was the daily round trip in the Humvee, riding through the winding streets of Baghdad to the power plant at the edge of the city. One contractor, a skinny guy from Ohio, was obsessed with getting killed on the ride—first thing in the morning, always, and then again at the end of day, when he was clearly tired from the heat and dust and chewing furiously on his fingernails as he told Alby and anyone in earshot about his solution for all their fears; he was the only one not masked. Just count to one hundred over and over and over until they got inside the gates of the plant or back to their hotel. Everyone already knew it was dangerous—the Iraqis were still angry at the US vaccine debacle around Covid-22, only fear of variants kept the demonstrations under control. The space was tight, but Alby always tried to sit away from him—but then so did everyone else. The Humvee was only so big. The skinny guy was like someone muttering over their rosary as the world was ending—it just made the ride worse.

Through the squared-off Humvee windows, Alby caught glimpses of busy sidewalks, interrupted by the occasional wreck—the aftermath of a car bomb. Even in the cool Humvee, sweat soaked into his clothes like there was a hose inside his shirt.

Ahmed Hussein was always the last to be picked up. He was college-educated, fluent in English, and oddly oblivious to all the turmoil going on around him (was it possible to be that optimistic, blind, or stupid?). No, Ahmed was *not* stupid. He was a trained electrical engineer and Alby's liaison for the rebuilding of the plant. Truth be told, Ahmed should have been the supervisor, but Alby was the "American contractor" and for some reason, Ahmed did not seem to resent that.

Alby was just not used to kindness. His well-honed North Jersey gruffness kept people away. But Ahmed said hello every morning with a hand to his heart and a slight bow—it was still considered a personal choice to shake hands and the traditional Iraqi kiss on both cheeks was long gone.

Not even settled in his seat, Ahmed went off like a rocket, speaking in one long sentence as they bumped their way to the power plant. It was as if he were the narrator of the trip, and in his monologue, he helped drown out the fool's counting. Although half of what he said was lost in the noise of the Humvee, Ahmed just had a relaxing manner. Everyone else was holding their breath, waiting for trouble. But not Ahmed. He would sit and mindlessly chat to Alby about dinner the night before, his family, nieces and nephews, sister, the plant, and the day's tasks. Never once did he bring up the war or politics or the failed treaty—or the fact that it was still Americans getting the well-paying Iraqi jobs. It was as if he were immune to the world. Alby admired him for his attitude in the middle of what looked like hell to him. Over time, he wore down Alby's barriers; it wasn't long before they were taking their lunch breaks together and soon after that, he invited Alby to his house on Sundays for coffee—which turned out to be a big cultural ceremony. Alby had never bothered to study Iraqi culture or history—it was just a job in a dusty, hot, and dangerous place.

"Come for coffee Sunday," Ahmed had said with a smile—a warm, welcoming, open smile. Alby was not used to being treated so well. It made him uncomfortable, but it had a pull he went with.

Over the last several weeks, after the coffee was prepared and served, Ahmed's sister began to join them for part of his visit. Aliyah. She had a college degree and had worked in the Hussein government as a bookkeeper before the invasion. Her English was perfect. Alby tried to look away but not before he saw her dark eyes greeting him, or how as she turned, her face became a perfect profile.

Relaxing in their courtyard at the center of the house, the small fountain cooling the air, drinking bitter, thick coffee, Ahmed's sister with them…this is what an oasis is, thought Alby, watching her retreat into the house.

Sundays became the thread that tied the weeks together—before that, the concept of time had meant nothing in Iraq. Day led to day led to day, a mindless circle, which he had been fine with…until now. Now he had Sundays.

That one Sunday, lunch and afternoon siesta done, he headed for Ahmed's house; it was only a five-minute walk from the Green Zone. Ahmed had always come and collected him at the Green Zone entrance. Now, after visiting these past months, he felt that he could go into the unguarded streets, despite what the mercs had told him at the hotel they lived in. The Iraqi guards on the street corner gave him a stare as he walked by alone. But Alby felt safe leaving the Green Zone—he was just a construction worker, not a soldier or merc.

The same storekeepers, always perched on a stool or old chair outside their stores, would nod to him, no expression but in a recognition that said it was okay to be there. Alby didn't care. All he could think of was Aliyah. He could only focus on how often he had had a peek of her or when she had joined them for longer than a few minutes.

Alby felt excited as he pushed the buzzer, with the door opening to a smiling Ahmed in response. Alby took three steps in, then something slammed into his right shoulder like a battering ram. He whirled like a windmill, arms spread wide. As he fell to his knees, a Marine, in full combat gear, appeared behind him in the doorway and he heard a shot ring out. Ahmed had immediately run into the house. Alby knew Aliyah was nearby. He had felt her presence, then had seen her black headdress. Now, a red bloom spread from the center of her chest. It was not a flower.

Before that moment, she had never quite looked at him, always slightly averting her eyes, other than when Ahmed had introduced them on his first visit to their home, that moment when Alby had been instantly struck by how beautiful she was. Now, her look froze him.

She moved first, rushing towards him, the flower spreading, headdress falling partially off, black hair coming loose from its tight bun. He couldn't connect thoughts. He tried to stand up, his right shoulder searing as if it had been branded and then smashed with the iron. Gravity's supremacy held him down. But he fought it and stood, wobbling, only to see Aliyah twist backward as another shot rang out. From his peripheral view, he could see Ahmed lunging at him, a silver and black switchblade in his right hand.

Alby went out of body just before seeing a second Marine cock his gun and shoot Ahmed in the head. Yet, the shot did little to slow his momentum in Alby's direction—instead his body arched even closer, and with horrifying ease, he sliced him like a scythe, the blade swinging straight across Alby's right side, right below his ribs.

A roaring blender of colors and images tumbled around him. A slowly rising tide of voices, up and down, up and down, and then sirens. No, not sirens, the wailing of women; the familiar chorus of grief he had heard too many times in Baghdad, as the news of another tragedy passed through the neighborhood.

After he woke up in the hospital, he spent the first three hours just staring straight ahead; the view was a gray wall. He knew what morphine felt like, so he ignored his pain and resisted the morphine pump he could feel lying by his middle finger; he needed to clear his head and find out what the hell happened. The creeping sensation of something along his side was nagging him; it felt wet. He refused to look at it.

Then the door opened and a Marine, gun at half-mast, and another guy in all-black jeans and flak jacket, the outfit topped off with black sunglasses, walked in. Alby had seen these types before—private mercenaries, former US government, the Marine was there for presence—they all worked for the same company; they did the security for Bechtel and many others.

"What do *you* want?"

The black-suited one flipped open a square wallet and Alby got a glimpse of the logo and the title "Regional Director." After that, he put up his palm for Alby not to speak and started in.

Alby couldn't be sure, foggy as he was, but it seemed like the guy didn't breathe—he just started talking at Alby like he wasn't there. Alby caught up by the second sentence: "Radicals—they were planning on taking out the power plant once it was done. They were using you. Your pal Hussein was setting it all up."

"No, Ahmed wasn't that way," was all Alby could think of saying—speaking made his side ache. It could not be true. "Who are you?" he asked again, with a firmer voice, mind clearing.

The guy smiled as did the Marine standing next to him. "We handle the big stuff—not the really big stuff, but the stuff that can blow up later. Like you. Even though, in my book, you're an idiot. Dumb American that got duped. As far as the public story goes, you're a hero. True, you missed the US news cycle, but the BBC and the local papers covered it." He shook his head like he was talking to a child. "After what has happened lately with them hating us for not sharing vaccines, and bad batches, all this bullshit, we decided we needed a hero. You fell into the job—the contractor who instead of being a victim uncovered this ISIS plot and helped us take it down."

"My friends were not ISIS." Trying to sit up, his right ribs told him to shut up.

"Whatever. Who knows? You're probably right. Pick a group, any group, and it's all the Allah Akbar crap." The Marine snickered like some cartoon character, but somehow, nothing moved on his face.

"First, they weren't your friends. Friends don't try and kill friends—well, not usually. Call me…" he paused… "your Handler." The words leaked out smoothly like a card shark's first hand and he smiled. Then he reached over to pull the covers back from Alby's left side; the bandage was already black with crusted dried blood. The stain winding down his side looked like the Tigris from a satellite view. Alby averted his eyes.

"As soon as the docs say you're good, you'll be shipped back to the States. Just gotta figure out where you're going. Then start covering your trail so they can't find you." He paused. "Yeah, this whole affair means we now run your life. You are ours until we decide otherwise. It's like Witness Protection. But not. Simple rules. We keep you hidden and alive until this blows over. We say you move; you move. We say anything, your only answer is yes. That is how you stay alive. The people who are after you?" He shrugged. "You wouldn't see the bullet coming."

Stopping suddenly, he felt around in his black blazer side pocket. "Got you a gift." The Handler took something out of his pocket and put it on a table across the room and out of Alby's reach. He struggled to see what it was. No matter how he strained, his body could not rise off the bed. He caught the Handler smiling at his obvious pain. Where did they find people like him?

"Now that is a gift! Ha! He's giving you evidence!" Obviously delighted, the Marine laughed, finally relaxing his stiff at attention posture. He walked over and picked it up off the table. It was a black-handled knife. He flipped a switch—the blade sprang out. "We were nice enough to wipe off your blood before we brought it here," said the Handler. Then they both laughed.

It was the knife Ahmed had cut him open with. It was just then he realized she was dead, too. And as the idiot of the heart he always tried to deny that he was, he also realized that he had been falling in love with her.

"We'll be back when you're less doped up." The black suit (his Handler?) paused at the door. "You are under my care now. Do not fuck with us. You are going to live a very small life; you can keep your name if you stay off the grid. Go on the grid, you die, that simple. Do not get sloppy." They left and, in that moment, that singular moment in time, in searing pain, heartbroken, all Alby could see was that knife lying out of his reach.

This was the moment when The Rules were born. Like all dogmas, The Rules were the creation of an idle mind in a disturbed state. Lying there in the hospital in Baghdad, each 24 hours passed while he suffered a catalogue of petty slights—the first stitches so sloppy that they had to redo them, staff rude or indifferent as they changed his bandages or bedpan, the unending ache in the jagged line of his wound, noisy patients, noisy nurses. The thought "why me" kept sneaking into his mind, but he swatted it away. Who cared? There was no one to rely on. He needed to make his own defenses.

So there he was in pain, half-drugged, caught in a crevasse between a dull awake and a heavy sleep, and it all became clear: everyone thought the world had *rules*… one set of *rules*. But it didn't. There were different rules for different people. He needed his own Rules. Yes, he thought, as he stared at the ceiling of the hospital room, feeling his pulse throb like a metronome, muscles singing with pain—he was alive. From here on in, he would make his own Rules to keep it that way.

A career in construction work proved fertile ground for creating his Rules. There was a natural hierarchy: workers, supervisors, Owners. And the guys above the Owners you never saw. Each had a highly defined role in the caste system of construction and subcontracting. Every day reminded him where *he* stood—at the bottom, lacking the money, power, or connections to change anything. That was fine. The powerful were the biggest pricks anyway.

When he returned from Iraq, he had three duffle bags: clothes, shoes, and a pile of cash (he had spent hardly any of his highly paid hazardous-duty salary), with the promise of a small stipend from the Handlers (there were now two): "Enough to keep you off the streets." They had handed him a no frills-looking credit card at the airport, admonishing him with the words, "Only for food, no rent, no gas, nothing but food." These two Handlers were as no-frills as the card, looking like poorly carved duplicates. He was pretty sure they didn't know about the cash he had saved; on the last visit to pack at his hotel, the room had not been touched.

They didn't like that he would be living near known family, but after checking Dorothy out, they agreed, though they never said why. He hadn't flown since before the Pandemic. Cheap shits put him in coach for the long flight, and yes, he was double-masked, but as hard as they tried, and study after study, air travel still didn't feel safe; he felt like he was in a variant cesspool. Falling asleep did not feel like an option, as if when he was asleep, one would sneak in and he would get infected. Although it hurt like hell, he kept himself awake the entire flight to JFK by occasionally using the seat belt to rub against his still-raw wound as a reminder.

From wheels down in JFK, they had given him only eight days to close up whatever was waiting for him to do in North Jersey (and do it so that no one knew he was even there) and get to Cherry Hill.

In Jersey City, he had to get busy. He craved seeing some old pals, but he had seen the fatwah video on YouTube—he swore never to watch it again—and he was damned if he was going to slip. The Handlers had driven it home; right before he left Baghdad one Handler played the YouTube clip of some guy ordaining in Arabic that Alby was to die—they would find him—it was only a matter of time. Knives and swords took over the screen. The vengeance of Allah would not be unanswered. There were subtitles, which Alby thought was odd. Nonetheless, as annoying as it was, he followed the Handlers' instructions, he avoided old friends or distant aunts and uncles—just when he needed them most. It only reinforced to him how truly alone he now was.

The Extended Stay America hotel was in Fort Lee, far enough away not to run into anyone he knew and just close enough to his family's storage facilities where he had left his and his mom's stuff. As low-end as it was, the hotel was a thousand times more comfortable than his room in the hotel in the Green Zone.

He tore through the family storage space, taking and tossing without much thought. Renting the truck was easy, but all the lifting and activity only served to make his wound ache more with each day, so much so that he had to lie perfectly still in bed at night. The weak-ass meds they gave him didn't work, so he threw those in the toilet.

By the time he had been back in the US for a week, the last of the good painkillers were gone—no refills—and the nightmares began.

Occasionally, he thought of old high school buddies he could call; he'd reach for the phone, then stop.

On day seven, all the contents of the storage unit had either been trashed or stored—either way never to be seen again, he knew. All he took was a leather boxing bag that his mom had given to him when he got engaged. He had been a little annoyed and had asked her why. "Relationships are a contact sport." She had paused and then given him that odd look she sometimes got: "you'll appreciate it when you get back." When he asked what she meant, she did the typical response: smirked and looked away. How had she known he was going to Iraq?

On the ride to Marlton, he kept things silent, his head empty.

They had given him eight days; he did it in seven. Was this what they had called a *new life*? It felt phony and hollow; the Jersey Turnpike didn't help.

Their words rang in his ears: "Your job is to hide. You are now going to live a small life."

He was beginning to suspect a small life meant no life.

Friday: 7 p.m.

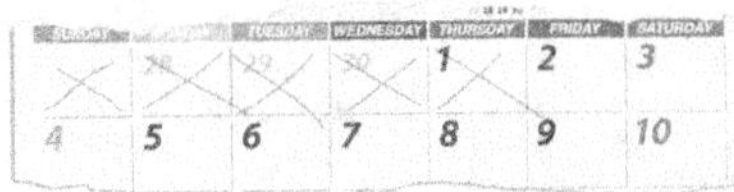

Stephen dropped down, exhausted, on the two-seater couch. "Damn, Alby!" he said, as he landed on the broken spring. "Where'd you find this? On a curb?" Alby said nothing because he *had* found it on a curb, but why admit it? Besides, Stephen had walked in just as he was finishing his morning virus Listerstrip routine. Stephen had used that line over a hundred times already. Alby went to the small refrigerator and offered him an iced tea. Stephen nodded and took it, swigging down half in one gulp. Alby never really liked cold drinks, so he went to the card table for his second coffee cup. Starbucks was an expensive habit, but he spent money on nothing else, so…

"Could've got me one, you know." Alby felt distracted; he had woken that morning with this deep sense that something wrong was going to happen. This feeling had lurked in his waking hours all his life, and every time had been proven right. He had once complained about it to his mom. She had given a sideways, unreadable glance and said: "Get used to it." The whole day had gone by and nothing bad happened; in one corner of his consciousness, he was waiting.

"Picked up only a couple. Besides, I didn't know you drank coffee."

Stephen could not help but groan. "You buy me one every time we have a morning job together."

"I stand corrected: I didn't know you drank coffee other than in the morning. It's dinner, right?" Stephen groaned again. He tossed his hair in a resigned nod. "Can I use your pisser?"

"You have to ask? Bathroom's small. No spraying!"

"If you hate it so much, move," Stephen told him. "I know plenty of apartment complexes you could probably afford. Get out of this hole in the wall."

A shadow passed over Alby's face. "Place is just fine." He had to change the topic. "Quiz time!" and continuing with a fake game show host voice exclaimed, "Rule number one!" Almost unconsciously, he took out the ebony switchblade and started opening and closing it as he waited. Alby had to wonder if Stephen was a masochist, the way he just kept wrestling with Alby's view on everything, which he knew Stephen was about to do again.

"Don't trust anyone." Stephen sighed and wiped a hand across his dirty forehead. "You really believe that?"

Alby held up a hand. "No, it's 'never trust anyone.'" He paused like it was an intellectual conundrum. "'Don't' implies there's some exceptions."

Stephen snarled, "Number two: Never do business with family or friends. You realize what a fucking hypocrite you are, right? I mean, I'm family and you spout out crap like that." Flashes of his mother colored Stephen's exasperation.

"Your grandmother hated foul language." Alby spoke with false solemnity; she had been as foul-mouthed a person as he had ever met. "I don't know where to start—on the nephew part or the fact that I made your mom a promise I'd get your sorry-ass some construction experience so you could work in this crazy economy. Teach you the trade so you can get a decent job with the infrastructure work." He realized he was getting sentimental. "Or is it the hypocrite part—oh, wait, I don't give a shit."

At that, Stephen got up and went to the bathroom. When he came out, it was like he'd never left the room…or the conversation. "Alby, you need to lighten up. That should be a Rule! It's like you just don't give a shit about anything. But I know you do." Stephen had taken his place back on the broken couch and was now crossing and uncrossing his long and currently stretched-out legs, knocking his feet against the floor in an attempt to loosen the dried dirt that had been caked into the heels of his steel-toed boots onto an already stained throw rug. Alby looked up and shook his head but only replied to Stephen's comment.

"Name one thing."

Stephen shrugged; he was not going to take the bait.

Alby picked up a pen and wrote on a piece of paper already covered in scribbles that was taped to the wall by the desk next to a cheap-looking gas station calendar highlighting a picture of an old DeSoto by a gas pump. "Yeah, I like that…Rule number seven: don't ever give a shit."

"And the good thing is," Stephen was on a roll now, his voice coated in sarcasm, "it doesn't run into that other Rule about not falling in love."

"Right. That's six."

"Yesterday it was seven. You make it up as you go along. You know, it just occurred to me—why would you of all people waste a whole "Rule" on love?"

Alby ignored him. Truth was, he didn't know why he had a Rule for love. He just did. "Not true. The first six are sacrosanct. Uncuttable."

"Immutable."

Alby cut him off. "Your vocabulary will make you a great foreman." He paused and then took the jab: "That is, when you get a real job." He closed the switchblade by folding back his fingers and forcing the blade into its sheath. Stephen had the impatient look of a man wanting to leave and his actions followed through accordingly. He got up and said, "Gotta go home and get ready." He nodded as if to confirm his thoughts, pulling back his right shoulder like it had been out of place—the body action of a contractor who worked his parts too hard. "How'd the Ghoul Crew work out? Still not sure how you landed it."

"You're cute." Alby gave him an unfunny smile. "Clever." He paused. "And useless."

"Hey, Alby, you gotta admit…picking up a crew on a corner in Camden at 7:30 at night is a little risky. Morning is fine, but night? No one goes into that place after the sun goes down, especially a white guy. And that asbestos is messed up."

"This isn't some zombie movie!"

"You sure? And we gotta keep you alive so you actually show up at my mom's party. No excuses." Stephen retorted, then cracked a smile.

"You done? It's my job. I got it. Money's good."

"Asbestos removal is bad shit. Bad. One lungful and you are done. And that bank you're working at, it's got a bad rep—"

"I am so glad I hired the EPA—you wanna switch jobs? That's why I hired the Crew to do the nasty work while I just hang out, sleep, and pick them up at dawn and make money. Take my cut off the top." Alby watched as Stephen passed by him and headed for the door, looking down at his phone. He began tapping away at the screen.

"One of our house frauen—I mean—customers?"

"Alby, I have a girlfriend. Let it go."

"Maybe I'll meet her someday." Stephen's face twisted a little, like he had eaten something sour, as he started to push on the screen door. But instead he turned and said, "See you later!" Then he paused. "You *are* coming, right? My mom really expects you." Stephen gave him a snide laugh. "She has someone she wants you to meet. Thinks you're perfect for each other."

The groan just slipped out: "I could not think of a more insane thing than my sister knowing what is 'perfect' for me—her as my matchmaker? Scariest thing I've heard today."

Stephen laughed his "be nice" laugh; after all it was his mother. "You can actually leave the cave occasionally, you know," he threw in as he exited the screen door.

The door slammed shut only to bounce off its frame and swing back open. Time to drive to Camden, Alby thought, and bent down to pat the sock on his right foot to feel the comfort of the switchblade.

He had been to Camden only twice, all in the last week. Although he lived less than five miles away, he hadn't known it was there; it was like some hidden island. Now, he understood why: they had constructed a force field around the ghetto part. It was cut off. The radical transition from glossy suburb to rotting ghetto was too abrupt—like passing through some psychic filter where you went from color to black-and-white.

Driving slowly was the only way to read the unfamiliar, graffiti-scarred street signs and the sun didn't help right then the way it was shining at that awkward angle when the shadows play tricks on the eyes. His left hand was tight on the steering wheel, the knuckles white; the other hand was loose, ready to slip down to his right side and grab the waiting crowbar. He twisted his body slightly to the right to feel the press of his switchblade, which he had moved to his jacket pocket. The Ben Franklin Bridge loomed like a metal arrow, one end sweeping into the ground in Camden. Seeing the bridge lights come on as dusk settled, he realized that after a year, he had yet to even go to Philadelphia. Explicitly ordered to keep a low profile, after he arrived in Marlton and Cherry Hill, the thing that was protecting him made him unable to score a big job in the huge infrastructure work being done in Philly and elsewhere in Jersey. But with the recent semi-lockdown in Philly, he wasn't going anywhere.

Growing up in Jersey City, he had seen plenty of ghettos: Orange was a disaster, as was Newark. Baghdad certainly had its share of the Iraqi version of ghettos; in Iraq it was easy to tell ghettos from bombed ruins. "It was easy," he recalled a GI telling him as they had driven to the plant, "because ghettos don't have big round holes in them." Even now, Alby could still remember the sweat in the overheated Humvee, even while feeling a chill at the laugh that the GI let loose after he spoke. But he was right; Camden felt different—a square-mile petri dish of Hell. Dangerous, but nothing near the danger he felt when he had taken the morning Humvee to the power plant. At least here he didn't have to worry about the same type of deadly man-made evils. It felt more desolate than dangerous. The Pandemic's impact on black people made the whole place feel abandoned. Like so much while he was away, he missed it, but he knew enough to know it was a bad, bad story.

Part of the eeriness of this part of Jersey was the way things changed so quickly from one extreme to the other. One block would look like people had enough money to keep up appearances, with neat row houses, all the same design, clearly built at the same time, and well-lit by streetlights. Then, the next block was as opposite as you could get; a corner streetlight would be out and any feeling of safety along with it. It seemed that in Camden, those kept-up stretches were the short ones.

As Alby drove farther down this particular block, he could see that there were some people around but mostly they were barely visible on their porches. Some were rocking in chairs, some were standing, but all were behind the cast iron bars closing in their tiny front spaces. A lot of them were holding onto the metal bars, and he could make out masks on some but most without them. They were the cheap kind, the blue tissue ones they originally used at hospitals before they got smart.

One-handed, he slowly spun the wheel to turn left at the corner into the empty lot on 4th Street. In the dusk, men milled about, glued together in small clusters. He eased to a stop.

He saw the bright, wide grin of the guy who was definitely the leader of the trio: a smiling Lucky with his two pals, Chance and Darnell, none with masks on. Instinctively, Alby slid his mask from the hook by the steering wheel and slipped it over his ears; he clicked the right side and the whole mask sprung around to click the open mouth shield into position with the frame on the other ear. These Warby Parker Plastimasks were expensive. To Alby, normally not given to shopping, with all this bubbling news and mis-news about a new deadly variant hitting the States, he wanted the best mask. It was worth it: you could actually see people's faces and read their expressions; whether they were honest reflections of what they were thinking was another story.

Alby had no idea how old any of these men were—they looked more worn down than old. Lucky had more lines on his face but that could just be the tracks of a tough life. He just wished that the man would stop smiling at him; it was like having a shark stare at a fresh meal.

"Mr. Alby!" Chance yelled, as if they were old friends, waving his hand and giving an annoying almost clown-like smile as he approached the truck. "Not too close," Alby called out. Even with six vaccines, half of which were new, who stood close to anyone these days? Between variants and efficacy curves, you felt like you were just a yard ahead of the Devil.

Lucky swatted Chance away. "You heard the man. He got Pandemic Jitters." Lucky laughed like he had known Alby for years…they had met once. Alby pointed to his mask, and they nodded and put theirs on; all had the cheapest ones, and Chance's had deep gray sweat stains. Alby rolled his window down halfway. Since everyone had a smartphone and his wasn't going off with the Covid Tracer alert, they had to be vaxxed. Or they could have had their phones hacked. Unconsciously, he adjusted his plastimask. He watched in the rearview mirror as the three of them climbed into the bed of the truck.

Alby felt good as he drove over to the bank; the job foreman, Fat Joe, had already faked all the paperwork and licenses needed to work on such a hazardous site. Of course, Alby didn't mention he was skimming twenty percent off the top of their four nights of graveyard shift work. From the looks of Camden, any money was good money. For Alby, it was all about getting fix-it jobs and keeping as busy as possible, which was tough with this hot-and-cold, open-and-shut, economy.

When they got to the bank, it surprised him to see the usually nondescript, square, four-story building turned into a full-fledged job site. The normally jet-black building was dressed in white. It was a scene caught in frantic motion—klieg lights, trucks, dumpsters, barrels, men in hazmat suits streaming into the building. Large translucent sheets of plastic fell from the roof over the windows and covered about a third of the exterior. Alby pulled his truck alongside the trailers where Fat Joe, his pear-shaped body swiveling around, mask hanging off each ear, pants hanging loose on his short body, sat on the steps outside his trailer. He shouted at Alby. "Drop them by the front door; the inspector will take it from there."

After he did that, Alby parked and walked up to the trailer. Taped to the door was a piece of paper with sloppy block letters in black marker on it: LIMIT TO 5 PEOPLE AT A TIME. Alby checked his plastimask. Last time he was here, Fat Joe hadn't worn a mask the whole time. Again, the tracer alert in his phone didn't go off; but if there were clear signs of a non-vaxxer, Fat Joe wore them loudly.

Alby knocked, walked in, and without asking stood on the faded red masking tape "X" that was about eight feet from Fat Joe's beaten metal desk. Alby positioned himself one foot to the left of the tape. "Paperwork all good?" Fat Joe's mask was crumpled on his desk next to a Bluetooth thermometer. Alby could see marks on the handle from greasy hands.

"More phony vaxxers from what I see. But I made it work; they're certified now! They're in a containment suit all night, so whatever. They're breathing their own air—they can make themselves sick!" He laughed. Alby winced. It sounded like glass in a garbage disposal. "That'd be a public service." Laugh over, he got a serious look on his face. "If I wasn't short on this job, I wouldn't even let you on this lot. Damn Infrastructure Bill hired all the good people."

"What time am I back?" Alby knew better than to engage with bullies.

"Six a.m.," said Fat Joe with a sigh. "Six goddamned a.m." He yanked his buckle on his worn-out leather belt as if bracing himself for the long night. Fat Joe had an ugly mouth, resembling more a grouper fish than a human. On his desk he had a cardboard box filled with the basic cloth masks, clearly not bothering with the newer ones, like his. The plastimask was a huge hit that combined cloth and plastic, comfortable and even fashionable. Warby Parker, working with Stanford Hospital and industrial designers, had copped a fortune making masks that were good-looking, safe, and focused on letting people see each other's mouths. It took the mental edge off hesitating and putting on a mask, a signal some people did not like. But the speed of the mechanism was so fast, that if you felt unsafe, a second later you weren't. With all the mask-wearing guidelines constantly shifting, the speed made all situations easy to deal with and make the judgment call. And it didn't fog up ever.

Alby hurried back to his truck; time for some take-out and Maker's.

While Fat Joe tried to stay awake at his desk in the trailer, inside the bank on the second floor, three men moved very slowly in their white hazmat suits, oxygen tanks on their backs. They looked like astronauts from a 1950s sci-fi movie. A fourth man stood, clipboard in hand, watching them work. The air ventilating machine that stood in the center of the room was meant to catch any loose fibers; it looked like a squat, square robot with a large mouth that acted like a vacuum, sucking anything the long, snaking tube could catch and blowing it into a sealed mylar bag attached to the machine. The ventilator vacuum emitted a slow, high-pitched sound, like a child's long wail.

Before every shift, Fat Joe would gather the men and give the same speech. He called it his "safety speech:" "One feather can kill you. One thread. One bad hose. One less-than-an-inch per pound of suction. Don't mess with it. Don't touch the equipment. You're dead if you do. I wouldn't give a shit, but the lawyers are like vultures and they smell stupid from way off. Don't be stupid."

Few of these men believed it. They had all seen the lawyer ads on TV for asbestos exposure for years. And Fat Joe knew it. But he also figured that half of these guys working here weren't even vaxxed but had their phones hacked to show they were. So he wasn't going to lose any sleep worrying about their health… he just wanted no worries about lawyers, so he harped on them about it.

Lucky heard the speech and had to hold back his usual barking laugh of disdain: asbestos was just another White Man scheme. But he had other things on his mind. He believed the "safety speech" was Fat Joe trying to keep them from stealing stuff from the offices—the only reason he had taken the job in the first place.

Back in the sealed room it was hot and noisy. Using a small garden shovel, they each dug their gloved hands into the soft material and scooped the asbestos away from the pipe, shaving it like sheep's wool, tiny fibers flying off each chunk. Like tiny feathers, they would start floating free, then get sucked into the black hole of the air purifier vacuum. The men dumped their work into a plastic bag with a small puddle of water in the bottom. The inspector moved around the room looking bored—well, walking like he was bored—you couldn't see his face with the mask and helmet on.

In a large conference room, Lucky held a mushy handful of asbestos-laden fire retardant pulled from an overhead pipe. In his large clumsy gloves, he twisted it between his hands like cookie dough.

"This shit looks like cotton candy, only rotten," he yelled out. But with the sounds of his oxygen system and the ventilator in the room, his words rang loudly as an echo inside his hazmat suit.

For hours, the three of them had been slowly yanking, pulling, and bagging the asbestos: methodically they tugged and ripped, gloves digging into the soft material from the ceiling crawl space—then knotting and taping shut the bags, rinsing any extra dust off the bags in the sealed shower before handing them to guys who just put them in a barrel and rolled them outside on a dolly. Lucky had ordered Chance to do the barrel work.

Even in the uniformly made white hazmat suits, each of the three men looked different. Lucky stood tallest; the suit hung off him like some poorly chosen clown outfit. He seemed to whip and jerk in his suit like he was hunting the asbestos, chasing it with a natural ferocity. Darnell was the exact opposite—slow and methodical, yanking off material in nice rectangular patterns, staring at it before he dropped it in his bag. Chance was like a white-suited twitch, moving from here to there, no rhyme or rhythm, no pattern. Occasionally, Lucky saw the inspector motion for Darnell to focus on one area; the guy knew to keep clear of Lucky.

Since shouting only worked when you were close, everyone used simple hand gestures. The inspector pointed toward his wrist and moved his hand to his mouth several times through the face shield then held up one finger.

One a.m. Lunch break.

The inspector moved into the shower chamber as fast as he could, clearly trying to get away from the crew. Lucky grabbed the arms of Darnell and Chance and mouthed the word "wait" through the clear face mask. A minute later, Lucky jerked his head and they followed him out of the sealed chamber. Without bothering to rinse off, they each stepped through into the hallway outside the office they were working in.

Lucky unzipped his helmet and said loudly: "Let's get to it. You see this room? There's got to be stuff everywhere."

"Nah," said Darnell, keeping his head gear on, "I saw the sign downstairs in the lobby. The executive offices are upstairs on four. We gotta go there. We gotta walk to go there," he reminded them. "No elevator powered on." He paused, "You wearing a mask at all?"

"Yeah, I'm wearing a mask, you dumb motherfucker." Lucky pulled out one of those cheap blue hospital masks but ignored the hazmat helmet—the pale blue had gone gray from overuse, just like the one Alby had seen on Chance's face hours before.

When Alby asked Lucky to find two other guys, it had been easy; Lucky picked Darnell because he was smart. He'd done his time, avoided a third strike, and had stayed straight for almost ten years. Lucky knew he had a new woman and needed money. Sometimes you need brains. Picking Chance was easy, too; he was always hanging around Lucky and he was pretty stupid. Lucky was sure he'd be able to get part of his pay from him. Sometimes you need dumb loyalty. Chance had had Covid twice and survived and was still not vaccinated—he was just dumb and blessed. And he'd thought that Chance's being a white guy might make Alby more likely to hire them.

At the stairs, Lucky waited, then gestured for the others to follow him up. The three moved to the stairwell to walk slowly to the fourth floor. Not quite sure what he was looking for, Lucky just trusted that his instincts would lead him to something valuable.

The floor was half-prepped with plastic. Fat Joe had made it clear that this weekend was for the first two floors: next weekend, they'd be on floors three and four. Fat Joe spoke to them like they were all idiots. But Lucky was a good listener; remembering the small stuff was a survival technique that had served him well.

After the blasting noise of the first two floors, in its absence, Lucky realized that his ears ached. He moved past some offices and approached a door with a nameplate. He took off his helmet and pressed the protective plastic against the surface to reveal the embossed gold letters of a name: Joseph Kurtz, Executive Vice President. Chance mimicked Lucky and took off his helmet. Darnell looked at them both with an expression that said he was looking at two of the stupidest people on Earth, but said nothing.

Lucky went in first and stumbled on a roll of plastic sheeting. Falling forward, his extended arm ripped through the plastic, exposing a wood-paneled office wall. Instead of pulling back, he paused, and used his arm to push down farther in and slice the plastic although it took some effort. The plastic was thick and resistant to tearing. Then, using both hands, he opened the sheet like a surgeon and stared intently for a good ten seconds. "Shit. I guess if we're gonna take anything, now's the time." Lucky smirked and went to the ripped plastic and peered through. Chance grabbed Darnell's shoulder and was pulling him over to stand near Lucky. The three looked at the ripped plastic. "We are screwed," he yelled.

"Nah, we use the electric tape, and no one'll know. Anyway, the way this job is run, no one's smart enough to look." Lucky nodded, as if affirming what he had just said. His entire expression changed.

"We got us some shopping to do," Lucky said with glee. "Look for desks, places with drawers we can check out."

Darnell took a step back and glanced nervously around. Chance was quick to nod his agreement. Darnell clearly felt very differently. Speaking loudly, he said, "I don't know. I'm kind of thinkin' we should go get lunch. Lucky, this is trouble—trouble we don't need. My third strike. I'm not comin' out."

"Shut the fuck up, Darnell. You knew that comin' in. Find some tape," he ordered, starting to size up the rip. He slipped two hands into the plastic and spread it open like it was a piece of rotted flesh, and it ripped more.

"Aw, Lucky, no more, man."

Lucky reached in and pulled out a large, expensive-looking silver frame holding a photo of a smiling family. The three men looked at it, expressionless. Lucky put it back through the plastic sheet, and they heard a smashing sound of glass breaking. He reached in with both hands, then extracted the empty silver frame and handed it to Darnell. "Just a little gift!" he laughed.

Chance leaned in. "Big bucks for this." Lucky cast a skeptical eye at him. This was all pocket change; he needed something of real value. "There's a bigger desk over here." He pointed as he squinted through the slit in the translucent plastic.

Darnell looked even more worried now and kept glancing at the double plastic containers ready for use that framed the doorway into the room. "You two better put your helmets back on. You'll get that nasty meso-themiola, or whatever it is."

Lucky wasn't listening. As he tugged at the sheet to get it out of the way, he reached through to get some leverage, leaning against the wall. But his hand slipped, then found something to grab onto. It was a handle. Slowly he folded back the split sheet.

A safe. It was a wall safe; he'd never seen one except in old movies his dad had made him watch. He reached in and slowly took hold of the handle, which faced upwards. Locked, he thought, as he turned the handle to the right. It didn't budge, like he expected. He exhaled loudly; it was like losing a scratch Lotto ticket, you just had to let it go. As an after-thought, Lucky turned it left. It moved. He yanked it down, and the small door swung open.

The other two men stepped closer, crowding him; Lucky brushed them back. He reached into the safe. Slowly, his hand, made clumsy by the puffy gloves, fumbled until he withdrew one piece of rectangular paper. A check. He had never had a checking account, but his second wife had, and he'd turned many a check in at PayDay. But this check was differ-ent—a weird size, oversized. He took it in both hands and studied it. Even as odd as it looked, it was still a check. The paper seemed frail in his bulky gloved hands.

"A check…Christ! It's signed," he suddenly exclaimed. Chance and Darnell stepped back.

"For how much?" asked Darnell.

"What?" Chance yelled.

Darnell gave Chance a disdainful look.

Then he looked at the check again. "They didn't write in a number. Just signed it." He paused and his face went blank, like he was searching for a thought.

Unzipping the front of his suit, he slipped the check inside his T-shirt and looked at the others. "Where's the tape?"

"Why are *you* holding it?" Darnell asked as he cast a threatening glance at Lucky's hand as it zipped the suit back up.

"I found it."

"What are we going to do with some dumb check?" Sweat ran

down Chance's face. "We need cash. Or something good to pawn."

"Then look for a gold ashtray."

"Good idea," said Chance.

Darnell and Lucky exchanged looks.

"Someone signed it." He got cocky. "Signed and waiting for me." He glanced at a glaring Darnell.

Lucky had no patience for their stupidity—except when it served him—so he calmly said, "A blank check, you dumb fucks. Fill in the blank and cash it and we are…"—he paused to consider how much to tell them. "We need to get out of here and talk later. That inspector's gonna be here checking on us soon." The two nodded their okays.

Chance, who had somehow already remembered to put his helmet back on, gestured for Lucky to do the same. Lucky hesitated. He hated being told anything by either of these two and besides, he could grab another cigarette. But he didn't think that he could afford another pack right now anyway. Then another thought came to him—maybe he'd be able to afford all the cigarettes in the world soon, and he grinned. Still, he resolutely shoved the helmet back in place. Gear on, they moved carefully down the hallway. Lucky took the lead, but he felt Darnell close behind him. Too close.

When they got back to the second floor, they could hear the shouts of men coming up the stairs from their break. It had to be near two a.m. The inspector showed up soon after and gave them all a strange look. "Where were you guys?" he yelled.

He was white and skinny and Lucky could tell black people made him nervous. "We ate up here."

The guy practically dropped his clipboard and his face went red as he shouted through the visor. "Are you nuts? Breathing this crap?" He shook his head as if speaking to a misbehaving and stupid child and scribbled something on the clipboard sheet.

The suit's plastic mask started to fog up; Lucky realized he was breathing too fast. Need to think: check, check, check; the words rolled over and over in Lucky's head, like being caught in a Jersey circle with no signs where he could get off. Alby, the ignorant fuck of a contractor, would be coming soon; he could see the pink glow of light coming through the pale plastic sheets that covered the windows. Dawn never looked so good. He needed to grab a beer, a donut, and a pillow.

The staging site in the back parking lot, painted by the reds and blues of sunrise, was as busy as if it were midday. People milled about—some talking, some smoking, some sitting slumped on the curb, looking like they were already asleep, people with masks half on, half off, and everything in between—like Chance. Lucky glanced over at him leaning on a barrel stuffed with asbestos, with his sleeping head bobbing like a marionette with its strings cut. Trucks and cars were pulling in and out, gears and lifts and thumping rolls of plastic sheets filled the air—if anyone could fall asleep in this noise it was Chance. He caught Darnell looking at him with an odd expression. Paranoia, Lucky figured; Darnell knew him well enough to know he'd try and screw them out of their cut. Lucky knew Darnell would be his big problem.

He suddenly felt like going over to the curb and slapping Chance awake. Just then Alby pulled in and yelled out the window of his truck. Lucky glanced at him as he walked by his window—he looked like hell, bags under bleary eyes, lips slightly crusty. Lucky recognized it right away and smiled: Alby was hungover.

"Camden Express! Time for bed, guys," Alby said with pretty obvious faked enthusiasm. He had almost slept through picking them up. Driving was not easy–his head ached from the forgotten number of tumblers of Maker's Mark he had lifted to his lips. One thought teased him: it was a new day and nothing had gone wrong yesterday, defying that feeling he always got. While he felt relieved, he also wondered why his intuition had been wrong. It had never been before. A smile wanted to creep onto his lips, but his head ached too much to let it in.

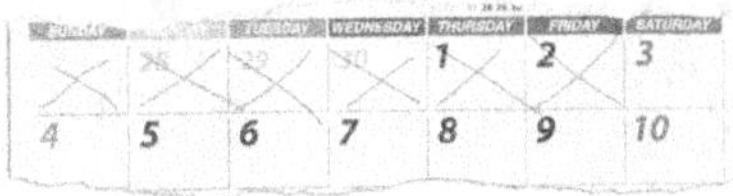

A few miles away in an all-too-perfect McMansion, Joseph Kurtz was half reading the paper and half listening to a cartoon playing in the nearby family room. He was thinking two thoughts at once: that did not sound like an ordinary cartoon (someone always yelling "Archer" and guns going off) and local politicians were all crooks. Putting down the paper, he came to two conclusions: he needed to change that channel before his wife got back from the gym and yes, they were all crooks. He would know—he had personally paid off a half-dozen in person over the past decade. Even recently, it cost him—well, the Owners—a fair amount to get the licenses for the asbestos work. The trifecta: the local state inspector, his supervisor, and his boss up in Trenton. That last one—he'd had to drive there with a white envelope stuffed with $100 bills and meet her at a Shake Shack.

When his phone rang, he picked it up to hear a voice he didn't recognize at first; the guy sounded like he was chewing glass. Then he realized it was Fat Joe, the night foreman for the asbestos work.

"You need to get over here. I think something in your office got stolen."

"What?" he asked impatiently. Kurtz took pride in the fact that he had perfected the executive impatient voice. Even though he had only met Fat Joe for construction work over the years—like updating the ventilation on the bank branch during the first Covid wave—he hated the man; he was just plain repulsive. But he knew that he was favored by the Owners. "Just keep out of his way," they told him when they let him know they were re-doing the bank interior to sell the building and move to a bigger one. They were expanding, which was good for Kurtz.

"How could anyone steal anything at night?"

"It's some small safe in the wall. They were prepping the executive floor. The door was open." A wave of panic rose from Kurtz's feet to his head.

His son shouted from the living room. "Dad, can I watch another half hour?"

"No!" He paused, feeling the panic build. "Yes, yes, yes! And tell your mother I went to work. Be back soon." Even as he felt his chest tighten and breath shorten, he paused as he passed the hallway mirror to catch a glance at himself. He didn't look panicked: slick black hair, trim personal trainer body, strong features a little roughhewn but softened by the cocky executive look.

"I thought you weren't supposed to leave me alone," his son yelled.

"Time to grow up!" Kurtz grabbed a jacket off a hook and ran out the door. His BMW liked high speeds and sharp turns, and it growled its thanks as he drove a little too fast and loose to the bank. But he wasn't listening.

One thought pushed everything aside: the check.

Last night, right before he left, almost as an afterthought, he had signed one check but not filled in the number; the final loan papers were due early Monday morning for a building loan they were going to give. He had been in a hurry, wife texting and pestering him about not missing another soccer match. It annoyed him that he had to rush for such a stupid game. Kid didn't even like the Eagles.

Now he could not remember if he had locked his office safe. He had opened and closed it a thousand times, knew the ritual of rolling the tumbler and yanking the small gold handle. It was muscle memory, but had he actually done that last night?

Fat Joe had warned him only the other day: personal belongings and valuables left around the office would disappear. "They all do it," he had said, yanking up his pants, like his personal exclamation point. "They just pick something up, put it in the bag of asbestos, and take it out later." He checked the belt loop like a nervous twitch. "Tell all your employees.

Don't leave anything around. Take it home. Locked drawers might not even be safe."

He tried to replay the scene. After a late staff meeting, where he had relayed Fat Joe's message, he had gone back into his office. He went right to the small safe embedded in the wood paneling, almost like a fixture or decorative element. He had turned the safe handle. It clicked and opened. His phone buzzed and he quickly read and typed a response to his wife: "Busy." The check went from jacket pocket to small shelf. His phone buzzed again. He texted her he was leaving soon. God, she is so annoying, he recalled thinking. What did he do next? Or, rather, what didn't he do? He only recalled thinking he would take care of it Monday.

He almost flew over the curb as he pulled up the driveway to the bank. He pulled into the fire zone in front of the building entrance, yanked his keys out of the ignition, and jumped out, swatting away the security guard who was about to tell him not to park there.

"Do you know who I am?" Kurtz plowed on through the lobby.

The check. The word kept repeating like a hammer pounding in his head.

Fat Joe was in the lobby, gesturing at two men who were putting away the plastic sheets rolled up like thick white logs. A guard didn't get up from the lobby desk but yelled for Kurtz to stop. "I run this place, you ant," he yelled over his shoulder. Suddenly he was stopped by a wall of thick plastic sheets, hung ceiling to floor.

"I don't care who you are," the guard said; "It is federally mandated for you to have to wear a suit to go in there." He paused. "Federally!"

Fat Joe shrugged and gestured to the far end of the lobby. A few rows of hazmat suits were hanging like suits on a store rack. The guard stood up, but Fat Joe waved him away and showed Kurtz how to suit up. "Just do what I do." He made him wear the oxygen tank version, so he didn't have to train him how to breathe. Kurtz groaned as he lifted the weight of the suit and tank.

"We need to get to my office," Kurtz whispered urgently, over and over, as they dressed.

"You need to calm down."

Kurtz mumbled on. Trying to put his first leg into the suit, he stumbled and fell twice. Fat Joe did not bother to help him, which earned him a glare. Fat Joe smelled trouble; this guy was just too nervous. To Fat Joe, nervous led to stupid. Besides, if what had happened really turned out bad, then Kurtz was radioactive. And this smelled bad from a mile off.

Wearing the baggy suits with the clown-like booties and weighed down with the oxygen tank, they slowly climbed the four flights to the executive floor. "Christ, you can't turn on the elevators?"

"Regulations."

"Don't we pay you to break those?"

Walls and railings were wrapped in the thick plastic. As heavy as the suit was, Kurtz rushed as fast as he could up the four flights of stairs ahead of Fat Joe, got to his floor, unzipped and moved through the plastic antechamber, and went into his office. The roar of the oxygen tank was actually making him nauseous, but he ignored it.

He went across the room, around the large freestanding ventilator with its two tubes, the short one sucking the air, the long one snaking up into a ceiling tube.

Fat Joe caught up with him in time to see him reaching out to try to rip the plastic apart to get to the wall behind. He could see that Kurtz was about to pull at the plastic—but it was already ripped—held together by a thin line of masking tape.

Kurtz's breath was labored, anxious, his face mask fogged up. Fat Joe went around him, got close to the plastic, and found the second line of tape the inspector had shown him earlier this morning. He reached out, and with his gloves, he scraped at the tape, peeling it back slowly.

The banker pushed him aside and grabbed for the exposed tear and pushed his hand into it; it opened like a blossom. Much more of the plastic sheet had been ripped; the clear adhesive tape left a thin scar for them to see how long the rip was.

Now Kurtz pushed both arms through the plastic; he fumbled around. He found the safe and with one hand grabbed the small handle. "Please be locked," he thought, but in his heart, he knew it wasn't. He grabbed the small handle. It opened easily. He looked inside: everything was there. He fumbled, only able to fit one gloved hand in easily, and scooped papers out. It was all there.

Except the check.

"I am going to kill whoever was working in this room last night!" Kurtz yelled, fogging up the visor again.

"I can hear you! This room wasn't scheduled to be done until next weekend," Fat Joe shouted and just shook his head. "What did they take?"

"A check. A signed bank check. Someone could cash it for anything!" After the words tumbled out, Kurtz drew back, realizing he should have kept his mouth shut. "What kind of lowlife people do you hire?"

"You wouldn't want to know."

Kurtz stuffed all the papers back in, shut the safe, spun the tumbler, and pulled away. The plastic fluttered back into place. He could hear the rush of blood in his ears and felt the sudden heaviness of the suit on him. "I have to make some calls," he shouted as he went out of the room.

Fat Joe stayed behind a moment; he turned slowly and took in the room. No other rips. A signed blank check was not going to make the Owners happy; Kurtz was now a liability. This was not going to end well, that much was sure. After working for them on and off for twenty years, he knew the Owners' patterns. If he wasn't careful, he'd be done. Fat Joe sighed and decided to check the other fourth floor offices for any theft, then he'd call them. They hated fear from an employee, so calling them in advance would make it clear that he wasn't scared. He'd give them his side, just in case Kurtz lied and blamed it on him. He knew the Owners would believe him over Kurtz. It was all about being the best at what you did—anything short of that could get you killed.

They both went downstairs. Once Kurtz hurried over to a bench to make those "calls," Fat Joe went back up to the other floors and did his best to check on what might or might not be there. Having done his due diligence, he went back downstairs, removed the hazmat suit, and quickly (well quickly for him) walked over to his trailer to call the Owners.

Meanwhile, Kurtz was busy tapping in a number. It was a number he almost never used and it wasn't written down anywhere. He had to try several times before he got through and he got more and more nervous as he waited. Finally, his call connected but it was a poor one. That didn't matter. The conference call would be brief; he knew how they hated extra commentary and adjectives. He waited on hold. He relayed the facts as he knew them and hoped they didn't hear the tremble in his voice. The call lasted four minutes and thirty-six seconds. They ended the call telling him that he was to wait, not to leave the site until someone arrived, and do everything they say; it would be several hours.

So he waited. Kurtz's phone buzzed several times—his wife. Eventually he turned it off. He sat in the lobby but had moved off the bench and onto a folding chair, near the hazmat suits, on the opposite side from the guard, who occasionally stared at him suspiciously. Kurtz felt like firing him just out of spite, but he resisted. That would cause a scene. After a while, he left the building and walked back to Fat Joe's trailer only to see his gold Lincoln gone.

Kurtz had been the bank's Executive Vice President for years and had secretly gloried in how invincible that title made him feel—until now. Now he felt like the walking dead. The Owners had just said get rid of any cops, wait for someone to arrive, and make things as normal as possible. The story? Nothing happened, human error. His.

Saturday: 6 p.m.

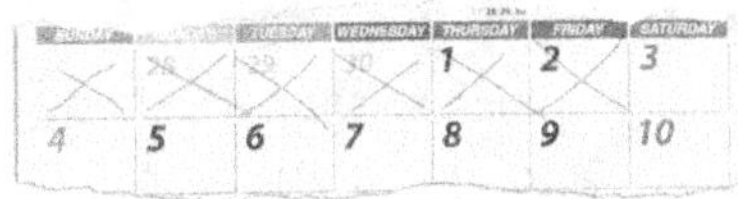

Kurtz paced back and forth in front of the bank. The sun was starting to light up the horizon. He had checked his phone for messages and saw that his wife had called and texted so much he would be surprised if she didn't have carpal tunnel pain by now.

Streaking with pink fingers, the sky lit up the trucks moving onto the site like some ugly Cinderella ball. A car pulled into the lot and parked at the far end of the sidewalk that ran the length of the building. A new Camry. Some guy in a gray suit in his late thirties—mid-forties maybe?—got out of the car and slowly swiveled his head until he fixed on the trailers. Kurtz ran to the car. The man raised his left hand, palm out, as his plastimask sprang out to click together. Kurtz grew self-conscious, tugged at his mask, and went from a run to a phony casual walk.

"Owners send you?"

"Jagger," the man announced himself, ignoring the question. "Where can we talk?"

"The trailer." Kurtz gestured to the one next to Fat Joe's. He knew it just held extra boxes and junk. Kurtz turned and Jagger followed him.

The Owners had woken him up this morning when they had called and laid out the assignment. They only ever called Jagger for one reason: he solved puzzles the typical hit men they had in their stable couldn't—they were all clumsy compared to him; he was surgical. The Owners had different experts to fit their various assignments; Jagger was not their blunt instrument…he was their scalpel. However, even after almost ten years in their employ he had never heard them so agitated. This idiot Kurtz had signed a formal bank cashier's check, had not entered an amount, then left the safe door unlocked. There was no way to cancel it, no way to stop anyone from cashing it for any amount in any bank. They thought it was one of the night shift workers, not an inside job. He had one week to take care of it, they told him. They wanted this cleared up before they finished re-stocking the yacht and going back to sea in ten days. Even after two rounds of vaccines, they had watched the tides of viruses come and go and avoided going on shore.

Jagger now thought about the man walking in front of him. While first impressions meant everything, for Jagger his first impressions were different from everyone else's: it was not clothes, stature, badges, personas, resumes. All the clichés. All he had to do was look at their faces. After a few moments he knew them better than they did themselves. What was nearly invisible or clouded about other people's state-of-mind was blaring and loud to him; everyone had an emotional map of Braille across their faces. People's lies, fears, secrets, everything, rolled across their faces so transparently to him. And if you asked the right kind of questions, the muscles would go into a chaos of emotions. Kurtz was disgusting to look at: the blatant fear was written on every muscle and line of his face. The fear was, on him, like bad cologne excreted from a man who was clearly a coward. Jagger had watched the pattern of jumping muscles along his jaw, noted the squinting line from the end of his eyes to his hairline.

"You called the FBI?" asked Jagger.

"No, county police. I know the Chief well."

Jagger shook his head: this guy was the worst kind of amateur.

"I called them back right after I spoke to the Owners. Told them I had made a mistake and had taken the check home." Kurtz paused, catching his breath. "I think they bought it."

Jagger leveled his gaze a foot over the banker's head and spoke in a slow monotone.

"Kurtz, Kurtz…You really would have to work hard to do a worse job." His words were harsh but his tone upbeat, like the sun had come out on a cloudy day. "You signed it. You signed it but did not fill it out. A bank check—A BANK CHECK." He had raised his voice like a cheer as if Kurtz was hard-of-hearing. "You did not lock the safe. You know the building is crawling at night with construction workers—losers and thieves—and yes, they steal the check. You come in, panic, call the cops."

"I—uh—uh, well," he stammered. Jagger waved his hand to cut him off.

"I'll make this simple. What I need you to do is one thing: Get whoever is running this clean-up to get me the names, addresses, all contact info for every single person who was on-site this weekend."

The banker leaned forward to speak. Jagger held up a single finger, his right index one, and continued, "After I get those addresses, I will do my part, find the check, and tidy up the mess." He paused; he liked watching his silence activate Kurtz' anxiety. "The mess *you* created."

The banker stepped back and half tripped over a box. But he pulled his phone out of his pocket and called Fat Joe. In a few seconds, he clicked off.

"What—what do I do now?"

"Now? You do nothing. Normal life. Nothing else. You will come to work. You will continue to run the bank, have meetings, you will go home, your typical incompetent work…" Jagger paused and thought, "…for a year. After that, you find another job and leave. Wait, I had that backwards: leave, then find a job. We don't care where you go. Just disappear."

"I…I…" Kurtz stammered.

"*We* do not care where the job is or whatever—just get a job and go."

"My family…I can fix this—"

"No, no, no, you can't. But I am glad you mentioned your family. If this does not go well, if anything else goes wrong, anything, anything, anything," Jagger twirled his index finger in the air, as if spinning the word like taffy, "then you will have an unfortunate accident, you and your whole family. I mean, a truly terrible accident that just makes everyone so, so sad. Gone. Long eulogies for everyone. Tragedy. Article in the local paper. Real. Sad. Stuff." He spoke the last three words very softly, with a sort of tenderness that made your blood run cold.

Jagger lowered his gaze a foot to see the eyes of the banker: he looked like everyone did when you told them you were going to kill them—the muscles around his eyes, cheeks, eyebrows, mouth were frozen in mid-step of running away—confused, scared.

Jagger turned to leave. He so wanted permission to kill this guy and maybe they would give it to him eventually, but not until the task was done. The world would be better without him.

"That's it?" the banker asked, then regretted speaking.

"That's not enough?" Jagger shook his head. "Yes. Now I'm going to the trailer—that foreman better be compiling lists for me."

"His name is Fat Joe. He had already started before I even called him. How are you going to find these people?"

Jagger casually pulled out and flipped open an FBI badge.

"How'd you get that?" asked the incredulous banker. Again, he immediately regretted asking.

"Counterfeit," he said, but thought: I killed an FBI agent and took it, what else? He waved his hands at Kurtz, like he was a gnat that needed to go. Kurtz, taking the very obvious and ominous hint, turned and fled to his car and took off.

When Jagger entered Fat Joe's trailer, he knew immediately why everyone called him that. Short, bulging in all the wrong places, a lumpy pear. No mask, though Jagger kept his on. The tracer software alert did not go off, so he intentionally ignored the red tape on the floor and moved closer to Fat Joe. The Owners insisted all employees get vaxxed and in fact, had an annual event where every employee did it in their presence to prove without question they had done it. No fakers. The Owners' file described him perfectly: a fat puppet, very effective and very canny at construction projects—he had a knack for bending but never breaking laws and regulations. Construction was one of the things the Owners cared a lot about— an easy way to launder cash. Jagger nodded in a businesslike manner as did Fat Joe, who was rifling through folders.

"I figured you'd want the contact info for the crews here"—the file had been correct, he was smart—"but it's gonna take a little while. The files aren't organized by shift. Some teams change each night. Here's what I got so far. Give me a few more hours."

"Next time I come, I want them in a binder."

After an hour, Jagger turned off the idling engine. The world moves too slowly, he thought, as he sat in his car and waited for the foreman to call him. The breeze coming in the driver's side window felt good, not the anvil hot breeze of a desert sunset, though he had it open as a caution in case someone hadn't cleaned the rental car well; he had sprayed it down when he rented it, but you can never be too sure. He was in month seven and lined up for the new booster at the yacht in a few months.

The construction site was in full bloom now, resembling the Big Top when the circus comes to town: klieg lights were being rolled around to the storage area at the far end of the large parking lot. Wind whipped and furled the plastic sheets like sails. Garbage trucks and flatbeds moved around the parking lot with barrels being loaded and unloaded. All the other contractors drifted in and out, one by one. He popped his head out of the car window and waved to Fat Joe who was near the lobby finishing up a conversation with a guy half in and half out of a hazmat suit.

Fat Joe moved towards the car, but Jagger got out and gestured to his trailer.

Once they were in the trailer, Fat Joe tried again. "This is the best list I got." He had about a dozen loose sheets. They were wrinkled. "Is it everyone? No. For all I know the guy you want comes back tonight."

"No one is that stupid…" began Jagger then stopped, realizing how stupid most people really were. "If you believe that is a possibility then I will see you later."

Fat Joe nodded his head, looking resigned but also a bit frightened. The clean-up guy was always the most dangerous. What was weird was that this guy looked as normal as normal can be—someone you would not even notice if you brushed by him on the street. Guess that was part of his angle.

"What time?"

"Not sure." Jagger enjoyed watching it—the fear and uncertainty filling Fat Joe's face like soup spilling from a can.

Jagger could see that Fat Joe was desperate not to look directly at him as he slipped the three-hole punched sheets into a binder and pushed it across the table. "Some of the Ghoul Crew guys don't exactly have addresses." Fat Joe looked up for approval, with an uncertain smile: "We call them Ghoul Crew because they're like zombies, get it?" He attempted a laugh. Jagger didn't move a muscle, instead stood like a pale, unmoving wax figure in his pale gray suit.

"Explain."

"Camden." Fat Joe shrugged, as if that was all self-evident.

"Yes, good work," he responded with cold sarcasm. "We are in the county of Camden."

"No, no, I meant—" he fumbled with some papers, dropping them on the floor. He pulled up his loose pants and bent down to get them.

With one swift motion, Jagger grabbed a bulging ring binder off a cabinet and hit Fat Joe squarely on the head. Fat Joe fell to the ground, hitting his forehead on the edge of the table.

"Please!" Fat Joe cringed.

"I'm here to do a job. I am a professional. I have no time for word play. Camden means what?" Jagger didn't care if the Owners liked this employee—Jagger didn't like games or wasting his time: efficiency first.

"Shithole. Ghetto. No man's land. Half these night crawlers don't have addresses."

"How many are you missing?"

"This is a big job. Day and night shifts, two weekends. This usually takes a month, and we're doing it in two weeks," Fat Joe said almost boastfully.

"How many not here?" Jagger lifted the binder with two hands and crashed it on the table where Fat Joe's fingers were holding the edge. Fat Joe fell on the floor, scrambling away like a bloated crab.

"Maybe ten. Twelve." He averted his eyes from Jagger and rubbed his sore fingers. "Give me a day. I've only had a few hours! Tomorrow." He looked at Jagger, which was a mistake. Jagger did not like it when people looked directly at him. Fat Joe figured that out instantly and quickly averted his eyes before he went on. "Some of the guys are ex-cons, bums, living with multiple women, families, on the street, you just don't know." Fat Joe felt a small worm of blood slipping down his forehead and he went to dab it.

"You will give it all to me in five hours, in a binder, when I will be back." Fat Joe was already pale, but he went an extra shade of pale.

After gently putting down the binder on the guy's desk, Jagger looked around for some sanitizer; Fat Joe was just the type not to be vaxxed and have his phone hacked to trick the Alert software everyone's phone came with. Not seeing any sanitizer, he reached into his pocket, took out a small bottle, and as he squirted some on his hands, he quietly asked, "Do you know what they stole?"

Fat Joe nodded.

"Then you know that Monday when other banks open, they can cash this check, right?"

Fat Joe nodded again.

As he turned to go, Jagger said, "Have a hazmat suit ready; we're going into the building." Fat Joe blubbered some chewed-up words—it was already sunset, how late was he going to be—but Jagger ignored him and walked out.

All Jagger cared about was getting as much information as fast as possible. Starting with incomplete information meant wasted time and incomplete results, which was always a sore point for him: it threw off his methodology and efficiency, things that defined him. Being the very best in terms of process and efficiency was the bull's-eye of his identity.

Already having chosen a local motel chain for the night, he'd wipe down the main "touch points" of the room later. Now was time for a true pleasure—pastrami, melted Swiss, coleslaw, toasted marble rye. A Reuben. On the flight he had Googled and found a deli just a few miles away. New Jersey: The best sandwiches in the world all trapped in one corner of the country. He shook his head as he drove away from the site…it seemed such a shame.

As Stephen got to the end of the driveway of Alby's garage, he yelled out the open window, "Watch out for that nasty Camden! Make sure you don't get killed. It'll ruin my ability to make money." Stephen laughed; certain his comment was genuinely funny. "Come to Mom's party! Just once."

Alby stood watching his nephew leave. The sun angled along the tree line. The one small street lamp in the back parking lot lit up with a dim spark. Working Saturdays meant more money, always a motivator. The main thing he didn't like about Saturday was that it led to Sunday. If he could, he'd be busy seven days a week—best to keep busy, best way to avoid thinking too much. Made his days easier: work, eat, drink, sleep. And box, he had to nod to that. Sunday was the day that irritated him the most—it annoyed him that everyone took the day off.

He ignored Stephen's throwaway mention of the party—his head was still in the work. It always amazed him how many driveways needed repaving. It was obvious why—people were still catching up to the post-Pandemic boom, which meant they wanted the work done, but all the handymen were busy or working on the big infrastructure projects—from pipes to bridges, America was one big construction site.

When it came to house repairs, people were suckers; they put their trust in some strangers' hands. After the final lockdown ended, everyone took the cheapest bid from the cheapest contractors who used the cheapest materials—after all, who was sure they would be around in a year? The cheap stuff barely made it through one or two rough winters and then the surface would crumble like a black pie crust. He mostly used real asphalt. Especially when the owners were older. If an asshole hired him, he sometimes used the bad stuff just to stick it to him.

As he thought about the work, he automatically moved to the bathroom, removed the panel from the wall, and climbed through to the garage. He still had a few hours before he had to pick up the crew, so why not let out a little frustration? Early autumn's yellow-tinged light came in sideways through the small windows up near the top of the garage doors. The neglected, overgrown bushes blocked any view from the service road that wound its way to Route 70.

After pounding the bag for fifteen minutes, he took one too many punches and cut the knuckle on his right index finger. He glanced at his boxing gloves on the metal shelf. He should have known better. Alby had been lost reciting The Rules ("…number seven, never fall in love—it costs too much…"). He had let himself get distracted.

His cursing reverberated through the empty garage. Not wanting to show any signs of his boxing he had been intentionally holding back. The less his sister knew about his life the better. Now he had a nice one-inch tear that would be impossible to hide. He'd blame it on the driveway work. That is if he went to her party at all.

Her party invite was messing up his usual Saturday routine—well, every night routine—because of some misguided obligation to his sister. The appeal of cozying up with a bottle of Maker's, hijacking his neighbor's Wi-Fi, and watching YouTube or Netflix—this held the comfort of the familiar. Going to his sister's for a party was low on his list of things to do—very, very low. But she'd had three parties since he moved to Marlton over a year ago and he'd turned her down every time—even for Easter, which would have pissed off his mom.

"Didn't you come here to be near family?" his sister had asked. He knew he couldn't turn down a fourth. Not because he cared about being rude. If anyone deserved to be blown off it was her. No, the real reason for this change of heart was, he suddenly realized, because he was sick of his "Maker's Saturday" routine and needed a break. One night off. Cleaning up, he mused, knowing that it was a self-lie. Plus, he was sure the party would only reinforce why he never went in the first place.

If the party was as bad as he knew it would be, he'd be happier than ever to use the old "Irish exit" routine: be very public then disappear without a word. This was a good plan, and knowing a Maker's bottle was waiting for him at the cave was a motivator.

As he tread carefully around the grease spots on the abandoned garage floor, he absentmindedly sucked on the cut on his knuckle until the blood stopped. He went to the wall, pulled open the panel, and climbed back through to his apartment shower.

No parties, over a year without socializing, no restaurants (diners didn't count), no dates, no movie theaters, no concerts, no sports events, no nothing… a year…of what? True, the Pandemic still screwed things up with crowds, but most everything was as close to normal as it was going to get. Everybody just accepted the warped normal. It was all "work and hide." Pandemics and shutdowns didn't bother him.

He tried not to think about the fact that he had gone to more parties in the Green Zone in Baghdad than in Cherry Hill, New Jersey.

And what a time to come back—just at the tail end of the shit pile wreck the eight Covid tsunamis did to the country. After the fourth, fifth, and sixth waves, the media switched from "waves" to "tsunami" when they finally understood "wave" did not capture the truly insidious nature of the water metaphor and how well it worked for the virus and variants. Waves roll in big and crash but they always pull back. Tsunamis build, grow, get deeper, higher, more violent, more dangerous, and just roll and roll and cover everything; it sometimes seemed too odd to think that he had left for Iraq a few months before it all started and then had come back to a place that looked the same in every way, yet wasn't the same at all.

Coming back to such a changed country, and feeling like he needed to get a sense of what actually happened while he was away, he had succumbed to wanting to go to one event—the new VP was going to be at Philly City Hall and this guy looked as close to the real deal as politicians could get. Alby wanted to see what "authentic" looked like in person. Alby hadn't figured out the president—yeah, she was doing the right things, but had the air of the zealot, a turn-it-on-its-head, make-things-right-in-America leader; she just annoyed him. The new VP was even younger than she was, but more cautious. His Midwestern manner was getting him a lot of media play. People filled the big open plaza area in front of City Hall, naturally spacing themselves (a new normal habitual behavior now) to see the guy and hear his speech. But with his usual single-minded focus on work and cave life, Alby had forgotten about the speech, only remembering at the last minute and was instead watching it all on his iPad. This crowd spacing still caught him off guard—the street had hundreds of red dots painted on the asphalt; it was not the America he left yet everyone made it seem natural; everyone knew how to triangulate.

If he was honest with himself, his "forgetting" about the speech was just a cover. Even wanting to go, he knew he couldn't. All he needed was some random news crew recognizing his face from that old photograph of him on that damned video, catching him on camera. That was not the way his life worked now. Different rules. Not his Rules, the Handlers' rules. He hated them. Just for that he would go be in public at his sister's party.

His body felt heavy and fell awkwardly into the contours of his lumpy sofa bed. Closing his eyes, he let his mind wander, needing a few minutes before he had to dress and go even though his stomach was motivating him with a grumble. He was sure she'd have plenty of food so he would not stop for dinner along the way—save a few bucks. An unwanted twinge of pain shot through his right side. His shirt must have rubbed against his scar the wrong way. It was like some insane alarm clock that went off randomly only to remind him it was there—that winding, six-inch red scar running along his right ribs. It was visible behind Alby's eyelids every time he closed them.

Perhaps socializing might help stop the nightmares. Not that he believed anything could, besides physical exhaustion and half a bottle of whiskey. Alby had tried everything else. Having a visceral hatred for being a victim, it ate away at him that it was these nightmares, dreams of his own creation, that haunted his life. The daytime hours were spent on his terms, in his way; but night created a darker pursuit dealt from his own mind he could not control.

Each nightmare was like a card dealt from the same deck—always the same half-dozen memories ordered in a different way—always with only slight variations of the same story. First there was Ahmed, Baghdad, and That Final Day—that last day of normal life in Baghdad, the images and impressions from that last evening, that last visit to Ahmed's family compound.

Then there were the massive gates of the Doura power plant, one hanging akimbo from the other, blown off its post by a bomb. The half-ruined remains of the electric plant had been his home every day, a power plant needed to feed the city with electricity. Keep the city alive.

In one, he saw his lunches with Ahmed at the plant, squatting in the shade of a huge turbine. Then that final moment again… a piercing sound, a man yelling, the doors creaking, a sharp crack. Doors to Ahmed's house, large and double-hinged, with a buzzer and a lock. He sees her. Aliyah. Is it the first time? Last time? No, last time was…

In his sleep's recall, she rushes at him, her headdress partially falling off, her black hair coming loose from its tight bun, then her head twisted the wrong way. Or did that happen? He tried to stay up. The supreme force of gravity pulled him down. He fought it and stood wobbling on his feet, only to see Ahmed lunge at him, a silver and black switchblade in his right hand.

Then the cries and screams of the neighborhood women as they carry him to a Humvee.

After moving to Cherry Hill, the good meds had run out and then the nightmares had taken over, becoming an endless loop of terror. The Internet gave him useful and useless information all wrapped together. Nightmares, psychological disorders, drugs he could take, doctors he could see, services he could tap into… especially if he had PTSD.

Then he read somewhere he should set the alarm to wake up every few hours to break a repetitive nightmare's cycle. The alarm clock was supposed to act like a nightmare stop sign. He tried it. It went off at two a.m., he got up to pee, closed his eyes, and slipped right back to the nightmares. Rang at four. Rang at six. Eventually, he had slapped the alarm clock across the room so many times that it broke.

As much as it had annoyed him, he decided that he had to do something, something had to give. So he called his Handlers about getting help. Alby knew it was the guy from the hospital from the way that he slid his words in that disguised southern accent. "Sorry, as non-military, you qualify for nothing." The bastard laughed. "Buy an Uzi and shoot up a mall," he said caustically. "At least you'll go out famous." He laughed again, and before he clicked off, he had added, "Also, don't call us. We don't want to hear from you."

Basically, suck it up.

Alby snapped back to the moment he was in—in the cave, exhausted beyond the physical. He had had enough of this road trip through hell.

Through the screen door, he could see the sun setting, the sky filled with tongues of red and blue—Day, he thought, meet Night. Time for a trip to Camden. He grabbed his keys, walked out, then spun around and walked back in, disgusted. Stinking masks. He slipped the two braces of his plastimask onto each ear. You read in the papers how everyone is supposed to get a vaccine super-boost—since so many got their first and some a second boost, they were advertising it everywhere. There were still stories declaring it all a conspiracy; even now, he knew not even three-quarters of the US had gotten even their second vaccine. Didn't help that the anti-vax, Neo-vaxxers movement was also spawning the Secessionist movement in several states. Adding to that, it didn't help that what you heard on the news kept changing—all the vaccines are different, how we're learning more and more, do this, do that, put this in your nose, shove this in your mouth. People were idiots, even the smart ones. It was that simple. Vaccinated, everyone still lived in uncertainty land: When would it stop working? And do the pills really stop it?

As Alby walked to the truck, he thought back to his first vax. A month after arriving in Baghdad, they had vaxxed him; he had barely heard of Covid. Before he left the hospital in Baghdad for the airport, he got his second one. His Handler had watched as the Iraqi doctor prepared and administered it. "Damn," Alby had exclaimed under his breath; it smacked his muscles like a professional boxer. The Handler laughed. "Ha! Always happens with this one. The Fauci 2.0. Sucker hurts like hell. You'll have a bad twenty-four hours and be fine." Alby had read online how the US government was holding back on this updated vaccine after having been burned by the last variant and poor global distribution.

"Take this, too." Now he was handed a small portable package of strips. "They're expensive. But you gotta test."

He had stopped at the truck door and his heart began to pound. Too many memories, too fast, too much. The Handlers coming into his room again, this time two of them, no introduction, wearing black flak jackets over white shirts and escorted by two Marines who looked like they would have almost made the final casting for *Robocop*. The memory of their voices was now muffled by the ringing in his ears, as the memory faded, some of it still came through… You're heading back to the States. But you have to disappear. Pick a place, any place. Just not a place where anyone knows you or where you lived before.

He leaned against the truck. He was confused; he was back in that bed, that hospital. He remembered what had happened. Sweat formed above his eyebrows as a cold chill swept his body.

"They're looking for you." The man who had spoken was wearing a white shirt puffing from the tight body armor. The black suit spoke in a matter-of-fact voice. "Fatwa kind of thing; vengeance on the infidel." The man had laughed, the Marine by the door chuckled. "Never thought you'd be an infidel, huh?"

Never believe a word, Alby had thought. These guys are trained liars. "I don't believe you." When he had applied for this job in Iraq, he had dealt with these quasi-government people before. The American army had moved out, to let the American contractors move in, and they were mostly ex-military.

Now, unaware that he was standing by his truck in Cherry Hill, USA, his mind had taken over again. He felt the heartache he had felt in the hospital that day. His heart ached for what had happened to the others, his friends. Or were they? Even in that fog of pain, he had known that nothing in Iraq was as it seemed. Where could he go? It occurred to him that he had secretly believed Baghdad was the end of the road for him. There would be nowhere else. The tears falling down his cheeks brought him back to the present with a jerk. He was momentarily lost between the past and the present. But only for a moment. Swiping away the tears in anger, he opened the truck door and got in. He would go to his sister's and make that exit in order to get home in time for some rest before picking up the Ghoul Crew at the bank.

Saturday: 9 p.m.

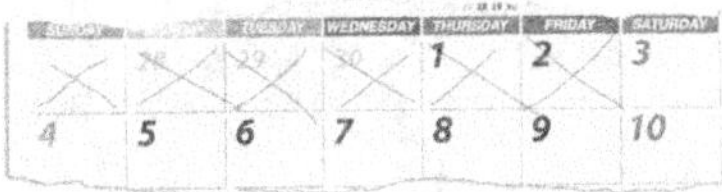

As Alby stared at her house—no, he was staring past it—he began to panic again. His sister's one-story ranch house sat in a nice tract of uniform homes between Cherry Hill and Haddonfield. Cherry Hill sounded so pastoral. Over the course of the twenty-five years Dorothy had lived here, he had only been there a dozen times for family parties: Stephen's high school graduation, the times he drove his mom down from Jersey City—while she was still able to travel—but not much else.

Alby was convinced that the person who named the place Cherry Hill was the master bullshitter of all time. For such a gentle name, Cherry Hill was the embodiment of a semi-chaotic, post–World War II, blemished, suburban sprawl. Alby knew how zoning and construction paired with corrupt local politicians: there were few regulations and even fewer regulators. Huge malls, tiny malls, strip malls, diners, big box stores—half of which were still deserted because of the Pandemic. Heavily trafficked routes, Jersey circles, side roads, highways, spill lanes had all been inserted among patterns of random tract housing. Huge, thick shrubbery worked to create a paper-thin green wall between stores and housing.

Like so many of the streets built back in the '50s, Dorothy's was one long winding curve giving way to a cul-de-sac. As you rounded each turn, the scene was littered with one ranch after another. Alby hated this type of architecture; the small windows were claustrophobic, an Eisenhower-era design detail that was probably meant to minimize the effects of nuclear blast. Each one-story ranch house had a short driveway and a flat roof with a stone patio overlooking a big backyard marred by the tacky above-ground pool. His sister's house was no exception.

He took a deep breath as he pulled up. Dorothy was five years older and had the Big Sister's Complex: always watching out, a little too much. Frankly she wasn't qualified to look out for anyone given how she treated their mom. This drippingly sweet pretext of caring—he was sure it was her secret guilt about her role in their mother's death—it had to be. So why the hell had he picked living near her?

There was no real answer to that question. It was happenstance; the Handler had just walked in—no greeting, no acknowledgement, all blunt. "Tomorrow you're outahere. Now? You have a minute to decide where you're going to go." His upper thigh had been constantly twinging, his shoulder had ached, and he hadn't even been able move his left side because of the huge bandage that covered a cut winding along his side like the Mississippi. Pain killers in a foreign hospital room do not make for good decisions. His mind had been so foggy from the morphine and lack of real sleep and he had felt a moment of blankness. His choice made no sense now but it was all he could call up then: South Jersey, Marlton, Cherry Hill. Dorothy's address had just appeared before him in his mind, kind of like a huge billboard, and he had heard himself repeat out loud what he had heard in his head, her full address: "Cherry Hill." He paused, "Jersey." Instinct not thought had driven those words.

He remembered a second man in a suit covered in a flak jacket had nodded okay. But then he'd come closer and said, "Wait. Aren't you from North Jersey? That's what it says here. What are you trying to pull?"

Somehow, what came out of his mouth was, "There are two Jerseys—north and south."

Flak jacket man seemed to buy it. "I've heard that. Okay, that makes no sense to me...your choice. But Jersey is so dense, no one would find you anyway. South Jersey it is." He scribbled something in a notebook and smiled at Alby. Alby had a talent for smiles; he knew how to read them. When you worked a lot of sites, you got a feeling for how people really were from their smile—they ranged from the begging to genuine thanks to screw-you. This one was not only phony but resembled an alligator that saw you as the appetizer.

The Handlers handed him a phone to make one call back to the States. Surprisingly, he had remembered Dorothy's number. On the phone, she squawked like a bird and laughed about her baby brother coming home—he had only called on the holidays the last two years. They could be a real family. She cried. This made Alby wince. He had a snapshot of her only child, Stephen, a grumpy, lanky kid. Stephen had always liked him; irreverent and funny, Alby had played the crazy Irish uncle role well. But Alby wasn't that person anymore. He also noticed the usual "Dorothy-edits-reality" behavior on the phone—she hadn't asked him why he was leaving Iraq so suddenly or moving near her or any question at all. They were siblings and both got it: she did not want to know.

While Dorothy was off like a rocket on the phone, excited about his moving nearby, Alby could hear the brother-in-law yell from his recliner, "I know family! I got family out the wazoo!" Vinnie the Slob had always made his disdain for Alby clear: Alby was Dorothy's bum brother—unreliable, bad influence, what was broken couldn't be fixed. Done.

Alby somehow dragged himself back to the present. He parked near his sister's unattractive driveway in front of her equally unattractive house. There were a lot of cars parked nearby. He sat there, not really ready to get out and knock at his sister's door.

Dorothy, he thought, what about her? She had left their childhood home in Jersey City as fast as she could, marrying Vinnie the Slob, and having one child—Stephen. Alby couldn't imagine a world where the two of them didn't fight over everything. He really had no idea why he had driven all those times to bring their mom to her house.

He had been careful never to dwell on all those years of rides, the obligatory, take-me-to-see-your-sister Sunday requests from his mom. It was mostly fun driving down the turnpike with his mom perched like a tiny porcelain figurine on the passenger seat of the truck cab, her old handbag neatly beside her on the seat, firing non-stop piss and vinegar about what she thought about the world. Alby was always quiet, figuring that one loud voice was enough but during those car ride years, he had finally gotten old enough to enjoy her monologues. She would settle down and get quieter as they got closer. She worried for her daughter, he knew. She had never liked South Jersey. "Bums," she would mutter sliding carefully out of his truck.

All the way back to Jersey City, the ride was a litany of judgment and worry—she hated Dorothy's husband, how she was raising Stephen, everything. His mom had a biting Irish tongue. She looked like a church lady but spoke like a sailor.

It had just become an accepted family reality that he was the one who would take care of their mother; after all, he was close by and Dorothy was just far enough away to not be able to pitch in.

Alby yanked the keys from the ignition. The sign on the lawn in front read "Vaxxernight !" The roaring tide of his pulse in his ears faded. His heart slowed. Control… he felt the word over and over. Control. He looked down on the fresh scab covering a knuckle on his right hand. Getting out, he paused to pull out the white strip container, placing one on his tongue. He counted to twenty and took it out: still white. If it was blue, he had It. Alby realized that if he tested positive, he had left his anti-viral pills at the cave. Instead of getting pissed off, he waited a minute: still negative. He hadn't tested that day and resented having to spend all that money on these test Listerstrips.

He saw he had parked with his truck tail sticking out a bit, but shrugged and figured if someone hit him, insurance would provide some easy money.

Still he sat in the truck, giving himself some time to change his mind and leave. Why the hell was he here? He'd even skipped Thanksgiving and Christmas last year. Maybe it was her unrelenting onslaughts, this one coming in one of her several thousand text messages—"I want to show off my baby brother!" Then with a very audible curse, he got out of his truck and walked down the sidewalk, noticing not for the first time how scuffed up his black loafers were. Besides his metal-toed boots, the only other shoes he had were sneakers and they looked like hell from too many tar roofs and paint jobs.

His mind drifted to a moment in time when he had enjoyed going out with better shoes on his feet, parties with old buddies, high school pals, guys at the bar from a site he was working on, even back on the base with the few Special Forces folks left in the Green Zone.

But that switch was off.

The "Vaxxer Celebration" was the anniversary of when the government announced herd immunity just a couple of years ago. Eighty percent. True, the double variant put that to rest soon enough with the race starting again. Still, people still celebrated; Dorothy had sent instructions in the invite with a code to type in before you entered the house; it gave his sister early warning if you had been vaccinated or not. He typed it in and waited for a half-minute until he heard the Tracer beep its approval. A hand-written note was taped to her door: "Be sure to 'strip'!" with a photo of Listerstrips.

He realized that he was still in the doorway. Move, Alby. Move.

Despite the vax, despite no buzzing alert, behind the door he sensed a crowd, so he decided to keep his mask on.

The front door was unlocked and as he stepped inside and walked towards the sound waves of conversation and music, like a calliope sliding up and down, he could see that he wasn't the only one wearing a mask. Everyone had Year One masks on—the blue paper ones. Dorothy had never mentioned a theme in any of her messages. The house was crowded, the party at full blast. He would have checked his watch if he had had one, just to time how long he'd make it before bailing. He took a big breath and told himself, "Survive the small talk and just go for the free food and drinks." He could only hope that this would satisfy his sister and even if he slipped out, she would let him alone for at least another year. It was like renewing his blow-her-off license for twelve months.

After squeezing through the crowded living room, he gave a fake smile through his plastimask and nodded to Vinnie the Slob on the other side of the room. Vinnie squeezed out his own fake smile that resembled a droopy accordion. Alby started to think he might have to create a Rule for parties. Something like, "never go to a party unless you've seen the invite list." That was a good one but unusable—too narrow and frivolous. The Rules were serious business.

Holding a tray next to her head, waitress-style, Dorothy tried to hug him with one arm and he had to catch the tray to keep the food from spilling. He could barely hear her greeting. It was a party moment. Cacophony and chaos, air filled with people trying to have conversations but shouting over the music. Alby was surprised by how many people were there. A few were neighbors he'd met over the years before he left for Iraq—the times that he'd brought his mom here. He nodded and smiled at them. Then he felt himself give an inner shrug, resigned to take advantage of what he could, and moved to where he thought he might find some food.

The kitchen was a messy but quiet haven. Even though various open coolers littered the floor, he opened the fridge: he knew where his brother-in-law's special beer stash was. Stella Artois did the job. Looking back into the living room, he nodded and smiled at several people, making eye contact, signaling that yes, they had met, which wasn't true, but he enjoyed leaving them confused and unsure. At least that part was fun. Vinnie the Slob came into the kitchen. "You know them?" Alby ignored him but parsed out a few more greetings as he bumped shoulders with a few couples in the kitchen and attached pantry.

He went back to the fridge and took stock of Dorothy's collection of refrigerator magnets; it was a point of pride that she collected them as magnet souvenirs of every trip she had ever made (none outside the US, a bigger point of pride for her).

The chatter of voices was annoying him. Being surrounded by people he did not know or care about triggered the signal—time to go. His appearance witnessed, now was the time for the Irish exit. To amuse himself, he started moving the magnets around to different positions. He noticed a woman standing just beside and behind him. He had that momentary jitter you get when you think you've been caught.

"Are you Dorothy's brother?"

"Yes, have we met?"

As if his question was a key in the ignition, she just took off and started to blab about their block, their kids, the schools, how viruses hung over everything, how she and Dorothy were best friends—on and on like banging a single-note cymbal. Alby nodded at the right beat to show that he was listening. All he could think of was how her mask, one of those old blue cloth PPE'ers, was half-off her mouth. The magnets were more interesting; he had the strongest urge to spin around and just keep playing with the magnets.

The music suddenly stopped, and the chatter came to a sudden halt. Then more music came on, even louder. The woman was asking him something. "Excuse me?"

She said that Dorothy told her he had gone overseas to work for a few years—where? He felt a showering rush of cold and hot, all at once. He should not be in public, he realized. He needed air.

"She told you that? I'd check with her. Maybe it's our other brother."

"You have another brother? She never told me."

"Because we don't." With that, he walked away, adjusted his mask, downed his beer, and tossed the bottle into the trash with a loud clunk. She took a look at him and smiled awkwardly and retreated.

As he stood in the kitchen corner, opening a Yuengling, his sister found him.

"Having a good time? I see you were talking to Becky—I *adore* her!"

He nodded yes, but meant no. He had not a clue why that woman would adore Dorothy in return. His face must have shown his disdain. Dorothy threw a hand on her hip and said, "You just want to be the difficult Alby. Why are you always so angry?"

He nodded as if he agreed.

"Everything seems to piss you off," she went on, with her usual casual but firm judgment as she reached to move a plate teetering on the edge of the marble kitchen counter. Alby was bemused. Her words had surprised him. She was rarely, if ever, so open and blunt. Where was she going with this?

"Can't you at least try and meet people and be pleasant? You know that's what parties are for, right?"

"Really? I thought they were excuses for people to talk at each other, not to each other." Alby had read that on a magazine cover at CVS.

She threw her arms up. "Why do I even bother! Did you meet the girl I wanted you to meet?"

"What girl? That one?" He pointed to the woman he had just cut off. She had already moved across the room.

"Her? She's married with kids. No, the one I mentioned. Name's Ginger." His face was blank. "Did you listen to a word I said when I invited you? *My dance teacher?*" She huffed and pushed her chest out like an offended bellows; this close, Alby realized that she was half-drunk. "I promised Mom I would watch over you, but you keep pushing me away," she said out of nowhere.

"You? Watch over me?" he asked incredulously. Do not bring up Mom, he thought.

She ignored him. "I met her when I started taking Zumba class. Remember yet?"

"Zumba? What the hell is that? No, don't tell me. I'm not sure I want to know."

"No, it's great stuff and I've lost five pounds. She is so great. She's cute, around your age, funny. She can be a bit sharp, but she's great."

"You said that already. What does 'sharp' mean?"

"Sarcastic." She waved her hand dismissively. "I really don't know why she's still single."

"So why the hell do you want me to meet her?" He did and didn't mean to sound so harsh. But this was just what he expected of his sister; when the need was there, when mom was going south, Dorothy was all phone and no show-up. Now, half-drunk in her own house, she was all talk, no action. He comes to one—just one—of her parties and she's trying to get him married. Why did he even bother?

"I don't know. Maybe because I worry about you. You're such a loner." No, he said in his head, swap an "s" for the "n." Loser, not loner. But who was he to interrupt his big sister? "I mean, I've never been to your apartment—"

He waved his hand and interrupted her: "It's not an apartment—it's behind a garage, a cave." He read her expression. "Yeah, I'm sure your son has had his say about the cave."

"Exactly! Who lives life like that? Vinnie thinks you're up to no good. You've been weird ever since you got back from Iraq." Her eyes narrowed. "And why aren't you working on one of those giant infrastructure projects? They need people like you." She was pleading. She looked like she was getting genuinely upset. Alby had seen this behavior before and had to intercept it.

"Dorothy—I appreciate it, but you don't have to worry about me. I'm doing okay. Ask your son." As usual, he had to be the peacemaker. Old patterns.

"Stephen said you're like fix-it men. He doesn't sound proud." She had opened the refrigerator door while she had been delivering her tirade, a caring one (even though he hated to admit it) but still a tirade. Now, slowly closing the refrigerator door, she looked at him as if she were counting in her head. "You live behind a garage in a hole in the wall. You have no friends. No hobbies. Do you even go to a bar? The work you do is way beneath what you've done before—didn't you tell me you were the manager of a power plant?"

"I was rebuilding it," he interrupted.

She shook her head like she was clearing water out of her ears. "What the hell happened to you?"

And there it was. The body on the floor. She'd said it: the unspoken question that had hung in the air for the past year. And she knew. Her left hand went up to cover her mouth, her eyes full of horror as if she had accused him of murder, which was true; he was the engineer of the self-death of the Alby he had been when he had left, replaced by the one that had returned.

They stared at each other; the wall of party sounds muted there in the now empty kitchen. They heard someone shout, "I will survive!" and on came Gloria Gaynor.

"Doesn't matter." Deflect, he thought, as his pulse started to rise like the tide. "Tell me more about her."

"No, I give up. You're trying to be nice. It's not working. It's phony. Live your life any way you want." She moved to pour drinks and grab some beers from the tiny faux-wood-paneled bar at the end of the kitchen. He felt a bit bad that he had given her a hard time.

"How about I go get you some ice?" He grabbed the large ice bucket. It had ice in it, but he ignored that.

"Thanks, Alby." She paused. "I know you have a good heart." She smiled at him and he saw a hint of his mom. That made him squirm. She turned back to the bar. "It's your attitude that sucks."

He hefted the bucket and tried to smile. "Where to?"

"Back porch."

Like a minnow going with the current, he moved back into the dining room and slid between and through conversations, making his way out to the patio. He slid back the glass door, looking for a light switch. A few strings of white holiday lights pretending to be a year-round decoration were on a trellis, casting a tiny glow. Putting down the bucket, he clipped back the mask into its ear holders—a deep inhale of cool suburban felt good—and decided to ignore his recent sixty-day-long streak of no smoking and lit a cigarette; the party had unnerved him. The lighter flared and showed him the hand with the bloody knuckle, shaking slightly. The pack was crumpled and the tobacco on the edge of stale, but the pressure of what Dorothy had said was pushing in on him.

A moment later, a woman's voice came out of the dark. "Filthy habit."

He didn't jump. He was surprised at that, but he took pride in not being startled like most people—the Humvee rides had perfected his non-reaction.

At the edge of the awning looking up at the sky, she stood in the shadows. He could only see a silhouette. Normal height, short angular nose, lots of hair, but that was all that was visible. Her mask, old-fashioned medical, hung from her ear like a flag at half-mast. The glow from a neighbor's yard cast enough light to make out a mid-knee dress and handbag held in the crook of her right arm. Who carried handbags anymore? She was a lefty, he bet.

It occurred to him that the light from the house was bathing his head so that she could see more of him than he could see of her.

"I have to agree." He held the cigarette away from his face. "I rarely do it." He dropped it and ground it with his heel.

"Rarely? Why now?"

"Party. Drove me to it." He felt relieved just saying it.

She snorted like a laugh got caught halfway up her throat. Not the most attractive sound, he thought.

"Actually, as filthy as it is, I like the smell. Reminds me of my dad," she said. "Though truth be told, he died of lung cancer. Mom, too."

She paused. Then laughed, "Kidding. Sorry, sick sense of humor. Enjoy your smoke. Have another. I don't care." She paused. He was confused—was she serious or kidding? "Actually, it is a filthy habit," she said with conviction. Again, she laughed. Listening to her skip around was like dancing on ice.

"Why are you out here? The party's inside." Feeling caught off-guard made Alby uncomfortable. He just wanted to be alone. If she hadn't appeared he would have found the back gate, done the Exit, and left. But now he felt stuck.

"It was a heart attack that got him, quick, no fuss. Don't you think that's the way to go? Fast. No lingering." She sounded casual even though she also sounded like she was lost in her head. Not being able to see her face, he could not read the emotion. He didn't know how to answer. He had to admit that he was pretty taken aback by her question, mostly because he agreed with her but had never heard anyone say what he thought so clearly. But now he realized that she hadn't asked it in a way that wanted an answer because she just plunged ahead.

"Truth is, I get sick of these suburban parties. I don't know anyone, and I have little or nothing in common with these people. Don't own a home, no kids, no husband, no complaining to do about bus schedules, juice boxes, soccer games. But it is good for business."

He nodded in firm agreement.

"What do you do?"

"Lots of things."

Was she playing coy? "Like what?"

"Well, I waitress, teach dance lessons, and have a few hobbies."

"Like what?" Squinting, he tried harder to see her against the wall of dark where she had melted into the trellis.

"Binge watching old movies. Old musicals."

"Huh."

"Huh, like 'that's interesting' huh or a 'that's stupid' huh?"

"No judgment. Just huh." He paused. "Well, why the old stuff? And what 'old' do you mean?"

"Classics. 1930s—some pre-code stuff—and all the great musicals."

Made sense; she just said that she was a dance teacher. He tried to remember the last time he had seen a movie. He couldn't. What was "pre-code"? he wondered.

"What do *you* do?" she asked.

They stood quiet for a minute. Quiet enough to hear the late summer crickets and the fading melodic chatter of the party that mixed in with the cicadas.

He was tempted to say: I hire the scum of the earth to do scum-of-the-earth jobs. Then he thought who cares and said it.

"Oh, you must be a contractor," she came back immediately.

Alby laughed. "Good one."

"Are you Dorothy's brother?"

"Yes." He paused: the dark had given her an anonymity to say things someone might not say, but he was in the light. "Sometimes."

She didn't take the bait. He thought it was funny.

"Alby…is that your name?"

"Yes. Crappy name, huh?"

She ignored his comment. "Is it short for something?"

He hesitated but then thought, what the hell. "Yeah, Aloysius."

She laughed lightly. "Wow, now that is so old school Irish! I am not sure I have ever met an Aloysius."

"Now you have." He felt stupid.

"Huh," she said.

"Huh as in 'good' huh or 'bad' huh?"

"Just huh. No judgment." There was a pause and then they both laughed softly. It caught him off guard… the laugh had just snuck out. He liked clever women but was not used to it.

The dark seemed to close in. Shadows with voices were pouring out of the house. He moved to look at the rows of coolers with ice bags in them.

"I guess I'll say goodbye."

"You're the Zumba teacher, huh?" It just came out. He couldn't help it. Not sure why. He suddenly didn't want her to leave.

She hesitated. "Yes, your sister takes—"

"—your class."

"Yes, Zumba. Ever try it?"

"No." He had to wonder; what kind of man took a dance class? Simple: divorced and on the make. "What kind of guy takes a Zumba class?" His tone had a phony innocence.

A disdainful noise came from her throat. "A divorced guy looking for dates."

Alby smiled.

Then, right there in the dark, in total stillness, she writhed and twisted her arms and whirled around for a few seconds; he could not make out much, but he could hear her humming, a thumping Latin sound in her throat, very quietly, as she did some sort of dance. The metal awning bar blocked most of her movements.

She stopped as suddenly as she had started. "Well, there you go."

"You invent that?" The edge in his words—he hadn't meant that. Talking like this felt clumsy—had he even held a conversation with a woman in the past year?

She took his comment seriously. "What rock have you been under?"

"Too many to count."

"Zumba. The person made a ton of money off of overweight suburban women who are bored to death and need exercise with a little indirect sexual spice thrown in."

A laugh was at the tip of his tongue before he held back. "Ouch. Nice scam. So, do you make a ton of money?"

"Nope. The scam? That would be the studio owner. The dance? It helps women feel like women, kind of what their husbands have forgotten." She shrugged. "And money is not my thing."

"Money," he said slowly, "…is everybody's thing."

Again, he saw her shoulders rise and fall in the dark in a shrug. "Root of all evil?" Her voice lifted upward, in a fake dramatic tone.

He'd never met anyone—not even the parish priest—who truly didn't care about money, no matter what they quoted. "So, you like being broke? You sound like someone who has first-hand experience."

"No, that's not what I meant. Money causes trouble." She moved away from the pole and stepped onto the patio. "Trouble…" she let her voice trail off into the dark.

"Sorry to hear that."

"Me too." Her voice moved down into the scale of sad and whimsical, and the quietness in it made it sound as if she had left the patio and was heading away. But then she spoke again. "Guess I am luckier than I thought."

"Rule number five: there is no such thing as luck." He spoke without even thinking.

"What rules?" She turned to face him, and part of her head came into the light: red hair, a bit wild, small nose, the outline of a face that seemed attractive. He regretted saying anything.

"Rules. The Rules," He had to get on another topic.

"You're a fine one…." She sounded curious, like a cat with a ball of emotional twine. "If that one's five, how many are there?"

"Nine." Wait, he thought. "Eight!"

"Aren't we creative." He could not read her tone: Cynical? Dismissive? Neutral?

Alby lit another cigarette just to do something, though he did not want to. He felt nervous, but not the kind of nervous he'd grown used to. After he lit it, he threw it away.

"Now you have me curious. These rules…."

"Never should have mentioned it. Where'd you grow up?"

She ignored the question. "Ah, but you did… so why not? We all need rules to live by."

"Yeah." Exactly, he thought. But he was suspicious of her interest.

"Why do I get the feeling that yours are particularly unusual?" She was toying with him—she was in the safety of the shadows, he was exposed.

"Depends upon your view of the world."

"True. What's yours?"

"Ha! No, I think I'll pass."

"C'mon. Rule number one?"

"Never trust anyone," he blurted out.

"Nice," she said. "Have children?"

"No. What's that got to do with it?"

"Nothing. Everything. How many rules again?"

Was she teasing him? She was teasing him. Irritating, but in an odd way he kind of liked it.

"Hmmm. Never trust anyone. You must have had a lot of healthy relationships."

He said nothing.

"What's number two?"

"Are you making fun of me?" Not being able to see her face because of the shadows, he was stuck because he could not read her voice.

"No, not really," she said ambivalently. "I'm just curious."

He went with it. "Never work with family," he declared.

"Doesn't Dorothy's son work for you?"

She had him. He chuckled. "I hate exceptions, but yes… jury is still out on that choice. You sure seem interested in this."

"Yeah, mostly because I have my own list."

He laughed, almost like her, a short bark like a gun going off. "Name one."

She didn't hesitate; she had been ready. "Rule number one? You got to believe."

Before he could stop himself, he guffawed and said, "You have to be kidding me. Believe in what?"

"Believe what you believe. Stick to it." She took a step back into the shadow of the awning pole she was once again leaning on.

"Guess we see life differently."

"No shit." Was that a sudden edge in her voice?

He sensed it first, a vibration in the air, then realized she was humming. He tried to pull the tune from his memory; it was familiar but ghosted.

"You've got to have heart! Miles and miles and miles of heart!" she sang quietly in perfect pitch.

"*Damn Yankees*," he snapped. Not altogether sure why, he instantly regretted speaking at all and especially in that tone of voice, then just as fast, he wondered why he regretted it. His mom had loved that musical.

"Good one. I grew up at sea. You?"

"Jersey City." He paused. "Navy brat?"

"Not exactly." She stretched the second word out in a curious way, then made a dismissive wave. "Another time."

How does a kid grow up at sea? Fisherman? Just then, he heard his sister shout from the house, "*Alby!* Where's the ice?"

The moment was lost. He could feel it, the movement of one moment turning into another that felt altogether different. He felt it as an actual loss. She glided past him. She didn't walk, she glided. In the dark, her feet seemed to float. He turned to the door to catch a glimpse of her; he hadn't felt this tinge…this…curiosity in a long time. She turned away from him as she drew nearer to the light, out of the shadows, revealing perfect legs, no stockings, blue skirt, powder blue blouse. But then she turned her head, saying, "Have a good night, Aloysius," over her shoulder. Her voice was coy and playful; she said his name in a way he had never heard before. She stepped sideways to brush by him to get to the door. Her hair was fiery red. He caught just a glimpse of her eyes peering out from under her curly mop, but it was enough to see they were blue and sharp. She passed through the door.

Seconds went by before he realized that he was standing stock still, as if someone had smacked him in the head. He shook himself and glancing into the forgotten ice chest, grabbed a bag and went inside, bumping into his sister.

"Where's the ice?"

"Melted." He hefted the bag up. She screwed up her face with disdain. Then she seemed to realize something and asked, "Hey, did I see—"

"Yeah, your Zumba teacher. Another reason why I hate parties."

"What? Why?"

"You meet people." Despite the cynicism in his words, he realized what they had really meant. He had felt something shift inside, an unfamiliar sense of something that he couldn't name but could certainly feel.

Bedtime, he thought, as he worked his way through the crowd. Gotta get the guys at six a.m. It wasn't the way he wanted to slip out—publicly. And it did not accomplish what he hadn't realized he was trying to accomplish; he did not see her anywhere.

Driving away without saying goodbye to his sister was like leaving the orbit of another planet, one that he had left long ago, one that he no longer belonged in.

What did "grew up at sea" mean?

Almost absentmindedly, the gray man patted the side pocket of his blazer, feeling the bulge of a small, worn notepad—his Check List for every new assignment. He knew the assignment and all the methodical steps he used by heart. The small, tattered notepad he kept only for sentimental reasons.

Very early this same Saturday morning, Jagger had been standing among palm trees and cactus. The Owners' private jets always seemed to be nearby, so getting here had been easy. From the beginning he had kept a bag packed and always had an open ticket in case their private jet wasn't available; but as with everything, Covid had changed that. Now a private jet was always available; given the severe germophobes they were, there was no way they would let any employee fly commercial. Even though the Owners were now completely stationary, sitting on their yacht off the Bermuda coast, they had shifted to make things Pandemic-proof. But that had changed nothing about their business; they had never been anything but *remote*; now they were global and busier than ever—he could tell because his assignments were increasing.

Saturday night had crept in and he needed to get to his motel room. But first, drive the streets. Get familiar. Break out the Check List. Then he would go back to the site.

Saturday Night: After Midnight

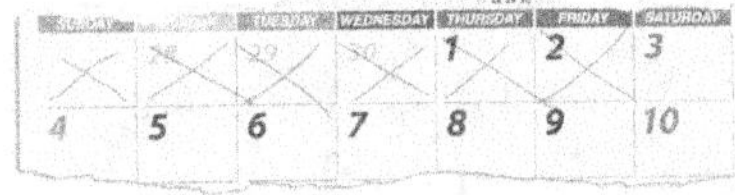

Nothing irritated Jagger more than incompetent people—which, unfortunately, was pretty much everyone. He often wondered if there was a never-ceasing epidemic of stupidity or it was just a trait built into mankind's wiring. For him, the Pandemic was the Earth putting out a contract on mankind. As sad a truth as it was, it did make sense anthropologically that stupid people would breed more, survive, and cause more trouble.

The Owners had thought Kurtz could run a bank, but he had demonstrated his incompetence on a grand scale. Someone had their hands on a genuine blank check: anyone with half a brain could fill in a very large amount, drive forty miles to where the bank check would be accepted without question, and with some double-talk, leave with cash—a lot of cash— enough cash to officially disappear forever. With the Owners' money.

But he had a hunch that whoever in the night crew had stolen it was as incompetent as everyone else. Jagger savored the gift of being the only person who had the clarity to see everyone else's incompetence with such utter brilliance. This theft had stupid written all over it and this usually meant a faster resolution—the thieves would show themselves, stumble. Then the script wrote itself: find the check, kill who you need to, clean up, go home. The Owners appreciated his efficiency—occasionally they complained about the body count, but he kept silent. He had the best job in the world.

Going into the building to inspect Kurtz's office would require putting on a hazmat suit. He had spent a few hours watching YouTube videos, educating himself. He had stood in front of the motel kitchen table, which was covered in road maps and the files from Fat Joe, looping several how-to videos over and over, dozens of times, as he mimicked the motions of each step in putting on this cumbersome suit. That was his definition of the utmost competence: doing something well you had never done before.

Now, while driving to the site and thinking more about it, Jagger decided that this assignment was going to prove to be one of the worst ones they had ever given him. Usually it was pure white-collar crime. Only lowlife scum and end-of-the-road addicts and ex-cons would do this kind of deadly, filthy work. In spite of how much time it had taken him to watch those videos about how to get into what was sure to be a clumsy get-up (and he hated to feel even a little clumsy), he knew that he would feel safer in it—the thought of even sharing the air with these people made him nauseous.

As Jagger approached the bank, he saw that the site was at the height of activity. In the darkness, losing itself in the lights from inside, the building's outer plastic sheathing rustled in the night wind, which had a ballooning effect on the building. The night was cool, but not cold, the kind of cool air that betokened early fall, where it rose from the earth instead of falling down on it. He pulled in and drove his car to the far end, the darkest part of the bank parking lot. It was nearly empty. He walked the length of the lot right to Fat Joe's trailer.

As he entered, Jagger immediately could tell that from his involuntary recoil, violence and fear motivated Fat Joe—easy enough, he thought.

"I want to see the fourth floor. Every executive office."

"They're still cleaning up the inside. You'll need a suit."

Jagger ignored him. "Start with the EVP office. Bring a scissors and tape." With that he walked out and strolled to the bank entrance, walked over to the rack, and took a hazmat suit off the hook. Pausing, in his mind, he played back the seven steps in the YouTube video he had watched. He started each one slowly and methodically. About then, Fat Joe hustled in, items in hand, and grabbed a suit.

"You're in charge?" Fat Joe began, with a question in his voice, and then thought better of it. "Right, you're in charge."

In response, Jagger cast a disdainful eye at him. "Yes." Have no doubt of that, he thought.

"Watch the suits—they rip easy," Fat Joe said. Jagger kept at his steady pace, one leg folded up like an accordion, foot in, suit pulled up. Left leg done. Repeat.

He could tell Fat Joe was looking at him, getting a chill at how automated Jagger made it look.

Jagger saw the elevator and headed towards it. Fat Joe, realizing what would happen if he told Jagger about the elevators being off at night while the construction was going on, decided to take the bull by the horns and called out, "Wait a minute while I throw the on switch for the elevator." Jagger shot him an impatient glance and then waited while Fat Joe moved towards another door as fast as his body in a hazmat suit allowed. As soon as he came out, Jagger continued walking to the elevator. Maybe that clown is beginning to understand who's who here. As they got into the elevator and rode to the fourth floor, his face, even from behind the mask, told an entire story to Jagger. "Kurtz and I went and checked the office."

"And?"

"That's when he admitted he had left the safe unlocked."

Jagger gazed at Fat Joe and then turned away. He was telling the truth; even through his faceplate, he could see that, although he could also see traces of other lies that must have been flitting around in his mind. But those lies were not of interest.

As they got out, Jagger turned to him. "What was his first reaction?"

Fat Joe stopped and looked at him curiously as the door slid closed behind them. Before he answered, he fitted the helmet over his head and watched as Jagger did the same. Now, speaking louder, standing nearer to him than he felt comfortable doing, he said, "I don't know—he was kinda scared, got nervous, made some calls, sat in the trailer then the lobby until you came." Jagger sighed. In his mind he was weighing all the options and the first to be looked at was: is this an inside job? He realized a person like Fat Joe was too oblivious to anything around him to answer such a probing question and he doubted that this guy would be part of any inside job anyway; all employees were all too aware of the Owners' track record for people caught screwing with them. When someone betrayed their trust, they videotaped the killing and posted it only for incognito viewing. Then sent a mandatory attend invite to all employees via email to watch it.

Leaving that issue behind for the moment, Jagger now spoke with added emphasis to his louder voice. "Before we go in, let me make our respective roles clear to you. You're a stupid foreman for a crummy late-night job. That barrel over there," he pointed out the window, "the bottom of that barrel over there sits higher than you on my food chain. When I ask you questions, you speak. If I don't ask, you don't speak. Take me in and show me his office."

Gesturing at an open door held together by a floor-to-ceiling zipper, Fat Joe yelled, "This is Kurtz's office." The zipper was oversized, big enough for hazmat fingers to pull up and down. This zipped piece of plastic led to more plastic—two small plastic chambers they would need to pass through. Jagger had a moment of claustrophobia, an old, old pain; he shook it off and stepped through the chamber that had a shower head on top, the chamber only large enough for one man at a time. It was like having someone put you in a plastic casket. Fluorescent lighting made the plastic seem even more opaque and the room cold and morgue-like.

Once they were through the chambers, Jagger turned towards Fat Joe and said, even louder this time (damn these helmets and now, what, an air purifier motor?), "Why were they up here? The floor looks empty."

"I think someone came looking for stuff to steal on their lunch break. Be the only time to rip stuff off."

Standing at the center of Kurtz's large office, Jagger turned slowly in a circle, taking in the entire space; he then looked up and turned in another circle, this time taking in the ceiling, the exposed ducts, the plastic not quite in place, the large air purifier not turned on yet. He could see the mummified-looking furniture molded by the plastic and knew where the safe was. "Give me something to cut this with!" he yelled.

"Already been cut!" Fat Joe yelled back, standing behind him. Jagger turned his head and about a foot away saw Fat Joe, gnome-like in the oversized suit, pointing at a fold in the plastic. With his gloved hands, he pulled the overlapping sheets apart, revealing a strip of tape. Leaning in and then back, he stretched and ripped the tape off. At first, he saw nothing but bare, wood-paneled walls. Then he tore it further, which caused Fat Joe to shout some warning or something. Jagger ignored him, especially as he now saw the small handle of the wall safe to his left.

Opening it was hard. The clumsy gloves made it difficult to grasp the small handle. He tugged on the small pen-length handle; it moved a half-inch and swung open; in the washed-out light of the white plastic sheets, the interior of the small safe was a black hole. Jagger reached in and slowly, clumsily extracted and examined each of the dozen items in it. He would be so glad when this job was done. Another bank check was there, also signed. He shook his head in stupefied amazement. Two signed checks? How could this guy have forgotten to lock the safe? Now he saw a white envelope with the flap open. Doing a fast visual count based on the thickness of the bills, he figured there was about twenty thousand dollars in one-hundred-dollar bills. Kurtz's escape money, he thought, in case things ever went south. Again, Jagger shook his head with a sense of pathetic resignation: they were all thieves. And idiots. They had grabbed the blank bank check but missed the cash. A few other items seemed out-of-place: Kurtz's MBA graduation diploma, a family photo from Disneyland, and a plastic bag with old coins in it.

Whoever had taken the check had to have taken off their glove to get it. In other circumstances, he might have tried to capture a fingerprint; he had back-door access to FBI files and could have matched it. But the poison air prevented that. With idiots like this, he did not need a fingerprint to find them. They would find themselves for him.

He pulled back and went to examine the rest of the plastic sheets on the walls carefully; he wanted to know how aggressive the thief was. They were all in crews of four...*was* it more than one thief?

Fat Joe watched Jagger move away from the man-sized tear he had created; the office air began slowly drawing tiny flakes of asbestos, like a virus. Fat Joe waddled over and re-taped it. Grabbing the giant roll of masking tape from his suit pocket, he went to work fixing the rip. For such a wobbly, clumsy figure, Jagger observed, his hands were fast and dexterous.

"I'm done!" he heard Jagger shout just as he smoothed over a single straight line down the plastic like it was the handiwork of an experienced surgeon. Silently, they both moved to the shower chamber, stepped through, and came out into the hallway. As Fat Joe zipped the last chamber shut, Jagger looked down the long hallway; a few guys were rolling barrels and one was checking an air gauge. "Already setting up for next weekend," yelled Fat Joe. "We'll be up on this floor by then." Because of the poor line of sight of the hazmat suit, he did not notice that one man was pushing a dolly right behind him.

Lucky hesitated as he saw the two men leave the executive office; but he just lowered his head and moved past them. He had snuck off at the break to see if he could find more stuff. He didn't realize they'd be setting up—too many people. He slowed his walk as he passed and glanced peripherally: he saw that the small, round-man suit was Fat Joe but he didn't know who the other one was, only that he was someone else who walked as if he was not wearing a heavy hazmat suit.

Lucky instantly understood that they knew the check was gone. Fat Joe was up here with that guy, probably a cop, looking for some evidence of who had taken it. The thought left him cold: they knew. Lucky had figured they wouldn't find anything missing until the end of next weekend when the job finished. What could he do? Lucky didn't have many choices. Trying to cash it at a local bodega would be stupid; the Dominican family that ran all the bodegas counterfeited their own checks and would cut his throat, and not before they would grab the oversized bank check and laugh at him. He could go to a pawn shop, but that was mob money and he wanted nothing to do with that. Besides, they all talked to each other. Lucky had figured that he would have the cash and be gone before anyone knew, but the chances of that happening just got slimmer.

Yet for every moment of doubt, he also found himself daydreaming of the possibilities and a warm feeling came over him. All the money, piles and piles; when he closed his eyes, he saw a suitcase with bills stacked in it. New car. New clothes. Out of Camden.

It was simple—he just needed someone with a bank account; he could go with them when they cashed the check, signed over to him, of course, and then just hand over the suitcase for the cash. He'd have to give whoever this was a cut, but with this much money, he could afford to be a little generous. That was the best plan. Now he just needed to find someone he knew who had a bank account—he wanted it to be someone other than his Uncle Charlie. He didn't want to go there and see his aunt; she always had it out for him. But it seemed like it would be the fastest way to go.

It was almost two a.m. and lunch break was almost over.

Lucky rushed to get down to the area in the parking lot where everyone was sitting on the grassy median, having their meal under the silver klieg lights. Nearly tearing off his hazmat suit, he rushed outside. He had to make sure the other two didn't steal anything else. As he did so, he heard Chance yell, "Lucky!" in that dumb you're-my-pal voice.

Lucky hustled Chance and Darnell to a curb and sat down to have a sandwich. Darnell was smart enough to survey the area around them before he spoke. "Wadda we doin' with the check?"

"How many times do I have to tell you? Tomorrow, I go see my aunt. Her husband has a bank account. Monday," Lucky repeated like a parrot. "Banks aren't open Sundays."

"All I know, Lucky, is that it won't be long before someone knows the check is gone. Then we're done."

"Darnell, grow some balls. No one saw us." Lucky decided there was no way he was going to share what he had seen.

"Yeah?"

"Yeah," Lucky said, sticking out his chest. "We got a week." He patted his chest; he could feel the check. "Nobody's finding anything." For Lucky, lying was like drinking water.

Chance just stared hard at him, mouth agape. "What?"

"It belongs to all three of us."

Lucky patted his right hand over his heart. "I know that."

"Let's decide who keeps it."

"Okay. Vote." Lucky glanced at Chance and let it turn slowly into a cold glare. Chance looked at both men confused.

Darnell shook his head, resigned to Chance's stupidity. "I vote I hold it. I'm more—"

"Don't get preachy on me, Darnell. Your hands are dirty, too. I hold it," declared Lucky, eyes never leaving Chance.

"Well…?" Darnell asked Chance. But Lucky broke in. "You know it's safe with me, Chance. I'm the best chance we got to cash this."

Darnell would not let it go. "Lucky, you'd steal from your dead mom's coffin if you knew money was there."

Lucky was still looking at the third member of the trio. "Chance." He said the name firmly.

"I vote Lucky!" Chance burst out. He immediately looked relieved as Lucky smiled.

"I got an idea—we meet each day at five at Sam's Diner. We check in on the check." Lucky said the last part with a laugh. Chance nodded, kept his eyes to the ground, and stepped back, spun, and walked away fast.

"Lucky." Darnell laid the name down like an ultimatum. Lucky paused, but instead of turning around, just said, "See you later at the diner. Six, right?" With the switch from five to six, to Darnell, it already sounded like what he had thought all along: Lucky had his own plans for the check.

Sunday: 6:30 a.m.

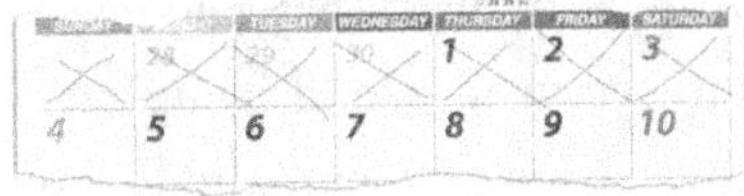

He glanced at his phone: Half past six. Crap, he was supposed to pick them up at six.

He hated Sundays.

Though you would think he had grown used to them by now, early mornings and a hangover were poor company. The chorus of birds outside was making a torturous noise. In Iraq, where everyone got up at dawn, there were no birds. Instead, there were the sounds of the city, the first call to prayer, construction, the grinding of old truck engines' gears. Your first thought was listening with anticipation for a roar of a bomb or a scream of an ambulance—which really did not happen often, but enough to make you pause. Give it up, he thought; Sunday was here, another week with the cocked-eye look of shit upon shit—the pattern turned over and stared back at him again. He had to move. He needed coffee and eggs, sausage, bread. More coffee. Then maybe a nap—maybe he could trick the nightmares with a round on the punching bag and set himself up for an exhausted, no-dreams nap.

Moving faster than he wanted to, he jumped into his truck and raced to the bank.

After a very whiney drop-off in Camden, he pulled his truck into the diner on the Jersey circle near where Route 70 and Marlton Pike met. He rarely went to this diner, but his head was fuzzy and it was closest to his place. Lots of coffee and a big breakfast, and that would weigh him down enough for a nap when he got back to the cave. Coffee could wake him up, but it never kept him awake.

With a nod, he went in the "Vaccinated" door, previously the front door, which was the dividing line between the no-Vax and Vax sides of the diner. He was glad there were no "Vax Rights" protesters who wanted those divisions removed; guess they didn't get up early. Story was, they had every right not to get vaxxed and have equal rights to everything, and Congress was arguing about it, calling it the new prejudice—separate but equal—and wanted legislation to give them equal access. Alby had read the story but didn't care: stupid was stupid; stupid only made more stupid; reading too much stupid made you stupider. He never ceased to be amazed at how ignorant people were; everyone thought they were invincible, he had too once, but he knew better now with the souvenir running along his side. As he pushed open the door, he stopped, realizing he had not snapped on his mask; he probably didn't need it here since it was segregated, but he clicked it in place anyway; there was too much news going around about a variant and a new form of Ebola in Africa. He moved past the old Greek owner at the cash register wearing no mask—he was paying more attention to the cash box than the piece of food hanging off the front of his white shirt. Alby smiled but got nothing back; the antique shiny aluminum register had the man's attention. So he slipped into the first empty booth he could find. The place was surprisingly busy. He sat for five minutes in a half-daze and realized no one had noticed him. As he felt someone near, he gave his order; he did not even look up. He made it clear, in a "No Talking Please" voice: "Coffee. Now. Then the full plate—eggs, bacon, toasted rye."

A minute later the owner slid a cup of coffee, slopping onto the saucer, under his nose.

Holding the cup, bent over, eyes closed, he breathed deeply. The scent of strong coffee—had to be the best invention ever.

"Boss says serve the rude man in booth six." It was Ginger (how could he know but he did). She slid the large, crowded plate over in front of him, all the food in an ugly riot competing for space. "No, he was wrong." Stepping back, she took a hard look at him. "You're not rude, you're hungover."

She didn't take a breath so he couldn't speak fast enough. "You don't strike me as an early bird. Yet, here you are." Staring at his eggs, the two yellow eyes stared back up at him.

"Look at those eggs any harder I am going to put them back in the shell and call the cops."

He sat up, shoulders back, eyes forward. It was for show, since he was sure he looked like hell.

She looked different in the washed-out blue waitress uniform; it was the same retro diner uniform that hadn't changed since the 1950s. Her red hair was pulled back and tucked under a pointy cap fighting to get free, her lips a bright red, her small nose looking sharper because it lined up with the point of the cap; a matching blue mask hung off her left ear.

"Hey," he said listlessly.

"Snappy comeback."

"Yeah, not as fast as you for sure. So this was the early work you mentioned?" And here he thought he'd been blown off when she left so abruptly. Get the no-hangover face, he said to himself.

"No, this is me impersonating a waitress in a cheap diner while my rich family searches for me." She placed her hand jauntily on her hip.

"Man, do you ever let up?" His head ached. Her words were like caffeinated bullets, coming at his throbbing head.

"Sorry. Here. Load up." She refilled his cup. He nodded and took a swig. "Looks like you had a bad night…bad date?" He looked at her sharply. "Sorry, sorry. I use humor to keep myself awake."

"Really. I would have called it a natural defense mechanism."

"Hmmm…that could be true." She pressed a thumb on her chin as if in thought. "Of course, how would you know since you're more closed up than a clam pissing at high tide?"

He couldn't help himself: he shook his head incredulously. How did she think of this stuff?

"It is way too early for this—anyway, clams open up at high tide. That's why they bubble in the sand." He took another gulp, picked up his fork, but kept trying but failing not to look at her. He noticed she had inched across the booth so he didn't have to crane his neck; it was so subtle he almost missed it. She was cute. And her eyes were a deep blue. Aliyah's eyes had been black. He shook his head: don't go there. Focus on the moment, or the coffee, the eggs, her eyes. No, not the eyes; Alby felt like he was getting lost in his mind.

"Never seen you here before." He kept waiting for the obligatory gum-smack sound from her mouth, but it did not come.

"I like the Marlton Diner." After he'd said it, he felt stupid.

"We feel honored by your presence. Heading off to early work?"

"It's Sunday. You just don't stop, do you?" But this time, a smile slowly moved across his lips; his head was clearing. "Actually, I am the part-time pastor at the local Presby church."

"Your sister is Catholic. You're Irish."

He laughed, contained at first but then like a bubble popping in his chest. The coffee finally hit home. She smiled and let out a short laugh, that bark again that he had heard last night. Just then, the manager called to her from behind the counter. "We have more than one customer! Coffee here, coffee there!" He said, gesticulating frantically.

Her grip tightened on the metal pot handle as she put on her cloth mask, same powder blue as her uniform; her knuckles were a bit white, and she made an exaggeratedly angry face that only Alby could see. He laughed quietly, which was all his head could take. She lifted one foot, spun in a perfect circle on her heel, landed with both feet and took off, coffee container straight ahead. "Who needs coffee?" she snarled over her shoulder, smiling. His lips moved to a smile before his mind caught up.

"I do!" He could not resist.

"You've had enough, pal."

No, he hadn't. He watched her walk away: damn if that blue waitress uniform didn't hug her hips just right.

Before he left, he looked for her and saw her at the other end of the diner, clearing plates from a table with a young family—even from where he stood, he could see that the table looked like a food war had erupted. He half-waved but was not sure she saw. Meanwhile, the owner—mask on now—was having an argument with some guy in his 50s—no mask of course—about why he couldn't sit in the Vaxxer area. Alby thought that wearing a hunting coat was a bad choice for someone looking for a fight.

He couldn't avoid hearing his loud voice—a neo-vaxxer. Bad news. As he slipped past them, his phone alert for someone not vaccinated went off—pretty obvious who, he thought. Then heads started to turn, masks were slipped on. Time to go.

Back inside his place, he dropped his windbreaker on the floor and went through the shower into the garage. Walking carefully around the oil stains, he grabbed the new boxing gloves that were sitting on a metal shelf. He stood in front of the rawhide-colored bag that hung from a chain over a metal beam running along the ceiling, set his feet in place—right in front of left—and started a series of jabs with each arm—right, left, right, left.

He had learned by now to hit the bag hard enough to not hurt his hands; the bloody knuckle thing, well, he hadn't mastered that. Especially when he just pounded mindlessly; he knew that he shouldn't box when he was drunk since in that state he often forgot to put the gloves on, but it happened. His knuckles told the tale. The usual routine was jab until his breath grew thinner and what he hoped was true exhaustion swept over him. Often, he pictured himself like those Rock 'Em Sock 'Em robots he had played with as a kid: jab, jab, jab. No roundhouse combinations or anything fancy. Just a simple machine-gun, left–right jab–uppercut.

Back in the room, he collapsed on the bed with his clothes on, then bounced up, grabbed some rope, and tied the screen door to keep it closed. This time he collapsed with conviction, not even taking off his shoes. He felt the food, coffee, air, and her slight fragrance cutting through his night-mares like a train on a raging night.

By afternoon, he was out back, beside the sandlot where he parked his truck, sitting on an old lawn chair his sister had given to him. Staring mindlessly at a tree and the broken bird's nest perched on one of the lower branches had been a good summer pastime. For some reason he could not stop staring at this family of birds. Having discovered it last spring, he was now involved in the family goings-on—it was his version of a National Geographic sitcom. They flew and grabbed twigs, then acted like a pair of interior decorators flitting about, trying to find the best place for that specific twig; they bickered, fed each other and their young. It helped that the sound of traffic was dull. The area behind the garage was a tiny sand lot—enough for a half-dozen cars. The whole area was corralled by rows of tall bushes that when bare in the winter revealed the backs of a development of what looked like newer, syncopated cookie-cutter ranch houses. In the summer, the bushes were a solid wall cutting him off. By keeping his truck in the back, away from the road, the garage looked deserted.

He slid his hand into his right boot and then withdrew it. The folded switchblade had some heft but felt light at the same time. With one finger, he tweaked the release, and the knife sprang open. The blade shone brightly as it caught the afternoon sun, in sharp contrast to its black ebony handle. He started to flip it in the air and catch it by the handle.

Rule number three, he thought: the money isn't real until it's in your hands. Immediately Fat Joe came to mind—the guy probably paid in counterfeit twenties. He was supposed to get it all next Sunday night. Cash. All under the table. This was fine for Alby because it was easier to skim his part from the crew. Alby felt a momentary twinge of guilt that he was being the kind of sleazebag he so virulently hated, but he quickly shook it off. If he hadn't gotten them the work, they'd have no money at all.

Stephen's old Toyota truck ruined his reverie. That thing needed a new muffler. Alby threw the knife into the ground near his left foot and reached for the Sunday paper, also on the ground—he stole the weekend paper from a different neighbor each week, just to keep it interesting. He liked the idea that they probably all blamed each other. They could afford to buy an extra newspaper. He placed his gaze on the page without really seeing any words.

Stephen got out and started to walk over to him. Seeing that he was reading the paper, he casually asked, "Any news?"

Alby kept looking down but nodded. "Looking for weather, deaths, and other events."

"Why?"

"Well, weather means emergency fix-it work. Deaths mean widows looking to fix up the house that the husbands never let them fix up. And other events? Hell, news is news. It's where I look for inspiration."

"That looks like the sports page."

"Huh. Sure does."

"You don't follow sports. Not even an Eagles' fan."

"Is it that time of year again? Those muscle-heads with concussions back on the field?"

Stephen shrugged and gave up. He was wearing an Eagles-green Randall Cunningham T-shirt.

"Why the visit? Sunday's your day off."

"Was on my way to my girlfriend's. Thought I'd say hello. Prep for Monday."

Inside the apartment, Alby's iPhone rang. He couldn't stand the damn thing, but the Handlers had given him one and said they were going to use a supercharged "Find My iPhone" feature to keep track of him. On more than one drunken night, he had stumbled to the screen door and tossed it hard into the night. Damned thing did not break. Since only a half-dozen people knew the number, this was a rare event for a Sunday.

"I guess since you were reading the weather, you heard about the nor'easter coming next weekend. They say it's going to be nasty. Could hit Atlantic City head-on."

Picking up a different section, Alby declared: "Huh. Should never watch the weather: it's all bullshit. It'll all change by Wednesday."

"Probably need a Rule for weather…something like, 'Weathermen are bullshit artists.' Big nor'easter is bad news, Alby."

"Believe it when I see it. Bad for roofs, good for us." Alby was matter-of-fact.

"Are you going to just ignore that call?" Stephen asked. Alby went inside. The ringing had stopped and then started again. Someone wanted him. He picked up the iPhone—it was a near-hysterical Fat Joe ordering him to the site. Only half his words made sense; they fell out of his mouth like rocks tumbling down a hill. NOW! NOW! Alby didn't like taking orders and he especially did not like being yelled at. But Fat Joe had a tone in his voice Alby hadn't heard before—fear. Fat Joe yelled one last time that he needed to get to the site and hung up.

A moment later, he spoke into the phone, "Wrong number," loudly enough for Stephen to hear, then came out with his keys and jacket.

Stephen followed him with his gaze. "That was the phoniest wrong number I have ever seen. Trying to get rid of me?" Alby needed to go; this was none of Stephen's business.

"Every number is wrong. Even phone calls that mean money. Rule number three: the money isn't real until it's in your hands." Alby raised his voice as if in a court of law: "Money's not real until it is in your hands."

Stephen nearly spit. "You really own assholedom."

"I'm an optimist. I look for good things, but unfortunately only find shit," Alby countered. "You're young and stupid. I am old and wise."

"Where're you heading? You usually hide on Sundays." Alby sensed Stephen knew something was wrong.

"Need some food."

As Alby got into his truck, Stephen slid into his chair, holding the newspaper. "Hey, I think my mom wants you over for dinner. My dad's on the road this week and she thought it might be good." As his uncle drove away, Stephen yelled, "Tuesday!"

Alby smiled and waved his hand out the window. Twice in a week? He'd made the effort already. The image of Ginger floated across his mind; it was like a loose balloon. Why think of her? He'd blown that one, he thought. Now what did that mean?

Pulling into the bank lot, all was quiet. He saw just a few cars, some new, empty dumpsters, and no one except the guard at the bank entrance.

He parked next to Fat Joe's old gold-painted Lincoln; it was in mint shape, probably late '60s, early '70s, the kind of car used by a *James Bond* bad guy.

He had barely gotten out one knock on the trailer door when it swung open and a frantic Fat Joe—mask on—unusual—said, "Get in here!" and pulled him in, furtively looking left and right as he did. Alby pulled himself free.

Alby did his best not to say anything; he had little patience for people screaming at him. He recoiled at being grabbed. People didn't do stuff like that anymore. Touching had become an unspoken barrier, never crossed without permission. Jersey even had laws about it—with jail time.

Fat Joe went behind his old metal desk. The trailer looked like a storm had blown through. But the desk was neat, with one three-ring binder sitting in the center.

"Where the hell were you all day? I called a million times." Fat Joe had an expensive plastimask—the plastic around the mouth seemed to buckle as he yelled.

"I usually turn my phone off on Sundays," Alby lied.

Fat Joe waved his paw and cut through the air. "None of your guys have real addresses." He smacked the paperwork on the desk in front of him.

"Did I miss something here? We had this discussion. You needed bodies, you dummied up the paperwork, I gave you a cut, all done!" Alby raised his voice a little; he felt anger, partially fueled by a growing sense that this conversation was leading to a place that he was not going to like.

Fat Joe threw open the binder; Alby saw the tab: O'Brien. It held the photos of Lucky, Darnell, and Chance clipped to the top of the paperwork.

"Where the hell do these guys live?"

"I don't know. I just pick them up at some lot in Camden."

"Bullshit. That's total bullshit." Fat Joe's face was red and bloated. Alby noticed he had a bruise on the side of his neck with a bandage behind his ear.

"No, it's not bullshit," Alby said very slowly as if speaking to a child. "It's their crap-ass reality. Don't act all innocent—you're the one who faked the paperwork. You telling me it's your first time doing that? Now that is real bullshit on top of bullshit." Alby hated bullies; and he could tell that as threatening as he was, Fat Joe needed him.

Fat Joe ignored him, but calmed down. "You need to find these guys and fast."

Just then the trailer door opened and another subcontractor entered, and even with his American flag mask on, Alby could see he wore a pissed-off look. Surprisingly enough, it was the same contractor he'd met at the gas station a few weeks ago who had recommended this job. They acknowledged each other with a nod. Alby could tell the guy did not remember him. He could picture the logo on his new truck: Delarosa Contracting.

Delarosa went right at Fat Joe. "Why the hell are you calling me on a Sunday and screaming at me? I had friends over for the Eagles' game and I was about to start the barbecue."

"Screw the Eagles—gonna lose anyway."

"Fat Joe—we've known each other a long time. You know the drill. Never on Sunday."

"Screw that! I need the addresses of your crew." Fat Joe snorted like a truck backfiring and yanked at his belt. "Listen, Delarosa, this is big trouble, so no shit, got it?"

"Why shouldn't I give you shit? I was having a nice BBQ. It's Sunday, for Christ's sake!"

"Eagles winning or losing?" Alby quietly interjected, enjoying dashing a little salt on the wound.

Both men spoke in unison, a duet of shared disgust: "Losing!"
Alby smiled inside.

Fat Joe banged the metal table, kicked his chair, and spun around as if looking for something else to hit. Then he turned back to them.

"Your shithead, lying-dog, screw-up crews stole something from the bank Friday night."

Delarosa didn't hesitate. "What does 'something' mean?"

"None of your business. I need to get hold of your crews fast."

Like he was in an elevator where the cables had been cut, his stomach dropped. Baghdad had taught him how to freeze his face so that nothing showed. He put that in place. This was bad. He looked at Fat Joe's bandage again. Someone had been very unhappy with this bully.

"Wasn't my guys," said the other contractor with utter confidence. "Seriously, what'd they steal? My guys"—he glanced skeptically at Alby—"are pretty good. No angels, but they keep it straight."

"Bullshit! How do I know that? I need their addresses. Six from you"—he pointed at Delarosa. "Three from you!" he said to Alby.

"Okay. I have most of them back at my office. Let me get back to you tomorrow." Delarosa turned to leave. He paused, "After I hand them over, what happens?"

"None of your damned business. It's taken care of. Done." Fat Joe spoke in a low ominous tone of finality. Both he and Delarosa had the same look on their faces. His voice dropped to a whisper. "You know who owns this bank." The room filled with the silence.

Alby felt stupid but had to ask. "Who owns the bank?"

"None of your fucking business," spat Fat Joe. "People you don't steal from."

Staring at the tan bandage on Fat Joe's head again, Alby figured the less he knew the better. Glancing over at Delarosa, he saw he also had a stone face: he was giving up nothing.

"God help you if you don't get me whatever you know by tomorrow. Call me the minute you know something."

"Joe, what are we *really* looking for? What was taken?" asked Delarosa.

"None of your fucking business."

"Oh, okay," Delarosa retorted sarcastically. "That makes it a lot easier."

Alby pictured Lucky, Chance, and Darnell. Lowlifes. Probably took the job as an easy way to steal something from the bank. Without a word, Delarosa moved out of the trailer and drove away.

Sitting in a shaded area of the parking lot, Jagger watched as Delarosa left, followed by Alby a few minutes later.

He drove over and went into Fat Joe's trailer. Fat Joe winced reflexively when he saw Jagger. Just that alone made Jagger want to hit him. "Those the two?"

Fat Joe nodded but kept his head slightly and unnaturally turned; he did not want Jagger to see the bandage over his right ear. "Yeah, I don't have their crew addresses—but they know how to find them." Jagger just stared at him. "The one—Delarosa—said he had some back at his office."

"Give me their addresses and phone numbers." Jagger took the slip from Fat Joe's hand, read it, and gave him a piercing but casual look:

"What is O'Brien's address?"

"He uses a PO box."

"People still do that?" Jagger had one; he was just surprised anyone else still did. "I need those addresses."

Jagger waited until Fat Joe pushed the binder across the desk, then picked it up. "I will be back. Tomorrow. In the morning."

He had to leave. The temptation to hit Fat Joe was too great. He had better things to do. As he got into the rented Camry, he checked the GPS and saw that Delarosa's office was only a mile away.

Oddly enough, it had been Delarosa who made him first aware of Camden.

A few weeks back, cruising for work, Alby had needed gas. This was the one thing (well maybe *one* of the things) that he wished the Handlers had included for credit card use. He pulled into a Lukoil for the gas and the conveniently placed Dunkin'. He got out to stretch his legs and rifle through his wallet as the attendant stood by impatiently. It may be an "electric" truck, but the engine still ate gas. "Twenty bucks." He had forty but needed dinner. As the guy started to pump, another flatbed truck pulled in. The logo on this new truck read Delarosa Contracting. The guy was older than Alby and rough-looking; he got out and didn't bother with the mask hanging on the rearview mirror. He walked with the slight limp of someone who needed a new hip. What the hell, he thought, ask the guy.

"Howdy," Alby said as he leisurely (he hoped) moved to the other side of the gas island. "You know where to get day workers?"

The guy looked him up and down. "Ha! Camden. Where else? Garbage can of the world. But a great place to pick up some day trash to do the real shit work." He lit a cigarette. A little too close to the gas pump, Alby thought, and took a half-conscious step back. The guy dropped his cigarette on the ground near a stain of dried gas and shook his head. "Just watch out."

"For what?"

"You'll know soon enough." The guy looked at Alby more closely now. "You a contractor?" His eyes slid over Alby's truck as he asked.

"Yeah." Alby wanted to say, "Just back from Iraq," but he remembered how his Handlers had insisted there were certain topics he *never* should mention: number one was Iraq. "Came down from North Jersey… still can't get used to someone pumping my gas." The guy gave him a quizzical look. "Don't they pump up north? State law."

"I don't like waiting."

"Never seen you on a site." Delarosa's eyes were narrow. "Army?"

Alby nodded; a small lie but it seemed to be where this guy was going.

"Me, too. Rangers. I did the first Gulf War." The guy pulled out his wallet and gave the small Mexican pumping his gas two twenties. "The guy can send the tip back to his family," he said to Alby with a harsh laugh. As he was putting his wallet back in his pocket, he hesitated and pulled out a card. "There's a big job, Bank of South Jersey, looking for subcontractors. We were supposed to do the electric, but when they opened it up, damned place was loaded with asbestos.

"Get some day workers and go see Fat Joe Genovese," he said as he pointed at the card. "Here's his card. He's the head contractor."

Alby took it from his hand. He didn't look at him; he didn't want to look like he needed the work as badly as he did. This asbestos job could be the break he needed, but the Rules always stepped in: never trust anyone. He gave him a phony smile.

"Don't just drive around. Go to 4th and York. That's a good corner." Delarosa lit another cigarette, turned to get back in his truck, and then paused. Over his shoulder he said, "That corner is also a drug mart, so keep your eyes open. Cops see a white guy in a truck, they'll assume you're buying."

"Thanks," Alby said quietly.

"Not doing you a favor, pal—I got a night crew there, too. Just want to get this shit out so we can get going with the real work."

Another asshole contractor. Another reason not to go to a gas station just because there's a Dunkin' there too, thought Alby. He'd only run into more like Delarosa there.

When Alby got back to the cave, he pulled out his old paper map of New Jersey and opened it up on the card table he used as a desk, kitchen table, and all-around open surface to put crap on. He had to push some take-out wrappers aside—the greatest thing about never cooking was you never had to wash any dishes. He turned to the map of Camden County and looked for the city.

"I'm new in the area," he explained to Fat Joe in his trailer on the bank site. Then he pictured the logo on that contractor's truck at the gas station. "Delarosa said you needed some extra hands," he added.

"What—you watch a video on YouTube? You and everybody else! Don't even know what the damn thing is, this YouTube, and it bites my ass at every job. Everybody watches some dumb video and they're the expert! You know you need a special license for this work? State regs."

Alby did not want to tell him he had spent an hour at Starbucks watching YouTube videos on asbestos removal, including a few that chilled his blood—in all his years, he'd avoided any asbestos jobs. Thankfully, most were promo videos from specialty law firms. But a couple were lonely-man videos, the kind where a guy sits in front of his laptop camera, so close it makes his face slightly distorted, then just vomits out his thoughts and emotions.

"What brought you from, uh, Maryland?"

Alby knew it was the moment of truth, the moment where he would or would not get this job. He needed it badly. "I relocated after coming back from Iraq."

"Bit old for a soldier."

"Contractor. Baghdad. Blackwater." Again, he knew he was not supposed to mention any of that, but he thought it might work in his favor.

Fat Joe nodded. He looked like he wanted to say something but

didn't. Then he muttered, "Tough stuff, there." A long moment went by—
Alby staring into space, while Fat Joe sized him up.

"Can you get three guys?"

Alby nodded slowly.

"Okay, okay, we're good here…just get here. Eight p.m. next
Friday. I don't care if they have paperwork. I'll get some photos and fake
IDs ready." He paused and gave Alby a squinty look. "You get one shot,
hear me?"

One shot. Alby walked out and felt the iron coil inside unwind.
This felt good—like good equals normal. A real job. His first real sub-con-
tracting job. Things were breaking his way. He couldn't wait to tell Dorothy and cut off her constant "You get any real work yet?" at the pass. He'd
have to drive to that address in Camden and try and get some guys set up
for tomorrow.

As he drove into the bowels of Camden, he rolled up his window
because sewage colored the air like bad burnt cauliflower. The corner
Delarosa mentioned was an empty lot. It was off the Admiral Wilson
Boulevard, just past one of the many massive, bunker-looking, cinder-block
liquor stores littering the roadway into Philly. He pulled up at the lot and
checked the map—it was the edge of a dense neighborhood—he could see
the straight line of row houses ahead.

Camden, or at least where he was, was like Baghdad, but worse. It
was midday and the streets were nearly empty. Wrecked cars were strewn
about like garbage cans; houses looked like tornadoes had blown through—
one would be worn but livable, next door was a disaster. Doors hanging off
hinges, partially burnt buildings. As he drove by, everyone stopped to stare
at him. Alby found himself shaking his head. This was America? Even
North Jersey had nothing this bad.

Baghdad. Suddenly, he could feel the coolness of the switchblade
steel and stone handle as it rested between his skin and boot.

Three guys in hoodies were milling about near the corner; one kneeling tying his shoes, while also looking at Alby's truck.

His radar went off, snapping him back. He focused on the three men, standing on the sidewalk. Somehow, he had driven back to the first lot he had gone to. They seemed to want to say something, yet they gave him a wide berth; probably thought he was some crazy man or on drugs. He rolled down his window halfway.

"What?" he barked at them. He knew danger well enough to know you had to go on the offense.

The guy put his hand inside his jacket; Alby reached down to grip the crowbar by his left foot, then realized it was probably drugs inside the jacket. "You looking?" asked the guy, eyes moving back and forth like rolling dice.

"No," Alby said as he composed himself. "Looking for day workers. Night job." Alby hated being nervous; he sounded stupid. His words were awkward.

"Yeah, we're looking for work," one said to him. He gave them a hard look: disheveled, two of them looking like they'd spent the first half of the day at a bar. All three looked like they could be anywhere between thirty and fifty. Alby suspected that people in Camden looked older than they were.

"Well, I need three guys, next Friday night at eight. Asbestos removal. Night shift. Two weekends."

One nodded and tried to do something that looked like a smile but seemed wrong. "I can get three guys easy." He paused like it was a joke with a punchline waiting, and then finally said, "Us." They all laughed. Alby smiled but it felt so forced he took it away quickly.

"Done that shit before," mumbled one not looking up.

"What's it pay?"

"$100 a night, four nights." Alby figured a forty percent skim was enough, "Shift is nighttime eight to six a.m. Over the next two weekends— get paid on the final Sunday. Four nights' work. Cash. That's the deal."

One guy's head started nodding up and down, up and down, like he was bobbing for apples. "Okay, you come back here Friday night. We'll be ready. But you pay *me*. I'll take care of them."

Everyone wants their cut. "Sure, sure. I just need three. What's your name?"

"George Floyd." He started laughing uncontrollably. The third, who had a worried look, rolled his eyes and sighed in disgust. Alby just stared with no expression until they were done. He had no idea who that was. Must've happened while he away—he had successfully ignored almost all news from the States. The main guy wiped tears from his eyes, "Lucky. Just call me Lucky. And this is Chance and Darnell."

Alby slid a few inches away from the window, his hand slipping down to grasp the iron crowbar. He smiled. The lot, the dust, the mess of cars and trash dislodged him again for a second…he could almost hear the call to prayer. He needed to get back to the cave. The stress was triggering him.

"Friday night. Seven-thirty p.m., at this corner."

"Got it," said Lucky, flashing his toothy, shark-like grin. The one who looked stupid waved limply as Alby drove away.

Maybe if he could pull this off, he could get into asbestos removal. Dirty, but good money. Hell, if he didn't have to touch the stuff and just supply a crew, he was good with that.

As he had driven back to the cave that day, after finding Lucky and his two chumps, it all played out so smoothly in his mind; it had seemed like a real break. That'll teach him to let his guard down. Those scumbags that *he* had brought onto the site had taken something so valuable that even tough Fat Joe was scared.

Alby felt a vice of bitterness tighten. What came to mind was that old Irish fortune that ended with, "and may you be dead twenty years before the Devil knows you're gone!" Alby never got that twenty years; the Devil had found him again. Now he had to find those three before someone else came and found him. Fat Joe had been squirrely, but his tone had been ominous when he mentioned the bank and its Owners. Clearly, whatever had been taken from the bank was important—Fat Joe was not the panicky type. Yet, no cops were at the bank. And who had hit him? Something didn't make sense.

Sunday afternoon was surrendering to night, with classic September blues. It felt like the sun was setting faster, rolling downwards towards the west. No way was he driving around here in the dark. Alby decided on take-out Chinese and Netflix on his iPad. Something stupid. Maybe *The Honeymooners*; he liked Ralph Kramden because Ralph was an even bigger loser than he was. Monday was a light workday. He had a few jobs to get him to the weekend—then pay day. Or maybe not…this whole job was going off the rails, he thought grimly.

What the hell had they taken from that bank? Putting the truck in park, he dropped his head into his hands. He could feel the lines and creases on his face pressing against his palms like rivers flowing down his cheeks.

Sunday Night: 6 p.m.

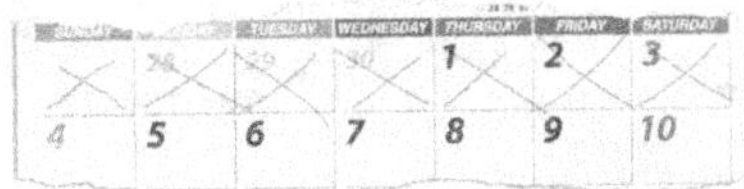

Alby was prepping for Monday, loading asphalt and tools and brushes onto the back of his truck. For Alby, life moved at two paces only: on or off. Off and stop were bad. On and fast were good. He liked it better when he was too busy to think. Construction work was particularly helpful, as it often required more instinct than thought and that suited him fine. Electrical work was harder, taking focus and effort, but it was still some-what automatic.

Arms loaded down, his phone rang. It was in the back pocket of his jeans but since only a half-dozen people had his number, caller ID didn't have to work so hard and he knew that he could call any of them back if he needed to. Then again, it might be another potential job from that cheap little ad he put in the local flyers. It was a New York area code, but this area was now full of former New Yorkers. He managed to get most of what he was carrying on the shelves and grab his phone—just as it went to voicemail.

He saw the number but didn't recognize it. Now that was strange. Stranger still was that when he heard the first few words of the message, he immediately knew that he was listening to Ginger's voice. Why was she calling him? And more to the point, how did she get his number? After that awkward conversation that morning at the diner after an equally weird one at Dorothy's party, you would think he'd be in her rearview mirror. He'd left both of those meetings feeling confused, part of him suppressing the fact that he had liked her attitude and that she was damned good-looking. But after how he knew he must have looked in the diner this morning, if he was her, he would have run screaming.

"Hey, Alby, it's me. From the diner. And your sister's. It's Ginger."

Why was she was calling him; but more than that, why was his pulse speeding up?

"Listen, I just got off the hook for my evening shift and wanted to catch a movie. I know it's Sunday but thought you might want to go—if you don't have other plans. Give me a call. I know it's last-minute, but what the hell. If you're up for it, give me a call."

He entered the number. She answered on the first ring. Must be one of those people who always holds their phone in their hand like a security blanket.

"Hey, you called back! Wasn't sure I got you in time."

"Yeah, just got back." He felt like he had to explain himself. "Work, getting ready for a busy week."

"Working on Sundays stinks." She laughed. "Even God takes it off!"

"I'd rather be busy."

She jumped right on that. "Good! Let's go to the movies. Cherry Hill Mall has a big complex. Lots of choices, but there's one I really want to see." She mentioned a title.

"Never heard of it, but sure." He said yes before he realized he'd said yes. Had he intended to? He was confusing himself; part of him just wanted to rest, finish his takeout then veg out and binge watch something on Amazon with his good friend, his only friend, Mr. Maker's—and drink until he fell asleep. In other words, his usual weekend night since he had gotten back.

"A date?" He said the words and immediately regretted them. It was as if his internal voice slipped out and he hoped she would not react. He felt a bit unnerved, not sure what to feel or say. A blankness fell over his brain and grew as he spoke. One thought kept revolving: why call me?

"No, just a movie—told you I love movies. And Sunday night is the least crowded." Alby noted the Pandemic caution in her voice. "I want to see one and your sister told me you have plenty of free time on your hands—tell me if I'm wrong—so I figured I'd ask."

He skipped the time comment and asked her, "How'd you get my number?"

Every promise he had made about lying low, staying out of life's main lanes in the past year yelled "No!"

"Called your sister, what else? She was happy to give it out. What are you, some Witness Protection Program guy?"

Matter of fact, I am, he thought, but said nothing. He decided to jump in with both feet, knowing instantly he would regret it.

"What time and where are we meeting?"

He heard her chuckle, as if surprised but not.

He kind of liked her sense of humor. At first it buzzed around your head, but now he saw it: sharp, clever, one step ahead. Not sure if he could get used to it, but he was starting to get it.

"My car is giving me trouble, so come pick me up. You know where the Gatewood Apartments are?"

He asked for directions. The movie was at the Cherry Hill Mall, pick-up at seven, movie at seven-thirty. No dinner, he thought. Which was good. He was short on cash.

As he clicked off the questions bubbled up. Considering he had just met her a day earlier, why did she call him so soon? Who was she really? How well did his sister know her and for how long?

But that last thought was kicked aside as he suddenly realized this was his first night out with a woman in years and he had absolutely no idea what he was going to talk to her about. Or wear. Looking around, he saw the pile of dirty clothes in the corner. Crap, he thought, no time to get to the laundromat. Before grabbing a quick shower to wash the stink off himself, he hung the shirt on a hanger and closed the door to the tiny bathroom to let the shower steam try and take some wrinkles out of his best flannel shirt.

When he got out of the shower, he yanked and gently tugged at the sleeves and the main part of the shirt while it was still on the hanger and managed to remove most of the wrinkles. Then he swiped his hand across the mirror to wipe the steam away; another contractor in Iraq had shown him.

He needed to shave. He hated shaving. It had once occurred to him that Iraqi men, who with cultural solidarity all wore thick mustaches, shaved the rest of their face because there could be few things more disgusting than a sweaty beard. And if there was one constant in Iraq, besides the never knowing what would happen next, it was sweat.

Alby checked his wallet, his eyebrows moving closer together as he saw how empty it was. He called Stephen.

"Really? You're that hard up for money?"

"Checks haven't cleared yet. The bank is closed anyway."

"Are you the only person on the planet without a debit or credit card?"

Alby figured silence would work best.

"Oh man, you are some uncle. I work for you and you are hitting me up for bucks for a date."

"How do you know it's for a date?"

"You have been back over a year and never gone to the movies. It's a date—though it is hard to imagine how you met anyone or why anyone would want to go out—"

"Stop." Alby said firmly, "Try this: play obedient nephew for five minutes, shut the hell up, and do as I ask."

Stephen laughed at him and with a distinctly teasing tone in his voice said, "Just don't forget Rule number three: don't ever work with family."

"That'll be number one soon if you keep this up. And it's 'never' not 'don't'—you're making me want to reconsider my exception." He paused. "I'll meet you at your mom's on my way out. I'll honk."

"Alby, I had plans. You know, with friends…you know what friends are, right?"

"Yeah, it sucks living at home. Your issue. Just either be there or leave me $50 in the mailbox." No way he wanted to see his sister right now. "And one more thing. You have a friend who works at the Cherry Hill Mall theater complex, right?"

There was a pause on the other end. "Right?" he asked again, louder this time like he was speaking to someone a bit slow.

"Yeah, and…" Stephen finally said.

"Just take care of that for me, please. It's the side door, right?"

There was another moment of silence and then Stephen said, "Knock three times…twice." Then he clicked off. Alby assumed that meant yes it would be taken care of. At least he hoped that it did. He looked at his phone: nearly six-thirty. He was going to be late. He grabbed his windbreaker and made his way into the garage and out the side door. He got in and pulled onto the service road—then realized that he hadn't checked his GPS for how to get to her complex. He pulled over. Getting a sense of where to go, he got back on the road. A chill went through him—what would he talk about?

The apartment complex was a low-slung, two-story affair, with a 1990s look. And right then it dawned on him: he didn't know the number of her apartment. Nervously, he glanced at the passenger seat and saw a coffee swizzle stick on the seat. He quickly brushed it on the floor, ready to call her and find out where to go.

Suddenly the passenger side door swung open and there was Ginger. Looking up at him she paused for a second, smiled, and then swung herself up into the truck cab and onto the seat in one smooth motion. Red hair blazing, bag on one arm, she was wearing a short-sleeved blue top buttoned nearly to the neck and a long, casual skirt that was only a shade lighter than the blue jean jacket she had over her other arm. She smiled. She had on a plastimask, so he could clearly see one side of her mouth, which was curled upward in a sly smile. She was good-looking. Just shy of beautiful, but definitely in the neighborhood, just a block over.

"Well, Alby…."

He sputtered like a bad engine for a second, caught himself, felt like an ass, and then took in a breath and said, "Yeah, yeah, movie theater," with a stupid smile that tried to disguise how she had caught him off guard. Again.

He fumbled with his phone on the half-lit front seat trying to set the GPS. She watched. "You really don't know where the Cherry Hill Mall is?"

The question crashed into him. Dropping his phone on the seat, he nodded. He *was* lost. In a momentary flash no one should feel, he felt how wrong this all was in every nerve, every cell of his body.

He recovered himself. The dim, half-light cast from the apartment complex spots should prevent her from seeing any emotion that had slipped onto his face.

"You look great." At the same moment he said this—and meant it—it occurred to him that maybe all she had wanted from him was a ride since her car was out of commission. Maybe she was just using him. It certainly made more sense to him than anything else. He didn't know what to do with this, so he just put up his radar for other signs.

"Thanks," she said then turned to glance at him. "No tux and tails for tonight, huh?"

"What?" He looked down at what he was wearing.

"Kidding."

"So, what are we seeing?"

She told him the title. He nodded knowingly.

"Never heard of it, have you," she said.

"Nope."

"Don't get out much, do you?" She carefully laid the jacket across her lap.

"Nope, I am saving myself for the right woman." He said it with fake conviction. She laughed, that single sharp bark he'd heard the night before. Here it was a bit loud for the small cab of the truck. He smiled and kept his eyes on the road. He made her laugh, good.

They spoke a little on the short drive to the mall theater. He asked how she'd become friends with his sister and was surprised at how she painted Dorothy as such a warm and generous person. "She's been great for business; she must have a hundred friends and I've picked up over a dozen new students because of her."

Alby was by now very used to watching other people's every gesture. He had to be. So he noticed that as she spoke—generalities of her day in dance class—she kept furtively glancing at his hand on the wheel.

"What?" he finally asked, slipping the question into a pause.

"What what?" she responded with a naïve tone.

"What are you staring at?"

"Oh!" With that one word, she sounded like a kid caught doing something bad. "Your knuckles—why are they so bruised?" She pointed at his right hand. "That one looks like it might be bleeding."

He removed the hand from sight. He didn't want to tell her the whole truth, so he told her one fact of the truth. "I'm teaching myself how to box."

"Really? Is boxing something you did before? Like a high school thing?"

"No." This time he was completely honest. "Just a way to work out the tension." Again, not the whole story, but close enough for someone he barely knew. The only other person who had ever asked about the punching bag and his knuckles was Stephen.

"Looks painful."

"It is." He shrugged, "Actually, it's not. You get used to it."

"Fun?"

"I wouldn't call it that. It's…it's more, uh, like a way to pass the time. Keep in shape."

"Most people go to the gym or jog."

"I'm not most people."

She paused, turning to face forward, and said: "Yeah, I'm getting that." She wouldn't let go. "Why boxing?"

He thought for a moment. "My crochet stitch is no good." She chuckled. Score one for him. Good. Wait. What was he keeping a score for?

"Here we are," he said, relieved that they were at the parking lot. For a Sunday night, it seemed odd that it was so jammed with cars, especially with some quota still in place. He had heard that movies were back now in the smaller theaters, with unlimited seating, now that the country was past herd immunity. That's why the Philly outbreak was all over the news—Jersey wanted none of it. Quotas.

He couldn't care less.

She kept silent.

He got lucky with a spot near the entrance but ignored it—which earned him a puzzled look from her—and drove to the rear of the complex. As she got out and made a move toward the ticket office, he gently touched her elbow and walked to the right of the theater, which earned him another quizzical look. He nodded as if to say, just follow me.

At the double-sided metal exit door, he paused, looked around, and knocked three times. Then waited. He knocked again. Waited. Time seemed to slow down; he refused to look at her.

Finally, the door swung open. A kid about Stephen's age looked at him. Alby smiled. "Get in," said the kid, looking around nervously. Alby took Ginger by the elbow and moved past him into the half-lit hallway between the many theaters. As he did so, he shoved a twenty in the kid's hand.

"Stephen said $30."

"Get the other ten from him."

He could feel Ginger's hard gaze on him, questioning what was going on. He decided he would act natural. "VIP."

"Really? Seems more VSE—very sneaky entrance." She chirped a laugh to herself and to him said, "Must be one of your Rules: Don't pay for movies. Ha!"

"Good one," he let out a short, fake laugh. Never should have shared The Rules with her; he did not like being mocked. He suddenly realized how absolutely asinine he looked doing this; it was as if he wanted to fail.

She said nothing else as they navigated the movie complex hallways, where everyone seemed to know the dance—never too close, not too far. It was just the way you had to move, weaving like a fish around others; he could tell the Philly outbreak had people a little more on edge; at the same time, it was the big test for the new Covid pill—the second generation they were rushing to distribute—since the first one had been a disaster. He made a beeline for the theater with the movie they were seeing. Checked his watch. Five minutes. "You want popcorn? A drink?"

"Gee, you sure know how to show a girl a good time. Sure. I'll grab the seats… over here good?" She pointed to a row in the half-lit room. "Diet Coke, no butter!" she threw over her shoulder as she walked into the theater.

"They don't put butter in Diet Coke," he said in a dry tone. She turned her head with that remark and smiled and this time she actually giggled.

The previews were either foreign or rom-com couples movies—she loves him, he loves her, she dumps him by mistake, he goes after her. Alby hated these things. He used to see the big action films. Now, with his Netflix choices, he could no longer stomach the fake set-ups and improbable endings; he had seen the real thing in Iraq, and that was enough for a lifetime. After Baghdad, they were just noise—although he still had a soft spot for Bruce Willis movies.

Watching the movie with Ginger was an adventure. She laughed a bit louder than everyone else, popped popcorn like gum drops, one kernel at a time, wriggled, fidgeted. He sat still, amazed that he was not only on a date, but one that had him watching and just barely tolerating such a stupid film. But then, with no warning, as the female lead was struggling with a new boyfriend, her old boyfriend returned from Iraq. In the dark, Alby sat up a bit straighter.

In the first scene where they were back together, she tried to tell him she had moved on. Like so many GIs Alby had met, it didn't take much for this guy to lose his cool. Tossing a chair across her apartment living room, he told her that the whole entire time he'd been overseas, thinking of her had kept him alive. Then the movie took a dark turn; the two guys, vying for her love, started to confront each other. The GI started following him to work and home, and the fiancé knew it. Their confrontation was ugly.

Alby began to feel the pressure on his chest, like a hand that was pushing him back in his seat—some invisible emotional g-force pushing the breath out of him. When the soldier kept appearing, acting out with episodes of irrational jealousy, the roaring of his pulse in his ears was almost louder than the movie. He could feel heat rising there. The dark was closing in. He had to leave. Without a word to Ginger, he just got up and pushed past people's outstretched legs, heading for the red letters— EXIT—and ignoring the comments about being rude.

If he had turned around, only for a second, he would have seen Ginger get up and follow him, making her own way past the others in the row, trailing him by just a few feet. "Excuse me. Sorry. Excuse me…What the hell?" Some woman had jerked her foot to kick her. "Excuse me!" she said, loud enough this time to have people saying shush all around her.

In the lobby, he looked for the nearest door. He moved so fast, he wobbled and carelessly bumped into people, who recoiled because touching just wasn't done. As he punched open the theater exit, she grabbed his elbow; he jerked it away. "Stop," she said. He kept moving. "*Stop!*" she shouted, which had the intended effect on him…and everyone else within a ten-foot radius. People stopped in their tracks, looking almost as if she were shouting at them. But no software alerts were going off, so people shook it off and moved on.

"Can we just get to my truck?" he implored, his heart thumping, the rush of blood in his ears now like a wave, making him almost dizzy. His words propelled him forward, not waiting for an answer. She quietly followed.

Without thinking, he went to the driver's side, then paused, shook his head as if to shake something off, went back to her side, and unlocked the door for her. She nodded and stepped up and slid in without looking at him. She placed her hands on her lap like she was waiting for a menu. After he got in, he blurted out, "This was a bad idea."

"Tell me about it! What the hell is your problem?" He didn't look at her.

"You don't want to know."

"Oh really? Let's see, I asked you out, to a movie I really want to see, and you pull this cheap-ass side-door routine like we're twelve and then walk out halfway through? I think I deserve an explanation."

He started the engine. Then he looked up and felt the sense of panic subsiding. He turned off the engine. "Yeah, I suppose you do."

"Yeah, I suppose I do."

"It's not something I talk about." She stared at him, arms folded like a tight pretzel.

"You were pretty talkative last night."

"That was different." He had no idea what she meant by that but this was not the time to ask. Instead, this was the kind of clueless moment Alby hated; he could not clear the brush from his brain.

"I… I…." He glanced over and suddenly felt like he saw her for the first time. Her eyes were angry blue seas, staring out at him through wide open lids. She couldn't possibly look any more different from Aliyah. No one looked like Aliyah. Her hair, peeking out from under her hijab, jet black, straight, like a deep, dark, calm river. And here was a woman named Ginger, with hair red, wavy, and with eyes like a stormy sea.

"Why are you staring at me?"

He quickly looked away. "Sorry."

"What is going on?" Her tone softened. "Come on, tell me."

A part of him wanted, no longed, to let out his story. About Iraq, Aliyah and Ahmed, broad strokes of what went down. He just didn't know how or where to start. The thought of trying to explain it all and the actual telling of the ending… a cold rush ran over his skin like an air conditioner running on high. He rushed to explain and then stopped.

He sat up suddenly and realized that he had never spoken to anyone about what had happened in Baghdad. No one. To Alby, a therapist was nothing more than an emotional bloodsucker—why else make a career of listening to people's dark, painful secrets? Besides, what he experienced should not be shared. No one else should have to have his garbage cluttering up their heads.

But he had to say something; she deserved it after the scene he had made in the theater.

"I was in Baghdad—for almost three years. I was foreman on a project to rebuild a power plant we bombed… bomb, build, bomb, build, that's how it was." He let his words drop in the air. "Things happened—bad things. I can't—" He clutched the steering wheel with both hands. "I can't—"

He grew quiet, then spoke in a low voice. "I had to get out. They called me a hero, like those engineers who got killed in Fallujah. Or to distract from the vaccine stupidity." He looked at her then just as quickly looked away. "That was years ago. Most people have forgotten about that.

Amazing what a war can do to your memory—and that movie was too close to home." He paused. "Yeah, it never made the news over here. Over there, no one forgets."

He heard a sound and turned. She'd been holding her breath and what he had heard was her loud exhale. "You're right. I couldn't possibly understand." Then she quickly added, "But thank you for telling me."

He shrugged, his shoulders slumping low as he relaxed. Breathe, he thought, breathe.

"Someday, tell me the whole story." She let her voice drift off in a softer tone. "But not now."

Finally, after a long but not uncomfortable silence, she said matter-of-factly, but with a tinge of guilt, "Definitely the wrong movie for you. Sorry."

He let his head drop to the steering wheel. He hadn't realized he'd been shaking, like some distant earthquake under his skin, until her cool hand touched his arm very lightly. With a soft, yet firm tone, she said, "Get out. Let me drive." Like a robot, he just moved.

It took a long ten minutes to get back to the Gatewood. She pulled into an open spot in front of a large wall of mailboxes that sat back under a wooden roof. The entire time, he'd had the passenger window down and had said nothing. His head had cleared on the drive. Now, besides a sense of shame and embarrassment, something else had crept in.

He felt lighter. And then that feeling disappeared as quickly as it had come, leaving him with the same feeling he'd had in the theater of wanting to get away, only this time without the panic. Now he just felt exhausted. Like packing it all up tonight and disappearing.

Did all that just really happen? Why had he left himself open to this disaster of an evening anyway? This was the price for stepping back onto the main roads. A good three fingers of Maker's was calling to him. Her, the bank, the crew, too much, too much.

It was like a homing pigeon—Maker's and the bag.

She put the truck in park. In the dashboard light, their faces were caught in angles of sharp light and darkness. Like in his sister's backyard.

"You are a mess. Get some rest."

"I think you're right. I— I am sorry this didn't work out."

She didn't turn off the engine, just swung open the door. She slid out and walked away. Walking in front of the bright headlights, she mouthed some words directly at him; he couldn't decipher them. As she smiled goodnight, the harsh glare of the truck bathing her in its headlights, he wondered why she was being so kind to him.

She casually waved at him and nearly ran, almost skipped, up the stairs to the second floor.

He got out and went around to the driver's side and got in. Then he backed the truck out. The only shaking was deep within his chest now. Except for his hands. They were vibrating like a train on metal rails. But he could drive.

Jagger had been watching a thriller in the theater next to Alby's. He hated the genre but for a few reasons felt it was necessary to see them when they came out. It was like professional Continuing Ed—but what he got from it was always the same: first, to see if he could pick up any new tricks; second, to have the fun of usually damning the movie, the director, writer, and everyone for creating such an untrue piece of excrement; and last, because he—and he always thought this consciously—was the only true professional sitting in the crowded dark theater, among the cattle and sheep. The amateurs around him were getting their thrills on watching what they believed were professionals. On the screen, they were only professional actors. Only one real killer was present, and they had no idea. He checked his watch: nine p.m. It was still early enough to make a surprise visit to Delarosa.

Sunday Night: 9 p.m.

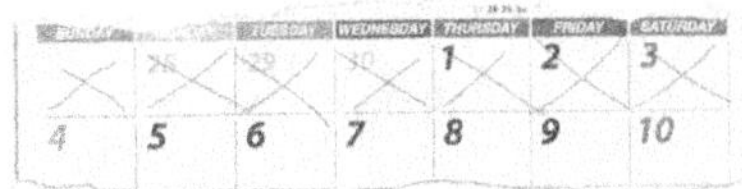

As he drove to Delarosa's office, he savored the simple act of driving a Camry. Back home in Phoenix, he didn't own a car. Instead, he always took the bus, to limit his electronic trail—except when he had to fly to a job. Then he always rented a Camry on the dummy card—one of his few sentimental acts. He always used Hertz because you could pick up the car and never have to interact with anyone.

He still had his room at the local motel; now he needed to transition to a base. Motels were too exposed. Records too easy to check. Someone always watching you come and go. Getting an apartment was tomorrow's first action—time to break out the Check List, settle in.

But even before he began his usual methodology of sequencing each step in his investigation of where to stay, it occurred to him that with Delarosa, he might have stumbled on a shortcut to part of his work. That meant a bonus. Fat Joe had mentioned Delarosa knowing some addresses of the illegal workers. He put in Delarosa's office address in the dashboard GPS. He turned the voice directions off—he didn't like anyone telling him what to do.

He ended up at a cinder block building, right off Route 30 near the Admiral Wilson Boulevard. Jagger started to wonder if they had invented cinder block in New Jersey. The place stood behind a much larger group of warehouses. Few cars and fewer people were around. He pulled up to the address and saw the truck with "Delarosa" spray-painted on the door. Lights off, he parked a dozen rows from Delarosa's truck and looked up at the three-story building. Lucky for him, only one light was on.

The small mag light he held in his mouth bit into his gums. Jagger rolled his mouth and moved it an inch without taking his eyes off the apartment rental ads on Craigslist. He needed a big innocuous apartment complex. He leaned the iPad on the steering wheel. The screen brightness turned low, so it would not show out of his car window; it didn't take him long to find a few places to rent.

For an hour, he occasionally looked up at what had to be Delarosa's office. Now something caught his attention—he looked up in time to see the light go out. He dropped the flashlight from his mouth and glanced around the parking lot. He had learned long ago that being patient was a virtue the amateurs rarely displayed. Delarosa hurried across the parking lot to get in his truck. Jagger waited until his rear lights were almost out of the lot. Leaving his headlights off until he moved onto the roadway made it easier to tail him.

Ten minutes later, Delarosa pulled into the driveway of a well-kept, split-level ranch house at the end of a cul-de-sac. Jagger held back, stopping, then slowly turned his car around to avoid turning at the dead end and being noticed.

Over the next fifteen minutes, three cars—all beaten up, old, and probably not insured—drove up to the house. From the light on the front porch, he could see the characters stream in with little more than a nod. Everyone stood socially distanced; even from this distance, Jagger could see Delarosa actually recoil as they streamed into the house. Six men—one was very big. Just the number Fat Joe had indicated. Clearly, he had called the bank night crew.

Jagger waited. In less than half an hour, all the men left. As they walked through the front door, no words were exchanged. Jagger slid down in his seat as they passed, but then sat up and jotted down their license plates as they drove past his side mirror.

It was nearly ten p.m. now. He coasted slowly toward the house, then turned off his lights and engine, using the momentum of the car to ease up the short driveway behind Delarosa's truck.

He must still be up, not that Jagger cared. He knocked...once. The hallway light went on again, casting light through the glass on his gray suit and plain tie. Delarosa looked out a side window and opened the door. "Are you lost?" he asked impatiently. Not the nicest thing to say, thought Jagger, who hated rude people.

"No, I don't think so." He pulled out his FBI badge and held it in front of him, arm straight. Delarosa's face shifted from annoyance to dismay; Jagger could see he knew instantly what it was about, the familiar muscle movements that made up a guilty look. Jagger smiled. "Can I come in?"

Delarosa hesitated. "Uh, sure, kids and wife are in the den… let's go on the back porch."

"Who is it, honey?" a woman called from downstairs.

"No one. Someone from work." He paused and growled, "Don't worry about it."

"A little late for more visitors!" she shouted back.

They walked silently upstairs, through the living room and kitchen to the back porch. Delarosa barely had the sliding door shut when he said, "What can I help you with?" Jagger had to admire the control it took for him to keep his voice level when he clearly was scrambling in his mind to figure out if a visit from the FBI had to do with the bank.

"The bank. What was taken." Jagger paused to watch his face; he said nothing but the face told the tale: it wasn't him. Being in the half-light was a disadvantage for Jagger: no way to get a clean read on his face but he was so good at this now, he could tell. Light spilled from the kitchen, but only on the other side of the porch. Jagger slowly strolled over, casually trying to peer into the house through the shades, as if weighing his words. Delarosa followed until his face was well lit.

"Something was stolen from the bank. And I have every reason to believe it was someone on your crew." He turned to look at Delarosa; his eyebrows had shot up, feigning surprise. Delarosa knew something, but how much? This assignment might get wrapped up in record time.

"Why would you think that? What was stolen?" The dance of muscles in the half-light was not easy to read; Delarosa had no idea what was stolen. That didn't make sense—why the initial show of guilt?

"That doesn't concern you. What should concern you is that an FBI agent is at your house, and if what I believe is true, you are an accomplice, meaning I can drag you out of here right now, cuffed and ready for a night in jail. Then tomorrow I get a court order and come back and ransack your house in front of your wife and kids."

"Hey, wait, woah, woah, slow down."

"I don't like working Sunday nights." Jagger said casually, dropping a nice non-sequitur to muddy the moment more. Delarosa was about to say something, but Jagger cut him off. "I need the addresses of your crew. Need to speak to each one."

"They are at my office. Meet me there tomorrow—"

Jagger saw the lie written large on his face—he had entered the house carrying a small binder. He had interviewed them all. No one had admitted guilt. Jagger's skill at facial emotional recognition made guilt as visible as a rainbow tattoo; it was one of the easiest emotions to read.

"Of course, I'll start with you."

Delarosa nodded and did not speak. Then he blurted out, "I had no idea about any of this until Fat Joe said something today!" The accomplice thing worked so well. Television had trained people to respond to these cliché statements and situations. Jagger smiled.

"If you cooperate, then we'll see what can be done. For now, let's focus on finding who did it."

"How do you know it's one of my crew? I know most of them well. What about that other guy?"

That's right, throw that Alby character under the bus; it is *always* everyone else's fault. Now Jagger genuinely disliked Delarosa, which changed nothing except for moving his eventual death from being neces-sary clean-up to an actual pleasure. Jagger cut him off with an open palm in front of his face. "That's for me to decide, not you. Do you have their numbers and addresses?"

He nodded, but in a non-committal sort of way and said, "Some."

"Some? What does that mean?"

He shrugged, "A few live in Camden."

Letting out a long breath, Jagger tried not to be irritated—the name "Camden" was starting to annoy him. The Owners only used him for big jobs, a lot of white-collar crimes kept him out of ghettos. There was that one assignment in Rio that did not go so well, the high body count did not sit well with the Owners. Too many locals. Too many dirt-poor people. Too many guilty faces. It made him feel dirty. Rio had taught him the limitations of his skills—that sometimes a bad lifetime created the same look as guilt and it was hard to distinguish guilt under so many scars.

This Camden theme did not bode well for a fast resolution; every bad road led to this Camden. He'd have to go see it for himself. This annoyed him because he had so little time and even though Delarosa seemed like a good lead, he had to pursue every path. He made a quick decision.

"Can you get them all here tomorrow night?"

"Uh, yeah, I guess."

"Okay, set it up. Nine p.m. tomorrow."

"Can we do it at my office?"

Jagger turned to watch the kitchen light pour across Delarosa's face. He looked scared. He's not afraid of me, he thought, he's afraid of his own crew, or at least someone on it. This was a new element; it had never occurred to Jagger that any of the workers would be so dangerous that his boss feared him. Maybe Delarosa was innocent: the crew would be the source. The other contractor—Alby—he only had three guys, while Delarosa had six. The odds were in his favor.

"Okay, your office." He could practically hear Delarosa exhale. But that was not the reaction he wanted. "Third floor, right? Behind Building 8. Two windows, so not a big space."

Jagger had the pleasure of watching the man's face melt like wax. Yes, Jagger thought, looking right at him, I have been to your office. "Give me your number and we'll confirm it tomorrow.

"I will be there at eight, but I won't come unless they are all there. Just wave out the window and I will come up."

Without another word, Jagger turned to walk away. He had to get to bed. The day would be early and long. He would call him in the morning and change the meeting place back to the house. That would throw Delarosa off.

Monday: 6:30 a.m.

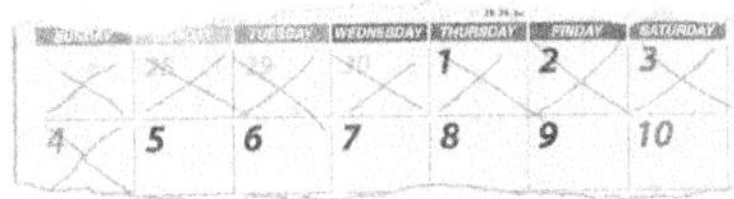

Dawn was not his friend. It was annoyingly upbeat. Nonetheless, he liked getting up early. He considered sleep a necessary waste. The instinct to stay in constant motion played forever on his mind.

Jagger enjoyed his internal alarm clock and always challenged it. It never broke. Every day, wherever he was, no matter how many time zones he had gone through, he'd open his eyes, turn his head sideways, and look at his watch: six-thirty a.m. Swinging his legs like a pendulum, he walked the two steps, put his pants back on, and slipped his feet into his shoes, then shirt, then jacket—all lined up in order of assembly. In the mirror, he took a moment to run the comb through his slightly mussed brown hair. Shaved, brushed his teeth. In five minutes, he was putting his suitcase into the Camry, which he had parked in front of his room. He walked over to the office to leave his key—perfect timing since the night duty guy at the front desk was half asleep. He knew this was when the guy would be so tired, he would not even look up as he prepared the bill. Anonymous. Gray. If ever asked, that would be all he would recall to say.

Returning to the bank site, Jagger watched from across the street as the final trucks carrying barrels of asbestos that had been pulled out left the parking lot. He could see Fat Joe directing workers to finish rolling up the huge plastic sheets. Everyone hustled like ants, but Fat Joe looked like Humpty Dumpty, round and waddling, ruling over his little kingdom of chaos. Jagger glanced at the folder on the seat next to him. The rubber band around it was purple; Jagger stared at it for a long time…why purple? What was Fat Joe doing with a purple rubber band? It seemed so feminine.

The morning was bright and sunny, with a clear and sparkling sky like bright blue lake water. The sun was barely up, but the roads were full of cars and trucks—fish darting in and out of lanes. Organizing his day was easy. First, find an apartment to rent. Then set up his maps and interview the remaining fifteen suspects; he grouped them in quadrants based on distance from where he was based, this made it more efficient to see more and eliminate them—literally if he had to—in a rapid fashion based on the list and what his instincts told him. Day planned and ready-to-go. Very professional, the way he liked it. Still, the chaos of this construction scene made him twitch with slight discomfort.

He'd told Fat Joe he'd be back at lunch to get all the information about the last missing crew members. First though, he decided to wait and follow Fat Joe home. He knew where he worked, now he would know where he lived. This would also give him some practice in memorizing the area's main routes—he had a feeling he would be back to the construction site before he found the check.

After watching Fat Joe roam the site, yelling and gesturing like a ventriloquist's dummy, he saw him walk over to his classic 1960s Lincoln—a brilliant golden hue, fins and everything. It was an easy car to follow at a distance; Fat Joe lived near Delarosa, another 1950s-style ranch.

On the way back to the site, Jagger stopped at the bank to get some cash: check another item off the list. Parked at the site, he counted the green edges sticking out from an envelope of $20 bills. He had another envelope of $50s that made the side pocket of his jacket bulge. Traveling to one of the Owners' businesses was rare but picking up the money from one of their teller's windows made everything far more convenient: $1,500 for the deposit on the apartment he had found on Craigslist; $500 for meals and gas; another $1,000 for "incidentals" like clothes, entertainment, any tools and bribes.

As he feathered the edges of the bills, deciding whether to go give the landlord the deposit or stop somewhere for breakfast first, he saw Fat Joe's Lincoln pull back into the lot. What was he doing back so soon? After a night shift, he should be asleep. A guy appeared by his car who looked a mess: it was Delarosa. Clearly, he was telling Fat Joe about his visit the night before. Fat Joe looked around furtively—Jagger smiled because he knew he was looking for him, fear rising around the guy like an invisible fog.

Fat Joe kept nodding, not saying much. Out of instinct, Jagger took out his smartphone and carefully got a picture of the two of them, as close as he could zoom. Delarosa was gesticulating wildly, but Fat Joe just shrugged and walked over to the trailer. Delarosa yelled something, but Fat Joe ignored him; this prompted the contractor to jump in his truck and nearly tear a hole in the parking lot as he drove away.

After counting to sixty fifteen times, he got out, crossed the parking lot, and knocked on the trailer door. Fat Joe yelled something, and Jagger entered. It pleased him that Fat Joe winced as he stepped in. "You're early."

Ignoring him, he just jumped right in with—"You look guilty." He paused like he was reciting a school lesson to a fifth grader, then declared, "You look guilty, because you are guilty."

"It's gas," Fat Joe said, patting his stomach, trying to use gruff humor. "The stomach bypass—it's a mess." The fear danced in his eyebrows, pulling down his cheek muscles until they looked taut. Jagger enjoyed the choreography of muscles.

"How are my files?" He scanned the sloppy piles of folders.

"All good. I had each contractor double-check, so you have the latest addresses, names, all that. You really going to visit all of them?"

Jagger gave him a droll look. "Do you really want to know what I am going to do?"

Fat Joe shook his head no and turned to neaten up his piles of folders. Jagger looked around. On top of a cabinet was a half-full metal binder. He lifted it and with Fat Joe's back to him, smashed it on the back of his head, right near the same spot where he'd hit him before. Fat Joe went down, nearly taking the metal table with him. Jagger smiled, which for him meant the left side of his lips curled up, and the right side stayed straight—lopsided, like an upended smile painted on a mannequin, frozen and oddly fake.

"Never ever, ever ask me another question." He paused. "You still don't have those addresses, do you? But those other contractors—"

"Delarosa. O'Brien." Fat Joe squeezed the names out.

"Yeah, one was here yesterday." Fat Joe tried to hide his surprise at realizing Jagger had been watching. "Delarosa. I will try and see him in a few days." Jagger had to place the lie just right.

"But that O'Brien—there's something off about him." Jagger thought the statement ironic; did Fat Joe know anyone who wasn't off? This was like taking a trip to tour a sewer. It seemed both he and Delarosa had something against this Alby O'Brien. He looked closer: caste system. Fat Joe felt Alby was a low-life. That simple prejudice was an easy emotion to read.

Jagger walked out, with Fat Joe carrying a pile of folders behind him. Jagger had him place them in his trunk. "See you soon!" Jagger said with false glee just to see the extra-frightened look engulf Fat Joe's entire body.

"When?" But by now, Fat Joe knew to ask it so quietly that only he could hear.

At that same moment, Stephen was jumping out of his truck. "Roof and driveway week!" he yelled to Alby as he entered the back room. Alby sighed and threw a shoe at him. "You're late."

"Hey, I brought you coffee, so cut me some slack."

"Rule number three, never work with family." Alby's head felt like a balloon. He tried to remember Sunday night after he had gotten back from dropping Ginger off, but couldn't and gave up.

"Wow, you are so amazingly smart. I was going to ask for those winning Lotto numbers you have."

This earned a grunt from Alby as he tied his work boots. "Let's go over the week. What we got." As he reached for a school notebook, Stephen dropped onto the couch next to his bed and asked, "How was the bank job?"

Alby winced—to himself. "Don't ask."

And so they went through what was going to be a busy week—two driveways, a roof of a garage, some fixer-upper interior painting for a widow whose husband hadn't lasted long enough to fix it up—they kept talking as they got in their trucks. Stephen tore off, kicking up dust onto Alby's truck.

The first job was someone they had worked for before. A nice old couple. Alby had sized up the job and given him an unusually low bid. Stephen always teased him— he never admitted it but he *did* have a soft spot for older people.

"You go all out for these people," Stephen said at one point, sweat pouring off him as he mixed the asphalt for the driveway. "And I just barely make beer money. We could just paint the driveway black and they wouldn't know any better." Alby ignored him. It was getting near time for him to find his excuse and go look for his crew. He told Stephen he had left his lunch at his place and would be back.

"Hey, forgot to tell you—my mom had extra and made you lunch." Stephen patted a cooler-bag, strewn with the Eagles logos.

Stopping on his last words, he said, "I also have to leave a little early today. Pick some stuff up." Stephen looked at him curiously, then shrugged as Alby walked away. He woke up with that familiar feeling—it was going to be a bad day. As always, he would try his best to ignore this instinct, especially as it always proved true.

Time to clear the Check List. Base was first—an apartment complex he had passed nearby had been perfect. Sprawling, low-slung, 1980s style, anonymous.

"This will do," he told the fidgety super as he looked inside over the Post-It note–sized "FDA clean" virus-cleaned approval seal taped across the door space. Apartment 15 was on the first floor of an enormous group of squat, two-level, ugly apartment buildings covered in worn wood like some shoddy ski chalet. It was a sterile and well-kept one-bedroom facing a row of shrubs that blocked a direct view of the front parking lot. The room was dusty, the beams of sunlight bisecting the room looked like some divine light filled with floating dust particles. The furnishings looked fine; the kitchen table was big enough for him to spread out.

"So?"

"I like it. I didn't think I'd be so lucky to find a place so fast."

"Relo, eh?"

"Yeah, for a year. Our branch in Cherry Hill is over-capacity. Needs staff."

"Huh. What company did you say?"

"Sanford Real Estate." Jagger had passed their office on Route 30 on his drive here.

"Mark Sanford? He sold me my house…well, before Covid when I had to sell it and move in here…." Jagger nodded sympathetically but could not have cared less; it took a lot of will power not to hit him as he blathered on. So, he smiled instead and got out his wallet. "Sorry, I meant Stanford Real Estate. With a 'T.' In Philly. Where do I sign?"

"Don't know them…." He got a worried look, "Philly? With that outbreak? You remote working?" Jagger nodded as if it was a forgone conclusion.

Suddenly, they were both startled by this near-machine-gun-sounding noise coming from the ceiling. The super grimaced. "That lady!"

"What?"

"A dancer. Loves tap dance—I don't know what century she thinks she's in. One reason I think I've not kept a tenant here more than a year—all the damn clatter on the ceiling. But she pays on time. I'll have to tell her she has a new neighbor—no more dancing."

"A stripper?"

The small man chuckled, "No, I wish. A dance instructor. Gyms." The tapping grew to form some sort of melody. Both of them looked like they were trying to figure out what song she was dancing to.

"This could get very annoying." While he said it, Jagger just wanted the complex manager to believe that. He actually liked tap dancing. "I hope this doesn't force me to leave."

"I'll stop by and tell her," the super said, while he looked almost hungrily at the thick wallet Jagger pulled out. He gave the man $1,000 in cash. The super raised an eyebrow. "Ha, haven't seen this much cash in years. This stuff's on the way out." He put the tablet on the table and stepped back to let Jagger add his electronic—fake—signature. He immediately started fingering the bills, looking like a dog with its last meal. "Can I get this to you later?" Jagger asked. "I have to get right to work."

As he scanned the room, he added, "What ventilation systems do you use?" The super named a reputable brand, but added his disgust at how much it cost. Jagger interrupted him. "I'll need a receipt for the rent—company expense."

The super nodded and gave him the keys. He explained that one was for the front door, the smaller one for the mailboxes lined up in a row between the main entrance and the parking lot. Mailboxes? Like PO boxes? He hadn't seen that in decades. All those lives in little rows. He had to explore this.

As the super left, Jagger closed his eyes and pictured his Check List.

Base. Set-up. Research. Plan. Prioritize. Act. Retrieve. Eliminate. Go home.

The tap dancing got louder, then quiet, then loud, then quiet. Jagger was curious: who tapped in this day and age? He shrugged and went to his car; he was glad the apartment faced the back parking lot. Coming and going would be easy.

Setting up a post for an assignment had become second nature; the Check List held his collected wisdom of how to settle into a new place and fast; it took years of him doing it, moving from town to town, city to city, country to country, always with a tight deadline and impatient Owners. Once they had gotten a sample of how he worked, they kept him busy. Now for the unpack and set-up-station phase.

Then there was the clothing issue; Jagger tended to go for whatever was the nearest thing to the "insurance salesman" look. Gray was a standard nearly everywhere. As obvious as it seemed, people simply do not recall the faces of men in plain gray suits with plain one-color ties and white shirts. The color, if applied right, can blur the person and the reality around them, like a photograph slightly out of focus. Most people don't pay much attention to those around them, anyway, but this was extra camouflage. Since his hair was bright gray at the temples with a small bald spot at the apex of his scalp, he felt that he had also entered an age that people would never associate with a killer. No one would even look at him.

A half-dozen assignments came to mind where there had been a witness nearby and he knew with utter certainty that when asked by the cops to describe the shooter, the cops probably got a blank stare and one word: "Gray."

But some places gray didn't work. Take Arizona for instance; you could wear a gray jacket with plain slacks, but a full suit and tie in gray (or any color for that matter) and you'd stick out like a cactus on a cowboy's ass. Whereas in California, black or white suits were the gray of choice, so overused and cliché it made him almost invisible. Gray suits worked well in the Northeast and Midwest. This was an expensive wardrobe—it cost him a lot to have every one of these suits made from Kevlar, which had never been tested but was worth the protection, so he had to be very strategic about his choices.

Jagger opened his two laptops and started doing his research. Earlier, right after the super had given him his key, he had quickly found a nearby idiot who left their wireless router unsecured. What a name, too: "tap lady." He glanced up at the ceiling and then clicked onto her signal. When he was bored, he would look into her private files.

He propped the two laptops on chairs on either side of him and spread out a map of Southern Jersey on the kitchen table. He then placed the binder with the fifteen addresses and paperwork on one corner of the map.

With his left hand, he called up Google Earth and opened it to the same geography as the map. On his right laptop, he called up the Bitstream threads of the Internet where he could browse incognito and secure. He stayed with Duckduckgo. After a moment, he went in the back door of a federal database of personal data. At least his Owners gave him the right tools; it was extremely useful that they had a side-business of hacking and then re-selling personal data.

Next he opened the binder and realized the hard part had arrived—he had to decipher Fat Joe's chaotic notes and bad handwriting. What a mess. Fat Joe clearly either did not know the alphabet's order, or he was just so dumb he didn't think it was important—probably that one. The three-hole-punch dividers were titled by contractors' names. Name: Delarosa. Name: O'Brien. Let's start with Delarosa…then he stopped. Even though Jagger was convinced that Delarosa was the guilty one, or somehow involved, he had a process to follow and quadrants to map out. Checking his watch, he saw it was nearly four p.m.—if he made headway, he could get at least a few quadrants done—about five guys—and then get ready for Delarosa.

After doing a quick and unsuccessful cruise through Camden, Alby realized that he was famished; he found himself back at Stephen's side, checking his watch constantly as they worked in the hot sun. "You have that lunch your mom made for me"

"I ate it an hour ago—it's after two," Stephen said stone-faced. Then he laughed, "Nah, it's here."

Alby nodded gratefully and trusted Dorothy knew how to make a lunch. With each hour that passed, Alby felt the curse of his natural bad luck settling over him and outpacing the descent of the sun and quitting time. Eventually, he told Stephen that he was tired and going to head out early. He could get a few more hours in Camden before it got dark.

He didn't have to look to know Stephen was shaking his head in resignation.

Alby needed to find Lucky and the other guys—not finding them yet was making him more than anxious. He knew one or all were guilty. Especially Lucky—he had the killer look. Alby had seen enough of that look in Iraq. He might be clueless about what they had stolen, but he was certain they had done it. When he had driven them home yesterday morning, Chance and Darnell had been too quiet while Lucky on the other hand had been too over-the-top noisy, singing some hip-hop song—off-key. There was no way they would show up for work next Friday, so he had to find them.

Back at his cave, waiting for darkness to settle in, Alby tossed his windbreaker on the folding chair by the card table. He glanced at the empty ashtray, stained with the memory of a thousand cigarettes, and felt a rare sense of accomplishment. Well, he thought, as bad as things are at least I quit that habit. Then he briefly thought of the party at his sister's. But that was the rare bump in the road. The time recovering in the hospital had forced him to detox and clean up; he had cleaned up his fiancée leaving him, his mom's death… but not Aliyah. He quickly went back to his thoughts on cigarettes.

Everyone had smoked in Baghdad: smoke was air. But he swore he would quit when he got home—and he had. He kept the ashtray as a souvenir and he kept it full to remind him not to light another. He had never been allowed back to his apartment in the Green Zone. Instead, the Handlers had gotten his clothes, a small radio, toiletries, some books, and this Persian glass ashtray that Ahmed had given him; he had said it was from the holy city of Qum in Iran, made of the same brilliant aquamarine blue stone the city was known for; Alby had secretly studied the history of Iraq/Iran—Persia—and was blown away by how much of today's world started there. Including the fall of several empires.

Alby's life had fit into two large duffel bags. A third one, carry-on, was filled with cash. The ashtray had been wrapped up in a pair of jeans.

As his Handler started telling him what he was and wasn't going to do, he delivered it like a practiced monologue. Watching how stiff the guy was, Alby realized guys like this worked in a black-and-white, good guy–bad guy world that made everything they did or said like applying the same template over and over. Alby's version was: "Alby, you're screwed: everyone believes you turned in the Hussein family. You helped take them out. Yeah, made you a minor league hero for the mercs and few remaining troops at the embassy. Never made the news cycle back home. You are now an official target for a lot of groups. Fatwah stuff." He paused and then said: "Avoid YouTube. You won't like what you see and they can track you."

Focus, he told himself, coming back to reality. Focus. He had to find a way to quit these time-drifts like he had found the way to quit the smokes. By now, the sun had set and it was time.

Driving around Camden was draining and his mind kept wandering. The neon glow homage to bodegas and fried chicken and pizza joints splayed out into a ghetto—it was too much. He had driven at least ten times around the same one-mile grid, like a rat in a maze. He gave up.

When Alby got back to the cave, Stephen's truck was there, and he was unloading the brushes and tar. "Where were you? Is it still Monday? Did you at least bring me the leftover food you got? I'm starving."

"Go home to your mamma." Alby just wanted him to go so he could start drinking. And when he finished unloading, he did just that.

Driving was boring; it was another reason that he didn't own a car. So he allowed himself to think about other things besides the assignment at hand. His mind went back to the day he stood in court and had his name officially changed. It was right after the Owners had hired him. Everything came together, and one day it occurred to him exactly who he was, or was about to be: the perfect archetype of the Hunter. The revelation had come to him in the middle of an assignment, quite by accident. In that moment, right before he finished his work, looking down on the two still bodies, a thought arose in his mind. A name. Jagger. The German word for the "Hunter." And wasn't the very essence of the need to pursue and hunt until all was complete perfectly distilled in him? The words just blew through his mind and lay over him. And with complete satisfaction, he knew then that his life had just become fully defined. He was made whole.

Going from being a discharged killer cop to a paid killer had been easy. He had worked on the Ft. Lauderdale force but had developed a pattern his bosses did not agree with—too many bodies. Soon after the dismissal of the charge—because the evidence against him disappeared—it occurred to him that if he needed work, the guys who he had heard were the worst in the city would probably want someone like him.

It all had begun after his trial, while he was starting to plan his exit from Lauderdale. He had been caught off-guard by a "No ID" caller. He was expected at Pier 66 at noon the next day. Click. That short. He went. As he drove closer, the yachts only seemed to grow larger. It was enormous—white, silver, with jet-black windows. A half-dozen men stood around in highly visible places, looking a bit too casual; halfwits with bulges in their windbreakers and chinos. Patted down twice, he was ushered into a large, gold-gilded-gaudy living room. Two men were situated at either end of the horseshoe-shaped leather couch; each had the exact same set-up in front of them on a large glass coffee table: two cell phones, a placemat with a plate of fruit, silverware, a clear drink, and a small mound of papers. He learned later that they were cousins.

They wasted no time: "We have followed you for a while." Pause. "We were the ones who made the evidence disappear." Pause. "You work for us now." Pause once more. "We need a specialist. One who ties up all the details."

That was all they said. What was odd was how they said it—one would finish a sentence and the other would pick up the next. They volleyed fluidly. All that was left were the details, which he would learn that they left to him. Jagger felt a deep sense of affirmation.

It only took one meeting to be hired and walk out with his first assignment. Lose a uniform, get a raise.

As he cleaned up the food wrappers—no mess allowed near the map and files—he pondered his first real day: doing his research, planning how to track down the remaining few. But the best targets were waiting for him tonight at Delarosa's. He had been given one week to find this missing check; with the cast of characters he had already met, he felt confident this would be done in record time. When they put a time limit on his assignments, it automatically meant that if he finished sooner, he got a bonus. He wanted to use cash to buy a house deep in the desert. This pandemic had only reminded him a thousand times over how much he hated what everyone called "civilization." He could order whatever he wanted. A bonus would make him able to move from Phoenix to… where? … Maybe outside of Cottonwood?

With fifteen known candidates, efficiency had to drive everything he did: research wide and narrow. The wide part was using the laptop on his right side for credit and criminal background checks on each name; the narrow was the laptop on the left using Google Maps and Google Earth. Up first, "Delarosa." Clean criminal record, a bad credit rating during the Great Recession when he blew off paying his mortgage for six months. He sold his Jersey Shore house. Delarosa had a bad spin, but that year everyone did. Knowing he was heading to his house tonight gave him a sense of calm; it was going to be his crew, he was certain. Delarosa rebuilt his business and life, got another house down in someplace called Ocean City.

He patted his chest for his gun, his father's WWII .45, and his left pocket for the badge. Then he bent and felt for the smaller .22 in the sock holster.

It took only a couple of hours; he narrowed the list into a few piles. He would start with the addresses farthest away.

He had printed out a smaller series of quadrant maps of the area where he had assigned names and addresses of the different workers' houses. Delarosa was Quadrant 4, one visit might knock a half-dozen off the list. And since he had the evening meeting set up, he could focus on his second level of suspects. His instincts said Delarosa's crew had the check, but he never trusted anything too obvious or easy—even though they were rarely wrong.

So, off to Quadrant 2, a five-mile radius from his apartment.

Over the next several hours, he combed the overlapping highways and winding streets and spoke to all five of the night workers that formed the inner circle of his suspects. While driving from house to house, apartment complex to complex, he felt refreshed by how the FBI badge always, without fail, solicited the same reaction: fear. If it didn't sicken him how transparent and weak they all were, it would have been funny.

Never once, to those few who answered their door, did he bring up anything about a check being stolen. He didn't need to; being indirect was the better way to elicit the kinds of truths he wanted. Since they were all guilty of something, it was like codebreaking for him. He had to use indirect, probing words to elicit any evidence of the theft he was interested in—the single guilty act he was looking for. He always embedded one key question into his interview:

"Did you see *anyone* take *anything* from the bank?" The emphasis was a trigger.

Then he would take a long pause to let the emotions show themselves, and they always did. Like a fast-growing vine, lines would appear and dance. The dozens of micro-gestures. The tiny motions that told Jagger all he needed to know. The Owners once asked: "How do you get these assignments done so fast?" He was not going to tell them about the face reading. If the assignments were finished ahead of schedule, you earned a bonus—and he always got one because of this skill. So he feigned ignorance. He knew that irritated them—both his unwillingness to tell them and the bonus they had to pay out.

He had honed this skill. Often, one question and the person would be revealed.

As such things always go, it happened by chance. It was a life-changing moment. He had found an article in the *New Yorker* magazine on detective work by a lone LAPD unit that focused on psychology and other unlikely things to solve crimes. In that article he had discovered Ekman and his book on what he called a facial action coding system. A fancy name but Jagger immediately read the re-issued version in 2002. And a new world opened up.

Ekman's book catalogued thousands of different expressions through a careful mapping of the muscles of the human face. Not every expression could be captured—some were too fast or the combinations unique to the individual. Thousands of photos, descriptions, the code on how to decipher them, break them down, and re-build to know what their truth was—it had all been in that book. The best question that got the best answer? It had been tested on criminals in LA:

"Are you guilty?"

Worked every time.

Jagger memorized everything he could find; his appetite for this subject became an obsession. And so few police departments or law enforcement agencies used it. Equally odd was the dearth of online information. This made no sense to him, but if it was his and his alone to have and use, so be it.

The results immediately showed—that's when the bonuses became a regular thing. That convinced him. So, he pursued the somewhat obscure topic of facial recognition. The local libraries were useless. On many weekends, he drove the four hours from Phoenix to LA and went to the university libraries—he had never thought of himself as someone who could have a "passion"—still didn't. But this was different. This was like learning how to breathe water; it separated him from all the others. He knew something none of them did. He could not read enough: it was like re-training the brain.

Then he came within inches of making a fatal error.

It was April, about five years before. He had been reading scholarly theses and other reference documents all day, and as he gathered up his papers at the UCLA library for the drive home, he was feeling quite charged about what he had just read: more analysis on the nuances of the laugh lines around people's eyes as another way to figure out whether they were telling the truth or not, hiding something or not... sometimes people revealed their thoughts before they even were aware of them. It was like the emotion or thought would start on the face or in the eyes and seep inwards to the brain.

As he went out through the library's turnstile, his eye caught the profile of a man going in. He did not hesitate; instead of exiting, he spun around, heading back in. Only a few yards ahead of him was the man he was sure had written a master's thesis on Ekman's work that he had found very helpful—he recalled the author's photo in the introduction.

Jagger wanted to meet him and ask him some questions. If he recalled the paper, it focused on the differences among cultures on how to interpret the emotions from the muscular combinations of the cheekbones and mouth. The guy's name escaped him, but he was sure it was the same professor of psychology that he had read. And he had taught at UCLA. It had to be him.

Once in the library's main room, the professor made a hurried turn to the small cafeteria. Jagger followed and watched as he got a bag of chips and a fruit drink and went to a corner of the room that looked out at a student-filled patch of lawn. The sun beamed in.

Jagger walked past him and sat back near the recycling and trash bins. No cameras visible. The plastics and recycling bin were big—just big enough. As he sat, he carefully marked his spot, yards from the nearest person. Then he got up, grabbed a tray, and hurriedly filled it with lunch items—juice, fries, pre-made salad.

As he paid for his food, the cashier glanced up—Jagger wanted to laugh! He could tell from one glance the guy was skimming the cash register. It was just so obvious.

Never having spoken to anyone about the science of facial recognition, he was thrilled that he could finally talk to an expert and get some questions answered.

He went back to the far corner and waited. Soon enough, the professor got up—he must have been in his mid-thirties—and headed towards Jagger and the trash bins. He lifted the lid and slid his garbage in, as he did so Jagger gently pushed his full tray off the tables to let it land on the man's shoe. Food went everywhere.

"Damn it," said Jagger, "I am so sorry." He bent down to try to both brush off the food and pick it up. The professor—Don Jergins he now recalled—kneeled to help. Typical California-nice.

"Wait, aren't you Dr. Jergins, the psychologist?"

That caught him off guard. He glanced at him, their two faces only inches apart. Jagger could barely contain himself, "I've read your work on the relationship between cheekbone types and smiling. You've done a great job with Ekman's theories! Fascinating, and so useful. I can't thank you enough."

"Uh—" and to Jagger's utter disbelief, the professor's face went through a series of micro-motions that he could read like a map. A wan smile appeared. "No PhD yet!" he said with false cheer. "Soon."

But Jagger froze on the spot, a feeling of disappointment that was totally unfamiliar pouring over him, rising to a sense of outrage. He could see it on Jergins' face so clearly. He had to speak: "You stole your research." He paused. "From a student." One edge of Jergins' mouth twitched. Then it shifted back to neutral and with false umbrage growing, he stood. "How dare you accuse me of that? Who do you think you are?"

Jagger didn't hesitate. Being in such proximity, at the back end of the cafeteria, he picked up his small plastic knife from the floor, wonderfully satisfied that this was the UCLA library cafeteria, so of course it was not one of those flimsy cheap ones, and standing up, plunged it deeply into Jergins' neck, all the way...until his index and thumb were pressed hard into his flesh. His head snapped back. Quickly, Jagger put one hand behind his head to push it back in place, held his shoulder, and then let his body fall loose to a kneeling position; the knife held the blood in for now, but Jergins' body was beginning to jerk a bit and sway where he knelt. Jagger lifted him and sat him at the table, gently resting his head on its surface. The body was still twitching, the blood forming a slowly radiating pool of red on the dull white plastic top.

Jagger rushed to the front of the cafeteria and pointed towards the back. "I think that man is having a heart attack! Call for an ambulance!" Of course, everyone turned and looked to where he was pointing. No one looked at *him*; no one saw his face. Someone screamed.

He was almost out of the cafeteria when he heard a second scream. "He's bleeding!"

Well. Can't come here anymore, he thought.

Now, the memory of that event passed through his mind as he drove back to his apartment, still twenty miles away. After that incident, he had let his assignments be his training, honing his facial recognition skills with each job. Today had been a good payoff of that work. He'd seen seven out of the fifteen—with their squiggly, work-worn faces etched in fear and guilt. The houses and apartments were all the same, the kind of place a low-life would live. And they could all be checked off the list Fat Joe had given him. Not guilty. Well, not completely true; he spoke to a couple who were guilty of something but not stealing from the bank.

As he finished each interview, Jagger ended with a disarming smile, where only a minute before he had been grilling them, making them uncomfortable. "The FBI appreciates your cooperation." It amused him to watch their faces reflect confusion as well as the ever-present fear.

Driving in rush-hour traffic, he knew he should be in a rush to get back to base to prep for the meeting at Delarosa's—where his assignment would finish, he hoped. Priority now was he needed a good deli sandwich and some great coleslaw, rare as diamonds out west where he lived; having such food every night was a big indulgence. He pulled into the first one he saw, figuring that in New Jersey, every deli did things right and he could expect to have the same tasty experience he'd had at the one that he'd Googled on the plane. And he was not disappointed. The Owners actually had a Pandemic Codebook; the dos and don'ts. Keeping distance between you and others was a big part. The place was a bit small for the Pandemic distancing thing, but a certificate on the door noted that it had the latest and best HVAC system in place. When he was through, he dabbed the corners of his mouth with a paper napkin and took his paper plate and plastic wrappers to the trash. As he prepared to leave, snapping his mask in place, he realized he was still hungry. He always got hungry before and after killing someone—sometimes the mere thought of taking someone out made him famished. Maybe he would grab another sandwich to take along to Delarosa's.

Back in Camden, Lucky was having one of those conversations that made him glad he had moved out when he was sixteen after his mom died. Since his Uncle Charlie had a bank account, this could work out. His aunt was standing behind the metal fencing that covered the front porch's screen door. Her look of disrespect was getting under his skin. If not for the metal fencing, he'd pop his fist through the screen and hit her right in her face. With his aunt's husband's bank account, he could move the check today and be gone from town. Go visit some woman he knew who had left Camden for Vegas; she'd sent him a postcard last year. In fact it was this aunt who had handed it to him, since it was the only address the old girlfriend had. His aunt had given him a sour look and had said, "Don't give out our address to your godless whores."

He hadn't spoken to her since, until today.

"My husband is not, and I repeat not, going to help you with one of your schemes. He's a good man. A God-fearing man. He has a good job now."

Yeah, cleaning the toilets at Cooper Hospital; Lucky just stared at her trying to look caring and convince her to let him speak to her toilet-wiping, ass-handed husband.

"Aunt Shirley, this is the real deal. I got this check; it just needs cashing."

"You'd have to sign it over to me. How much is it for?" His Uncle Charlie had come out to stand in front of his aunt and he was speaking now—well, not really his uncle, but he and his aunt had lived together for so long and he'd helped her take care of his mom when she was dying. Lucky got stuck on the first statement he said and did not directly respond to the question.

"Lot more than you have in your account." Sign it over to him? Lucky couldn't figure this out. This seemed wrong. It was so obvious to him. "You just cash it."

"You gotta sign it over to me, son, to cash it." His uncle sounded resigned.

"That makes no sense. Are you bullshitting me?" He leaned forward and put his hand on the inside of his zippered and very worn black jacket. It had no collar and there were some faded stains on the front. He kept the zipper locked at the bottom. He slipped his hand around his knife. "Let me in, Auntie."

She pushed her husband behind her and stepped back from the black iron gate. "Lucky, I don't think you understand—"

"No, you don't understand. I hit some big money and I need your help."

"How did you ever hit payday?" asked his uncle incredulously.

Lucky ignored him, keeping his eyes on his aunt.

"Let me in." They were playing games with him, but he was the smart one. With it known that the check was gone, they'd come looking. Before he had come over, he had gone through it in his head: he thought he might be able to get him to sign the check, kill them both, and stay there for a few days, covering for their absence and any visitors, then head out of town. Greyhound and Vegas. His aunt eyed him and noted where his hand had disappeared.

"Lucky…."

He put his other hand on the gate and rattled it. "Open!" Then he calmed his voice. "This would make Momma and Gran feel good knowing I'd hit it."

"Show me the check," his uncle said.

Lucky hadn't considered that, so he let go of the knife handle, elevated his hand, and removed the check from his T-shirt pocket. He held it up and opened it with two hands. It felt odd because it was so much bigger than a normal check, but who cared.

"Oh my…." His uncle looked closely through the grate and then stepped back. "That's a bank check. One of those cashier's checks." He looked scared.

"All checks are bank checks. Isn't that the point?" His uncle was stupid. Just open the gate, he willed him with his eyes. Instead, his uncle took a step away from the gate. "Bank checks are from the bank. Not like personal checks. Those are smaller. You had to get this from someone at a bank."

"Okay, okay, it's a bank check. Good friend gave it to me. Owed me a favor. Let me in and I'll do just as you said and sign it over."

"I don't know…." His uncle pleaded with Lucky's aunt with his eyes.

He rattled the gate. "Let me in!" he ordered.

His aunt just shook her head. "You are a dangerous boy. Your mother would be ashamed."

"Let. Me. In." She had called him a boy. He snarled at them from behind the gate.

His aunt smiled that nasty, churchgoing, back-stabbing smile that only she could do and backed into her house. As she did so, she said in the kindest tone, "Go fuck yourself, Lucky."

Lucky stood there for a minute. His mind was blank, which meant he was thinking. He needed a plan. It was nearly time to go meet Darnell and Chance at the diner. He was so sure his uncle was the answer. What now? What would he tell them? Didn't matter. He just needed time and he was not giving up the check to either of those idiots.

How the hell was he going to cash this check? This was supposed to be easy. He even had a pen with him to fill in the amount: ninety-nine thousand dollars.

As Jagger drove, all he could think about was how long the sandwich in the seat next to him would stay fresh. Arriving to see that Delarosa's truck was not at his house yet, he parked a block away. He took out the sandwich and started eating—a true Reuben in a world of poor imitators. When he came East, he always worked to find a good Reuben sandwich. All these years in the desert, and he still couldn't find a good deli near enough to him. Chompies, the only good one in Phoenix, was nowhere near a bus line and he never took Uber because of the credit card trail.

Dabbing at the drip of Russian dressing on his lips, Jagger saw Delarosa drive past him. And in a slow parade following him came the same motley crew of cars he had seen the night before. They filled the driveway and spilled out onto the street. It was eight p.m. Once they were all inside, Jagger counted to sixty ten times, then got out of the Camry and walked briskly to the front door—he caught the movement of a curtain over the door's window before climbing the steps. With a flick, he clicked on his Warby Plastimask.

As his fist moved in for the knock, the door opened. Delarosa had a very tense look on his face—no mask, but Jagger's phone didn't go off. Delarosa was working hard to keep his emotions in check; Jagger could see them running in patterns that spoke of fear. And guilt.

"Everyone here?" He pushed past Delarosa and went down the three steps into a den designed in all-white, including a wraparound leather couch facing a huge TV. Eagles memorabilia lined the walls. Seven men sat there, three black, two Hispanic, two white, all eyes on him, faces well-controlled. Collectively, these faces were almost impossible to read, something he rarely came up against. He would have to ask some seriously direct questions to each one, then look for cracks and clues. He liked that. A challenge. In doing his research, he had learned that each had a criminal record. Jagger knew from experience that the deeper the criminal heart, the easier it was for them to put on a chiseled-face—a sort of plastic surgery that removed some of the layers of life, along with the lies and the scars that would normally mark it; a lie could be made to look innocent. To a degree. When real fear was created, and he was very, very good at creating real fear, the mask came away—as always, even here, fear took over all muscular controls.

"You know why you are here. Something was taken from the bank"—he flipped his FBI badge open and closed in one motion—and said wearily, "Yes, FBI. I am here to find out what you do or do not know." He paused, but not one expression in the room changed.

"You have a separate room? I'll use the kitchen. One man at a time. You." He pointed to the one on a chair to the left of the couch. He jerked his thumb over his shoulder, spun on his heel, and walked up the steps. He could hear the guy get up—the chair creaked slightly. The others quietly started to talk.

In the kitchen, he gestured at the cheap-looking chair standing at the ready at the cheap-looking linoleum table. The guy was thin as a pencil, but sinewy. "Name, address, and show me whatever paperwork you have."

"Joey," he said, but then he threw up his hands. "Delarosa said nothing about no paperwork, nothing about no FBI."

"Get over it. Answer my questions. If you're not guilty, you have nothing to worry about." Jagger glanced at that man's face. "Are you guilty of theft at the bank?" Instantly, he knew he was guilty. This elated him to no end—first interview. Jagger held back his smile. He would be on the

Owners' private plane heading home as soon as he got the check back. After his earlier outburst, the man became extremely docile. Jagger got his address and asked him some perfunctory questions and dismissed him with a nod. "Go get the guy next to you."

"Don't mess with Turk," Joey mumbled. Jagger cleared his throat. "Excuse me?"

"You just remember who warned you." Genuine fear peeked through the wall of scars, oozing like invisible wax between the cracks along his cheekbones, along the folds of skin under his tired eyes.

See you soon, Joey, thought Jagger. He knew where he worked during the day. Joey might not be returning from lunch tomorrow.

The next guy walked in—it was more a stomp than a walk. He was very tall and big in all places. It looked like equal amounts of fat and muscle were competing to own his body. "I'm Turk," he announced as he stood next to the chair. Turk's hands were so large, they covered the top of the chair. Jagger waved his hand for him to sit down. Turk did not move. Intentionally, Jagger kept his eyes on the notepad in front of him, knowing this dismissive approach put people on the defensive. Finally, after a long silence, he looked up at Turk's face.

He was guilty, too. So, he and Joey were partners. He'd have to take Turk from behind. "I said sit."

"Do I look like your dog?" As he said it, he practically growled. Jagger wanted to laugh and say yes.

"We do this the hard way or the easy way." Jagger played the FBI cliché game.

Turk was silent and did not move.

"The hard way is we go downtown, and you spend the night in jail."

"Like that would scare me?" Turk barked a big short laugh, his enormous shoulders and belly swaying in opposite direction. "My initials are probably on the walls of every cell there."

Jagger decided on a different tack. He smiled and nodded as if he got the joke, even though for Turk the last thing in the world he wanted was to be funny. "Turk, let's just do this and get it done. I don't think you are guilty of stealing from the bank, right?" He hesitated dramatically, like an opera singer taking a breath. "I have to interview everyone on that shift. That's the deal."

Turk nodded and slowly sat down; he poured like lava over the small seat. Less than five minutes later, after some yeses and nos, he dismissed Turk. That was two; they had worked together, both guilty. Excellent. He was done. Now he had to figure out how to get them both.

Without being called, the next man stepped in and moved swiftly and slid into the seat. His fingers immediately played on his right knee like a piano. Jagger looked at his face: guilty… was this like some shared Lotto ticket? Were they all in on it?

Jagger sped up. He had to see if they were all involved. This was a scenario he had not planned for. Six men and one had the check. Or six men splitting the check.

Twenty minutes later, he was done. Dismissing the last man, he leaned back against the linoleum counter, closing his notebook of names, addresses, day job locations…how could they all be guilty? Confusion was not an acceptable state. Only resolution mattered.

Head shaking in disbelief, he got up, slid both chairs back to their original positions—careful to wipe them free of his fingerprints—and moved to the short steps to the den. It was dead silent. Everyone was sitting either on the long wraparound couch or on the other couple of chairs in the room, all in different states of agitation, except Delarosa. He stood near Jagger by the steps. Jagger had to subtly position himself.

They were all guilty, but of what? They all stole *something* recently. But when he brought up the theft at the bank, by the time he got to the third or fourth one, he realized that what had been missing right from the first one on was the usual and expected visual and muscle clues that evidenced themselves—no slight twitch, or the line of the mouth curling down on the right, or the eyes narrowing, with the mouth following a moment later…nothing. They were all innocent. And guilty. For a moment, he was extremely annoyed at himself for not recognizing this absence right from the first one. It occurred to him that these might be the most pathological humans he had ever met. Reptilian. Nonetheless, Jagger knew what he had to do.

Delarosa, leaning against the wall, stepped forward and said: "So what's next?"

"Whoever has the check, give it to me now and you walk." Promising freedom was always a winning strategy. He surveyed every face. They all shared a naïve look: what check? They all had varying shades of questions on their face. They glanced at each other, like they each hoped the other knew what was going on. The word "check" clearly surprised them all. Only Turk didn't move—his body was leaning slightly forward and he had his eyes locked on Jagger.

Turk was carrying a gun. Jagger had missed it while the guy had been standing in the kitchen, but when he had sat down, his pants rode up his leg a few inches, exposing the bulge of what was probably a .38 tucked into his left sock.

"You." He pointed at Turk. "Give me the gun." Turk's eyes bulged out in surprise and maybe even in a hint of panic. Jagger put out his hand, palm open. Turk slowly leaned forward, pulled up his pant leg, and removed the small gun from his sock. Yes, a .38.

"Holy Christ!" Delarosa declared. "I could fucking kill you. You brought a gun into my house?"

"Not to worry," Jagger said, waving his arm dismissively. "I am a professional. I'll take care of it."

He put out his left hand and walked over to Turk, who dropped the gun into his open palm.

Jagger stared at it for a moment, then swiftly switched it to his right hand and shot Turk between the eyes. He swiveled, his arm following the line of the couch and chairs. Five more bullets, six men gone. As he swiveled to Delarosa—who was getting close—he pulled out his own gun and shot him in the eye.

"Guilty," he whispered. "All guilty." One of them was supposed to have the check—that was the whole point of the night. Yet, no check. He went through the clothes of all of them just in case. No one had even known that what was missing was a check until he had said it.

He took the gun and wiped it with his handkerchief. Then he placed it in Turk's hand, wrapping his finger around the trigger. He reached into his jacket pocket and took out a simple Glock and put it in Delarosa's hand as he lay sprawled on the couch. Cupping his fingers gently around Delarosa's limp hand, he raised his arm and shot the gun three times into three different bodies. The white couch was covered with growing splotches of red, like some mad Jackson Pollack painting.

He momentarily paused, feeling very frustrated—something that he rarely felt on the job. Another day had passed, and he still had to find the check. Back at the starting line.

Jagger walked up the steps into the kitchen. He used his elbow to slide back the glass door and stepped out onto the back porch. He carefully lifted the giant Weber grill and rolled it slowly until it was close to the glass. Reaching around the back, he loosened the hose and then turned on the grill, smiling at the hissing sound of escaping gas. He went back and looked in the refrigerator; he took out a half-dozen bottles of beer, opened each of them and placed them on the living room carpet by the bodies, carefully pouring out different amounts from each bottle onto the floor. Slowly, he surveyed the scene, then went back up into the kitchen and backed out of the door, slowly backtracking until he was off the porch steps, feet on the ground. The windbreaker he wore was dark gray, a cloth material, something inexpensive-looking that he had purchased at the Men's Wearhouse. He patted his left pocket, took out the butane lighter, flicked it on, slipped a pin in the lighting mechanism so it wouldn't go out, and threw it at the Weber.

He turned and ran, low to the ground…one, two…and up it all went—the gas tank blasted through the glass door, immediately engulfing the porch and kitchen in a mass of flames. Truly the worst party any of them had ever been to, and he'd planned it; but screw that plan because now his plan, his methodology, had to be revised.

In a matter of minutes, the entire house was in flames.

He had to get back to the apartment. Confusion was clouding him. All his instincts had told him that someone tonight would be The One. And he had been wrong. Amateurs were wrong. Professionals were not. For him, doubt was as uncomfortable as an untreatable rash. Action was all that mattered. As he drove back to the apartment, Jagger did his best to contain the simmering anger he felt at not being right. But every mile of driving was like an odometer of anger ticking higher. By the time he got to the apartment complex, parked in the back, and turned the key in the door, the simmer had turned into a full boil of red-hot anger, an emotion he did not like nor had a lot of practice catering to; he had to wrestle it into some compartment so that he could use that energy to focus on his renewed search. Amateurs were guided by emotion.

He threw the keys at the sink across the room as hard as he could. In one continuous motion and not without a little disgust, he took off his gray jacket, loosened his tie, and sat down in the chair—his laptops, maps, and files all around him. Without looking, each hand landed on its rightful place on the keyboard, like a well-rehearsed pianist playing two pianos at once.

The map of Camden County lay before him; it held answers he could not yet, anyway, see. The previously marked quadrants, with all the night shift crews' known addresses, were overlapping circles made with a red marker. He took the red marker to the area where Delarosa lived and drew an X over it very slowly.

More research was needed. Only two contractors had had no addresses for their crews. With Delarosa gone, that left Alby O'Brien.

His hands moved like twisting serpents over the keyboards; on the left… Alby O'Brien. Google him and follow the trail through the small bits and bytes of his life. It was so much like playing Alice in Wonderland, rushing behind the rabbit, not knowing what was next. This was the part he enjoyed the most—no, that was not true. He shifted left in his chair and felt his handgun rub against his upper ribs. Both thoughts began to calm him. His right hand opened the concealing Tor software, and then the backdoors to the databases and servers only his Owners knew how to get into. Jagger knew how to hunt online.

But thirty minutes later, Jagger pushed back his chair in frustration, his temporary state of calmness lost. This was not right or possible. These trails made no sense. They led everywhere and nowhere.

O'Brien's path started as straight as most. Growing up in Northern Jersey, Jersey City, both parents Irish immigrants. Jagger knew how to find old documents, school newspapers, report cards. It all existed somewhere; you just had to go through the trash heap to find it. This guy was very average—his parents both union members, his dad dying while he was in high school—right about when he joined the football team and did well as a running back. Channeling his anger, thought Jagger.

Jagger had needed to go into the hacked databases for deeper information. There he had found that O'Brien did two years at a nearby community college—mediocre grades—and bought a used truck. A business license for construction was issued within a month of him finishing his second year of college. Jagger moved between laptops—one following O'Brien's history, the other his official records, credit reports, loans, credit cards… it went up and down, up and down. Looking at his life and finances was like watching a bad game of whack-a-mole. The man sometimes had lots of money—big construction jobs—then would spend it stupidly until he was near broke.

At one point, he did settle down. A woman co-signed a house lease. Jagger snorted, went looking and found what he suspected: a credit card statement with a $2,000 engagement ring from Diamond Street Jewelers, which nailed down that neither he nor the woman had any taste. With his left hand, he spent five minutes doing a basic search on her—a nobody. Jagger kept looking but instead of a path that was heading for marriage—the money trail was easiest to follow for this—it led to a year later: he moved out. Bank account went empty. New lease was issued in her name.

Break up. Wedding's off. Just out of curiosity, Jagger followed the woman and found an application for a wedding license a year later. Cheating on this loser O'Brien, most likely.

But then something else showed up. Right before the break-up, the guy's credit card debt shot up. Soon, he had a huge debt. Hospital bills? Jagger hacked the hospital records for O'Brien: it was his mother. Since she had a union pension and insurance and still ran up some huge bills, it must have been a huge sickness. Cancer.

The cost of a funeral came up a few months later. Funeral home, parish priest, coffin, burial plot, a bill for a big memorial lunch at a union hall.

Then the path zigged. A passport application. Then nothing until he reappeared a few months later through pay deposits, working a Bechtel job in Baghdad. The medical bills suddenly got paid off in large amounts—hazard pay. Whatever he had been doing must have been dangerous. What the hell made him go to Iraq? Money? No, that was too big a change for just money. The conclusion seemed obvious: he was running away. Had to be.

And then the bottom of the search just dropped away. Jagger couldn't find any trace of him. ADP payroll for Bechtel stopped. His work visa ran out with no renewal. No plane tickets, no credit card charges… nothing.

Where did he go?

With a few more taps and incognito browsing, he found a mention of Alby O'Brien in an obscure Army base weekly news rag. This was beyond belief: he had uncovered and taken down an ISIS terror cell about to blow up the power station he was managing. A contractor. A hero. This did not make sense. This guy was a runner, a loser, a shadow in the world.

Soon after that Army article, he appeared again about a year ago in a Jersey City hotel getting new driver's and construction licenses. He put down nearly $40K in cash for a new, double cab, Ford F-150e hybrid electric pick-up.

How did he get all that cash? How did he get back to the States? Jagger could find no visa, air ticket, customs records…with his right hand, he pecked away in the airlines and federal databases at the same time. Nothing.

It was impossible that anyone could get from Iraq to New Jersey with no trail. Jagger filed that away. It smacked of some government work; maybe somebody had helped him disappear. Although it took a while, and several aliases, Jagger went on YouTube and found a video of an Arab in the shadows holding a short, scrawled list of names. Jagger stopped the video and zoomed in. There it was: Alby O'Brien. Was he really a hero? Someone was spending a fair effort to declare vengeance on him. This just did not seem believable.

Next he saw a lease signed for a garage on Route 70 in Marlton. Jagger memorized the address; O'Brien must be a mechanic and some kind of sub-contractor. He had a new driver's license, but the address on that was his sister's house. Why there? And the PO box bill showed up. Knowing where the guy worked made him feel better. He shut down the browsers and then the laptops, pondering which would be the best path— do what he did with Delarosa and try to get him and his crew all together and confront them? Or follow him?

Just then, a sharp clicking sounded overhead. He looked up.

The tapping started quite slowly, then suddenly sped up then slowed again. Jagger cocked his head and tried to hear the music. It was faint. Could he make out the song? Sounded like Cole Porter—maybe Irving Berlin? He went into his suitcase, retrieved a small object and pulling the chair right under where the loudest sound was located, he climbed onto the chair and placed the object on the ceiling. Grabbing the AirPod with his free hand, he stuck it in his ear and listened for a few minutes. Then he got down from the chair. And in another few minutes he was in bed. He had been wrong on both guesses: Gershwin. In the bedroom, the clicking from her shoes was distant and soothing, like drops of rain on a glass pane. A loser and a hero, he thought. He had just unfurled the flag of Alby O'Brien's life and found a patchwork of actions, mistakes, and mysteries. O'Brien was a loser and he, Jagger, could not be wrong, so…

Following him would tell the real story. That meant up early and at that garage before Mr. Alby O'Brien went to work.

Tuesday: 7 a.m.

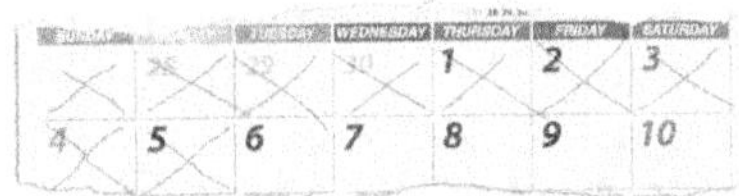

Marlton, where Alby slept, was about a mile from the construction site, two miles from his sister's house, a little over three to Gatewood Apartments.

At this time of the morning, caught in the limbo between sleep and wakefulness, he always felt completely disoriented. Okay, the Maker's might play a role. He rolled over and filed away another night of nightmares. Same theme, same characters, same palette of pale colors of orange dust and white walls exploding with red-washed surfaces… just re-shuffled each night like a deck of marked cards. Having spent the evening watching Netflix, he finished by exhausting himself with the punching bag. None of it did any good. It was like someone tied him up right after he fell asleep and then cut him loose in the moments right before he woke up: his body was stiff and uncomfortable. His knuckles were sore, the scar on his side ached—he had to stop extending his right arm to the bag.

Sitting up, he slipped his socked feet into his boots and stood up, and almost blindly walked over to the chair.

"I hate mornings," he muttered. Instantly he knew it was going to be a good day. Something good was going to happen. He tried to ignore it, but at least this felt good, believe it or not.

"Then how about a free coffee from Dunkin'?" Stephen suddenly appeared in the doorway, bag of donuts and a tray with four coffees. Alby nearly fell into the chair—he had not heard him come in.

"Jeezus Christ! What are you doing here so early?" He wanted to smack the kid, but the lure of coffee and donuts made him hesitate. Surreptitiously, he kicked the empty Maker's bottle under the couch. It clinked loudly as it collided with another empty bottle. He winced. Stephen said nothing but shook his head.

He took the large Dunkin' cup. "You always bring me Dunkin'. You know I like Starbucks."

"Too expensive for my budget. Pay me more and I'll go." He laughed. "You probably go there to steal the sugars." Alby kept looking at him, trying to look innocent.

Stephen rolled his eyes this time and then a little proudly answered Alby's question. "Early at the job. Gotta finish this morning… because last night I got us a new job—should take up most of this week and next."

Alby semi-wrestled the second coffee cup from the cardboard tray. "Who—how the hell did you get us a job? What kind?"

"Connections, baby. Local boy." Stephen moved to his usual chair—the only other chair in the room—next to the side where all the tools and gear were kept. "Garage roof. Re-build."

"Great." He responded with sincerity—so much so that Stephen's head snapped his way. "I mean it, good job."

"Thanks, Alby. Maybe I am getting the hang of this construction business."

"It's Uncle Alby to you, you smart shit, and don't get too cocky." He rubbed his chin. "We still have to finish that driveway."

Stephen got an awkward look on his face. "I finished it yesterday. The old man liked it so much he showed it off to his neighbor. That's the garage."

"Nice." Alby was surprised at his nephew's initiative.

"We can grab some day workers from Camden and just check in on them. The two jobs are only a neighborhood apart."

"No!" Alby barked, then in a quieter, calmer voice, he said again, "No day workers. We'll divide and conquer. Better we pocket the cash. I can start the driveway we had planned, you start the garage. Tomorrow we're both there."

Stephen nodded, sipping his coffee. He looked a bit surprised by

Alby's outburst and Alby noticed. So he re-directed. "You didn't get one of those girly drinks—the chai, mocha, blocha, flocha crap now, did you?"

Stephen put down his cup with a resigned sigh. "You're lucky you're family."

This made Alby lift his head and look at his nephew as if seeing him for the first time: never work with family was his Rule. Then a single thought stopped him cold: Was he putting Stephen in any danger? It was like he was looking down through a microscope. Every detail of his nephew's face, the slight scar on his forehead where a foul ball had hit him in eighth grade—Alby had been there, it was the playoffs—the beginning of laugh lines by his eyes, the way his mouth looked like his mother's... Alby's mother. Those laugh lines had skipped a generation. His sister only had two expressions: deep frown and exuberant open-faced joy. What an annoying mother she must be.

Soon, the trucks were each loaded. Alby strapped the ladder onto Stephen's truck with bungee cords. "Try not to lose the ladder on the road—"

"Funny!" Stephen yelled back as he drove away. Maybe it was better that they worked separately; Alby could sense that Stephen knew he was on edge.

Alby was the first to find the address and saw the owner already on the lawn, moving things out of the garage and behind the house. "Hey, I'll help!" shouted Alby as he pulled up. Hopping out, snapping on his mask, he ran over and took the paint cans from the old man's hands. "I got it." The man started to look ashamed, knowing he was too old to do this work, but Alby smiled. "It's what you're paying us to do."

The man nodded, with a half-frown, half-smile and they chatted away as he led Alby to the back.

A half-block away, Jagger witnessed their movements. As Stephen unloaded the truck, Jagger opened his laptop, loaded photos of him into it, and looked for an unprotected Wi-Fi signal. He found several that had no lock on them. Yet again, he wondered how people could be such idiots as he logged onto an incognito browser window and started running the facial recognition software on the FBI database.

His laptop made a ping sound, letting him know his search had found something. He looked down and read the name on the report: Stephen O'Brien Calabrese. Jagger read the file; he never would have guessed.

As they finished setting up, Stephen and Alby discussed their game plan, as they usually did. This time though, Alby claimed he forgot something and had to go back to the garage. The old man was outside again, and he smiled and said, "My wife made iced tea for you and your boss."

"He's my uncle! Get me at lunch time, thanks!" A disgruntled Stephen went up the ladder, carpentry bag on his shoulder.

The roof was in bad shape; there were even a few spots where he could see through to the garage. Alby had prepped part of it already by piling the long nails, tar paper, and some rotten boards. The only answer was to remove at least half of the roof, board by board. Stephen grabbed a large hammer and dove right in, prying the long nails out. This was going to be a day where his arms would feel like anchors by five.

An hour later, Alby, without a word of explanation, joined him.

Around noon, Alby's phone rang. Seeing it was his sister's number, his first impulse was to let it go to voicemail. She practically owned his voicemail—he hadn't deleted any of her messages from the past year. But Stephen looked up, and he felt he could not be disrespectful to his sister in front of her son.

"Come over for dinner."

"I don't know, sis—" But she was ahead of him, having been turned down several times before; her husband was away, and she wanted some company. Reluctantly, he shook his head no and said yes. After he clicked off, he looked at his watch and saw that it was nearly one p.m. "Hey, I gotta run back to that other site. Also buy some supplies."

"That job is done. I told you I finished it this morning."

"Yeah, well, did you collect the check?"

"You never told me to."

Alby grunted as if to say I'm always right. "Be back in a few hours."

"Sure, just like this morning."

Alby, already climbing down the ladder, said nothing.

After a while, Stephen got hungry. The sun was that last bearing-down heat of the tail end of summer. He stood and took careful steps. His lunch box was near the ladder. Just as he was reaching for it, a head rose up before him; he hadn't heard the ladder squeak. That ladder always squeaked. It caught him so off guard, he nearly jumped.

Then he saw half the torso of a man on the ladder, a man in a gray suit jacket and a gray tie. He could not see his pants.

Stephen stared at him for a moment with an "Are you kidding me?" look on his face.

"Stephen O'Brien Calabrese." His voice, look, color, were all flat. Stephen could not tell if he was an undertaker or… what? An insurance salesman?

"You can't come up here." Stephen waved his hammer in a circle as if to demonstrate what should have been obvious from the supplies, nails, loose boards, and toolbox; he quickly put his mask on. The man said nothing but kept climbing until he was standing on the roof. The gray suit did not quite fit him; his tie was slightly crooked. Something was clearly not right, and the fact was that he said nothing and looked out of place—why would a businessman like him be standing on a roof?

"Up here for the sun? Get lost on your way to Subway for lunch?" He'd learned these verbal tricks from his uncle; Alby called it verbal stiletto—keep jabbing until you drew a reaction.

Maybe this wasn't the best approach, thought Stephen. The man knew his name and now that he thought about it, he had that "Law" look—the hairs on his arms rose to attention as the man spoke: "FBI." He reached into his jacket and flashed the badge.

"Shit, what do you want?" He glanced around, over the roof, up and down the street, "We had an agreement—"

"Shut the hell up." The man let it drift off. It seemed uncanny that he was so close to the roof's edge and seemed unaware of it. Or maybe he didn't care.

Stephen put down the hammer. He sat down and edged a foot higher up the roof.

"I've never seen you before."

"Do you know what trouble your uncle is involved in?"

Without thinking, Stephen straightened his back and sat straight up. "Uncle Alby? He's up to his usual bullshit—making deals, doing crap work, dragging me along."

"I don't think so."

"Can we talk somewhere else? Like, can we both drive down the street and have this conversation?" He started to stand.

"No. Here. Now."

"Oh—kaaay…." He sat down again.

"What do you know about the work at the bank?"

"The asbestos job? I don't know, easy money, fast job, it just sucks that he has to get up early to pick up the crew."

"Six a.m." Jagger said matter-of-factly.

"Yeah." What was he getting at?

The man walked over closer to him and surveyed the neighborhood like a sailor taking in the horizon. His eyes moved into slits as he turned towards the west and the sun shone down on him. He talked but didn't look at Stephen.

"Well, getting up early is the least of his—or your—worries. What you need to worry about is, are you two going to jail?"

"Could you make sense?"

The man quickly turned and took a long step, landing his black shoe right on top of Stephen's hand as it propped him up as he sat. He yanked it away with a curse and scurried away like a crab, scrambling backwards on his hands and feet. Reflexively he grabbed the hammer and lifted it.

"Stephen, Stephen," the FBI agent said paternalistically. "What I need to know and what I need you to do begins with the following: Your uncle stole something from the bank. We know it. The only reason we haven't arrested him is that we're trying to find the other men involved."

"My uncle is a lot of things, but he's not a thief." The snap image of his crew came into his mind. "If anything was stolen, it's those scum buckets from Camden, not Alby."

The mention of Camden seemed to annoy the agent, but he waved his hand and cut him off. "Your only choice to help him is to help me. Help me keep an eye on your uncle and find out where the others are. I need all of them."

"I knew something was wrong." Stephen shook his head.

"What?" the agent asked impatiently.

"With his crew. He's been ducking out of jobs. Now I get it. He's looking for them. I'll bet that's what he's doing. He's been acting all weird and shit the last few days. Ever since Sunday."

"This crew…do you know where they live?"

Stephen laughed and then saw the agent's glare and cut it off. "Camden, you know how it is. One father, four families, three girlfriends, a grandmom, and an abandoned house…pick your address. They could be anywhere. He sure doesn't know where they are. Crap, they don't know where they are day to day. He just goes to the same place to pick them up and drop them off."

"And that would be where?"

"Where you don't want to go." Stephen looked up and really looked at the guy. "You're not from around here? Which office are you out of? I usually deal with Agent Blonder."

The agent waved a dismissive hand as if wiping a table clean. "He's busy. I'm out of North Jersey. Where?" he asked again.

"4th and York."

Stephen sat silently now. His uncle was in some deep shit and he knew he was too, but Alby had been good to him and he knew in his heart that he was the same uncle who had come to his weekend baseball games all through high school, taken him to Manhattan for the first time when he was twelve and then again on his 21st birthday…right before Grandmom died and he'd disappeared to Iraq.

Stephen knew he had to do something. He just didn't know what. But he knew what to say for now.

He looked at the agent. "Okay, give me a number to call. I'll start asking around and see what I can learn."

The agent smiled and Stephen almost recoiled—it was like watching a boa constrictor unfurl to release a dead animal. It bore no resemblance to any smile he had ever seen.

The agent wrote a number on the back of a card and gave it to Stephen.

He moved to the ladder and started down. Again it seemed like he had no sense of concern about being on a second-story roof. Stephen waved his hand to stop him, "Wait—say hello to Agent Blonder."

"I will. He'll be back from vacation soon."

"I like him," Stephen said abruptly, awkwardly.

"Yes, me too." And with that, the man's head disappeared down the ladder.

Stephen did like Agent Blonder. Except he was a she—and cute as hell. Alby was in some big trouble. This guy was no FBI agent. A fake agent packing a gun, holding a fake FBI ID. What the hell had Alby fallen into? And he couldn't tell him, because then he would have to open up about the FBI.

In Camden, Lucky, Chance, and Darnell had agreed to meet a block away from Santorini's bodega and deli, where they had agreed to the night before at the diner. As they stood outside, it was after one p.m. and most of the lunch crowd was gone—mostly low-wage workers from nearby Cooper Hospital getting a cheap sandwich. As they moved slowly down the block, Chance suddenly said, "Hear about that guy and his crew who all got killed last night?"

"No," said Darnell, a hundred miles away. He was busy trying to think of what to say when he walked in.

"Bad shit. House burned to the ground. He worked on the site, too. Said it was an explosion from his gas grill—"

"Shut up, Chance," said Lucky. "Who needs to hear about this shit."

But he went on, deaf to anything but the flow of words emptying out of his mouth like a river. "…and he had his crew there. They worked at the bank job, too—I knew Turk. Man, hard to believe anyone could take him out." Lucky rolled his eyes. "Yeah, barbecue for the crew! All six of 'em! Now how come Alby never does that for us?"

Lucky stopped and stepped into a dirt lane between two row houses. Darnell silently took the check from Lucky's outstretched hand. "Don't let them have it. I'm giving you ten minutes then we're coming in." He yanked up his jacket and showed the knife handle. Darnell didn't even glance at the knife; now he knew that Lucky didn't own a gun. The knife was for show.

Too much experience had taught him that the Guatemalan gangs were more than dangerous—they'd kill him in a second and for no reason. They just liked killing, like those weird Russians that dealt heroin near the hospital. He'd dealt with them, too. Fronted stolen stuff. They always ripped him off and laughed him out of the store, but he made cash.

The door ringer went off as Darnell stepped into the store. He glanced at the saggy-eyed guy behind the deli counter as he moved towards the back, past an armored door that was half-open. He looked in.

Santorini was directly ahead of him, sitting with his crew at a table, each staring at their phones. Darnell stepped into the sparsely furnished room, with its one folding table and a few chairs. The guys weren't playing cards; he caught a glimpse of one screen. They were playing "Words with Friends" on their phones, in Spanish.

"I remember you," Santorini said, slowly eying him up and down. "You still alive?" he asked with mild surprise.

Darnell didn't want to think about those days. He knew this check thing was bad business—more of that poisoned water he used to drink every day—but he was in. No getting out.

Words would be meaningless, most likely be dead before he fin-ished a sentence, so he simply held up the check. Santorini—a short man who clearly looked Mexican but always boasted his grandfather was Italian—turned and reached out to take it. Darnell pulled back and held onto it. Santorini snorted through his nose and shook his head back and forth. "You think that's real? Don't believe it's real; we make checks all the time. That's bullshit. Why don't you buy some milk and get the fuck out of here?"

Another guy at the metal table laughed disdainfully; he gestured at the check: "Look at that size! What's that? Super-Check?"

They all laughed. Santorini walked over and smacked the guy on the head. "That's a bank cashier's check." Darnell smiled. Santorini was interested.

"I'm here to make you a lot of money," Darnell said slowly.

One guy pocketed his phone and stood up. Santorini stepped closer, eyeing the check hard; he resembled a panther stealthily moving forward, assessing his prey. He moved his eyes side to side, carefully, along its width. He stepped back and rubbed the small tuft of beard on his chin.

"You got the balls to come in here and pass us a bad check?" He rubbed his chin again and turned his head slightly to the side, like he was thinking. "I'll take it off your hands. Twenty bucks."

"It's real and you know it."

"I'll tell you what I know. It takes a lot of nerve to come in here, shoveling this shit."

The third guy, still sitting, had slowly pulled out a gun and rested it on his lap.

Darnell calmly told them he had two guys packing out front with a ten-minute window. "You're about at four minutes. It's that simple. Deal or no deal, I walk. I'll sign $100,000 and you cash it and keep $25K for me just showin' up."

Santorini looked at his crew then lunged at the check. Darnell stepped aside, and he stumbled past him. As Darnell backed quickly to the door, the crew got up and aimed their guns at him. Santorini recovered, red-faced with anger, and spat at him: "I know now where you got that check. I know that bank. Those people are…" he paused. Darnell was shocked to see Santorini freeze in momentary fear. "Shit, I don't want you even in here. If that's real, then it's like a bomb in your hands, bro. It's going to blow you up. Bang!" He threw his arms in the air. "Bang!" Santorini waved one hand at his crew and they lowered their guns. "Don't want anything with those people. They're bad news." He paused, then yelled, "Out!"

Darnell immediately turned and headed out of the back room, moving quickly down the store's narrow aisles. Watching him from the doorway, Santorini roared: "I should turn you in for a laugh."

As he pushed open the outer door, he heard Santorini speak again, this time not to him. "Next time we see him, it'll be on the TV—dead on the sidewalk!" He could just catch the sound of the men laughing at the man's words as he stepped onto the sidewalk to face Lucky and Chance. Lucky had a look of both satisfaction and disgust.

Four blocks away, Alby was cruising Camden in what was fast becoming a twice-a-day ritual. By now, it was getting familiar—that was not good.

Cruising so slow was making him a target for people's stares; he ignored them just as he tried to ignore the growing churning in his gut that said the longer he took, the more trouble he would be in. But he was getting nowhere looking for those three… yet again. Time to give it up… again.

As he headed back to the cave, he decided that it might be a good idea to bring his sister a gift, so he pulled over at one of the many bodegas at the edge of Camden. A six-pack of imported beer was as good as he was going to do, he thought, feeling generous, and clicked on his mask.

The tinny bell jangled as he opened the door, but no one was at the front counter, which was encased in thick plexiglass to prevent robberies from the days long before Covid would have necessitated it for health reasons. He saw the freezers in the back and slipped down the narrow aisles; it amazed him how much crap was shoved onto tight shelves and how dusty everything was. The store had nothing imported, but there had been a Heineken's sticker on the front door. He looked around for someone to show him where it was when he heard sounds of laughter in the back.

He wasn't sure what to do but knew that he absolutely did not have time to go someplace else. He edged down a tiny hallway where he could see a metal door mostly open. He heard voices.

"Who the fuck he thinks he is? Next time we see him, we cut him. No one will miss his ass." They all laughed. It sounded like maybe three guys. "We turn Darnell and the check in and we are on the inside with those bank guys."

Alby froze. Darnell? He'd been there? A different Darnell?

Okay. Decision time. Go forward or quietly turn around and head back out the front door? Either one was a bad decision. It was just which one was worse. Three days he'd been looking for Darnell and the other two. Hell. He stepped through the metal doorway.

The three men stopped in mid-laughter. One, clearly the boss, stood up and pushed out his chest. "Whadda *you* want?"

"I came here for some beer—"

"Get it and get the hell out."

"I heard you say Darnell was here. I'm looking for him."

"Who the hell are you?"

"Was Darnell here?" He had to push. Alby, raised in good old Jersey City, had enough street smarts to figure how long he had before the situation went bad. It had served him well in Iraq. He could feel the other two men tense up. Keeping his eyes on the boss, he reached his hand slowly into his jacket pocket, found the handle of his knife, and placed his finger on the blade release.

"So *what* if Darnell was here? Why don't you buy your beer and get the fuck out of here. We're busy." He laughed, the other men echoing him. Alby glanced up at the large screen showing a soccer match.

"I need to find Darnell." Now he palmed the switchblade.

The boss stopped smiling and stepped close to Alby. He was short, muscular, with a pointed chin that was now jutting up and out arrogantly. A hospital mask was hanging down from his ears but he didn't put it on. "I don't think I want you in my store. Are you sure you know where you are? This is Camden, man. Folks like you don't come here, and when they do, they can disappear." He snapped his fingers in Alby's face. "Just like that."

Out of the corner of his left eye, he saw one guy reach behind his pants and Alby knew he was reaching for a gun. In spite of a racing pulse, he welcomed the coolness that settled inside. The risk of leaving was greater than staying—it was that simple.

That cool, calm wave must have been showing on the outside because the guy kept talking.

"Hey, for some dumb old white guy, even you should know better. Yeah, Darnell was here, and he left. He was smarter than you and left when he should have."

One of the other two men moved slowly to shut the metal door that led back to the store.

"No." Alby said with a firmness even he couldn't believe. He'd seen these scenes a hundred times at checkpoints. Everyone was spring-loaded and ready.

"What?" the boss asked incredulously, with a half-smile.

"This," answered Alby. With a practiced motion, a smooth softball motion, he swung his arm up, released the blade, and by the time it opened to its full six inches, the point nestled in the hairs under the boss's chin.

Everyone in the room froze.

"You shouldn't mess with Santorini," said one of the guys, hand behind his back.

"You pull that gun out there will be no Santorini," said Alby calmly, not sure where that came from. But this was his first lead. He had to push. "Tell me about Darnell and we all walk." Run, a voice in him said, you mean run.

Santorini didn't move a muscle; the blade hovered less than an inch away from the underside of his jaw. Then he smiled and with a casual wave of his hand, the other two backed away. Then Santorini took a step back, away from the blade.

"Okay, crazy man, Darnell came in here with some fake check. From that bank. You know, the one run by those bad dudes."

Unfortunately, Alby knew the bank too well. "A check?"

"Nah, it was fake. No check looks that big. It was like a check on steroids." Then he laughed and Alby had the distinct feeling that he was lying. It all came out too easily. Santorini lifted his arms in an open gesture, almost as if on a cross.

"We good?"

Alby held the knife still, his mind momentarily on hold. A big check? A bank check? No way. They had stolen a bank check? He snapped back to the knife in his hand.

"You know where to find him?"

"Nah. He's like all those trash, hiding out in some alley or house or with some aunt." He laughed and the other two echoed it. The air grew less tense.

"We good?" asked Santorini again, but more firmly this time.

Alby took a step back but kept the knife aimed at his throat.

"Yeah, good."

Santorini exhaled and then he smiled again. "You are one brave fucker coming in on me like this."

Alby couldn't help himself. "I was just looking for a six-pack of Heineken."

They all howled with laughter, the energy in the room turning on its head. Nonetheless, he kept the knife at arm's length.

Santorini smiled at Alby like they were old friends. "Beer?" He shook his head. "Beer? Wow. Hector, get the man the six-pack. On me." He smacked his chest with one fist like Tarzan.

Without taking his eyes off Santorini, Alby stepped aside to let one of the other men leave the room

"Just for that, you leave in one piece. Man, you got some nerve. I like that. Crazy old white guy."

Hector returned and began to hand him the six-pack. It wasn't Heineken. "I wanted Heineken." They laughed again and the guy got the Heineken.

In one quick motion, he folded and stashed the switchblade back in his jacket pocket, still focusing on Santorini. "You're good with that thing," Santorini said admiringly.

Alby stepped backwards.

"It's okay. Go! Go!" As Alby moved quickly through the store,

Santorini's voice grew dark. "But don't ever come back."

Getting into his truck, he floored it and nearly ran a light as it turned red—his breathing was hard and his chest ached, but slowly his head cleared and he pulled over into a gas station near the air pump where he couldn't be seen.

Breathe… the only thing he could think of was the punching bag: jab left, jab right, left, right, left right. He could feel his body twitch like he was really punching. He heard the sounds and his racing pulse subsided in waves until some semblance of calm took over.

Glancing at his phone, he saw that he had to be at his sister's in less than an hour. Of course, those three idiots didn't steal something small— they had to steal something that would cause *big* trouble, and he knew that it was Lucky leading the charge. It pissed him off when he remembered that big smile he had given Alby when he had picked him up Saturday morning. That bastard had the check on him then.

A bank check. What do you do with a bank check?

You can't *cash* it! It would be too noticeable. Stupid. And those guys probably all had police records. What could they possibly do? If it wasn't signed, it was worthless. It couldn't be signed. No way it was signed. It got under his skin that while one mystery was solved—a sonavabitch bank check—it only opened the door to more questions. Darnell going to that scummy bodega meant the crew was shopping it around.

It was nearly six p.m. and he needed some food and gas. He drove the few miles back into the suburbs. The truck hit the curb of the Lukoil station, and his cell phone went flying from the seat onto the floor. Of course, that's when it rang.

"Christ," he muttered, pulling over to the pump. Reaching for it on the floor, he saw that it was his sister. He hesitated, then picked it up.

"How are you, sis?"

"Alby, you actually sound civil. I figured you were just going to ignore me. Let me leave my one-hundredth message." She didn't have to say it. He heard the unspoken echo of "as usual" at the end of her comment.

"Actually…" and she let the word linger as if it had special meaning. "You still coming over tonight?"

"The slob's not going to be home, right?" Looking down, he noticed his hand was shaking slightly.

"*Alby!*" she yelled, "He is my husband. Be nice. He just happens to be going bowling. Big tournament."

"I said I'd be there, I'll be there." He felt kind of bad about how he had acted at her party. Maybe she was making the effort; and she *was* his only family…well almost. "Stephen going to be there?"

"He'll show up. That girlfriend of his—well, another time on that—she's not really welcome around here, but…"

"Yes?" asked Alby, waiting.

"They'll be coming."

She paused, and the air seemed to get heavier on the phone. "Alby, I think it's time we talked about Iraq. I'm your only sister and I know some bad things must have happened there—"

He cleared his throat loud enough to stop her. "You're bringing this up now? On the phone? What—your therapist tell you to? No. No. Not gonna happen, sis." Iraq? Holding back, he wanted to shout: The hell with Iraq! How about almost being killed in a bodega in Camden, right off your doorstep? He knew this outburst of anger he was directing at her was partly fueled by what had just happened—but he also knew that his mother's death held the real burn, and it was like an engine just waiting for the on switch to let loose. They would have it out one day. But not today. What a coward to try do it on the phone, not in person. He hit back.

"You know, if we're going to talk about anything let's talk about mom!"

There. He'd opened the door he knew she wouldn't go through.

Silence. He could hear her breathing. He pictured her standing in her kitchen, travel-magnet-covered refrigerator door half open, food ready to be cooked. Then she spoke. "No, yourself. We've gone over this. Nothing happened. She died, and you need to accept that."

"Go screw yourself, Dorothy!" he yelled into the phone. "You need to own what happened"—then he stopped, deflated, the phone line silent. Like the call had fallen off a cliff. After a long pause, she asked in a tight, but calm voice, "Are you still coming?"

"I'll be there." And he clicked off. She sure was full of surprises; he'd been here over a year and she had never invited him for dinner, only parties. And she had never mentioned Iraq before. He glanced up at the gas ticker, even though he was trying to ignore it; it chapped his ass every time he filled his truck. Inflation was back with a fury, as bad as it was during the oil recessions of the 1970s; he had to look away as it ate at his wallet. But bigger problems loomed that were greater than an empty wallet.

There would be no parking in his sister's driveway. A green Honda Civic CRV sat there. It looked like it was at least twenty years old, but someone had kept it in mint condition. Must be Stephen's girlfriend's car. He parked his truck on the street.

"Alby!" his sister called out as she opened her front door, her arms spread like wings to welcome him. In spite of her welcoming tone, her body language and the tension on her face told him that she was still holding onto their conversation. She was always too loud and had always been that way. They called her megaphone mouth in high school. He stepped into her embrace but only half returned it. "Smells good, sis. Stephen here?"

He had to be civil. As much as he hated it, he knew small talk was the only plan for surviving the next few hours and if Stephen and his girl-friend had already shown up, they could fill the chasm between Dorothy and him. Just the two of us? he mused. I mean, why would she do that? She avoided him as much as he did her.

"No. He's late. Out with that liberal feminist white trash girlfriend of his." Alby had never heard that particular grouping of damning per-sonality flaws strung together before. "Oh...kaaay..." he said. Not being a statement that had a response, it was all he could manage to say.

As she moved past him and went around the corner to the living room, he followed her and continued, "So, it's just you and me for din—"

He stopped.

Sitting on the couch, looking awkward, was Ginger. She was

squirming ever so slightly. She smiled a phony half smile, then dropped it. They locked eyes, briefly, and she nodded hello. She did not get up. She had a drink in front of her, something brown with ice. It was *her* old Honda in the driveway. He nodded back. Should he smile? Was he supposed to?

Dorothy made a sweeping gesture, "Aren't you glad you met at my party last weekend?"

"Alby…well, he doesn't tell me anything. Him and his 'cave!' Mr. Mystery!" With a meager attempt at a laugh, she turned and moved to the kitchen.

"Alby, you know where the bar is."

Dorothy's small dining room was attached to the living room; as he went around the couch, he noted that there were five places set.

Ginger spoke first. "How's the hangover?"

"That was Sunday. Today's Tuesday in case you hadn't noticed." Had he been that bad?

She harrumphed.

"Don't I get a beer?" he shouted towards the kitchen. "No booze! Beer!" In his peripheral vision, he could see Ginger raise an eyebrow.

"Hold your horses, baby brother," Dorothy shouted back. "Beer? Okay."

"Not that cheap piss your husband drinks. Anything left over from the party? Somebody must have left you a spare Heineken." After the phone call, he had decided to keep the six-pack for himself—why give her a gift? It was his trophy for surviving the bodega.

"Alby, stop being so mean. And yes, it is the cheap piss he drinks." He heard her laugh and a bottle cap hit the floor. She carried the bottle out and handed it to him, standing over them both as they sat facing each other. She put her hands on her hips, triumphantly. "I am so glad you two could come over. I wasn't sure, but I just had to have you both over, you two are so alike, so…." And with that, one hand rotating in the air, she realized she had run out of words. She had painted herself into a corner with her big mouth, he thought. She just moved her head back and forth as if looking for them to fill in the blank.

He decided to play it straight. "We caught a movie Sunday night." Dorothy looked relieved.

"I didn't know—Ginger, why didn't you say anything at class?"

Ginger shrugged. "You didn't ask."

"See," Dorothy exploded, "you two *are* alike. Both smarty pants. See? I am always so right with these sorts of things. A match!" And with that she blew past them and headed back into the kitchen.

"A real coincidence."

"Alignment of the star," Ginger threw in.

"Stars, you mean," and he smiled.

"No," she smiled smugly back and turned a little with one shoulder pulled back and her chin up, striking a celebrity pose. "Star. Singular."

His smile went away. Then it crept back—so, she knew how to be silly funny as well as sharp funny.

Dorothy just couldn't stay away; she came back into the living room and plopped herself down on the edge of the couch near Ginger. "Dinner's almost ready. So. You two went out to the movies. What did you see?"

They exchanged a glance, as if to say, who's going to speak first? And what do you say?

It was Ginger who spoke. "We planned on going to a movie, but it didn't quite work out."

"Oh…." Dorothy seemed at a loss, but only for a moment. She perked up and smiled. "Well, this is a good chance to get to know each other better. I know both of you don't have many friends—" and at this, both Alby and Ginger swiveled their heads and just stared, expressionless, at her, but Dorothy was oblivious—"and keep to yourselves. Not healthy. Just not. So, let's eat and have some fun."

Did he really share the same gene pool as her? Alby slowly stood, waiting for Ginger. When she did not rise, he walked to the table. She waited until he was three steps from it and then got up quickly to follow. Dorothy had them sit opposite each other while she sat at the end.

Alby sat down, as uncomfortable as a thirteen-year-old boy having to sit with his parents when there was a ball game going on… or when the mom had invited the new girl at church to dinner. And then to make it worse, he heard Dorothy announce, "Lasagna—Mom's recipe." Alby twitched when she said "Mom." He didn't want to think about the resentment towards her that always lay in wait—about how he'd been all in. There by her side. Taking care of things, losing his relationship, his savings, his friends, and being left with the bills. Forgiving was out and so was forgetting. Glancing at Ginger, though, he pulled back; maybe he could give Dorothy a form of emotional parole and let it go for tonight. No need to drag anyone else into this hell hole, especially a stranger. Especially *this* stranger.

They served their own food and began eating in silence. Seated at the end, like some referee, Dorothy kept furtively glancing from left to right, as if looking for a spark, a word, anything to start a conversation.

After a few bites, Alby had to admit to himself that it was like his mom's lasagna.

"Ginger is a dancer. Did you know that?"

Mouth full, he grunted no. He glanced at Ginger as he lied.

"Tell him about it."

Ginger rolled her eyes, then caught herself. He suddenly realized that she was equally annoyed by his sister's conversation. At least they had that in common. He had to give her a hand.

"Go ahead, tell me."

For a long while, they kept it all to small talk. Ginger was round-about, mentioning working for the past year at the Zumba place where she had met Dorothy; before that she was a co-owner of a dance studio in Brooklyn, when she spoke of it, a shadow of sadness brushed her face, shrugging with the resignation of accepting a past lost relationship as she said it went out of business. Killed by Covid, she said.

"Why don't you open your own studio again?" asked Dorothy.

Ginger smiled, but it was a sad, tired smile: "That's the plan. Just needs to be the right place—I'll know it when I see it."

"I am sure it's very expensive to build one, all that wood, and the mirrors, you know."

Ginger wrinkled her mouth in an odd way, "Not worried about the money."

"What's the plan right now?" he asked, truly curious; that was a second time on the money thing, it was like a switch for her.

"This is in-between time."

He had no clue what that meant, so he nodded and looked at his food. Then he grew stunned: was he in in-between time? He realized he never thought about any future, just a week at a time.

Sensing an impending silence, Dorothy launched into anecdotes of their childhood—sanitized, of course. Once she finished recounting most of her childhood (as *she* remembered it, of course), it was time to dive into Alby's. He gave her the evil eye, but as usual, like a wind-up doll, she just went on and on and on. As she got near to high school, he cleared his throat. She stopped and looked at him, surprised. He gave her the "time-to-clear-the-plates" look. Dorothy scanned the table, shrugged, and then looked at Ginger.

"Let's *all* share tonight! Ginger, where did you grow up?" she exclaimed. Alby wanted to throw up.

Alby looked at Ginger. She sat up straight, like she had been caught off guard, staring at her empty plate, as if trying to find something. Alby could sense a shift in the air around her—clearly, she did not want to share her past. Dorothy teased, even badgered her. Finally, probably sensing Dorothy would not give up on her pursuit, Ginger spoke. Her voice dropped down a few gears, low and slow. Dorothy's frown told him this was not what she had expected.

"I grew up in a few places—lots of time with my grandparents in Ohio—mom's side." She smiled and gave Alby a shy look. He was surprised she had a shy bone in her. "But every summer, right after school let out, I'd be on a plane or train to the nearest major port, wherever I could pick up whatever Cunard ship they were on."

"That's a ship company," Dorothy said with authority. Ginger looked surprised, then laughed lightly and nodded.

"Yes, a very big ship company with very big ships." Alby noticed her slight sarcasm was of course lost on his sister, and he enjoyed it. Ginger told them that her parents were professional ballroom dancers for the Cunard line. "From six years old until I was a teenager, they took me on the crossings with them— one time, a Cunard liner had lost its dance couple at the last minute and my parents got the call. So there wasn't time to find a place for me to stay." Her tone shifted, softened, which Alby immediately registered. She pushed at some food that was left on her plate with her fork as she spoke. "The QM2. It was amazing. It is amazing. Seven days crossing the Atlantic. They named it 'The Crossing.' That was my favorite. But we did them all—Cape Horn, the Caribbean, the fjords, the Baltic. And we danced. And danced. I practiced with them all the time. The three of us would fill the empty ballroom with all kinds of dances: salsa, flamenco, tango. But it always came back to ballroom dancing. It was a big part of the cruise." Alby watched her closely. She was and wasn't looking at them—really, it was almost like she was looking past them, like she was seeing some scene unfold. Then she was silent, but there was a big smile on her face; he noticed again how wide and full her mouth was. Then he noticed her lips, and suddenly he saw nothing else. But a second later, his sister's loud voice distracted him.

"That sounds amazing!" Dorothy looked at Ginger as if she were looking at royalty. Alby had never been on anything larger than a fishing boat and had always had this perception that cruises were cheesy. Besides, that industry had just begun to recover in a really noticeable way from the debacle that had scarred them when Covid began.

Ginger seemed to come back from her reverie and continued speaking. "I always spent the first day on the deck, just amazed at how much water there was—especially after being in Ohio for most of the year. Sounds silly, I'm sure."

"Not at all!" Dorothy said, too loudly as usual.

"Most nights, I ate with the crew and just went to the cabin and read. My parents practiced all day, every day. All the different nationalities had their own dining room—I always liked the Filipino one best. They were all so warm and funny. I even learned some Tagalog." She paused, and her tone changed. "That's their language." She smiled winsomely. "Anyway,

I think I was always the youngest person on the boat. I wasn't supposed to go to the upper decks with the passengers. They kinda had to bend some policies for me—but whatever ship we were on, we always got a special card and visit from the captain." She sighed. "It was always before some big event, and he wanted to discuss the dancers, routines, whom they should focus on—like the old Cunarders." She tossed the term aside then caught herself, laughing with the memory. Alby couldn't help but smile. Her laugh was infectious.

"Yeah?" he asked. "What's a 'Cunarder'"?

"Oh, those are the ones who've done endless trips—some have spent months and years on the ships. It always amazed me. Seemed kind of romantic to forever sail the world. Anyway," her face becoming soft again, "the captain always loomed large, with his white tuxedo and his medals and his creased black pants…." She let her voice drift off.

Alby picked up the ball. "Nice way to spend your summers." He could not imagine being such a vagabond—ship to ship, crew to crew all summer, and a kid, too. The only summers he knew were weekends at the Jersey Shore, mostly Ocean City, and the second week in August when his parents rented a small bungalow in Belmar. In fact, going to Iraq was his first trip outside US borders.

"So, you're a second-generation dancer! Your parents must be so proud!" He could tell that Ginger liked his sister but liking her did not stop her from giving Dorothy a withering glare and her voice changed. "Last thing in the world they wanted. I guess it's good they're both dead and haven't seen what a mess my life has been." She caught herself and smiled as Dorothy looked aghast at the comment. "It's not a mess. I'm just being dramatic." She waved her hand dismissively.

Alby was hooked. He had to ask. "This may seem like an obvious question to you, but what inspired you to pick dance as a career?"

"Wellll…." She drew the word out; she seemed pleased he had asked. "One night, the last night of one of the crossings, I snuck up the stairs and went to the big ballroom. I knew my parents were giving a performance. Oddly enough, I had only seen them dance in performance a few times; mostly I saw them in rehearsal. Yeah, when they had their off-season breaks from the cruises, they kept a small apartment near my grandparents; even then, every night they practiced. Stop, start, stop, start. I was either doing homework or shuffled off to bed. But I'd hear the record player start and my father's low voice, "One two three, one two three, one two three…."

"I always wanted to go on a cruise," Dorothy burst out, "but my husband, he gets seasick. Personally, I really think he gets wallet sick." She giggled at her own joke. "Plus, the Covid thing, even vaxxed a few times and I still don't trust those ships."

Acting as if Dorothy weren't even there, Alby asked, "What happened?" Alby genuinely wanted to know; he watched as her face softened, the furrows between her eyebrows opened and drew back into the smoothness of her forehead like two wings.

"Oh, it's nothing," she said. But he made a gesture telling her to go on. "Well, that one time, I snuck up from the crew quarters. Dressed in my best clothes so no one would suspect—although given my age, everyone of course stared for a second—I went into the ballroom. It was eleven o'clock. And they were just being announced. Then the music started. The band was big, the room seemed huge, full of bright lights, men in tuxedos and women in gowns and jewelry. In the center of the dance floor, my parents stood still, like statues. The band began a waltz. Then they just moved. They floated. They were perfect. Like they were a few inches above the ground. I don't know who the composer was but I was mesmerized by the music and them. Everyone seemed to hold their breath. Everyone had their eyes on my parents as they glided across the floor; I saw the looks and how envious people were and how magical it all seemed. At that moment a man, a prince, glided up to me and with impressive skills, we danced the night away. That was it. I knew I was going to be a dancer." She laughed as if lost in time and in the scene that she was describing.

Dorothy's mouth was half-open: "A real prince?"

Ginger laughed, but quietly, and looked down. "Yeah, a real prince." Then she shifted her body and expression, like letting go of the line that tied the ship to the dock. "I needed that; I needed to share it. I had never seen them that way. They weren't my parents, they were…stars." Her voice dropped off. And then she nodded, as if bringing herself back to the table. "I wanted that magic. Silly, huh?"

Shocked by her honesty, Alby could only nod.

Alby wanted to do something to counter those last words. "Why not try out for a Cunarder?"

"Oh, I did… chorus, theatrical players, shoe-in dancers who grabbed the shy husbands and got them to dance." She sighed, and very quietly, almost too quietly, said, "But I wasn't my parents." She paused and as a kind of afterthought, added, "I never had the right partner."

"You are very, very talented," said Dorothy, reaching over and patting her hand.

"I teach Zumba for God's sake!" Alby could feel the disgust in her voice. "And I'm stuck loving an art form that hasn't been popular in fifty years!" They must have both had questions written on their faces. "Tap. Tap dancing. Obsolete," she said with disgust.

"I've seen you practice between classes. You're the best! The best!" Gesticulating while picking up two plates, Dorothy resembled a drunken octopus, tentacles whirling. "I've seen you at the studio on our breaks."

After she left the room, Alby let the silence hang for a moment and then asked quietly, "Do you still feel the magic?"

She gave him a curious look and nodded, with a bit of remorse on her face. "Yes, sometimes. Mostly when I am alone and practicing."

"But the best dancing is with a partner?" She nodded. He nodded as if he understood, but of course he didn't.

With that, the front door opened, and the moment popped like a balloon with the sounds of Stephen entering with a girl's voice accompanying him. Alby's first thought was that this was a welcome interruption, but as the thought arose, a very different feeling accompanied it. If he were to give it a name, he would call it…disappointment. Ginger, also seemingly interrupted in mid-thought, fumbled with her napkin and looked at her lap. Alby turned in his chair to face the door. Maybe it was better this way; he might have started running out of things to say.

"Hey Mom, sorry I'm late! I'm hungry! Got any leftovers for Jill and me?" But before Dorothy could answer, he saw Alby. "Uncle Alby, holy shit. What are you doing here?" His eyes were red: Stoned. Realization spread across his face as he saw the two empty settings. His face said it all, he had forgotten his uncle might be there until now and he knew that his uncle knew it too.

"Having dinner with your mom. What does it look like?" But suddenly the girl came from behind him and sat down at the other end of the table. She took the chair meant for Stephen. He looked around awkwardly and pulled up another chair to sit next to her.

"You got a lot a nerve telling me to come to dinner and you forget!" Alby said, teasing him.

The girlfriend, shoulders thrown back and her long black hair uncombed enough to reveal a long tattoo that ran down her neck and disappeared into her collar, barked: "Don't speak to him like that. You might treat him like shit all day, but you don't have to when you're not working… or do you?" Alby felt like he'd been hit with a brick.

The girl was clearly sizing him up as she spoke, and then a slow, not-so-nice smile appeared in all its glorious phoniness. Ouch, he thought. What Stephen must say about him.

He looked at Stephen, who was studying the tablecloth like it was a map. A little more quietly this time, Stephen asked, "Got any food?" His mom, still standing in the kitchen doorway, responded with teeth clenched as she glanced at his girlfriend. "Sit there. Hand me your plates."

The silence held firm until she returned. The girl just kept her eyes on Alby; he robotically moved his eyes from the plate to his glass.

"Didn't see much of you today," Stephen said.

"Had business to take care of."

"Like the crew?"

This caught Alby off guard. "What makes you say that?"

"I don't know. I thought you said you were heading to Camden." Alby had said no such thing. He made a point never to tell anyone where he was going. How could he have figured that out so easily?

"Nope, not today. Not till Friday night."

"Oh." Stephen struggled to find things to say. Stoned, thought Alby again.

"That's that mob bank, right?" the girl interjected. Alby grew still. That was two people. Was it true? He felt like a ditchdigger who's just realized that he'd dug down so deep he can't climb out. "Good job—from mercenary in Iraq to working for the mob." There was the sound of triumph in her voice as if she'd just unlocked a treasure chest so she could rifle through it.

"Do you have a name?" Alby asked her. Stephen sat between them. He looked both ways like he didn't know where to look or what to say. "Jill," he said. "Meet my Uncle Alby."

She nodded. Stared at him. He hadn't seen her blink—just drill her eyes into him. He hadn't seen that since Iraq.

"I'm Ginger, just in case you want to stare at me."

Alby nearly fell out of his chair. He had to swallow his laugh, which made it sound like he was choking. He looked up at her in surprise. She looked back and screwed up her nose like she was twelve years old. Then he looked back down at his plate.

Jill ignored Ginger and kept her eyes on Alby.

"How'd the roof job go?" Alby asked casually. He figured he had to try and move this conversation in a different direction.

Stephen began to speak when Jill cut him off. "You know it's a mob bank, right? Everyone does. It's been in the news a few times."

"Ever been able to prove anything?" Alby spoke deliberately and slowly lifted his eyes to meet hers.

She grunted. "Guess you don't read the papers."

"Why bother? Same stuff every day—death, disaster, end of the world, war…."

Stephen seemed confused. "Alby, you read the paper every day—you just told me…." One look from Alby and even he knew to shut up.

Ginger moved uneasily in her chair. Dorothy said nothing, for a change. Her face seemed to be getting a brighter pale and her left hand was flitting across the serving dishes as if she was ready to collect them and go to the kitchen but couldn't move.

Stephen started to rise. "Jill, let's go. We can eat later."

"No wait…you were in the war, the latest one, right?" Stephen sighed and sat down again.

"I was in Baghdad. I wasn't fighting."

"Really?" She said it skeptically and didn't wait for him to respond. "You think there's a difference? You weren't part of the crew that destroyed that country? So, what *did* you do?"

"That's a stupid question." He stared hard at her. He could feel his pulse start speeding up, that distant sense of losing control rising all around him. His hands felt itchy and sweaty.

"Uncle Alby," begged Stephen.

Still this girl Jill would not relinquish her icy, unbroken stare; he could see the coat of anger painted all over her. She had too many hard lines in her forehead for someone so young—he knew a miserable person when he saw one.

"You know, you screwed that whole country for decades. You know that, right? I mean, you were there." She leaned on Stephen and waved her arm in a big, sweeping gesture. "Ever see the *Onion* headline? 'Americans kill more Iraqis than Saddam Hussein.' Hilarious...."

Alby held back out of respect for his nephew; but he glanced at him repeatedly—after all it was his dog to muzzle. Stephen avoided eye contact; he patted Jill's arm, and asked for the salt. She ignored him and leaned over the table, coming closer to Alby.

"What did you do? Build army bases? Prisons? I'll bet you made a killing!" she said with a bite.

"Construction. Electrical. Fixed a power plant." He didn't know why he shared that. He wasn't sure what to do—her dog-with-a-bone attitude was too much. Despite having lived it, Alby had no conclusion or opinion on the war in Iraq; it was too confusing and the lines were all blurred; he had just kept his head down. The less he thought about it the better.

"Good men and women served their country. And good Iraqis tried to do the right thing."

Jill shot back, "Good people who died for nothing."

"Did you have any family in the wars?" asked Ginger innocently. Jill didn't take the bait and wouldn't take her eyes off Alby but rapidly shook her head no.

"So…." Alby had begun to feel his words form like the curl of a viper's tongue; it was the Jersey City in him that he hadn't seen for a while. "You're the one with the advanced degree in Right and Wrong? How much money do you make off Right and Wrong?"

"I have another question." Ginger's innocent tone was so sharply phony that it could have cut through bone. "Does any of the garbage coming out of your mouth make sense?" She paused and smiled at Jill the most insincere smile a person could. Dorothy was as white as a sheet and looked like she had been borrowed from Madame Tussaud's wax museum, but Ginger continued. "If you're looking for a bone to pick, I think you'll find it shoved up your ass."

Dorothy gasped.

Stephen finally woke up: the train wreck had happened. He stood up. "We gotta go." She didn't budge.

Without taking his eyes off the girl and without thinking, Alby stood up. He pulled up the left side of his shirt, exposing his side and the six-inch scar that ran down it like an extra rib; it was raw, jagged, red, and uneven.

"My gift from the war," was all he said, in a flat voice. He locked his eyes on her.

Everyone gasped. "Alby, my God!" His sister looked like she was about to faint. Ginger sat straight up in her chair, but her eyes never left the scar. Her face was expressionless.

Only Stephen spoke. "Holy crap, Alby, what happened to you?"

As though his words were a spark, the dining room practically blew up—his sister jumped up and started grabbing plates. Stephen grabbed the arm of his now sheet-white and finally stunned-into-silence girlfriend and pulled her away from the table, backing them hurriedly out the door and mumbling about a movie.

"Just shut up!" were the last words he heard Stephen saying to her as he slammed the door behind them.

Slowly, carefully, Alby tucked his shirt back into his pants and sat down. He folded his hands on the table and just stared at them. He felt a hundred pounds heavier. He could hear his sister tossing things in the sink and muttering; she always fell apart and retreated when something-not-so-nice happened; same thing she did when their dad got into screaming battles with Mom.

His mind retreated back there. Right to the kitchen she'd go and start cleaning. She did it right after the funeral: went to their house, cleaned it top-to-bottom for the whole entire day, then left without a word to Alby. Other than a thank-you note for sending half of the money from Mom's house sale—which he thought was damned strange—Alby hadn't spoken to her until a few years later when he had called her from the hospital in Baghdad to tell her that he was coming home. He hadn't even told her about going to Iraq. He could have called her, but her whole attitude and that lingering doubt kept nagging at him. What *had* really happened the day he left Dorothy alone with their mom—what the hell had happened? Coming up about once a week, Dorothy had been helpful in spelling him, so he could go to work. He was running through money faster than he could make it—mostly due to the lousy insurance and the rip-off hospital. Dorothy had arrived that last day and woken him up in the hospital lounge chair they had rolled in for him and he had left for work, as usual. Yes, his mom had started the day dying; she had been near the end for a week. But he had not expected to return to the hospital later and find her dead. And the doctors never gave a straight answer to anything: "It was her time." That expression pissed him off. No one had a "time"—did these assholes own some Death Watch? Something had happened, and Mom was dead. He had been sure that she had weeks left in her. He would never have gone to work if he didn't believe that.

Now he looked up and then over at Ginger. She was staring at him with a look that gave no hint of what she was thinking or feeling, which surprised him since she seemed so naturally outgoing and emotional. He now realized that she could hide herself well; he knew that trick, too.

"Well?" he finally asked.

"Well what?"

"You have anything you want to ask me?"

"Oh, I've got plenty I want to ask." She shook her head repeatedly, almost like she was trying to clear her mind. Her red hair lightly slapped her left cheek like a series of overlapping curly waves.

"Go ahead."

"You told me what happened, but you never mentioned getting hurt."

"Didn't seem important."

"Oh really?" Her red eyebrows arched up, and her nose scrunched a little; for a moment he was taken aback at how cute she looked.

"Am I going to get that"—and she pointed at his right ribs—"part of the story sometime?"

"Some time. But not tonight." He shook his own head and sighed loudly. "I shouldn't have done that." After he spoke, he regretted saying anything. Just the concept of regret repulsed him: you live with your decisions. The secret was avoiding having to make tough decisions.

Suddenly, with no warning, she laughed; it just spilled out of her like a broken fountain. Now it was his turn to be shocked into silence.

She looked over at him, caught herself, and stopped abruptly. She put the back of her hand to her forehead in a dramatic gesture. "You should have seen that girl's face. You scared the living shit out of her." It took him a long few seconds, but he started to laugh, too. Her laugh was like the first voice in a chorus that you had to join. The laugh had a meaning they both got: it was all so stupid, a waste, the entire scene. And sick funny. Those were some odd things to have in common. But he liked it.

His sister came back into the dining room, her face aghast. "What the hell are you both laughing at?"

Alby stood up and pushed back his chair. "Ginger and I are going out for a drink."

His sister's face lit up. Ginger looked surprised.

"Ginger, I am so sorry for my son's behavior—"

"He wasn't the problem," she said firmly, closing the topic. Dorothy seemed taken aback by her curt reply but just nodded.

"See you at class?" Dorothy asked sheepishly. Ginger smiled a big, wide, fake grin. "You bet. Thanks for dinner."

In the driveway, Alby started laughing again.

"*Now* what's funny?"

"Stephen! He has to spend the night with that witch. Teach him a lesson."

"Bet she's got one helluva broom!"

They both laughed, a laugh of innocent mischief as the pale light from the porch poured over them like a pair of show lights on center stage.

"So, where should we go?" He caught Dorothy sneaking a peak through the living room drapes.

"I have an early morning. Follow me back to my place, and we can talk a little."

Trying not to follow her car too closely, he thought: I am a fool. Why didn't I tell her the whole thing? Why did I tell her anything? And *her* story. What was she running from? He knew that scent all too well and it was on her.

She drove to the rear of the complex and pulled into an empty parking spot. She turned off her car, got out, and climbed into the truck. He turned to tell her perhaps they should not see each other again. He didn't have a single clue why she should like him, and he was bad news, especially now with the stolen check.

Without pausing, she slid over on the cab bench, grabbed his face in both hands, and kissed him. Hard. No mask, no distance, no permissions, no discussion about her last Listerstrip test, which vaccine they got, when, efficacy, variants, how long did it last, boosters—all the stuff everyone talked about now before they had any contact or intimacy. She broke every unspoken rule. After a few seconds, she broke the kiss and whispered, "Alby...I am so sorry. No one deserves such bad stuff. You're a good soul."

He barely heard her words as she leaned forward and he felt her press against his lips again, light this time, almost a brush stroke on a painting; he caught himself falling into it. It unwrapped him, like metal sheeting being pried back from his skin. Her red lips on his, her red hair falling across his cheek. Even her scent smelled red...a spicy, flowery fragrance. Completely lost for a second, he knew he had to focus. They broke away. Suddenly self-conscious, she conspicuously slid back to the far end of her side of the cab.

"Don't be sorry for me. My bad luck. Fate."

"We make our own fate," she said emphatically.

Silence hung there for a moment. His lips tingled. He was still lost in their kiss.

"I know you like me." The boldness of these five words after the sweet moment of those two kisses was spinning his brain and he had no clue how to respond. Then she pivoted again. "Do you dance?" She asked the question like they had never spoken about Iraq or kissed.

"No, um, dance? No, but I guess I can learn…uh…Dumba. I mean, Zumba!" She gave him a nasty stare. Then she laughed… loudly; it reverberated through the truck. Unlike the last time, when he had felt that her laugh was way too big for the cab, now he felt like a vacuum seal had popped and the truck was filling with air that he hadn't even known he'd needed.

"Next week we dance," she declared.

"I don't think you want me doing that."

"Try."

"Not worth it."

"Stop being an ass, and just go with me on this." Then she paused, as if in deep thought, and opening her eyes wide, as if she had just come up with some radically wonderful idea, she said, "I know. I'll spare you the public scene and give you a private lesson." Then she opened the door and slipped down, her skirt lingering on the seat behind her for a moment, exposing her knees, until her feet hit the ground.

"Hey!" he called. She turned around. "You want to go grab that drink?"

She must have seen his crestfallen look, and her cynical tone turned gentler. "Sorry, but tomorrow's a workday; gotta get up early." She paused, biting her lower lip. "But call me, okay?"

As Alby drove away, he tried to feel it, he wanted it in his memory, a photo, a feeling, the first kiss he had had in…four years? Some prostitute in Baghdad, at a private club, and he had pushed her away. He tried to re-live Ginger's lips, her kiss, to hold onto it. He touched his lips. They were soft. How odd that he had never known that. He had never considered the notion that his lips could be soft; it was as if Ginger's were made of a lotion that had somehow softened his. He realized he had not shaved and thought that she must have felt the rough bristles.

For a moment, his thoughts drifted to The Rules. It was there in neon: never fall in love. It costs too much. What number Rule was that? A kiss was not love. Damn. She was challenging The Rules. He thought about all the protocols she had not addressed and yet was so a part of how life was now. With a free hand, he automatically went for the strips to test if she had infected him. When he pulled them out, he looked at them for a second, then opened the window and threw them out. Screw you, he thought—the kiss was worth it whatever happens.

The truck rolled smoothly on the night road; he almost wanted to call his sister and thank her. Then the thought turned, and he felt like calling Stephen and reaming him out. Then he thought again about Dorothy and how angry he was with her. It was a jumble of emotions, stealing away the thrill of the kiss, so he chose to shut down and drive. The closer he got to the Route 70 garage, the closer he felt to the abyss of sleep, and a slightly frightened chill went through his body—the check. Always the check. Waiting for him was the black, eyes-closed pit crowded with demons. As tired as he felt, he knew he had to go to the punching bag.

Later, when he dropped half-dressed into bed, he had one final thought: it had been a good day. His lips told him so.

Wednesday Morning: 5:00 a.m.

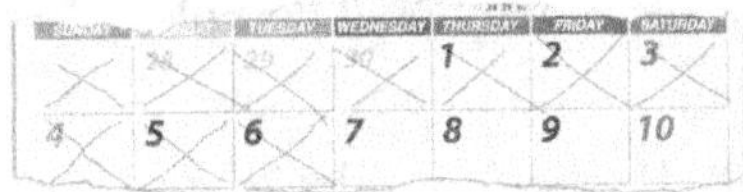

She always overslept. She and the morning were in a lifelong wrestling match. No matter how hard she tried, she just could not make herself be a morning person. When she had the studio, she could skip the early morning classes and it worked just fine. Waitressing was another matter entirely. Nearly all shifts that the newbies got were at dawn, and before arriving in Cherry Hill, she hadn't waitressed in nearly twenty years, definitely making her a newbie. Who the hell gets up that early and goes to a diner? Who would want to be seen in public that early? This early morning wrestling match had gotten easier for her to win when she went to high school in Phoenix—high school started earlier because of the heat. But come college, she fell back to sleeping in and that had been the clincher, locking her into a pattern that she had not been able to break out of since. Now, in her current life role as "waitress," she had dug in her heels even deeper. Not gonna budge, she thought, enjoying the comfort of stubbornness. For anyone to be up this early, it was just wrong, against Man and God, she would say to herself—until she got to the diner and had to listen to the shouting of Tony, the Greek owner. Luckily, he had a soft spot for her, but his heart was shaped like a cash register. He didn't abide by anyone being late for their shift.

Already behind, she hurried her strip test—not that she thought Alby had infected her—it was just another morning ritual, usually before she brushed her teeth. As she practically skipped down the steps to her car, juggling a metal coffee container, a light sweater, and her red diner uniform cap, she recalled their kiss; she still had no idea why she had done it. True, she had always been impulsive, but this was different, though she couldn't name how. Working at two diners meant you always had to keep straight which uniform was right. As she (carefully) glided down the steps (dancing has many benefits, she thought), she glanced at the apartment complex's rows of small shiny mailboxes affixed to a single, wide wooden base. A wood surface jutted out from the bottom, with its shelf for piles of junk mail and flyers, and letters and bills sent there for people who unbeknownst to their senders had packed up and moved on. The seventy-five or so small boxes all faced the parking lot, away from her sight. Facing her was the community bulletin board where she could see the slightly frayed flyer for her Zumba class. She had not checked her mail in days—it's not like she was getting thank-you notes or party invitations. But she should check. Mid-thought, she turned the corner and nearly ran into a slightly older man wearing a gray suit, white shirt, and tie. Suits had come back since herd immunity had reopened offices. He was very... tidy; that was the only word that came to mind.

"Oh, excuse me!" she said, then stopped and pulled back. He had a small screwdriver in his hand and was standing along a row of several pried-open box doors. Mail was piled on the side, categorized by magazine, bills, and personal letters.

"What the hell?" She could not believe it. She had seen this guy, maybe once, and he looked like an insurance salesman, kind of wimpy and bland, like an institutional version of vanilla ice cream. In a full suit and tie, he seemed starched head to toe, including his facial expression, also smooth and bland.

He straightened up and palmed the screwdriver and looked her in the eye. He did not look guilty or surprised.

She glared at him. "Tell me you are not ripping off people's mail." He said nothing but stepped away from her. She noticed some envelopes in his jacket side pockets. "Personal mail? Are you kidding me?"

"It's no big deal," he said calmly, blank in stare and tone. His stare started to disturb her; she felt he wasn't so much looking at her but almost through her. She nodded and with both anger and sarcasm in her voice said, "I see… and you would be the judge of that because…?"

"I just moved in and had forgotten which box was mine."

"Good try," she said with more anger than sarcasm this time. "Let me give you the big clue: it's the same as the number of your apartment." She was glancing around him, trying to see if he was hiding anything else. She glanced at her watch. She was now super late, but how could she leave him here? This was just plain wrong. Plain wrong stuff always made her stomach twist. Someone had to stick up for what was right, though she couldn't explain why it was always her. It seemed like she always tripped over the world's small wrongs.

"I think I need to go get the super." She turned to go down the front row.

"I don't think you should." His voice had a slight change in it, like the road hit a sudden curve and the driver hit the brakes. She kept walking, ignoring him. She'd seen a thousand bland men like him at the diners she worked at—bland but full of the undercurrent of perversity.

"You're in 25, right?"

This stopped her. She slowly pivoted around to face him.

He smiled: it made her skin crawl. "I'm in 15—is that you tap-dancing on the ceiling? You like to tap-dance?"

She thought 15 was empty, or else she never would have danced that hard. A momentary feeling of embarrassment settled on her, and she was going to say something, when she saw the entire ruse. The art of distraction. He was keeping her attention on his eyes and voice, while one hand behind his back was slowly closing each mailbox door.

"Well, yes," she said slowly, "I do tap dance." She was trying to decide if this was all worth it. He had a major creepiness factor and she had survived long enough to pay attention to her radar: he was trouble. "Are you a fan? If not, sorry."

"I am a fan."

She looked at him in dread: he was going to say Gene Kelly.

"Gene Kelly mostly."

She shuddered. She hated Gene Kelly. That overdone helicopter move just got under her skin; he didn't hold a candle to Fred Astaire.

Knowing that he liked Gene Kelly didn't help his case. But that wasn't the reason she began to feel the hair on the back of her neck rise. This felt risky.

"Listen, what gives with the mailbox jackings? Come on, share."

"I have no idea what you are talking about."

"Really? What about—" She stepped forward and looked behind him.

He stepped aside. His jacket pockets were empty of the earlier bulges and edges of white envelopes; his hands were palms up, almost in a gesture of helplessness. All the boxes that had been open…were shut.

She felt her ears tingle—her trouble radar. How had he done that without her noticing? She had to get away and fast.

"Uh, right, so right! What could I have been thinking?" She stepped back. He stepped forward. She stepped back.

"Well, welcome neighbor! I'll cut the tapping out." He nodded and stepped closer; she turned her body towards her car when he suddenly took hold of her elbow. She could see he held something small in his right hand. It wasn't the screwdriver from before. Whatever this was, he was palming it so she could not quite make it out. But she knew it was danger coming at her hard and fast.

"I wasn't doing anything. Nothing at all." His voice was silky and warm. But she had faced many a bad situation and knew what to do. Even if he made her skin crawl, she could deal.

"Cut the Kung Fu death grip." It didn't hurt, but he pressed her muscles just shy of that. She could not detach herself. His fingers were like glue. He was staring intently at her face, like a man looking at a map, his eyes seeming to travel up and down as if deciding which way to go. What was this about? It was too early in the morning to start the day with a true nutcase.

"But don't you agree? Absolutely nothing."

As she was starting to consider yelling for help, a door slammed nearby. She could hear a guy whistling—on key, too—and instantly she knew who it was. Not many people can whistle on key. The mailbox man released her arm and stepped back.

The guy came around the corner—they had gone out a few times when she first moved here from New York; eventually, she realized that they bored each other. He was nice, but she just could not deal with his hair bearing the faint remnants of a mullet haircut. "Nick!" she exclaimed a little too loudly.

"Hey, Ginger, how are you?" he shouted back as he walked up to her. Clearly he was a morning person. "Surprised to see you up this early."

The man in the suit took two steps straight back, turned like a compass on his heel, and disappeared around the corner of the building.

She felt the breath rush out of her. That was weird. Now she regretted three things: being so late, running into some nut job, and having to owe a guy who probably shopped for cologne at the dollar store.

As she got to her car, she gave Nick a gentle brush off. As she drove, she started to fume; she would have to move. Her Creep Radar was still going off. He was that bad. She would have to park somewhere else to avoid him. If she was lucky, she'd never see him again. She had moved around enough to know how to avoid people.

Jagger had not gone back to his apartment. Instead, he had circled the building, gotten in his car, and quickly driven to a spot near the entrance of Gatewood. Then he sat in his car, slumping low in his seat. He waited.

After a few minutes, the red-haired woman drove past him in her Honda. She looked like she was in a hurry. She had been wearing a waitress outfit, so he assumed it had to be some breakfast joint nearby.

He pulled out slowly and followed her. He knew where she lived; now he would know where she worked.

Jagger rarely felt any emotion such as pleasure at a few indulgences or anger at phonies or amateurs. Emotions, at their most turbulent were all like watching a storm in the distance. But what really irked him, with sheer disgust, was the rampant stupidity of mankind. Even though he considered himself an atheist, in his heart, he often wondered if God was speaking to him, giving him his Mission; remove these beasts.

But this was a little different: she had actually caught him in the act. Highly unusual. Would she turn him into the super? That would be awkward. She had no evidence, but any attention was bad attention. He had clearly frightened her; he'd seen it from the way she'd locked her emotions on her face. But he also saw a determined defiance; she was a survivor. He might have to deal with her soon. An accident.

In his travels to interview more site workers—Quadrant 3, the farthest out—he would have time to consider some options. What kind of accident does a tap-dancing, single waitress have?

In a few minutes, she pulled into the Marlton Diner. Jagger drove in and turned around. Enough of this—he needed to finish the interviews and find Mr. O'Brien.

Alby got it—he should invent the "Why Today Sucks" calendar and make a fortune. This was one of those todays. Alby had spent hours stuck in his round-and-round touring cycle of Camden in his truck, all one square mile of it over and over. Despite the repeated stares he got, he kept circling. Fortunately, Stephen was finishing one roof and he had ostensibly gone to prep for a new job. It was easy to work, then slip off and head to Camden.

At one point, he got hungry and left his touring to go have an early lunch at a Panera's that was next to the Cooper Hospital, the developed side of Camden. He passed the blue light scanner and the AI voice welcoming him (meaning he was vaxxed) and over to their two entrances—one for vax and one for non-vax. It was a noticeable relief to see people dressed in neat clothes and speaking in civilized voices, lots of white lab coats. As usual, no one noticed him for a little while. He let the minutes roll on until someone glanced his way—looking surprised, as if Alby had suddenly appeared out of nowhere. Now, he took his order. The panini was good—a little greasy but it was the atmosphere he appreciated. Like a man returning from space, he just needed to see what the other "normal" part of Camden looked like.

On his way back to Marlton, down the Admiral Wilson Boulevard, he saw the bright yellow cinder block liquor mart and decided to stop for a bottle of Maker's. He always kept an extra bottle around on hand—you never knew when you might run out. Not familiar with this place, he pulled into the lot, making a point to put his tool bag on the cab floor under an old jacket so no one would be tempted to break the window and steal it.

He went in and nodded at the scruffy-looking white guy behind the plexiglass, hands resting on the cash register like silent piano keys. Wonder what kind of gun he kept back there? Shotgun would be messy. Most likely a pistol. How he would use it with the plexiglass, which had a turnstile built into it, Alby had no idea. But, in this neighborhood, not being armed would be stupid.

The aisles were narrow and packed with every conceivable form of booze, liqueur, aperitif—who around here was buying Grand Marnier?— and row after row of cheap wine. Beer was in coolers lining the back of the store. The rest was filled with snack food.

As he rounded one corner—heading straight for the bourbon—he nearly bumped into a scruffy guy holding a case of beer on his shoulder. "Excuse me—" he began, then stopped. "Chance!"

"Mr. O'Brien." His voice started normal, but then went up nervously.

"Chance, I've been looking for you guys." Chance took a step back, his eyes got wide, and he shifted the case on his shoulder. He was taller than Alby and half his age, yet somehow, he looked intimidated—he literally shrank away from him, like a scared rabbit. Alby smiled. "What are you up to on your day off? You work here?"

"Same ole."

Alby nodded as if he had a clue as to what that meant.

"Can I give you a ride somewhere?" Alby smiled again, nodding at the beer. "You, Lucky, and Darnell having a party?"

Chance had always seemed the highest strung of the three workers. His sudden action proved Alby's instinct right: Chance jumped forward and then slid the case of beer off his shoulder and shoved it hard into Alby's stomach.

Alby caught the case but fell back into the metal frames holding all the booze. The noise of glass hitting glass filled the store. The steel frame bit into his shoulders. "What's going on back there?" someone shouted. Alby dropped the case and tried to catch his breath—Chance was already at the door, leaping over the turnstile. The guy in the plastic booth was reaching under the counter. Alby did not want to get involved in this, but he knew he could not get out in time. He yelled, "That guy just tried to rob me!"

Behind the counter, the skinny white guy now had a large, very old six-shooter in his bony little hand; it looked like some overblown toy gun. But the way he held it told Alby that he knew how to handle it.

"I know the sonofabitch! Seen him here plenty! Probably been ripping me off!"

Alby staggered to the front and leaned on the counter to get his breath back. Screw the Maker's. He needed to find Chance, but he couldn't move yet. There were two empty blocks of rubble between the liquor mart and the neighborhood. So he had to play the white guy victim.

"Damned Camden bastards," he muttered.

"Trash, all of 'em! If I didn't have to work here, I swear I'd go out with Old Missy here"—he waved the gun—"and just shoot and shoot until I could take as many down as possible. Public Service killings, that's what the cops call 'em." His voice rose as he spoke. Other than the loaded weapon and being an evil bastard, he looked almost comical, all flesh and bone, squeezed into a booth so tight he could barely move, like a marionette in a box doing a sideshow. Alby regretted playing the privilege card—he had uncorked the wrong bottle. But if a nut job rant got him out of the situation, that would work for him.

"Maybe I can catch up to him."

"He take your wallet?"

Alby patted his pants—it was there—but he turned to the guy, incredulous. "Damned if he didn't pickpocket me!" Alby pushed off the counter and raced through the turnstile. The sun momentarily blinded him, and he almost ran into two guys coming in. One gave him a shove. Alby stumbled, shook it off, and ran for his truck.

Racing out of the store driveway, he turned right towards Camden. As he drove, he squinted but could see no one ahead; he looked left and right across the rubble: nothing.

He sped up and turned into the side streets. Nothing. Dust, flat empty lots, remnants of abandoned buildings. There was no way Chance could have gotten more than a few blocks away.

He slowed and went around the block. People on their porches stared at him. A kid intentionally walked across the street in front of his truck, forcing him to hit his breaks. He glared at the kid, who slowly strolled a foot or so from his front grill and casually gave him the finger.

This was confusing. How could he have disappeared so fast?

Heading back to the liquor store, he found the store clerk just putting his gun away and staring at the phone. Alby, not wanting any cop contact, said, "We don't need the cops. What you going to tell them anyway?"

The guy squinted and pinched his face so tightly that now he looked like a corkscrew. "Yeah, you're right. Why bother." Alby nodded, got his Maker's and left.

Having come through the plastic curtain from the beer warehouse just seconds before, Darnell now stood still. The clerk looked over at him. "You didn't know him, did you? The guy who robbed him?"

Shaking his head no, Darnell went quickly into the back storeroom. Grabbing a mop and bucket, he came out to clean up the shattered case of beer.

Jagger slowly turned his car towards the waterfront. It had been pure luck that he had seen O'Brien's truck at the liquor store. When he saw someone run out, he instantly knew it was Chance—Fat Joe had photos in their files. He could hear the kicking from inside his trunk. It annoyed him that this new Camry would be damaged by that idiot. "Let's you and me have a chat by the water!" he shouted over the back seat. It was easy to find the right place around here—it was deserted and ruined and full of great places to leave a body. So many cities were so cleaned up today, it made it hard sometimes for Jagger to find a good dumping ground.

The night before, he had turned on Google Earth on his iPad and just moved around Camden neighborhoods as if driving them from above. He took the elevated view to isolate the different neighborhoods and abandoned industrial areas. Then he went to the street level and moved around as if driving, marking visual cues to let him know where he was. So now, he knew just where to go. Heading towards Weeks Marina, he saw the rotting piers in the distance and drove until he spotted what looked like an abandoned dock.

He had to get out and cut open a metal chain—he made sure to get back out and re-string it after he drove in. He moved slowly past the piles of junk until he got near the half-rotting dock.

An hour later, sitting on a log between two derelict buildings by the Delaware River, across from the Sugar House casino, Jagger was still admiring the view but was also getting tired. Even worse, he was getting bored. Usually, the act of torture and torment gave him a sense of satisfaction and purpose, but today it tired him. Not physically—he was just weary of dealing with idiots. Tired of always being right about everything. Tired of beating this man—what kind of name was Chance?—and getting nowhere. Chance was a rootless, useless creature—had no idea where his pals lived, only saw them at night on the corner. A corner? Okay, now we have a clue. Which corner? Any, answered Chance; you never knew. You just walked until you found them. What was most frustrating was Jagger could see that Chance was not lying. In fact, he was too dumb to lie well; his face read raw and red with fear, his features seemed to be made of the most pliable clay that screamed fear.

Jagger took off his jacket and hung it on a piling. He went back to the waterside where Chance lay bound on the ground. He rolled him over and undid the handcuffs. He left on the ankle locks.

"Oh, thank you, thank you, I can help you find them—just come back tonight and I'll show you."

Sure, Jagger thought, you will be just waiting for me.

"Know how to swim?" he asked Chance casually.

"No," he answered as he tried to sit up. Jagger took his leg and pushed him in the center of his back and watched him tumble ten feet into the water. He tried to scream, but he smacked his head on a wooden piling and fell in, the water filling his open mouth as he went down.

Another failure of our education system, thought Jagger; not only stupid, but never learned how to swim.

He waited to be sure Chance did not surface. Following the contractor was his best strategy after all. Chance had come running out of the liquor store and Jagger, who had been tailing the other, had intercepted him.

One crew member down. Alby O'Brien, where are you now? Not knowing where he lived annoyed him and having only a PO Box and garage was not enough. But there were a lot of things about Alby O'Brien that annoyed him: his lack of a home address, the empty garage, the missing pieces in his recent past, this Iraq Fatwah story. This just did not happen to Jagger; somehow this guy Alby, as a person, a profile, had eluded him. He could not see him in focus; he was blurry. This kind of thing had never occurred before and it made Jagger uncomfortable. In most instances, people were unaware of their footprint in the world—and thus were too sloppy, too public. But Alby was different. He had figured out how to either be the biggest loser or simply fall off the edge of the world, or both. Or… he was successfully hiding from something that Jagger just could not see. For the first time, Jagger suspected Alby had nothing to do with the blank check.

Yet he had done something. Why else be so elusive?

As he drove down the service road off Route 70, he slowed as he neared Alby's garage. He pulled off the road to the front: as before, he saw an empty garage with weeds starting to poke through the black parking lot tar; an abandoned business, two large bay doors with narrow glass windows near the top. Jagger got out and peered through the windows. The place was half-lit from the parking lot, so all he could see was a mess; trash and oil stains were the main inhabitants. Thinking he had seen enough, he turned to leave but something caught his eye. He cupped his hand over his eyes, letting them adjust to the dark, and looked deeper into the garage. Near the back, hanging from a chain attached to a metal beam was a boxing bag. Why would someone leave that? What was a boxing bag doing in a garage anyway? Jagger was getting tired of things he couldn't make sense of, so he filed it as a trace item, possibly useful later.

At that exact moment, only a few miles apart, both Alby and Jagger shared the same thought: I'm hungry. For Jagger, as usual, killing someone always made him famished. He had no idea why, and at one point, earlier in his career, as he studied his every move, emotion, motivation, he became obsessed with this specific reaction. So, he had gone to a psychiatrist. Using a pseudonym, of course.

As a professional, he admired other professionals; he figured giving one a chance to solve his question was worth it; this therapist he found had very high ratings on HealthGrades and an impressive CV. The doctor was casually dressed, perhaps a bit too casually considering what he cost per hour. Thick bound books lined the walls as the main motif in his office. After brief introductions, the psychiatrist casually said, "Tell me why you're here."

Jagger looked aimlessly around as he described a recent murder he had committed and the extreme—he really emphasized this—extreme hunger he had felt afterwards. Why hunger, doc?

The doctor at first gently chastised him for using such strong metaphors as "killing someone" when clearly that wasn't the real trigger.

Jagger frowned; he had been completely honest, and this was his reaction? "I kill and then I am famished. Not much more to it than that. But why?" He could not have been more straightforward.

The doctor arched his back slightly, like something pushed him back into his seat: his face muscles had gone from professional neutrality to a jumble of open fear—the real emotion peeking through the professional mask. Jagger leaned forward, just to see if he recoiled—he did. Jagger almost sighed out loud—not a true professional. A true professional would have just engaged and made little of the murder and instead focused on the question: why the hunger? It was an honest, serious question; one you should be able to ask a professional therapist and get a professional answer. Even worse, the muscles on his face revealed way too many emotions way too fast, like the rapid-fire staccato of a machine gun; this guy was a shrink who couldn't even hide his own emotions! That sense of disgust Jagger felt for people not acting to the level their profession demanded overcame him. After a few awkward minutes, when Jagger knew the session was in the back half, the doctor said this was beyond his experience but perhaps he could recommend someone.

He got up and went to his desk, took out a small pad, and started scribbling down a number. "I have to say, I have never had anyone come in here and admit they murder people. Astounding." He got flustered. "Hopefully not true! But client-patient discussions and the law—they limit what I can do. I hope you understand." The doctor picked up the phone and turned toward the desk and away from Jagger's chair. Jagger quietly stood up, picked out a heavy tome from the shelf (*Writings of the Talmud*, it said on the leather binding) and in one swift downward movement, hit the doctor as hard as possible on the head with it. Blood spattered out like a meteor tail of red spray over the Oriental carpet.

The doctor fell hard, bounced off the desk, hit a table, and crumpled to the floor.

Jagger liked books.

He watched for a moment to make sure he was dead. Then he went to the desk, foraged in the top drawer until he found his appointment book. He looked at the day and time slot. The fake name Jagger had given him was next to a sloppier note: "new patient."

Surveying the room, he saw the doctors' iPhone and wallet. He took a tissue and picked it up and left the office. Outside the small anonymous business park, he crossed the parking lot, pausing at a flatbed Chevy truck. Jagger took the phone and wallet and wedged it in the corner. Let the police track it to this person, he thought.

Pausing by the truck, he took in the bright light, the heat, the nearby large palm tree, and the sound of traffic. Inhaling the hot air, the moment was perfect. Nearby was a bus line that would take him to a nearby restaurant for lunch. Bar food, but good. He was famished. All he could think about was what to order. Hungry again. Someday he would have his question answered.

Now, letting go of his therapist reminiscences, here he was leaving the garage, incredibly hungry. As much as he knew that he had to find Alby, his hunger won out. There was a diner listed on Yelp that said it was great for corned beef; not the one he'd followed the tap dancer to. He typed in the address and let the AI lead him.

Alby had gone back to the driveway work to let Stephen go and prep tomorrow's job—a sagging patio roof on an old 1950s rancher. But he could not concentrate. The episode at the liquor store confirmed his worse fear: he was not going to find the check. He was screwed. He kept envisioning Chance running out of the store. The scene ran over and over in his head. After a bit, he gave up, got in the truck, and headed toward the Marlton Diner, secretly hoping that Ginger was working the current shift.

He had to cool down; it pissed him off that Chance had gotten away from him. He was using the anger to distract him from the pain of where the case of beer had struck: right on the scar. He was sure nothing was cracked. It just hurt like hell.

All this felt way too familiar. Was this the same nightmare of Iraq just wearing a different costume? It surprised him that his anger was greater than his fear. In Iraq, it had been the opposite; his fear had been omnipresent, with him morning, noon, and night. If something dangerous or deadly hadn't happened to you, it had happened to someone you knew. You were next. Always next. The only time he really exhaled was at Ahmed's house.

Alby knew the drill: good news is dropped fast; bad news burns like wildfire. People talked. Delarosa's pals, Fat Joe, the Crew knew—and probably a half-dozen more. Half his friends had grown up being cops in Hoboken or New York, and they had always said it: eventually, everyone talks. Whether it was some inspector, a cop, a bank employee, someone was going to find out, and soon, and then come looking for the crews and…

Alby had to pull over, the floodgates of panic sent fragments of plans flooding his mind.

Maybe this was the wrong approach; maybe he should go to the cops. But dealing with cops was always dicey. It's always who you knew. And in his case, he knew no one; only an idiot would think that he wasn't a prime suspect—all this time living like a hermit, scraping by, anti-social. He was a profiling dream. That left his Handlers. They were pricks and a wild card; he could appeal to them to let him disappear. Was that becoming the best choice?

Then he realized it: there was no right answer.

Every path led to a bad ending. So, it became a pick-the-least-bad choice. It was either cut-and-run or stay and take his chances. Staying meant having some say in his fate—jump back in the lane and try and do something. It broke every Rule, every plan, every defense he had so carefully built up. It felt like the resistance of the rawhide and the solid weight of the punching bag behind it.

It all came down to his crew. How was he going to find them? And once he did, what would he do with what they stole? For as hard as he tried, he could not figure out why he was doing what he was doing; he just knew it had to be this way. Crazy. Pulling into a small empty lot to clear his head, he looked both ways and slipped into traffic near the ramp that split—one way to Cherry Hill, the other way to the Atlantic City Expressway on 42.

Glancing at his watch, he saw it was nearly after five. He hoped she was on duty. He could go to the Sage Diner if she wasn't here. He pulled into the parking lot, a tight ramp, with him nearly clipping a small Hyundai. The old lady driver with wraparound dark sunglasses and a black mask gave him the finger. She looked like an old vampire. Maybe she was, he mused; even they have to get out. Wonder what she ordered at the diner. Probably blood sausage.

Walking into the vaxxed entrance, he thought he caught a flash of red hair going back into the kitchen. He sidled up and onto a spinning stool at the shiny black-and-white Formica counter, which was near the door, and plopped down. Every other stool was pasted with a "NO SIT-TING" sign.

As he swiveled around, he casually took in the long, rectangular diner; a waitress passed by and dropped a menu in front of him and kept moving. He started to say thanks, but she was gone. A busboy lifted it up, and in one move wiped the surface with disinfectant, dropped the menu, and swung a glass of ice water in front of him from below the counter. He had a mask on.

Seated near the front door, he had the best eye on traffic coming and going. He recalled several Sundays when he had hidden in those booths in the back, hungover. He could not see past the last seat of the center or the first booth beyond it. A door from the kitchen swung in and out, only a few feet away.

Where was she?

"Hello, big boy." Her voice came from behind him. Who was she impersonating? Ahh. Mae West; it was like muscle memory. His dad had once made him binge-watch a W.C. Fields movie marathon and she was *the* sex goddess of the 1930s. He swiveled towards the front door. She stood there in what was the exact same uniform as the other diner, only pink. Her hair just did not like caps, like it was waiting to burst free of the pins that held it. As usual, her hair and lipstick mirrored the same red.

"An old movie quote?" He hesitated to say Mae West.

"Good guess. Mae West, 1931. How'd I do?" He smiled and gestured wordlessly with his hands—she cut him off. "You don't remember her. That's okay, I'm used to it."

"No, I do, I do." Alby felt like he was having an out-of-body experience; he never stumbled verbally. "Never give a sucker an even break," he snarled.

"W.C. Fields. Funny man. Terrible alcoholic." Gesturing at his glass of water, she kept going. "One time, a bunch of reporters were interviewing him, and as a famous drunk, they asked why he never drank water? 'Fish fuck in it' was his answer." Throwing her head back, she let out a short, sharp laugh. Then she was all business. "Early for dinner—late for lunch. Unless you're here for the Blue Plate special? And you're too young to qualify by the way."

"Yes." He could see she was tired. Her words were upbeat, and bullet-sharp, but they were carried by a harried tone, her ears were a little red around the edges, and her hair less neat than he had seen before—one curly red tuft had sprung free of a hair clip, making it look like she had a small antenna rising from the right side of her head. She pushed it back in place unconsciously. It sprung back out. Then the burdened look of a long day fell from her face and she smiled at him. A true smile. His heart hiccupped.

That was when he actually *felt* his own smile. It seeped through him from his belly to his lips to his face and then back down his neck. It felt completely unfamiliar.

Seemingly out of nowhere, she stopped, her eyes widened, and she stared at him. "Alby. I'll be damned—you came here looking for me."

Every lesson in his entire life told him to say no, deny it.

"Yes," he answered. "Got hungry and wanted to see you. Two in one." He couldn't tell if that was stupid sounding or casual.

In the rear of the diner, Jagger had just finished a delicious meat loaf with peas and mashed potatoes—he had decided against the corned beef. He always appreciated a diner's variety over any one repeated meal; meat loaf was one of the litmus test meals—if it was good, everything on the menu was probably good, and vice versa. Picking up the check, he stood and reached in his pocket for his wallet. As he did so his gaze drifted upwards just in time to take in Alby on one of the swivel counter seats. Straight ahead. He took a step back towards the booth as he locked onto the bright blue eyes of the waitress standing next to Alby: the neighbor from the mailboxes. This was not good. He needed to disappear. He fumbled for two twenties and threw them on the table and turned towards the back exit sign. It always paid to sit near the exit.

Across the diner, eyes gunslinger-narrow, she was looking past Alby, her face suddenly frozen, her profile sharper. She looked like she had skewered something with her long nasty gaze. She breathed deeply, her nose even flared like a bull having just seen red as she said, "Excuse me," without even looking at him.

Crossing the length of the diner, she went right up to Jagger, who was in mid-stride towards the rear exit, exclaiming, "Why are you here? Are you harassing me? Following me? You really creeped me out this morning—if you ever come near me again, I am calling the cops." Her face was red, even redder than her hair.

Jagger had heard enough and without thinking he moved quickly—quickly enough to turn heads in his wake. This could work; it had worked before. A man in gray, a loud woman, a busy diner. Order became chaos.

Jagger had his eyes on her raging face; clearly, he had struck a nerve from her past. He could see it written deeply in lines of anger. He kept his eyes locked on hers but slipped one hand back, cupped the knife from an empty table setting; he was ready to shove it between her ribs in a way that no one else would see.

"Innocent mistake. I didn't know you worked here," he said as he waited for her to move a few inches closer. Her anger and protests were dangerous—people were starting to look.

He needed to get a step or two closer to the fire exit.

She stuck by him, which was good since it would make it easier to stab her once and go.

He pulled back his arm and maneuvered the knife around until the sharp edge peaked between his two-fingered grip. This way he could easily push the edge in and thrust the rest with his palm.

"What the hell is going on?" He looked away from her eyes and over her shoulder. Coming towards them was a very agitated Alby. His Alby.

This was not going according to plan.

For the first time in a very, very long time, Jagger had no idea what to do. He tried not to stare at Alby.

He scrambled, "I had no idea you worked here; anyway, I am leaving now. Money on the table." He gestured at the money on the table and confidently strode through the fire exit. A short alarm sounded, jarring everyone in the restaurant.

"You better run," she practically shouted, with everyone at the diner now staring at her. She gestured at Alby. "This is my boyfriend and he's gonna kick your ass!"

Alby looked at her, "What the hell was that about?"

"Nothing. A creep." She smoothed her outfit, pushed a hand through her hair, and adjusted her cap, trying to gain some semblance of control. "Creep," she said again, under her breath. Clearly this was a live nerve. Gone was any sense of humor, or gentle chiding. She was full-on mad.

"Was he an old boyfriend?"

"No, you're my boyfriend," she said absentmindedly, dismissively. Then she realized what she had said.

"I'm your boyfriend?" He was dumbfounded.

She got wide-eyed like she had been caught shoplifting. Then her features fell back into place and she looked at him and her eyes were smiling, but her mouth held a straight, tight line: "I'll tell you later. Here to ask me out tonight?"

"Uh…."

She puckered her lips at him impatiently then pushed harder for him to answer her with a short, "Yes?" He knew he had taken too long.

She gave him a pass. "No movies."

"No movies."

"I pick the restaurant." He nodded. "Get me at eight." He nodded again.

"What was that all about?" he asked again, feeling a little lost. Who was that guy and why was she so angry? She quickly told him about finding the gray man illegally opening mailboxes. While it was weird in a bad way, there was a deeper thread of anger the man had triggered in her.

"Dinner then!" She eased up and smiled at him. "I have to teach a quick class then I'm good to go." She paused and considered her next words: "You know, like the one your sister goes to." She paused. "Except hers is tomorrow."

Outside, Jagger took out his handkerchief, wiped down the handle of the dinner knife, and tossed it into the dumpster. He jogged to his car and took off. A half-block away he pulled into a gas station and parked near the air machine. From his seat, using an adjusted side mirror, he watched the one open sidewalk where patrons came and went from the diner.

It was an oddly confusing feeling for Jagger. He did not know where to focus. Alby was his key to getting the blank check back, *and* he knew the tap-dancing neighbor? This was getting to be too small a geography for him, like being in a shrinking room at a fun house. It made him uncomfortable. Too much randomness. Random was bad: you couldn't see it coming, didn't know what it would look like or do. It had no flavor, color, words, or predictability.

This job needed to be over, he told himself. This was going to require a push to get this whole situation out of random and back to where he could control events.

He had figured on killing her right after he found the check and killing Alby, too. Since they knew each other, perhaps there was an even tidier plan.

Back at the diner, Ginger was nose-to-nose with the manager who was giving Ginger a hard time about making a scene, and in doing so, was making a new scene. Alby stepped between them.

"Back off! The guy was gonna skip his check. She caught him."

"Oh really? Explain the two twenties on the table." He waved them in Alby's face. He looked past Alby at Ginger. "You need to leave."

"For the day?" she asked, quietly.

"Forever!" the manager yelled. "Out."

Ginger's face fell, but then she sighed and handed him the blue hat. "You give Greeks a bad name."

"*Out!*" he yelled. People looked uncomfortable sitting in their booths. She moved around Alby to go out the back.

He glared at the manager, turned, but before he left, he paused at the door and shouted, "And your coffee sucks!" As lame as it sounded, Alby figured this had to be a big insult to a diner owner. Truth be told, it did suck.

In the parking lot, he felt like an idiot. What was with him doing stupid crap like that? Picking a fight was a long-ago thing, or so he had thought. He pictured the scene at the bodega; who was that guy who pulled out the switchblade so easily?

In the minute, she came out a rear door and came around the front. Walking past Alby, she just glared at him.

"What did I do?"

"Got me fired."

"It wasn't your ex-boyfriend who started you off? You have some temper."

"Not. Ex. Boyfriend." The words were like nails piercing wood. She moved fast down the row of cars. He could see her old Honda. "Well, I'm done! I needed that job. And you helped get me fired!"

"I might have lost my cool, but you had already let loose."

She stopped so abruptly that he almost bumped into her. She dropped her chin.

"Some things just set me off," her voice was wistful, weary. Just standing there seemed awkward, but she had planted herself on the sidewalk. She suddenly looked drained. The Honda was a few feet away. "Creeps." She stated it in a factual tone and let the word hang in the air of self-definition. But he could tell there were movies going through her head.

"You know, people are jerks." He could not believe himself. He had lost his cool for a minute. He had believed he'd tamed his anger, but once again there it was, always waiting for the right key to open the waiting door.

Taking a deep breath, he asked, "We still on for dinner?" trying to sound like nothing had happened. A big no was what he was expecting.

She nodded silently, then shook herself. "Yes, yes, at eight. In front of my place. By the mailboxes."

She practically ran to get in her car, but just before she slipped in, she looked at him sternly and said, "This didn't happen."

He just nodded, faking a half-smile. But it did, he thought. He had Iraq. What was holding her down? She looked heavy, like she was carrying a 500-pound bag on her back. Was this how he looked?

After sitting in the front seat of his truck for a few minutes, empty-headed, Alby left the parking lot. He was still wondering if that other guy she had gone off on *was* a former boyfriend; though it did not make sense, the guy was so…bland. Like an insurance salesman. Last person he could see her with. He would ask her again. Might as well be honest.

From a distance, Jagger had taken in the entire scene between them and read them both: he didn't need words, their bodies told the story. Alby liked the redhead and she liked him. Ginger: she hadn't known that he had already opened her mailbox before she had caught him and that he had learned what her name was. He eased into traffic a block behind Alby. Was this his chance to learn where he lived? After a minute he knew where he was going.

Seated with the window open, wind blowing back her red hair, Ginger's eyes shifted from the road to Alby, her face emotionless but open. He felt like she was going to say, "Cold? I'll shut the window." But she didn't. He smiled wanly, trying to shake the slideshow of silent sounds in his head. Why was he even out?

She turned back to gaze out the window.

They had gone to a Chinese restaurant, shared their orders, laughed, told a few stories about their childhoods, and laughed some more. He would smile: she would smile. They didn't even speak of that afternoon's diner debacle. The topic of dance and how integral it was to her life was never far away as something to talk about. When he asked what she watched, she didn't hesitate and told him TCM. Old classics. When she spoke of Hollywood musicals, a genuine smile lit her face and she got very animated, like she wanted to get up and dance a scene from the movie. Alby was pretty sure she could do it.

The fortune cookies came, and she chuckled as he read his—which was stupid and immediately forgetful. His cookie was stale, but he ate it anyway.

She opened hers and hesitated, then seemed to make a decision and read it out loud: "Someone special will come into your life."

"Corny," he said, making the comment before he thought, not wanting to focus on the obvious meaning. She looked hurt, then shifted back. It *was* corny, he thought. He hated feeling so awkward. "Dinner good?"

"What? Are we speaking Caveman now?" she laughed.

He nodded. "Ug."

"You must know a lot about Middle Eastern food… do you like it?" The instant the words left her mouth he could see she regretted them. They both sensed the shift. She looked at him with pursed lips, brow furrowed slightly and heading towards more concern. But she couldn't take it back. He bobbed his head several times, not a yes, not a no—he was buying a moment to get control of the rushing sound rising in his ears; it was like someone asking, "How's your nightmare? Black-and-white or in color?" Focus on the here, the now, he told himself; you are in a Chinese restaurant in New Jersey with Ginger. Nowhere else. A cloud of silence settled over what had been a noisy table; he had to say something. But after losing it in the movie theater, he hesitated saying anything about any of this. So he went for dismissiveness.

"You sure know how to pick a topic."

"Sorry, should've known better." He knew she got it. She understood.

"Yeah."

She looked at him, concerned, then her face changed to a smile.

"Didn't I tell you we'd dance soon, or that you would try? How about it?"

He heard the contrition in her voice. He was still a bit shaken but figured that he could try to hide it and maybe succeed in hiding it from himself too. So he nodded. A part of him wanted the evening to go back to where it had been. Seeing her round face, red hair bubbling all around it, he focused in on her lips: he wanted to kiss her right then and there. To hell with the vax conversation.

"Head to my place and then go to the back parking lot," she ordered. "I have an idea."

When they pulled into the complex, she guided him to the far back parking lot. "Turn your truck so it faces the fence and keep the lights on." That area of the parking lot was half-empty and near two dumpsters. He did as he was told, the headlights flooding a high white fence. She hopped out of the cab of his truck, waving for him to join her. As she stood in the bright area cast by the lights, she made a flourishing motion with her arms and spun on her heel. Looking at her in front of the fence, he realized that the headlights made the fence look like a stage backdrop with their large shadows. And then he looked back at her, taking her in: knee-length deep green dress, cut to be open at her shoulders—unadorned but striking against her pale skin and red hair. No jewelry except for a small green pearl around her neck—at dinner, she had told him that her parents had brought it back from a cruise to Bora Bora. He got out and shivered a little in the cool September air. As he rounded the hood and stepped into the headlights, he saw that she had put on her jean jacket.

"What now?"

"Hmmm…where should we start?" Walking back over to the truck, she pulled out her iPhone, tapping at the screen for a second. She jabbed at the screen and on came an orchestra playing a waltz—at least he thought it was a waltz. He had never done a waltz so he wasn't exactly sure. Even in the small amount of light that came from the periphery of the headlights, she must have seen the uncertainty on his face. "We are going to do a box step, not a waltz. Same beat though. A simple square with my feet following yours." She spoke this quite casually as if he had heard it a million times before, somehow knowing that assumption was better than explanation. "Let's start. Best I lead."

"Start what?" Hands on hips, she just stared at him. They stood sideways to the car lights; each half light, half dark. "I really have to dance?" Yeah, he was whining, and he knew it.

"Yes, you said you would." She paused and said gleefully, "At the studio."

She was lying and they both knew it.

"No, I didn't," he said with a false firmness. "I never said I was coming to your studio."

"Yes. You. Did." Her hands digging deeper into her hips, she defiantly leaned forward on her tiptoes. He was waiting for the grade school teacher's wagging index finger move. But a moment later, she just smiled and then yelled, "Box step! Nice and simple." She threw up her arms in akimbo like a mannequin and moved towards him. He mimicked her in reverse and they locked hands and hips. She gently nudged him back, a formal distance apart. "Let me lead." She glanced at the scab on one of his knuckles. "That looks painful."

"I'm good." But she was right; where she grabbed it was painful.

"If you say so," her tone doubtful.

He needed to change subjects. "I appreciate you not making me do Zumba," he said dryly.

She ignored him. "Just go slow and follow me. You can look at your feet—for now at least. Until you get it. We are going to do a simple square."

"Okay." They did this for a while and although he repeatedly kicked her toes, she said nothing; guess she was used to it being a dance instructor. This went on for a bit, her quietly repeating, "One, two, three, four. Again."

The song ended. She pulled away and examined her phone. "Let's do something more romantic, slightly waltzy, still a box-step," she hit the button, her phone wobbled a moment on the truck hood. The music sounded grainy and old.

"Who's singing?"

She looked at him like he was an idiot. "Really? Fred. Fred Astaire." She didn't even try to keep the incredulity out of her voice. With that, she stepped forward to the left, slid to the right, stepped back, slid left and stopped, all while humming the melody—it literally was a box wrapping around the music. He could do this—a simple box. He could tell she wanted to sing along. The man sang slowly, his voice smooth and melancholy.

> *Must you dance every dance*
> *With the same fortunate man?**

As he held onto her, he realized what a sad but beautiful song it was and inched closer to her. Alby wanted to say something about the song but couldn't find the words. He skimmed one of her shoes but managed not to crush her toes. She had the song on a loop.

"Again."

They squared themselves, paused, and moved slowly. Again. And again. Ever so slowly, she sped them up, occasionally muttering "1, 2, 3, 4…" under her breath like a metronome. He followed the beat, trying his hardest to let go, and slowly he began to feel less clumsy. At one point, she turned a little, he fumbled but recovered quickly. The truck lights were sharp, falling across them like sheets of white light as they slowly spun around.

As they danced, he got a sudden view of their shadow casting an enormous silhouette on the white fence. "Hey, it looks like we're really dancing."

"We are, you goof. On the Big Screen." She cocked her head towards the fence, laughed and kept moving. Suddenly, Alby felt it flow, fluid and calm. He got it. He could see her face, half in and out of shadow. She was keeping her eyes on his face, intently, like she was measuring something, but he could not tell what she was thinking. Light, dark, light dark—it was like watching mercury spin. He took his focus away for a second and promptly stepped hard on her right foot.

She let him go and jumped back, "Ow!"

"Sorry!"

* *(Listen: evenapandemic.com/changepartners)*

"Next time don't wear your work boots, for crying out loud," she said, and sounded annoyed as she said it. But she came back to him, arms open. "Maybe without music." She went to her phone and stopped it. They began again, slower this time. She hummed the "1, 2, 3, 4…"

He could get used to this. As he thought that, she suddenly stopped, leaned in and up and brushed her lips sideways across his, like a breeze fanning across his mouth. All his senses sang. She moved away as if nothing had happened and started to dance again. His body followed her back, wanting more. She smiled and locked her arms giving the signal that it was dance time. Except for her low humming—she was repeating the rhythm of the song—they danced for another few minutes in silence. The muscles in his arms and shoulders released tension he didn't know he had.

"What was your mother like?" she asked casually.

He stopped. "My mother?"

"Wasn't she the first woman in your life? Most influential? I mean, I barely know anything about you, so start at the beginning, right? You know what they say about guys and their moms."

She was genuinely interested in getting to know him better but unknowingly started with the wrong question. She seemed to have a knack for that. But he went along. "Mom was a tough, Irish-off-the-boat type—except she flew here!" He guffawed. She smiled. "Married young, kids young."

"Family back in Ireland?"

"Yep. In the North. That's the family farm. My mom went once and said it was big. Never been there myself, but they visited us once when I was in high school."

"You have siblings?"

"You mean like my sister who introduced us?" he asked sarcastical-ly. She grimaced. He felt the immediate retreat of her muscles, though she still held on and led.

"Only her."

She must have detected his tone. "Sorry. I seem to have a real talent for picking bad topics with you. Maybe you should give me an 'off limits' list."

"It's okay… Mom lived a good life, though it wasn't easy. She never really got a break." He felt his heart sink, stopped dancing, and dropped his arms to his sides, like wood boards, stiff, straight. Looking at the ground, he continued. "She went pretty fast. Dorothy…." He couldn't badmouth his sister. "One day it's 'must be a sciatic nerve,' and bam, she's in the hospital with cancer, then hospice, and within three months she's done."

"I am truly sorry." He felt she said it in a way that she truly understood it.

"Nah," he said, in a tone that was supposed to let her know that he had shrugged it off and then offered his arms again in the box step pose. "We all should go that fast."

"Good point. Is that when you went to Baghdad?"

She connected that dot, he thought. She was fast. Was she also thinking he had run away? It was the truth, but he did not want to admit it—his life had gone to shit, and Iraq was the final flush. Or so he had thought until now. Alby didn't like where this dark hole was going. He nodded as he took a step; she waited and nodded back when she took her step.

"So, a mother tells you something about a guy. Huh! Makes sense." He was trying to focus on his feet; he was losing the connection between brain and feet.

She stepped into the pose and began to move. His hands were a bit tighter than before. They went back to dancing in silence.

"Sooo…." He let the word draw out and linger in the air. "The guy at the diner—what's his mother like?"

"Do you know how stupid and childish that comment sounds? Did you just turn fifteen?" She let go and stepped back.

"You were the one shouting, 'Stop stalking me.' That's usually a crazy old boyfriend thing."

"You have no clue…." Her disgust was evident—but she changed her tone. "I can't stand jealous boyfriends."

"I thought you couldn't stand creeps."

"What's the difference?"

"How many jealous boyfriends have you had?"

"Boy, you're just full of nasty! He's a new neighbor and I caught him breaking into the mailboxes—checking people's personal mail! I told you. I knew he was creepy, but when I saw him at the diner, it freaked me out and I just let it all out." She stood stiff, defiant, her body saying, "So there!"

Alby stepped back and took in her words and her posture. He felt at a complete loss as to what to do. The evening was heading down the drain, just like at the movies. Hearing his own voice, he started to realize what an ass he was.

"I...." He had to try something. "I get it, I get it. Not a boyfriend. I don't care." He moved one step closer to her; she practically jumped back.

"No, it's not that easy. You get to be the asshole and then shrug, and all is good again in the world. That's not how it's done."

The words started to fill his head from The Rules: never fall in...

He interrupted his own thought. "Maybe we should—" and it was then that he understood she was angry at herself.

She swiped the air with her arm, carving an invisible line between them, and took another step back. "You're messed up, you know? You're carrying all sorts of scars—it's written all over you. That Baghdad story, okay, all good, got it, but you know what? You left a lot out...." Her voice dropped. Their moment was running out of gas.

Silently, they stared at each other. His arms felt leaden.

"Who was she?"

He snapped. "Cut it out," he growled at her like a chained dog. Alby felt like someone had poured ice onto his chest. He felt his mind detach from the air and the night around him. He didn't even look at her. He just turned, waved his hand dismissively, basically ending the date. Even though his nerves were jangling with nervous energy he didn't show it. She had stepped back and was giving him an up-and-down assessment like he was insane.

"I'll walk you to your door," he said calmly. They had both stepped backwards and away from each other and the headlights, both now in the dark made even darker by the glare of the lights on the white fence.

She didn't say anything but instead shook her head and turned and walked towards the side steps leading to the second level of the complex. He watched her as she walked through the parking lot, up the steps, and around a corner. Not a word, not a glance back. Fine. Teach *him* a lesson in trying to live a normal life. What did he care. I mean what the hell was he thinking? Dating, women, friends, socializing, all off the table: that was someone else's life. She had just smacked him back in line. He should thank her. What he really needed to be doing was focusing on that check—that was life and death. Having gone on this date was a frivolous waste of time.

The truck engine roared a little too loudly, his foot a little too heavy on the gas as he put it into gear; he hit reverse and wheeled around and roared out of the parking lot; as he drove, his phone lit up. For a second, he hoped it was Ginger, but the caller ID read "Fat Joe." Ignoring it, he looked back up at the road.

Yet, the question lingered like her slight flowery scent—did she want to change partners in real life? Was that the message? That song said more about her than she let on.

Seated half a parking lot away, Jagger had watched this all play out in pantomime through his side mirror. An afternoon and evening following first Alby, then the two of them, had paid off. He nodded. This was good, this was very good. New relationship… two losers drifting through life, they meet, get together, fight, he is some nut job back from Iraq, gets violent and kills her in her apartment. His body? Suicide next to her. Simple bullet to the head, no note, and body goes unfound for days. Once Jagger got the check, he could do it. The plan was so neat. He felt that warming glow of professional pride.

Giving Alby a little distance, Jagger eased out of the parking lot. Ten minutes later, he was surprised to see him pull into the empty parking lot of the abandoned garage. Slowing down to make the turn, he lost site of the truck. As he turned, he switched off his headlights and glided into the far end of the parking lot. Getting out of his car and gently closing the door, he crept along the walls until he came to the first of the garage bay doors. Suddenly, he saw the gleam of a flashlight through the top windows as it cut through the dark garage; he put his back to the wall, waited, then stole a look into the half-lit room. Rarely did he get genuinely surprised, but he was now as he watched Alby jabbing away, flashlight casting light across him and the punching bag. He couldn't see his face, but the jabs were short and angry.

Jagger crept further along, finding the small drive that went behind the building. Moving carefully in the dark, he looked around the far corner to see the single light coming through a door in the cinder block building. Alby lived in the back. Again, Jagger could not understand why he went to such attempts to hide, but he had to admire how thoroughly Alby had done it—admiration was a feeling that he was very unfamiliar with.

Thursday: 5:30 a.m.

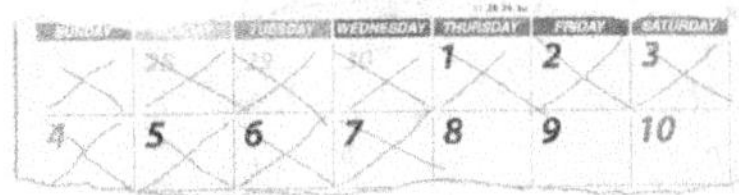

Jagger woke with a deep feeling of impatience. Gone was any feeling of admiration for anyone or anything. He hated the dawn. It tried to speak to him, but he was tone deaf to the voices of brilliant colors and the cool fresh air. Not just because he was color blind, but because it simply irritated him. He wasn't a night person either. The best part of the day was sunset, clouds going from brilliant to lifeless, dark birds flying in chaotic flocks, the darkness devouring the light; it was all so deeply satisfying.

"Thursday," he thought in disgust. The looping trails and twists and turns were starting to frustrate him. The very fact that he had to find and remove a simpleton like this Chance; this job was below him. Not that he would get emotional about it; he was too much the professional for that. It was more like a small electrical current running through him with a higher vibration than he liked. True, he had eliminated—literally—several of the potential sources of the missing check but had gotten only peripherally closer to it. It was Thursday and he had only until Sunday.

His annoyance grew when the Owners called 30 minutes later, just as he was tying his Windsor knot. Hearing from them in the middle of a project was unusual; but on the other hand, as usual, they were short on words and clear on meaning. They did not like the body count he was racking up. "Too messy. Cleaner. Get it done and go home. You're taking longer than normal," was all they said. He made no excuses, just quietly agreed, and hung up. Same as any call, only this time they sounded a little on edge. He wished he had been able to see their faces; then he would know what their real concern was.

He had his way of doing things, it worked, and he was going to stick to it. The list he had made the night before was short: find and follow Alby. It had worked once, it would again.

Jagger was thirsty from dinner earlier. He always kept the refrigerator empty, or close to it, making it a point to occupy the least amount of any apartment's footprint; the less he touched, the better. Coffee might help his thinking. He liked Starbucks, and they opened early near his place. He thought the company did a great job—their employees all wore uniforms, were polite, and smiled like the sheep they were. Starbucks was the anti-Dunkin', where he used to get his coffee until one day he saw a roach on the place's floor—true, it was the desert and the roaches were everywhere, but dirty is dirty.

When Alby awoke, it was with a deep sense of relief. He liked the dawn. The light meant he'd made it through one more night. Daylight was like psychological parole. No amount of Maker's Mark made the nightmares go away but it sure made coming in and out of Hell smoother. He sat up and swung his legs over the side of the bed. Cupping his head in his hands, he emptied his mind as best he could. Thursday. No sleep, no rest, no thoughts—a chorus of nos sang in his mind. He was grateful he didn't have a hangover. But not nearly as grateful as he was that the nightmares had seemed less frequent last night. Suddenly his breath caught. He hadn't dreamt at all. What had happened? In that moment, it was almost like the response of a child used to being beaten—he almost missed it. But he jettisoned that thought quickly enough.

"You are such an asshole!" He could still hear her words ringing in his ears and boy, was she right. What *was* his problem? Or maybe he was such a mess that he should be asking himself what wasn't his problem. Scratch that—no nightmares for the first time in over a year was nothing he should be turning into a problem. But that thought was only temporary.

In its place, he felt the wall of problems rise up again in his head. He *was* an asshole. No matter how you looked at it, that was the fact.

Was Ginger… a distraction? His suppressed loneliness biting him to get attention? He wasn't sure. She just spoke to some part of him; she had that edge he liked, yet she also really got under his skin; he could tell she would be the kind of girl who would always demand honesty, and he wasn't sure he could handle that. After last night, he couldn't say whether he ever wanted to see her again. But then he recalled the brush of her lips against his, and like a not-so-distant echo. The night before had been a moment left incomplete. But a glance at the dried blood on his knuckles kicked in reality and he knew in his head that he could never make it work with her.

Ever so slowly, he slipped his feet into the unlaced metal-toed boots he wore and moved to the bathroom. The floor was too cold to walk on. Kicking off the boots, he stripped and got into the shower. He aimed the showerhead at the center of his chest and did what he did every day: turned the handle all the way to cold and let it rip. The blow of the water was always a punch to the stomach; as much as he had made it part of his morning ritual since returning from Iraq, he never grew used to it. The jolt was the only way he'd found to shock the nightmares from his body and mind. Then, after a minute, he would turn it back to warm. Wait a few and turn it back for another minute of cold. This knocked his system around and cleared any clouds from his head.

After he dried himself off, he slipped his boots back on and walked naked into the main room. The air felt good on his scar.

The check.

Lucky, Darnell, and Chance—where are you, you bastards? There was no doubt in his mind they had the check. He knew Lucky had it; he was the savviest.

Stephen would arrive soon, so he needed a plan for how to keep working while looking for the crew. Should he tell Stephen about the check? He would have to be stupid not to know something was wrong— Alby never left a job and disappeared for lunch, as he had been doing all week.

"Uncle Alby!" The shout came from the parking lot outside.

Stephen's truck was barely in the back lot before he came bursting in holding a newspaper. "Did you see this?"

"Stephen, you know I don't read the paper." They both knew he was lying. Stephen glanced at the pile of last week's newspapers on the floor near the trash can by the door. Alby saw the glance but kept going. "Nothing ever changes. You might as well buy the paper and wipe your ass with it. It's cheaper than toilet paper."

"Cut the bullshit. I don't think so. Not this time." He threw the paper on the table, then handed Alby a large cup of Starbucks. On the front page was a picture of a typical suburban development of neat rows of triplex houses, all the same design, like rows of neat teeth—except one area had a vicious gap that looked like a missing tooth—a charred ruin of a house.

"Some fire."

"Yeah, except it was Delarosa's house. He and his whole crew were there. All dead. I've seen him around. Isn't he the one who gave you the lead for the asbestos job?"

Alby tried not to show any reaction. He felt momentarily light-headed—he had a clear picture of standing next to him in Fat Joe's trailer on Sunday. Whoever it was out there, they had killed six construction workers, actually seven with Delarosa. No small feat. This felt like when you left the Green Zone in Baghdad—the air tightened, the fear filling your senses like latent electricity under your feet; you knew, even though it was unlikely, that killers were all around you. Alby felt it again, now. This was a big deal. These were real killers. They had their own rules, and that was not good.

Alby had the urge to throw Stephen out, pack a bag, and run.

"Didn't really know him."

"Alby, he and his crew worked the bank last weekend. Like you."

"So? You think we're drinking buddies? What's your point?" He realized he sounded defensive and shifted tone. "What do they think happened?"

"Well, first they thought it was his barbecue grill tank that blew up—faulty line or a leak or something. But now they think it was all a set-up to cover up their murder. Autopsy showed each had a bullet to the head."

"Hmmm…" Alby murmured as he sipped his coffee. Below his neutral surface his heart was racing and his mind was still thinking about the moment in the trailer. This was bad. And getting worse by the hour. Who was doing this? And who the hell can take out seven guys and try to make it look like an accident? He didn't know what to think—did this mean he was off the hook? Maybe Delarosa's crew were the thieves. Maybe whoever was doing all this bad shit had found what they wanted. There was one way to find out.

"Hope his family didn't get hurt."

Stephen picked up the paper and read some more. "No, it says Delarosa had sent them away for the night. Seems weird to me."

"Yeah, real weird." Delarosa had been no idiot; he knew someone was coming for him. Alby downed his hot coffee, tried not to choke, and stood up. "Let's get going. Think we can finish that garage roof and the driveway today?"

Stephen gave him an odd look—Alby couldn't make it out.

"Sure. Yeah, we can get it done. Unless you're gonna do your daily disappearing act. Is it that Zumba lady Mom set you up with?" Stephen had gotten nosier in the last few days; he had lousy acting skills and his questions felt like clumsy disguises for what he really wanted to know.

I miss her, Alby thought randomly as Stephen mentioned her, completely surprised by the thought.

Stephen interpreted his silence in a different way. He fumbled for words, "About the other night, she, you know, she was bad, really out of line. I—"

Alby just stared at him. It occurred to him that Stephen was his only friend.

"Just keep us apart and do your thing." Alby waved his hand in a nonchalant way, dismissively. It was as close as he could get to a forgiving statement.

Stephen shrugged but then tried a smile: "You and that lady—"

"Ginger."

"Yeah, Ginger—you two seemed to be getting along. She really likes you, that's for sure."

"How would you know that?"

"She defended you, Alby. Why do you look so surprised?" Quickly, Alby shifted the expression on his face, which for a moment had probably looked hopeful. But inside the edge of a thought was like a paper cut to his soul: when was the last time anyone had stood up for him? Taken his side? Been at his side? He was so cut off from the world he didn't even notice.

Stephen turned to leave, and Alby called after him, "I'll be over in a few minutes. Gotta make a call."

Stephen shrugged like he couldn't care less, pushed the creaking screen door open, and let it slam shut.

Alby waited until he heard the truck's tires on the gravel fade before he grabbed his phone and called Fat Joe. "Joe—it's Al—"

"What? Find those bastards yet? I've called you every day."

"No. I just heard about what happened to Delarosa. What the hell is going on?"

"You don't want to know. Just find at least one of those bastards and call me the minute you do."

"Then what happens?"

"Since when do you care? They're all animals anyway." With that, he hung up.

By the time Alby arrived, Stephen had most of the tools on the roof. Alby handed up the half-dozen planks and then carried up a bucket of shingles. The rib that had been hardest hit by Chance's case of beer ached with each step up the ladder.

"There's a rumor going around something bad happened at the bank."

Now that came out of nowhere, thought Alby. What was he up to?

"Like what?"

"Not sure. Just bad."

"That's a pretty broad category, don't you think?" With that they fell into silence and hammered away. Each downward strike of the hammer on a nail seemed filled with a sense of purpose—for Alby it was anger. He had to stop thinking about the "what if" around Ginger and stay focused. Why was she getting under his skin?

How many times can you drive one square mile. That wasn't a question because by now he knew. He felt like a rat in a laboratory maze.

Strangely enough, as chaotic as it seemed, he now saw there was a pattern to the chaos—it was like a canvas full of wrecked cars, garbage, dirt, and pits where homes once were. The litter on one corner seemed to disappear on another like some calico blanket of decay. Today, bored, Alby had tried touring Camden as a grid—the streets were laid out with east-west numbers crossing—but it tired him out after an hour. So, he just went randomly. At each stop sign he'd turn the opposite way he'd turned before.

At best, he knew finding Lucky would be the equivalent of winning the lottery. Fifty million to one. But he had to try. The monotony of driving gave his mind the chance to wander. Why hadn't some FBI agent showed up—if there was a bad guy loose, then the law should be set loose too. Yet no one had mentioned anything about the police. Fat Joe's scheme of fake documents would blow up and Alby knew he'd be the natural next person to investigate. At the very least, they could charge him with accessory, and there would be no way to prove it wasn't true because he was!

But what the hell was he supposed to do? Whoever had taken out Delarosa and his crew had to know about him. He felt a small flash of pride because it may be that by keeping himself off the main street of life, he was probably hard to find. That had to be why on Thursday he was still alive and looking. Whoever took care of Delarosa Monday night had yet to find him.

That would not last. Alby took one hand off the wheel and slipped it around the handle of the knife.

Thoughts tumbling around, his anxiety was worn down by the monotony of driving up and down every block—boredom and anxiety. His mind drifted to his usual nightmares; he saw the massacre and felt the colors and singe of heat—his senses saw everything, and her eyes, he saw her eyes. They were blue. But he knew they weren't blue. Why were they blue now? And with the scarf, he only got glimpses of her hair. Why could he not see her black hair?

Then his heart pulled a trick on him: he had to see Ginger. The impulse was too strong, though he didn't know what he was going to say to her; she'd expect an apology, but he felt like she owed him one, too. He had no idea what he was doing, so he just did it.

At the next stop sign he pulled over and called his sister. He cradled the phone on his shoulder and turned the truck around. For some reason, Vinnie the Slob answered. "Hey, is my sister there?" He told him that she was at her dance class. Exactly what he was hoping for.

As hard as he was trying to follow the directions her husband had given him, he almost flew by the lot entrance and had to hit his brakes and turn suddenly, with no time to click on the turn signal. This earned him several angry honks, with a long trailing one as he moved down the row of storefronts. "Elaine's Dance Studio" was at the end; above the dance sign he could see traces of letters from an earlier iteration of this space. There were faint etches of cats and dogs on the windows. Snapping on his mask, he got out of the truck; they had their "mask mandate" government sign on the door. The Philly thing was creeping in.

The door jingled as he opened it. He was immediately assaulted with heavy, thumping, Brazilian-sounding dance music. It came from behind a thickly beaded curtain.

"Can I help you?" asked a small voice over the sound. He saw a skinny young woman, wearing exercise tights with a T-shirt that said, "Dance Your Ass Off!"

He had read it quickly, trying not to stare at her chest.

"Is there a Zumba class going on?" She looked him up and down—

sizing him up and surely, he thought, she knew he was not there for a class.

"It just started. You need your wife?"

He laughed; that was a good one. She looked a bit put off, as though he were making fun of her.

"No, my sister. Dorothy." He lied but couldn't help it.

"Dottie? I love her. Let me get her." She stood up and moved from behind the counter to the doorway into the studio. A former deli, he thought by the way it was laid out. But how'd it become a veterinarian's office? Jersey, he thought. Trail after trail leading nowhere. A state of cul-de-sacs and dead ends. Not waiting, he followed her through the beads and the noise got even louder.

The studio was one square room, variant unfriendly. It was laid out with a wall of mirrors and a balance beam facing the main area. Around the corners were free weights and other equipment. He stood by the side of the door, so no one noticed him.

And there were a lot who might have. In front of him was a truly scary tableau: a dozen suburban housewives, ranging from wide to thin, different body shapes accentuated by multicolored tights, all swaying and thrusting their hips to some throbbing music that sounded like the bastard in-breeding of disco and salsa. It hurt the ears. And in the front, between them and the mirrors, eyes ahead so she could see the class, was Ginger in a leopard-patterned body suit over a black leotard. Everyone had a mask on: except Ginger.

"ZUMBA!" she suddenly yelled.

"ZUMBA!" they all responded at the top of their lungs, with a few laughing and a few puffing.

Alby felt like he had just landed on the wrong planet. He considered retreat.

"*Alby!*" His sister emerged from the center of the group and rushed towards him. "What are you doing here?" She smelled like sweat and perfume enclosed in cacophonous patterned tights, like a pillow someone had squeezed into a case that was way too small for it, her excess weight pouring over and out in all the wrong places. She pulled her mask down to smile at him.

"I, uh, came to give you some money for Stephen." Seeing her in public, remembering what the receptionist had said about her, made him feel a twinge of guilt. She was a good person…then it snapped back. Yeah, a good person who let their mother die.

"Oh, really? And to think I was just hearing from Ginger how you two have been seeing each other. Am I the best? True, she won't say much, but I can tell!" She leaned forward but her bulging, multi-hued tights made him pull back. "Give me the money after the class."

"Okay." He had made a mistake. Every muscle said go. Just then, the music died down and stopped.

"Are you kidding me?" He turned to see Ginger walk towards him. Flat out gorgeous, he thought. It wasn't that she just looked beautiful—she *was* beautiful. She flowed as she walked. It was pure motion. How can someone do that, he thought. Her red hair was pulled back, but he recognized the battle the waves fought to get free and dance. Her face was flushed from the dancing, a slight sheen of sweat glittering there—it made her cheeks rosy. She was utterly beautiful.

"I, uh…." The ability to speak had left him, so he started looking around in pretended interest.

"Why are you interrupting my class? What are you doing here anyway?" She stepped back and then, as the class watched, said in a loud whisper, "Are you stalking me?" And she smiled.

"Ouch!" he said, and then she smiled again, successfully wiping her words away as far as he was concerned.

"We need to talk."

"Why?" she asked, looking less than interested.

"I came to apologize." She stood up straighter, genuinely surprised.

"Don't strike me as the type that does that often."

"Yeah, I'm out of practice," he half-smiled back, "but I was a real jerk—"

"Ginger!" Alby nearly jumped at the thunder-crack of a voice coming from a side room. A woman in her late 50s emerged, wearing tights but with fat layers cascading like small tsunamis down her body. She too had on an Elaine's T-shirt and it looked bad. "What are you doing? Why did the music stop?"

"Hold on, Elaine. A breather, okay?"

Ginger looked panicked for a second, then looked back at Alby. "Are you going to get me in trouble everywhere I work? Listen, the only way you can stay here is if you join the class. Elaine's a real bitch."

"Excuse me?" He did feel guilty about the diner job. "Listen, if you need some help—a little short—" He was fumbling with his words again, but he knew he was getting his point across.

"I don't need money! Money is unimportant." She waved her arm dismissively. This caught him off guard—who doesn't need money? This was just odd that she said that every time. "Just shut up, take off your boots, and come here," she said, tapping her foot impatiently. He quickly untied his boots and tossed them by the nearest wall, where they hit with a heavy thud. Then she grabbed his hand and yanked him onto the dance floor. The women giggled as he came onto the floor, trying to untuck his flannel shirt from inside his jeans with his one free hand, and then socially distanced themselves to make room for him: it had become second nature by now for everyone. Ginger leaned in and whispered quickly, "You'll have to pay, too." Before he could react, she pulled him next to her in the front, to her left, and grabbed the remote control from the floor near her feet.

"Let's pick it up where we left off." Ginger glanced over her shoulder at Elaine who was still half in the room, standing in the doorway to her office. "Remember girls, just dance your ass off! The pounds are flying!" On cue, they all laughed and took positions, hands on hips, legs apart. Like waiting for the pitcher to throw, thought Alby. He also was aware that they were all taking furtive glances at him. He couldn't blame them. Then Ginger hit the remote control and the Brazilian music leapt from the wall speaker. Everyone started swaying.

Last night, after going home in a foul mood, he had spent some time on Zumba.com trying to learn as much as he could. There had been some videos, but they were all short, frenetic, and promotional. They barely captured what was in full force now—a raw throbbing syncopation, pure, heavy on percussion, filled with intense energy.

"Hands in the air, now sway those hips!"

The whole group mimicked her every move as she barked orders and advice, held her arms up, elbows slightly bent and slowly built up an ever-widening rotation of her hips. "Dottie, stop staring at your brother! Janice, move those hips, you're not dead!"

Alby just stood there, bemused and a bit confused. This had to be one big joke. He was about to say something, when she yelled at him, "Arms up! Like this, like this! Reach for the heavens!"

He realized she was serious when he saw her cast her eyes in the mirror towards her boss, still leaning in the doorway, face still skeptical. Whatever it took, he had to avoid getting her in trouble.

"Oh yeah!" she shouted and the class refocused. Some kept repeating it like a chant. Alby held his arms up and tried to speak again. Ginger interrupted him: "Hips!" She glared at him. He tried to move his hips a little, it felt like two rusty cogs that couldn't catch hold. His jerking motions elicited a few giggles from the class. Quickly, he untucked the rest of his shirt and stretched his arms to loosen up.

"I wanted—" She pointed at her ears as if to say she could not hear. He followed her lead but moved a step closer. "I felt bad about last night," he said, chin down and trying to aim his voice at her, while she kept a fake-looking, wry half-smile as she danced. Could she hear him? He couldn't believe how uncomfortable he felt. But then he saw a bead of sweat rolling down her forehead. She was working harder than anyone.

"Everyone—to the left!" They all clapped and turned and started moving one foot to slide to the left. The class had done this before, he could tell; they switched both their arm angles and the hip movement as they shimmied left, then right. Try as hard as he could, he was one beat behind and sure that he looked ridiculous.

"Lame," she mouthed—he could easily read her lips and the accompanying expression.

They turned as a group and moved back with the heavy sound of drums, and she almost ran into him. "Hey, watch out!" he said. "I just wanted to apologize."

"You keep saying that, so do it."

He cleared his throat, and just as he uttered the words, "I am really,

really sorry," the music abruptly paused in beat; his words loudly filled the void and seemed to bounce off the glass and reverberate around the room. The women all burst out laughing, especially his sister. He had to recover. "Uh, for being a bad dancer."

No one fell for it; the class laughed again as they got back into position: back straight, hands on hips. Surprisingly, Alby didn't feel humiliated. Ginger just shook her head in disbelief; he could tell she was pursing her lips to control the corners of her mouth from breaking into a full smile.

"You can't even apologize well. To the right!"

The music started right where it left off.

"You really had to come here." She glanced at him in the mirror, eyes flashing angry again.

"I had to come and tell you."

"I heard you!" she yelled and spun around, then stopped to glare at him and spun again; the class followed. He was frozen, but then looked for Elaine—who was now going back into her office. The door shut behind her.

He stopped faking it and turned to Ginger. But she would have none of it.

"Dance or out!"

"Come on!" he pleaded.

She stopped and waved the class to continue. Facing him, her mouth scrunched up, as did her nose, and she drew her full lips into a thin line—she looked like a determined kid again. "You wouldn't dance last night, so do it now." She paused. "You are either all in, or out." Still moving, but resisting, he saw how serious her face was. This wasn't about dancing at all.

Alby bent over in resignation. Hands on knees, he took note of his stitched left side and took a deep breath; the music changed tempo and got deeper—more jungle-sounding. He paused, then began to shake his butt left to right. He jumped up and turned towards the mirror. Now he was shaking his butt right at the class of young and middle-aged women. A mild ripple of laughter moved across the room, but everyone seemed to hold back.

Screw it, he thought, he was going to show them that he could let go of his stupid male pride. Anyway, there were no other guys there; if he had to make a fool out of himself, this was the right moment with the right crowd.

With that, he threw himself right into it. "ZUMBA!" he yelled. The class hesitated then returned his shout. He could see his sister laughing. Ginger kept moving—now in circles with one arm held high, fist pumping and twirling—but she gave him an uncertain look; she was confused by his sudden enthusiasm.

Alby looked back at her and stuck out his tongue. He started doing an exaggerated imitation of her circling and swaying her hips; his version looked like he had a rat trapped in his underwear. The room roared with music, laughter, and sweat.

"Glide to the left!" They all stopped and turned their feet outwards and started moving left.

Alby shouted at her, "What about that guy at the diner?"

She threw him a biting glance but lowered her voice. "I told you! Downstairs neighbor. Loser." Then she yelled, "To the right!" They all changed direction, including Alby who was struggling to keep up. His thick white socks didn't help any; they were slipping on the waxed floor.

"What about the girl in Iraq?" she retorted.

Alby stopped moving. She had figured it out. He had no choice: "Dead!" he shouted, turning a few heads in the class. Ginger nodded affirmatively, lips pursed tight, as if she had known all along. She looked at him as she moved; she mouthed the words "I'm sorry."

"Back it up!" Ginger yelled. And everyone stopped, bent over, placed hands on knees and paced backwards with exaggerated steps, like a retreating lion. Alby stopped and fell in. After ten steps, without urging, they all marched forward. His socks kept slipping slightly on the varnished floor, and he nearly bumped into the woman who came up from behind him. "Sorry." He took a fast step forward and was again nearly at the mirror. Mirrors don't lie—he saw himself and he looked like a sweaty jackass. Then he burst into laughter—and let it roll with the music. A real laugh. A deep, long laugh. He couldn't recall the last time he felt a laugh go that deep. The whole class joined in.

That was when he fell. His sock slipped, his feet flew forward, and he hit the ground hard, right on his ass bone. The room suddenly turned from a dance studio to chaos—Ginger grabbing the remote to turn off the music, women crowding around him to help him up, his sister pushing through yelling, "He's my brother!"

Ginger was the first to stop all the commotion and buffer him from the rest. She stood over him, hands on hips. "What the hell was that?"

The entire right side of his ribs ached, the scar felt stretched to the limit. His tailbone ached. She smiled. It softened her face and opened it like a flower after the rain. Her eyes sparkled, or at least it looked that way from the floor.

"Break," she ordered the class. "Two minutes!"

"Alby, are you okay?" His sister pushed through and held his shoulder. He grimaced; she had put her thumb right on the bullet scar. "I'm good." He gently moved his sister's hand away.

Reaching over to her remote, Ginger laid her phone flat on a speaker and pecked away for a few seconds. A new song came on. It jumped right out of the speakers from the 1930s with the tinny sound of horns—a brassy, upbeat cadence but with a kind of scratchy quality to it.

She put her hands on her hips, looked down at him, and in a sing-song voice said, "Here's some words of wisdom from the composer Jerome Kern." Then she cleared her throat and began to sing words of advice in a clear, big Broadway kind of voice, she told him to pick himself up, dust himself off, and start over again....

Alby was absolutely dumbfounded; he didn't know what to say. Other than a few drunks, no one had ever sung to him; it was like being in a musical. She continued to sing, wagging her index finger at him, then singing the next verse and closing it all with the same advice this had all started with.

...so, pick yourself up, dust yourself off, start all over again!

* *(Listen: evenapandemic.com/pickyourselfup)*

She ended with a full spin and landed smack on one foot flat, one on an arched toe point. At this point the entire class, watching with mixed looks of awe, appreciation, and confusion, burst out clapping.

She looked over at him again, the left side of her curly hair bobbing along, having broken loose from a clip. She seemed to have become a mixture of Ginger waitress, Ginger Zumba instructor, and Ginger just plain fun woman who merely said, "Okay, Alby?" Then she walked over to him and extended her arm, which he grabbed onto her forearm so he could stand back up. "You apologized, danced, and did what I asked. Come over tonight and we'll check out the Aquarium—Thursday is Shark Night. Over in Camden."

An aquarium in Camden? Bet it was part of some tax-abated, government "urban renewal" infrastructure project; you couldn't drive a mile without seeing a new bridge, school, library, major road, or even a side road, all being rebuilt, expanded or completely re-designed. He had seen plenty of government urban renewal projects in Iraq—more went to payoffs than actual construction. Clearly people were being paid off here, too, he thought. More good money after bad. But that didn't matter—he had gotten another date out of it.

And once again he felt a lightning bolt of surprise. Whatever it was with Ginger, it was turning out better than he had ever imagined it might. And not for the first time, it crept into his mind that he had been hoping it would turn out to be something from that very first night at the party.

"Deal," he confirmed with a big nod and a smile. She walked him silently to the beaded doorway. Ruefully, he kept smiling. He had to resist the urge to rub his ass; it ached deep into the tailbone. As he passed through the beads, she smiled, and then her entire face opened up into her usual "I've got one on you" grin. He felt the intensity of her wrap around him in full force.

"Feeling rather chagrined, are we?" she said triumphantly. "Just think! We've seen each other almost every night this past week. Get me at eight. And oh," she added, nodding over towards the girl at the desk, "don't forget to pay."

Alby paused in his thoughts. Chagrined was a word he had never heard anyone use other than his mother. Hearing it coming from Ginger surprised him and caught him a bit unprepared for the combined presence of both women in his mind at the same time—but then Ginger had a way of keeping him in a totally unprepared state. His mom would have liked her, and she had not been easy on anyone.

Then another thought overtook any comparison between Ginger and his mother. That thing about "almost every night this week" was Ginger's way of sending him a message. The problem was that part of the "my brain is connected to my heart" messenger connection that she was speaking to was rusted out. He had not realized they had been together every night. And now that she had apprised him of that remarkable point, he began to worry that she had just been acting impetuously. After all, what the hell did she see in him? She was cute; he was sure he looked like a rag doll. He had no money, no real job, hid in the back of a garage, and had more scars—both visible and invisible—than any dozen people could collect in a lifetime; she was making money by working several real jobs at once and lived in a real apartment. He was broken, lived like he was broke, and she knew it. She wasn't exactly without her problems but she was not broken and he knew that. So why bother with a guy like him? It just made no sense.

And then his mind suddenly clicked out of whatever orbit it had just been in. What the hell was he thinking? Some crazed killers running around looking for the check and he's making plans to go on a date? Maybe he shouldn't see her; no, he had to see her, but to do that he had to some-how track his crew down—especially Lucky—and get this time bomb off his back.

Too many questions with no answers, he thought. One thing was clear—it was back to Camden before seeing Ginger.

And in the way of his world, he came back to reality realizing that he was not in his truck looking for Lucky, but instead standing at a counter. At the dance studio. And the young woman was filling out a receipt.

"Sixty bucks."

He almost choked. "Are you kidding me? Sixty bucks for me falling on my ass?" She smiled obliquely like she couldn't hear him. He handed over three twenties.

Sixty bucks. As much as he thought that was highway robbery, he remembered the woman Elaine standing by to make sure that Ginger was "working hard." Alby had to wonder just how much Ginger got; it couldn't be much. No wonder she took on the waitress work. Yet, she kept dismissing money as something to worry about.

As he headed for the door, he knew he had two choices: back to the job with Stephen or back to Camden. He sighed. It was obvious. There was no choice. He started down onto the first step and then paused, looking around nervously, as if he were being watched—was he? Now he was getting paranoid. He had to pick up the pace and find this damned check; it was *his* life on the line. As good as he had done hiding in the cave, how long before these bad guys found his garage?

Before he could reach the pavement, Dorothy came out, breathless. "You said you had money for Ste…" then, stopping in mid-sentence, she suddenly looked smug. "You came to see Ginger—admit it!" Staring at her a whole catalogue of comments went through his head, most of them mean, and he decided that it wasn't worth it. He smiled a phony smile, turned, and just left.

As the Zumba-induced sweat began to dry, he suddenly realized how hungry and thirsty he was, so he headed for a Thai place not far away. Once inside, with menu in hand, he was lost again: Ginger Chicken, Ginger Pork, Ginger Stir-Fry…it was as if the entire menu had her name on it.

What Ginger had said about his mom's death driving him from the country had burrowed itself deeply under his skin. Mostly because it was true. In his whole adult life, he had never taken care of anyone; he was raised to be independent. As loving as his mom had been, she had had no illusions about the world and the nets of negative entanglements it could create and so she had encouraged that indepedence in him. Yet, in her last months, his life had become consumed by playing the role of all-in caregiver. And that was how it should have been, right?—she was his mom, after all. That's what you did. Loving someone who cared about you was also something that she had taught him by her own example. But what if you just have no stupid single idea of what to do.

Knowing that and letting it ease his guilt, though, were two very different things. Watching the decay of her sharp mind following the decline of her body was a torture that he had ignored. Her decline had accompanied the decline of his bank account; now he realized that somehow, he must have done a lousy job at it all. He'd failed her, although he was not sure how. Maybe he had done his best. Maybe he just wasn't capable. Maybe he could have used some help. And that always led to Dorothy.

After the doctor had told him that his mom had only a few months to live, he moved her to hospice and sold the house as fast as possible; it was in poor shape because she never let him do any major repairs, so he didn't get much for it. She had also taken out a line of credit he hadn't known about, and when he asked her why she just growled, "It's just damned money." After paying everyone off—he had never written so many checks in his life—he took what was left and sent half to Dorothy. But it wasn't much. His half he used to start whittling down the momentous number of medical bills.

Standing next to each other at the graveside, he and Dorothy had seemed both siblings and strangers to each other; they had barely spoken a word. Mom had drawn a big crowd, but even then, Alby hadn't really been aware of who had come. He'd been in a fog and had tuned them all out. He was planning his escape—off to a high-paying job in Iraq re-building the country's infrastructure—an old pal who worked for Bechtel had approached him only a few days earlier.

"Can I get your order?" asked a young Asian man.

Startled back into the here and now, Alby looked again at the menu, mindlessly, while he began inwardly berating himself for doing what he hated most: thinking. Alby and thinking did not have a good track record. More times than not, it only led to bad decisions, regrets, second-guesses, self-doubts—a trash heap of scenarios considered and tossed. So at some point during these past years he had trained himself not to think, not to give himself time to ponder who he was, wasn't, where he was, wasn't....

Now he couldn't stop thinking. The missing check was darkening the surface of everything. Then came Ginger, like a roll of the dice that promised something more than he had had in a very long time. The waiter impatiently tapped his pen on the order pad. The plastic cover on the menu—with photos of the platters—fell from his hand. "Ginger with basic brown sauce—I mean Ginger chicken." His mouth could move but his mind was clearly elsewhere.

As the waiter walked away, a voice in his head told him, "Run! You *know* how to do it." But he could feel that the impulse was distant and small—it was not too distant, though, to know that part of him was frightened. He didn't like what he saw, the pettiness of what it was, what it said about him, who he was and who he wasn't, his life, his everything, the whole whirling cyclone of Alby shit.

He had run before. He knew all about it. But he had not been raised to be a runner. His mom had never walked away from a challenge; she had always declared—and loudly—that she made her own luck—a confidence he wished he'd picked up.

His mind skipped like a stone across the water, but in a jagged line like the scar on his side. At least the food, the reminder of Ginger, was very good. He turned to the waiter and motioned for the check. From the light coming through the front window, he guessed he had a few hours of daylight left.

He gave the waiter the Handlers' credit card and smiled at him. "Add a twenty-five percent tip." He always did that as his own way to stick it to his Handlers. Then quickly he caught himself smiling and immediately willed his expression back to grim neutral, his World Face. But inside… inside something different was being willed to come out. Without noticing, he had already begun to reconstruct his life—winter meant less work, so maybe he should try for a steady job. Get out of that dumpy garage hell-hole. Buy some clothes.

That was the "Be with Ginger" plan. What that meant, he had no idea and frankly did not care. He—they'd—figure it out later. Anything was better than how he was living now—when the only company he was regularly keeping were the demons that chased him every night, bourbon and a punching bag.

If he ran, what would that plan look like? Call the Handlers? They would sniff trouble in a second and send him to some godforsaken place. Or hell, they might laugh at him, tell him he's on his own, and change their phone number hoping he'd get killed. Still, it was so tempting. It would be so easy to run—call the Handlers, grab his cash duffel, grab a few bags, and go. Just drive.

Running…staying…his mind got cloudy; he couldn't see a future in either choice. But he saw one stark difference between them. And that difference was Ginger.

One last shot, he thought as he got into his truck, one last attempt to find Lucky and the check. He knew that if he did find Lucky he was not going to just roll over and hand it over. He felt around for his switchblade. The check was Lucky's way out. And there was also the fact that it was Thursday night, so he *had* to look, because if he didn't find him, there would be even more hell to pay from Fat Joe. He would need a new crew—if he even let him back.

More than a few times over the years, Alby had wondered whether he had a killer somewhere inside him, next to all the other Albys in there. This thought had started in Iraq—anyone claiming that it wasn't a war zone was blind; it may have stabilized for a few years, but Covid and the follow-up vaccine roll-outs, new variants, the US sending bad batches, not sharing the anti-virals—it upended what little peace there was. Even when things seemed calm, you would suddenly hear the pop of gunfire, or the more disturbing rumble of a car bomb or IED. The story behind it would filter in later, usually at the hotel restaurant.

Bechtel wouldn't assign you until you did a week of training, and it wasn't on any topic related to construction. It should have been called: "Being paranoid means you survive." It was taught by a US soldier, no rank or identifiers on his uniform. He lectured them on the litany of what hell waited for them outside the Green Zone; the government's collapse due to the vaccine debacle, strongmen, Special Forces going back in, all looked bad for anyone from the US. Yet the guy was arrogant as hell.

Could he kill Lucky? He had surprised himself with Santorini and he'd come pretty close. But for all he had seen and done, he wasn't sure he could go all the way.

A better idea occurred to him: a third way. If he didn't find them this last time, then head home and start packing. When he picked up Ginger at eight, it wouldn't be the date that she was expecting. It would be a sit-in-the-truck discussion.

He would ask her to come with him. She had to come with him.

He eased the truck off the last exit just before the Walt Whitman toll booths; he could see the cars piling up due to the infection checkpoints going both ways. He drove slowly, swiveling his head left to right and back, taking in every detail and watching out for that lanky frame of Lucky. Plenty of bodies walking the streets, but not the one he was looking for. He drove slowly past the trash-strewn lot at 4th and York. Empty.

It was taking real concentration for him to keep driving in circles—he had this feeling that he was descending a hill of sand, with little hope of climbing out. A large part of him had already given up and was cataloguing his belongings and the escape plan.

Suddenly, the missing ball fell into the side pocket: If he got the check what would he do with it?

Then, a siren went off, and he saw flashing lights in his side mirror. A cop? He pulled over. A momentary wave of anxiety flashed through him as he thought of the switchblade in his pocket and the crowbar on the floor by his right hand.

In the rearview mirror, he could see that only one cop was in the car; he was clearly punching the keys of his laptop—probably entering Alby's license plate.

Alby exhaled and rolled down his window. He tried to look casual, left elbow on the window frame, right hand at two o'clock on the steering wheel. The slightly rotund cop slid out of the seat, hand on holster, and walked slowly to stand a half-step back from Alby's window. The cop was white and around Alby's age, which made Alby sure that whatever was going on, it was nothing.

"Both hands on the wheel," he said firmly.

Alby complied. "Officer—"

"Shut up," he said but in a matter-of-fact way as he slid closer to the window, peeked in, and scanned the interior of the truck cab. "What are you doing around here?"

"Looking for day workers." A version of the truth.

"At sunset?" The cop grunted and moved in front of the window, so he could look Alby in the face. There was a scent of menace—Alby had felt it many times before, but this time he could not figure out what the source was.

"Getting reports all week about a white pick-up truck floating around the neighborhood." He glanced at it. "White. Cruising around Camden with some white guy in it. Is that you?"

"I guess." Alby wasn't sure what to do or say. He saw the holster clip was off and one hand was resting on the handle of his 9-millimeter gun.

"Looking for that many day workers? You know they're all illegals or ex-cons, right?"

Now he knew he was busting his chops; there wasn't a small business contractor, landscaper, snow plower, cleaning service dude, farmer, who didn't collect day workers. And always at a public place.

"License and registration." Alby carefully leaned over to the glove compartment, got them out, and handed them over. Unlike most drivers, Alby kept his license in the glove compartment with his registration. The fewer people who might see any details on it when he got out the credit card, the better.

"Don't move," the cop said, a hint of threat in his voice.

The cop walked slowly back to his car and took a few minutes as he looked Alby up. This was not good; though Alby had registered everything through his sister's house, he knew his record had empty spots, which if you were already suspicious would be damning.

The cop sauntered back, handed him his cards, and said: "Listen, and don't bullshit me. You're a white guy cruising Camden. That takes it down to a few reasons. One, you're looking for drugs. Two, hookers. Or both. The day worker thing is more bullshit so don't bother. You stick out here. People don't like it."

Alby must have looked dumbfounded. The cop squinted at him, Alby's expression was so genuine. "Officer, I'm—"

The cop raised his hand, palm open outward, telling him to stop.

"Your record's clean, so my best advice is: whatever the hell you are looking for, give it up. Get the hell out of here. If I see you again, I'm taking you in." And with that, he walked away.

All Alby could think, and feel, was: screwed again. There was no Rule to account for this situation; the cop only confirmed what he knew to be true: he had to get out—before someone, and he didn't even know who, caught up with him.

He exhaled, realizing that he had stopped breathing. His breath had caught somewhere in his throat. Pushing himself back into his seat, he felt his shoulders tighten; the sound of water in his ears rose, rushing faster with each breath. He had to get out. Out of Camden, out of Jersey, out of everywhere. He put the truck in drive, hit the gas pedal a little too fast and hard, and took off for the garage.

Rush hour delayed and annoyed him every mile of the way, but he finally pulled in at the back of the garage and quickly went inside. He had to pack, but what? Feeling the tide of panic still on the edges of his senses, he kept glancing around the room as if something would jump out and he'd grab it. But after a minute, he realized that there was nothing to take besides some clothes, his laptop, a couple of chargers for his iPhone, and of course, the duffel from Iraq stuffed with hundred-dollar bills. He would leave the ashtray. There was the punching bag—couldn't leave that, it was like family at this point. The knife he already had on him; unconsciously, his hand moved into his right jacket pocket to finger the ebony handle.

He filled the two duffel bags he had grabbed and then fell hard on the couch. He couldn't take his eyes off the ground. He felt a noticeable tremor, like the slight shaking from a distant earthquake. He knew what to do: he would go to her. They would run together.

Lifting the chipped white coffee cup, Lucky got the waitress's attention. Just then, in came Darnell, eyes scanning the room, glancing at the half-dozen people at different stages of ordering and eating before he saw Lucky and headed over to him.

"Lucky, this shit—"

Lucky waved his hand in Darnell's face. "Calm down, man. You look so scared, you look almost white." He laughed.

"Alby came in the store at lunch yesterday. Something happened with him and Chance. They both ran out. Haven't seen Chance since."

"Where'd they go?"

"Don't know. Alby was in his truck, Chance just ran."

"He'll be here."

"Don't think so." He leaned forward: "Story is going round they found him dead by the old docks."

Lucky put down his fork and leaned back in the booth; he could feel the tear in the vinyl seat cover press into his shoulder blade. "What?"

"Yeah."

"Shit."

"Found him in the river."

"Shit."

"Yeah, you got a plan besides saying shit over and over?" asked Darnell, leaning forward, challenging his space. He leaned back when the waitress came for his order. "Coffee," was all he said, not taking his eyes off Lucky.

"I'm thinking." It was an awkward moment. Lucky did not like Darnell and really did not like feeling the guy had the upper hand in some way. Nothing he had suggested had gotten them any closer to cashing the check. In fact, if he added up Chance's death to what happened to that other contractor's crew on Monday night, it smelled like the bank Owners had sent their own crew to find the check.

Reality sunk in. The lock had found the key, but it had turned the wrong way for him: they had no time. They had to get rid of the check any way they could, try to get some cash, and run. Running was something he knew how to do. He needed to stay calm in front of Darnell. "At least we only have to split in two ways. That's good news."

"Half of nothin' is still nothin'," said Darnell as he lifted his coffee, blew the faint steam away, and sipped, still with his eyes on Lucky. Lucky wanted him to stop staring. Darnell spoke slowly. "Lucky…every day this week you had some new plan to get that check cashed. First your uncle. Then the bodega—"

"Those Mexicans are low as shit."

"Guatemalans," Darnell corrected him. Lucky just looked away. Darnell reached out an open hand. "Give me the check."

"No!" Lucky hadn't meant to react so fast.

"All week you had it, all week the only thing keepin' you here was you just don't have no money to run away. Nowhere to go. What good is you havin' the check?"

Lucky just stared at him

Then Darnell said, "I got an idea."

"About time…."

"We give it back."

"What the fuck!" Ignoring Darnell's outstretched hand, Lucky patted his chest pocket, almost like rubbing a good luck charm. "No way. Why the hell would we do that?"

Lucky was as upset as Darnell had ever seen. Darnell looked at him fiercely. "I have a good job. Don't pay much, but I got a job. That's somethin'. I even got a woman and a place to lay my head. I was thinkin' last night. What the hell is gonna happen? Somebody's got to notice the check is gone and is lookin' for it. Somebody did notice. Why else is Chance dead?"

"Because he's stupid. Probably was trying to get some smoke on credit."

"No, someone is lookin' for that check. Alby for sure. He knows. And those Delarosa guys…" Darnell's voice trailed off.

"Then we go kill him."

"Who?" Darnell was confused.

"Alby, you stupid shit." Lucky smacked the table and the cup jumped and rattled, drawing some stares.

"Alby's no killer; he's not our problem." With a dismissive shake of the head, Darnell lay his arm on the table, palm upwards, and pushed his hand out closer to Lucky. "Give me the check."

"No." Lucky's hand slipped over the knife on the table. "What?

You wanna fight for it here? You're as dumb as Chance."

"We can find a way."

"Tomorrow's Friday—you goin' back to the bank?"

"Don't know; hadn't thought about it."

"We gotta figure a way to get the money but not get with the law." Lucky's brain was moving faster than his mouth.

The waitress floated too close to the booth; Lucky slipped his hand and the knife onto his lap. He was calculating whether he could reach under the table and shove the knife in Darnell's stomach. It was too far.

"I know your shit, Lucky. Do not try it on me. You think you're gonna kill me with that butter knife you're hidin'?" He laughed. With one hand, he pushed the empty cup to the edge of the table. "I'm not stupid. I survived this long for a reason. But we keep playin' games with that check and we're dead. Whoever got Chance is lookin' for us, too."

Lucky hadn't thought of that yet. Taking a deep breath, he sat up straighter in the booth.

"You done?" The waitress startled him. He nodded, and she took his plate and the empty coffee cup.

"Two checks."

As if she knew he would say that, she threw them on the table. "Let's go outside—I'll give your plan a hear."

Eyes locked on each other, and in silent unison, they slipped out of the booth. Lucky left the table knife behind. The bill was for almost $5, so Lucky threw two ones on the bill and stared down the waitress as she watched.

The streets were still crowded with commuters as they walked outside, but the sidewalk was deserted. Lucky jerked his head right and the two of them walked side by side down the street.

"Let's go in here," he said without warning, and he took a sudden right into the first alleyway. He walked ahead of Darnell past the dumpster. "You want the check. Hold on."

He bent down, acting as if he were tying his shoes and slowly withdrew the sharp steak knife he'd put in his sock alongside his ankle. As he stood, he whirled around and lunged at Darnell.

Darnell jumped back a foot and stood his ground. Lucky froze. Darnell had a small .22 in his hand aimed at Lucky's stomach.

"Yeah, you're smart, Lucky. People don't know you're a cold-blooded killer? I'm on my third time. Like I said…I don't want no trouble. I want the money, but I want this all to go away. Give me the check."

"Why?"

"I'm goin' to the site tomorrow night and gonna put it back where we took it from."

"How you gonna do that?'

"I'll figure it out. Check."

Lucky dropped the hand holding the knife to his side and used his left to reach into his jacket pocket. He pulled out the oblong paper—the edges were getting frayed. He held it out for Darnell to take it.

Giving him a hard look, Darnell cautiously reached out. But as his fingers got just inches away, Lucky lunged at him with the knife. Darnell turned sideways and tried to use the gun to push away the knife. Lucky swept left then right and downwards to slash Darnell's forearm.

Darnell staggered back, but then surprised Lucky by jumping forward and grabbing the check that was in his other hand. "I'm gonna shoot your ass, Lucky."

"Not today!" The knife swung in a big arc across Darnell, just missing his chest. He pulled back, and since they both held an end of the check, it ripped in half. As the paper split, they both stumbled backwards.

There was silence except for the cars and trucks going by, an occasional honk, someone's voice calling a name.

They each held half the check.

Darnell stared at the jagged edge of the ripped check. "How we ever gonna cash this now?"

"Get some tape."

Lucky slid the knife back in his boot. There was no way he was giving up. Suddenly, his mind cleared, and it clicked open. "Darnell, you said you was gonna give it back?'

"Try to."

All week Lucky had worked his ass off to try and cash the check and he realized he had the answer at last—he knew that if he had thought about it long enough, he'd solve the problem.

"I got an idea…." He gestured for Darnell to shut up. "We *will* give it back. But not to the bank. Somebody wants this bad enough to kill. That means they'd be willing to give up some money to get it back."

"Like a reward?"

"Yeah…like a reward." Darnell gave him a half-smile, but Lucky could tell he had hit the winning number. "Ransom!"

He could see that Darnell was thinking hard, so he said, "Remember that silver picture frame you gave Chance? That was a family photo. What was that guy's name whose office we took it from? He left it. He must be in big trouble, too."

"Yeah. Something with a K," Darnell said.

They both thought in silence.

"*Kurtz!*" Lucky finally shouted.

"Yeah!"

"We call him. Tell him we got the check. Arrange a meet."

"Yeah." Darnell was smiling now. He slid the gun back into his pants pocket.

They left the alley and looked around for a pay phone. "Nearest one is over in Cooper Hospital."

"It's almost six. Think the guy is still at the bank?"

It took them fifteen minutes of fast walking to get to the hospital. The guard gave them a long look as they entered the lobby. "Darnell, you and him ain't allowed in here."

"Just gotta use the pay phone." Darnell pointed to a booth across the huge open lobby. Everything was clean-looking and new. People in white jackets, wheelchairs, all coming and going…it was like rush hour at the hospital. Even though it was a place for sick people, it felt bright and happy. Always a sunny day, colorful wallpaper, and everyone knows it's a big lie. They're all dying. What bullshit, thought Lucky.

"You got some money?" Lucky put out his hand. Darnell dropped four quarters in it.

Holding his breath, Lucky entered the bank number and asked

for Kurtz; it was a night operator for online banking customers; she tried to follow a script, but Lucky interrupted her: "Your boss—Kurtz. I have an emergency and it's gonna hurt the bank; he needs to know *now!*" She got flustered and then asked him to wait on the line. He was put on hold for what seemed forever. Then he heard the phone ring once, twice, three times—then heard a voice.

"Hello?"

"Kurtz?"

"Yes. Who is this?"

"I got the check."

There was a long silence. Then in a dead tone: "Who is this?"

"Like I'm gonna say? We got your damned check. What you want for it?"

"I don't—Wait, wait, you really have it?" The banker fell silent. Lucky waited.

"Yeah. So how much for the reward?"

The banker laughed loudly. "Do you have any idea who you are dealing with?"

This pissed Lucky off. "Yeah, the dumb fuck who left the safe open."

Darnell nudged his shoulder. "Lucky, we gotta move. The guard's comin' over." Not only was he starting to slowly walk across the long lobby, but Darnell could see his hand was slipping onto his holster. Lucky shook his arm off.

"We were gonna cash it for 99,000 dollars."

Kurtz laughed and laughed, like a wellspring opening and the water spouting out in a gush. He could not believe his luck. If he got it back, he could make the whole problem go away—maybe he'd tell the Owners he'd misplaced it in another drawer. Honest mistake. Stupid, but honest. He would make Lucky disappear. Then maybe they'd call off the killer in gray and everything would go back to normal. What had been looking like another dark, bad day had just turned bright and in his favor.

Then he realized that this was going to cost him personally. "I'll give you fifty grand." He said it with finality, in his "no-negotiating" voice.

Lucky cupped the receiver. "Fifty grand." Darnell nodded profusely. He was getting nervous. He'd done time with the guard a long time ago; they shared a cell and got along. But he knew he was tough. This was not the time for a run-in or trouble.

"Just say yes, Lucky." He did.

Kurtz paused, then said, "We'll meet at the bank tomorrow night."

"Why there?" Lucky didn't like the sound of this.

"I have to get the money. That's where we keep it," he added sarcastically. "After hours, when it's closed for the crews."

"Get it tomorrow, at work."

"No," Kurtz quickly responded—too quick, Lucky thought. "I can't take out that much while other people are around. I can get in the bank after everyone goes home and get the money then." Now Kurtz was seeing how it could play out. He kept going. "Meet me during the night shift lunch break. No one will know. Behind the bank, near the loading dock."

Lucky began to object. "I don't like this…." But before he could say more Kurtz pushed on. "How will we know each other?"

At this, Lucky laughed like he'd just stepped on a bug. "You'll be the only white guy carrying a bag of money."

There was a pause. "Okay. One a.m. No tricks." Another pause and then, "In the back, by the loading docks."

Lucky had the last word. "We both want something. Don't fuck this by doin' something stupid."

As he clicked off, Darnell tugged on his sleeve. "We gotta go." They quickly moved across the lobby; the guard swerved to intercept them.

"What the hell are you two still doing here?"

"Using the phone."

"Go somewhere else next time. This place is for decent folks." He didn't even look at Lucky. "Darnell, I thought you had gone right."

Darnell ignored his comment but moved faster to reach the revolving door.

As they left the hospital, Lucky turned to the right, back to the neighborhood.

Darnell walked with a bigger stride. They both moved briskly through the dusk. With each block, the decay got worse until they were back closer to the heart of the neighborhood.

"Feelin' good?" Lucky asked Darnell, putting his hand on his shoulder.

"Yeah. Now we just gotta pull this off tomorrow. Man, twenty-five thousand dollars. Man!" Darnell rubbed his hands together. "Might have to take my love and go for a long visit to her relatives in North Carolina. Let things quiet down."

They crossed an open lot, and as they passed a neglected, overflowing dumpster, Lucky turned toward Darnell and said: "Glad you didn't shoot me?" He laughed.

"Yeah, no harm, Lucky. Anyway, I borrowed the gun. It didn't have no bullets." He laughed, too.

Lucky reacted. As Darnell moved one step ahead of him, he bent down, took out his knife, and stuck it right in Darnell's back. Darnell buckled. Lucky pulled it out and thrust it back in. Moving closer to him, he grabbed him by the coat collar and in one heave-ho threw Darnell into the dumpster. Bending down, he cleaned the knife edge, first one side then the other, on the rough, uncut weeds. He stood and peered over the edge of the dumpster, looking around until he found an old newspaper. He took a handful of pages and wiped them all over the areas of Darnell's coat he thought he might have touched. One item he didn't want to forget—he dug into the dead man's pocket and grabbed the empty gun. Might be useful, even without bullets.

"Not twenty-five. Fifty!" he said triumphantly as he stared at the blood-soaked parka and a very dead Darnell. Then he turned and hurried away.

If he was really going to bolt, Alby had to clean up some messes before he called his Handlers. First on that list was Dorothy. The air between them stunk of things unsaid and unresolved. If he was going to do a disappearing act, then he needed once and for all to confront her about his mom. As he drove nearer to her house, he noted the slip…*his* mom—as if she were his alone. But Dorothy had run away to South Jersey as fast as she could after community college, got married, and stayed there.

It was *his* mom she had killed.

"Dorothy!" he yelled as he banged on her front door. Her Mazda was in the driveway; not for the first time he wondered what was she doing with such a slick kid's car at her age. She swung open the door, obviously surprised it was him.

"Alby? How nice!" she said with pretended enthusiasm; he must have had an odd look on his face. He pushed past her into the living room. "What?" she asked. Vinnie the Slob yelled something from the kitchen. "Hold on!" she yelled back.

In frustration, Alby moved back to the door, facing her. "Tell me what happened that day." He could feel the anger in his voice, the red heat of it swelling up his throat.

"What day?" But her eyes told him she knew.

"Don't bullshit me."

"Why can't you let this go?" she pleaded. Now tears began to fill her eyes.

"Oh, I don't know—let's see—Mom's dying of cancer. I ask you to come up and watch her, so I can actually earn some money—*to pay for her bills!*" he yelled at her, then calmed down. His phone started to ring, and it was like a bee caught in his inner ear. He ignored it, certain it was Fat Joe.

"And then you finally come. Mom's in and out of the coma. Doctors saying she's holding on. That was your job, Dorothy, to help her hold on. Just one stinking day."

"For what, Alby? For what?"

"What do you mean, for *what?*" he yelled. Then…suddenly…what she meant sunk in. And he could feel his whole body start to heat up.

"She was in horrible pain. There was nothing they could do. She wasn't living like she wanted to, in any way. It was horrible. She told me!" Dorothy began to cry, burying her face in her hands.

"Still *our* mother. Ours," he pleaded, the reality continuing to hit him. But still he needed to know. "What did you do, Dorothy?"

"I did nothing." She was gulping in air now, between the sobs. "I did what she wanted done!" Tears were streaming down her cheeks, but now she looked up at him, and in that moment, her eyes were directing as much anger and frustration at him as his had ever directed at her.

"It's what I had to do. She knew you couldn't do it—not her beloved son!" She stopped, the next words caught in her throat. Between sobs, she took in a deep breath. "I couldn't say no to her. You know how Mom was." Dorothy struggled to drag in air. "You weren't there. You didn't know. It was horrible."

"She never would—" Then he stopped. All this time he had put it on Dorothy, but it was his mother. She was tough and knew her own mind and was stubborn as hell. If she had decided it was time to go…his mom, the most willful person he ever knew…

Dorothy was holding her face in her hands again, but her sobs had quieted.

"I have to sit down." He strode back out the door onto her front path and sat on a small bench. But that wasn't working. He got up and walked over to her. He hesitated for just a moment, then he opened his arms. She fell into them.

Head burrowed into his chest, she spoke softly. "Once she knew I was coming, she called me. She could barely speak. I heard her thank the nurse for dialing then yell at her to leave the room. Mom told me…." She stopped.

"Yeah." Alby's eyes got watery. He would not let himself cry. "Sounds like her."

"She said she couldn't take the pain anymore and wanted out. I tried talking to her, but she was still sharp. She remembered that I'd had knee surgery and asked if I had any pain pills left."

"And you did."

"Doesn't everyone? Anyway, she told me to bring them up next time. When I got there, I told her no way was I giving them to her, but she…she…." Dorothy just let it out—the flood gates opening, the pain pouring out. "Oh, Alby, I can't believe I killed our mother."

Seeing her like this was hard to take. Her pain was visceral—like a puppet with all its strings cut, her body was loose and seemed to droop, yet not even with enough energy to collapse to the ground.

Alby wiped his eyes. This hadn't been what he expected at all. It had never occurred to him it had been his mom's doing. She took herself out. He was momentarily in shock, finally knowing what was true. He shook his head. Yeah, that was just like his mom. Being such a devout Catholic, weekly Mass, tea with the priest, the whole thing—he would never have guessed it, but now it made sense. That day, after a chemo session, getting her home, when she was too weak to climb the stairs, she had suddenly admitted to him that she was an atheist. That she saw no Heaven or Hell. Only darkness. And that she was fine with that. Alby had been absolutely stunned. "At least I'm not bullshitting myself," she had said with a ragged chemo-cough. Now he felt just as stunned with the realization that Dorothy, contrary to everything he had ever believed, had been the strong one, a strong one just like his mom had been.

Dorothy was crying now like the dam had finally broken. He gently pushed her away from him and walked her back up the steps. Then keeping her at arm's length, he zipped up his jacket and made noises like he was leaving. She took her hands away from her face.

"Sis," he began, "I'm heading out. Away. Won't be back." No matter what had just happened he had to follow through.

"What? Why?"

"Good question. I need to get going," He added, "*Really* away."

"Alby, I don't understand—"

"Good. It's not that important." He felt a twinge of the "big" brother, the protector, the role he'd played with her most of his life, even if she was the older one.

"Where are you going?" He didn't answer, just stared at her like it was the last time he'd see her.

"Somewhere where no one can find me," he said finally. "Think of how it was with Iraq."

"You're in trouble, aren't you?" He nodded before he thought about it. "What do I tell Stephen?" This caught him in mid-stride. As he held the screen door open for her, he said, "Tell him his uncle is gonna miss him." He said it with much more emotion than the words by themselves conveyed.

As he walked back to his truck, the cooler air and darkening sky reminded him about that nor'easter that was coming. It had been so long since he had experienced this type of storm—but go through a few and you never forget they were the most unpredictable storms of all; he only now realized that this could be a major hit.

Next was Ginger.

As he drew nearer to her apartment complex, his heart rate began to speed up. But it wasn't the usual panic attack or that sense of rushing water in his ears—his brain becoming disoriented, his eyesight fuzzy. This was different. He felt sure of his decision. Yet the closer he got to her, the words for what he was going to tell her slipped farther and farther away: I'm leaving, and I want you to go with me. Now. But that seemed too confrontational and bossy to say to Ginger. And that made him feel more clearly than ever that cut-and-run alone was the only choice he had.

He walked so slowly to her door that it felt like he was slogging through mud before even one drop of this nor'easter had begun to hit land. He stood in front of it for a minute or two, debating. Then he raised his hand and pounded on the door, twice. A little look of surprise spread across her face as she opened the door and it told him everything he needed to know. "Uh, Alby, I'm not ready. You're really early." Her hair was in a tight bun, clearing the way for her round face to shine. Her make-up was half done. He realized he had never seen a woman with only half her make-up on; it was surprisingly honest.

"I am," he said, abruptly pushing his way in; he'd never been in her apartment and was immediately taken with a full wall of Hollywood memorabilia—color posters, framed black and white photos—and there were other smaller items on a glass shelf in front of it. The wall was dominated by a large framed movie poster—"Barkleys of Broadway with Fred Astaire and Ginger Rogers." Clearly an original. She watched him staring at it. "My prize," she said proudly. "It is the actual movie marquee poster." Then quickly, she turned back. "Why are you here *now*?"

"Sit down. I have something to say."

"Oh really? Do you want me on the chair or the couch or the floor?" She was being coy, but serious. And for the first time, she looked nervous.

"I don't care."

"Then come in the kitchen. I'll sit on a chair in there."

Once they were both in the kitchen, he started to pace. "Ginger…." He paused because he realized that he could actually feel her name roll smoothly across his tongue and then out into the air; it left him feeling disorientated. "I…I need to leave town now, and I want you to go with me!" He looked away. It had all just tumbled out. He let out a deep breath. There. He had said it. He felt better. Then he looked back at her. Her mouth was open, and he could see that she was at a loss for words.

"So?" he demanded too firmly.

That loss for words quickly disappeared. She used both barrels. "Are you nuts? Well, I knew you were nuts, but I thought it was a good nuts. This is not good nuts, this is *nuts* nuts. Why in God's name do you"— she paused for emphasis—"*we* have to leave town?"

Alby felt like someone had slapped him awake.

"Well?" She stood up and put her hands on her hips.

"I think I better sit." He waved a hand at her and they both sat down at her small kitchen table. Figuring the best place to start was at the beginning, he talked about meeting Delarosa, getting the bank job, hiring Lucky and his crew, and on and on. She interrupted him once.

"Delarosa? That's the guy who was part of that mass murder scene in Medford Lake?" Alby nodded.

When he had come to the end of his words, Ginger just stared at him blankly. Then she said calmly, "Wow, you are in some big shit trouble. No wonder you want to bail." She shook her head, taking it in, and he could see she was understanding it. Then her face changed. "Wait. You ex- pect me to bail, too? You're pulling me into your crap? Why the hell would I do that?"

Alby had no answer. He kept his gaze on his boots.

"You are asking a lot," she said very slowly. "I don't have a home. Never have." A complete non-sequitur. She said it with finality, and not a little tinge of regret. A cold recognition was there too. But hope began to grow somewhere inside him.

"The sea? The ocean?" he asked quietly, in a voice he didn't quite recognize.

She looked stunned. Then she started to laugh. "That was the sweetest thing you have said to me yet." He looked at her in surprise. She had a sly smile on her face; how the hell could she smile after all he'd just told her?

"Why Alby O'Brien—are you falling in love with me?"

The room became very quiet. Suddenly all he heard was the tick of a clock. He realized the sound was coming from an old MGM clock sitting on the table in front of the poster wall.

"No. Wait. What did you just say?" He had paused too long and now jumped too quickly. She laughed again. "Why else are you here? Sweep me away on the shining horse to ride away from this nightmare and a mob bank?" He just shook his head back and forth. A resigned no. But she knew he meant yes.

"I know none of this is funny, but you should see your face." This time she had the decency to cover her mouth, but it didn't stifle her laughter.

"Ginger—" he pleaded, as tenderly as he knew how. This stopped the laughter; she saw how serious he was.

"Bad men—who the hell knows who—I have to go." This was a mistake, he thought.

She hesitated. "You came here telling me *we* have to go."

"I — you — you're —" He could see what she was waiting for. "You're the best thing that's happened to me in a long while…no, that's not right…it's…you're…." He was at a loss for words…again.

Staring at him, she slowly unfolded her arms and reached over to touch his knee. He almost jumped.

"I don't know if I can just up and leave, Alby. I don't have much here, but what I have is mine. And I've moved around more than any twenty people I know. I can do it easily, but I just don't want to. I'm tired of being a vagabond. I'm sorry."

He nodded, as if his head weighed a thousand pounds and his neck couldn't hold it up. Now his gaze moved from his boots to the carpet. This was not how he pictured this conversation. "…Never fall in love." He heard The Rule in his head; he should have known better.

There was a long silence, then her hand retreated. "Alby," she said gently, "you can't run. You have to make this right. From what you said, I think you already know that. You have to find the check."

"Who says I can't run?"

"Me." This stopped him. His eyes took her in—a fiery red landscape with twin blue stars focused solely on him. She was serious. And with that single word, it came with a message: she wanted to be with him, too.

"And if I find the check, do what with it? Keep it?"

She got wide-eyed. He shrugged. Then she shook her head like he had said something naughty. "No, that won't work either. You're the only one who can clean up this mess. And until you do, you will not only be on the run, but on the run with a target on your back."

He already was a target with the Jihadists, but she was right. This was different. Damn, he thought, he would have to tell her about that, too.

"Ginger…" he said, then stood up. "Yeah, you're right about this."

She arched her eyebrows and waited.

"Okay, on a few things."

"I usually am," she snuck in, but there was nothing smug in her voice. He nodded.

He had to say it: "But don't talk about this love stuff—"

"I see, I see. Like most men you can only handle one major emotion at a time." He winced. "Sorry. Uncalled for."

There was an awkward silence. "I guess I better get back to Camden. If I can find Lucky…."

"You don't have a gun, do you? How are you going to get it if you find him? Maybe the police…."

"They'll think I'm guilty." She nodded in agreement, which he wished she hadn't.

He felt helpless. Almost subconsciously he pulled out the switchblade from his jacket pocket. Her eyes went wide as she leaned in to stare at it, now stretched across his palm; the silver Arabic lettering was clear to see. "Wow, tell me that isn't—" she pointed uncomfortably at her ribs, then her eyes moved to his right ribs.

"Yeah, it is. Good guess."

"You carry that with you? After what it did? Who the hell gave that to you? Those goons in Iraq?" As he nodded, she carefully reached out and stroked one finger along the rough lines of the ebony handle. She avoided the silver lettering.

"That'll work," she said with finality. He was puzzled. "Saves me letting you borrow my bat."

"You like baseball?"

"No, but I like my bat." She made a fake gesture of swinging a bat and whacking someone on the head, then she repeated and went under for the balls. Alby, like any man would, winced. Pointing at the knife handle, she asked: "Can you work that thing?"

With his right thumb, he flicked the release and the six-inch blade flew out. She jumped back a half-step.

"I've practiced…but more as a hobby."

"Some hobby. You couldn't pick up bowling?" She may have sounded flippant, but her eyes were focused on the knife like it was an alien artifact.

Ginger looked around; near the door entrance where they were now standing, there was a table with several magazines on it. She went and took two and stood them up on a shelf about ten feet away. "Can you hit them?" They were old Hollywood star magazines. "They're not worth anything."

"You're kidding, right?" He was nervous as hell. With a pensive look, she shook her head. Alby, having little idea what to expect, stood up, casually swung his right arm back, like a softball pitcher, then swung forward releasing the knife. It slid smoothly across his palm. It hit with a loud smack, dead center in some movie star's forehead.

Trying to seem nonchalant, she let out a long, low whistle, nodding as if to confirm that he could handle whatever came, but even he was surprised.

As they both stood there, Alby knew she knew that he was think-ing about kissing her. Eyes glued to his shoes, he scuffed the ground lightly and turned to leave.

"You know we never even talked about our vaccines." As he said it, it felt like a deflated balloon had landed in the room. Like he'd just said the stupidest thing he had said in a long, long time.

"Alby. I may be my own crazy, like you are yours, but I am not stupid. Science rules. I have Neo-Vaxxers in my family. It's horrible. I've seen the way you move—you're careful." Then she smiled in a fake but encouraging way. "Come back." He turned to face her, starting to reach.

She held up an arm. "No, I mean later. Clean this damned mess up. Then come back. For me."

"For you?"

"Yes," she said firmly, looking past him. Was she talking to him or herself?

"To do what?"

"We'll figure it out—"

"—fast. We won't have much time."

She puckered up her lips, formed a kiss, and gently blew it at him. Not a clue as to what to do, Alby nodded, and left to do one final round of Camden. But there was a smile on his face. He had felt her kiss.

Clearly, Alby needed a very different approach to finding these three, since his endless circling had gotten him nowhere. And now he knew that the last thing he needed was to be noticed by the cops again. Cops and ghettos were a bad combination. So this time, as he went around the corner to the empty lot, he slowed and stopped, slowly rolling his win-dow down. Halfway.

A man approached the truck. He was young, or younger than Stephen at least. His pants were slung low with underwear showing. The T-shirt proclaimed the name of a band Alby had never heard of.

"You the one looking for Lucky?"

Alby figured subtlety was not worth it. "Yes."

They stared at each other. Taking measure. Alby knew that his hand was less than two seconds from floor to window with the crowbar.

"We know," he jerked his head to show another guy coming from the shadows, "where he is."

"And?"

"I ain't stupid and neither is my pal here."

Alby felt it would be better suited not to follow the obvious response to that statement. "I am not paying—"

"Everybody knows about the bank." He spat the words.

"Right. That's where we worked. I want to talk to him about work this weekend. He didn't give me a number."

The men both laughed and the first guy said, "He'd steal a phone before using one!"

Alby tried a chuckle in response, but even he heard the nervousness in the sound.

"Give us a hundred bucks cash and we show him to you." He put out his hand. By this time, Alby had already gotten the crowbar in his right hand and his grip tightened on the handle.

"Find him for me first."

"Ha! Sure!"

The distance between the men and the truck window was just about right, thought Alby. He could easily get away unless they pulled a gun. He couldn't see any bulges in their shirts or anywhere on their pants, but they could easily have something jammed in their back waistband.

"You want what he stole. His boys have been talking shit all week about some check."

"What kind of check did he say it was?" Alby hurriedly added, "Just making sure you're not bullshitting me."

"$100."

"No. Talk."

The guy shook his head and ran his hand across his hair. "Some weird-shaped check."

They knew. Everyone knew.

"Pay now." The guy's tone said he had read Alby's face. He put out his hand. Alby laughed disdainfully. The man jerked back his hand, like an animal used to not getting the treat and instead pointed down an alley across the street.

"He's in the old schoolyard."

"Show me." They started walking, then picked it up, jogging down the street, then into the alley. He had to rush the truck to catch up, then go slowly behind them. If from all the crap he had seen go down in his life, he had any radar built in, now was the time to use it. Of course it was screaming drive the other way. He ignored it.

At the next corner, they cut left and were out of his sight until he turned the corner onto a dead-end street, facing a closed primary school. On one side of the small graffiti-covered building, he could see the remnants of a playground, though the one streetlight was a dim one; the wind picked up and shook it and the bulb flickered like a warning. They went through the broken chain-link fence and walked briskly, then stopped and looked back at him on the other side of the windshield. He got out of the truck slowly, crowbar in hand. He could barely see their outlines in the dark; the streetlight cast an angular shadow across the ground nearby, next to a broken merry-go-round.

"Where?" He walked only a couple of feet towards them, keeping a few feet distant and looked around quickly so as not to take his eyes off the two men. As he did so, they fluidly moved apart, a pincer movement, one on each side. Alby was still within leaping distance of his truck door but knew they had gotten too close for that to matter. His pulse was getting louder in his ears, and his right hand slid over the handle of the switchblade. But he did not take it out of his pocket. Waving the crowbar, he tried to keep them at a distance, but the way they moved in the settling dark, he couldn't keep his eyes on both.

"You don't want to do this," he said. And that's when the guy on the left feinted a move— Alby saw the glint of a box cutter in his hand before it grazed his right shoulder and he shouted in pain. Meanwhile the one on the right took a swing and connected solidly with Alby's chin. He had always been pretty good in a fight, but two guys was too much. As they hit him, he fell and dropped the crowbar, and all he could think of was how stupid he was. They started to kick him; one had grazed his ribs and he screamed in pain. All that he could think of was his Rules: Four…everyone is a liar. Five…If someone screws you once, they will do it every time.

Then his head hit the weedy grass and his body followed. He could barely feel anything as they rolled him over and started going through his pockets.

"Man's gotta have a wallet."

"He keeps it in his belt in the back. He's the cautious type." The one guy opened it and took out the two twenties, then tossed the empty wallet next to Alby's body.

"Let's check the truck!" They both stood up and turned towards the truck. As an afterthought, one of the men kicked Alby in the side; right on the scar…. And that's when he passed out.

"What the—"

Jagger had stepped out of the shadows of the school building. His Camry was in the parking lot behind the school.

"You said you knew where Lucky was? Where."

"We just—you know…yeah, all right, we know where he is!" The one man looked nervous. Jagger kept the revolver in his right hand in plain sight. Their faces told the truth: they did not have a clue.

"Not far, just a block or two," the other guy threw in.

"Let me guess, you want me to follow you?" Jagger said with a disarming smile. They stopped talking. Their faces were plaster masks of emotional scars; the fear of this moment was like watching glue seep through the mask, breaking through the surface.

"You don't know where he is, which is unfortunate for everyone— except for Alby here. He is the one I know who can find him. So not only have you wasted my time—" he glanced down to see that Alby was just starting to groan and stir— "but… you also saw my face."

"I'm telling you—" one man started, but Jagger slowly squeezed the trigger nice and steady-like, the way a professional does it—neither fast nor slow but just right—then swiveled to his right and did the same thing. Done. True, it was noisy, but Camden struck him as a place with few cop patrols and where sounds like gunshots went unheard.

He bent down next to one man, took a small plastic bag of white powder out of his gray jacket pocket. Feeling around in the near dark, he slipped the packet into the man's left hand. The gun he had used, he placed in the man's right hand.

"Sad, sad, sad," he mumbled to himself, feeling quite self-satisfied—more amateurs removed from the world.

Quietly, he turned to take a closer look at Alby; he was stirring but his eyes were still closed. He did not even bother rifling through his clothes: Alby did not have the check. But he knew who had it, and that was all that mattered. "You're done for the night, Alby. Crawl back to your cage," he whispered before walking away.

When Alby opened his eyes, he rolled onto his side and came face-to-face with one of the guys who had robbed him. Except the guy did not have much face left. He jumped up, and almost fell as he tried to get his balance back. He knew there was a second body near him, but he didn't look.

Pure instinct moved his body to the truck; he leaned on the hood, got in, took a deep breath, and took off, tires screeching. His jaw hurt, his lip felt swollen, the cut in his right shoulder burned like he had been slashed by a hot branding iron; his side hurt from being kicked—it hurt so badly that he was scared to look down and maybe see red seeping through his shirt.

He had nowhere else to go, or maybe his brain was off, or maybe any number of synapses were firing in too many different directions. Who the hell knew. But he found himself pulling into her complex and parking. He wasn't even sure how he had found it. He slumped on the steering wheel and counted to twenty; he didn't feel any less dizzy, so he tried to count to one hundred, but couldn't get past forty. Muscles were locking up from pain. He opened the door and slid out, holding on tightly so as not to fall. He waited until he had his balance and then somehow, one step at a time, made it down the walkway and agonizingly up each step until he stood in front of number 25. He took in a deep breath that hurt everywhere and said to himself: *now.*

An order was an order.

Lifting his left arm, he pounded three times, then leaned his head against the door. A few seconds passed—either she was looking out through the glass peephole or she wasn't home—and then thankfully he heard the lock slide back. He painfully jerked his head off the door just a split second before it opened. Ginger stood in the doorway, the apartment light streaming from behind her. She had her hands on her hips. "Last time, you're early; this time you're late!"

"I…I didn't know where else to go."

"Oh my God, Alby, you're all beat up." She grabbed his right arm, pulled him in, and shut the door while he barely managed to stifle a groan. When she had yanked his arm, it had pulled on the scars that had been kicked. Looking down in response to the pain, he could see that blood was forming a thin line along the seam of his shoulder where the box cutter had caught him. Ginger took it all in, gently sat him on the couch, and began racing about her apartment, practically running from kitchen to bathroom and back.

"I was scared this was going to happen. What the hell happened to you? I know I have the stuff here—come on, come on…." Finally, she found the box of bandages and gauze and came back to the couch. Together, without words, they got his windbreaker off over his shoulders—only to be faced with a bleeding wound. "Box cutter," he said matter-of-factly, trying to sound calm. "Maybe a razor—it's just a cut, nothing went deep." She pursed her lips, her face a jumble of expressions and emotions. Was it concern like anyone would have, he wondered and then winced as she tore open his sleeve, but now she was smiling. "I know this is an odd time to say this—but I always wanted to do that." He could tell she wanted to look away. But she was tough, he saw. She grabbed the cotton ball and soaked it in alcohol and pushed hard on his shoulder blade.

"Jesus Christ, are you trying to kill me?"

"No, you idiot, someone already took my turn at *that* tonight. Now shut up!"

He did so, trying not to show the pain, which, having had such long practice living with a scar on his right side, came easier than he would have liked. Pain shouldn't feel normal, but he had resigned himself to that being his reality a long time ago.

"I appreciate this," he mumbled without thinking, and the minute he said it he knew it sounded stupid. She snorted and dabbed.

"Yes, no doubt you do. I don't often get many wounded gentleman callers."

"But you do get *some* wounded gentleman callers, right?" He was trying to smile but it hurt. A little humor distracted from the pain.

"Give you credit, Alby—you do have an inappropriate, poorly timed, sick sense of humor." She smiled through her worry. "And I like it."

She tore off some tape and then wrapped fresh gauze on the shoulder wound. "No, no guys with these kinds of wounds—usually emotional wounds; the kind you don't see until it's almost too late." Then she glared at him, as if to say, "And you know who I mean."

As dizzy as he was, he kept from leaning back and getting blood on the couch. Lids half closed, he stared at her; she kept busy, now aiming another drenched cotton ball for the cut above his right eye. "You know, Alby. You came to me. For help, right? Now stop being an asshole and let me patch you up. And tell me what happened."

"My—damn it that hurts!" He paused. "My sister calls me that."

"Dorothy? What?"

"Asshole.

"Yes, because she loves you. Alby, it all hurts. Life, luck, bad luck, no luck, no breaks. It all hurts. What the hell happened?"

He told her. Her face was blank as she listened; but when he said he woke up to find the two muggers dead, she almost jumped.

"That is not good. Who saved you? Not a cop." He could see her mind racing.

Her eyes wandering around the room, they both sat in silence.

Ginger finally broke the quiet. "Someone is following you."

They both stopped and listened as if this was the moment to hear something sinister. Nothing.

"I'm not sure…the only creepy thing around here is that neighbor downstairs—you know, the guy who we ran into at the diner yesterday."

"That guy lives below you?" He looked at the floor, as if he could see through it.

She nodded. "Yeah, creepy little shit. I mean, who rifles through people's mailboxes."

"Seemed kind of bland to me." He paused. "Sorry, let me rephrase that—creepy bland."

"We're being paranoid. I'm being paranoid."

Then, as if in answer to a question he hadn't even asked, and more to break the tension, she said, "I learned it on the ships; practice drills."

"Ever consider being a nurse? It probably pays better than the dance thing."

"With all this going on, I may. You seem to draw trouble to you like flies to honey, and yet, and yet…." She paused and smiled in a phonily sweet manner as she closed up the first-aid kit, "…you love me," she finished as if it were a comedian's punchline.

"Stop bringing that up."

"But the man does not say no! Okay. We can put that aside for now. Another time," she said lightly. "Now…now it's bedtime."

Without a word, she went to a closet and pulled out a sheet, a blanket, and a pillow. She was very business-like about it. The pain in his ribs—which he hadn't even mentioned—and shoulder were subsiding from full, teeth-clenching agony to a tormenting wince when he breathed. Dizziness passing, he realized how tired he was. When she came back, she motioned for him to get up, then quickly made up the couch and told him to sit.

After a few idle words and a comment about sleeping in, she was gone. She closed her bedroom door; a moment passed and Alby heard the light sound of a turned lock. A minute later he heard it turn back.

Exhausted, having to sleep sitting up, he knew that sleep was not in the cards. There was no doubt someone was following him—why else was he alive and those scum dead? It had to be the same killers who took out Delarosa and his crew. They could have easily followed him here. He reached over and grabbed the bat she left leaning against the coffee table. He sat straight up and pushed back into the cushions to find some way to get halfway comfortable, but he would have to settle for not totally uncomfortable. He rested the knife, blade open, on his right, the bat, hand on the grip, by his left knee.

And waited.

Directly below Alby, Jagger took out his earpiece for the night. He needed sleep; tomorrow was the day it would all come together. And with the two upstairs, it all wrapped up into a nice package of love and murder.

Friday: 6 a.m.

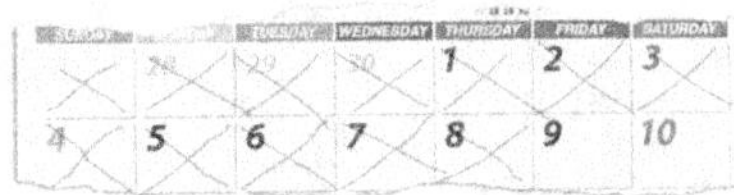

Waking up was like being on a roller coaster moving through quicksand—gravity was grabbing him with an extra pull—slow, ponderous, jerky. It was all the muscles in his body, each an anchor. Alby could not make out where he was—he just knew it was someplace different. So he sat straight up. After a disorienting moment, he realized he was on her couch, bat on the floor where he had dropped it sometime during the night. The knife was on the floor too. Luckily it had fallen on its side and not lodged itself in the rug. The couch smelled of dust and Febreze blended in some odd mixture that was still in his nose. It wasn't the stinky cover-up Febreze like his couch, but clean smelling. He took a deep breath. Facing him was that clock—the one with the MGM lion on it—and it said six a.m.

Falling back to sleep sounded so good but staying here and exposing Ginger was stupid. He had to go. If someone was following him, he had to get away from her.

Light peeked through the slats of the window blinds. He could hear nothing. The door to her room was closed. She was still asleep. He stood and then dropped down again on the couch. Every inch of him ached. His ribs, his jaw, his nose, his cheekbone—all the places they had hit and the parts of him that had hit the ground first when he fell. Steeling himself again, he knew he had to get out before she woke up. And he needed several Advil.

Since he was fully dressed, he only had to put on his boots. Bending over and tugging his laces felt like he was pulling a truck uphill—tying them hadn't been this hard since first grade. With each yank of a lace, his arms felt like they were lifting a ton. The cut in his right shoulder ached. He glanced at his right side. The bandage was soaked but drying. He pulled on his windbreaker over the shoulder with the wound. The bleeding had stopped, which was a good sign.

It took him a moment to realize that every time he moved, he grunted a little. As he finished tying his second boot, he took a deep breath and stood. He shook his head and body like a dog shaking the water off—he was hoping the aches would go with it, but they didn't. He turned to check and see if he left anything on the couch and saw her standing silently by her bedroom doorway, arms folded. She was wearing a bright red full-length silk robe. He could not read her expression but saw the puffy sleepiness around her eyes and a slight crease running down her left cheek from her pillow. She looked like she hadn't slept much.

"Heading out?" she asked casually.

"Yeah…Lots to do." Ugh, what a stupid thing to say.

"I'm sure." There was a moment's silence. Then she said, "You know, I've had a lot of set-ups aimed at getting in my pants but last night's was a first." He could tell she was trying to be funny.

"Thanks for—" and he waved his good arm around like a small windmill, feeling awkward and stupid.

"You going to the police?"

He looked at her, expressionless, and said nothing for a very long minute. Was this the moment? That second where either a yes or no steps up to make it all crystal clear. Run? Stay? Call his Handlers now? Say something, he ordered himself, just say something. Nothing was clear.

"Thanks for patching me up." And he truly meant it; he could not recall the last time he'd asked anyone for any kind of help. He knew without a doubt that this was not what she wanted to hear. But now he felt like he needed to get away from her as fast as possible.

"We're not the types to ask for help," she said slowly as if reading his mind. He nodded slowly, and silence filled the room.

"I have to go…."

"Sure, of course you do. Door's right there. Same place as it was when you knocked on it last night, looking like a train wreck."

He walked to the door and moved to put his hand on the knob and turned back to her. She was standing by the couch now. "Thanks," he said. He just couldn't think of anything else to say. She nodded, as if acknowledging his response, arms now folded again.

He started to open the door. "See you later."

"I work till four. Then back here. Got some food shopping planned. Exciting stuff. Stock up for the storm like every other idiot." While she made it sound like she was reading an agenda, they both knew she was inviting him back.

"I gotta try and fix this…." The words slipped out. He was surprised at the pleading he heard in his voice.

"I know…and what you need now is rest," she answered tenderly but firmly. She reached one arm out and took his hand. "So get this over with." She looked at his face, her blue eyes locked onto his, silently squeezing his hand. A long moment passed. "Then we can talk about going or staying." And with those words, she cracked open the unspoken with a flourish. Then she reached down and handed him her bat, which was leaning against the couch. But he gave it back to her.

At the threshold, he turned halfway and caught her staring at him.

"What?" he asked, unsure.

She inhaled, then smiled a sad but warm smile: "Alby, we're both broken. And that's okay." She inhaled, then loudly exhaled. "I need a dance partner."

His heart dropped with a thud. "I don't dance."

He didn't know what else to say. Nothing seemed adequate; every word sounded empty in his head.

She looked at him like he had just fallen off the dumb truck. "I'm not talking about dancing."

For some reason that was way beyond him, she saw him as the partner she needed. He got it. All he could do was nod in silent agreement. Then he left.

He got in his truck, feeling every movement as he hauled himself in. By the time he turned on the radio he was already on the main road.

He turned it up—all everyone was talking about was the nor'easter heading their way. He never understood the obsession everyone had with weather—something you couldn't do anything about. It usually annoyed him, but now he was grateful because it took his mind off how much he hurt.

Driving back to the cave, he kept checking to see if anyone was following him. When he got to the back parking lot, he saw the screen door swiveling slowly back and forth, occasionally slamming into the door jamb—his usual alarm clock. When he left here last night, he figured that he would never be coming back. Now here he was, like it was a regular workday just about to begin.

He went in and started taking off his clothes—almost in slow motion to keep from passing out from the pain that every movement caused. But as he did so, he realized that the slowness was not because he felt tired. He did not feel tired at all.

He had slept… with no nightmares. Again.

A second night with no nightmares.

This time it felt a little like a loss, a death, the loss an addict must feel when they realize they have ended their addiction. But he figured that he could get over that feeling pretty fast.

In the silence of his room, he paused, feeling an odd kind of emptiness. There were the regular sounds seeping in from outside—a tree rustling in the wind, the screen door, a murmur of traffic from Route 70. But what really silenced him was the realization that a break had occurred, a break between where he had been and where he was right now, this very second. Ginger had called it "in-between time" at Dorothy's. She was right. He had grown so used to being frozen in life. The movement back into it was jarring.

Then he was jolted back—if he was being followed, he might not have much time. He headed to the shower.

After the shower, he put on a few new bandages as fast as he could and went outside into the bright sun. Around the corner of the back side of the garage, the full, choking mess of sounds came in from the late morning commute. He decided to go to Starbucks and load up on coffee. When they had seen each other last, Stephen had told him he had some errands to run this morning, and they had no jobs planned until Monday.

When he got back, he parked his truck as close to his back door as he could and as out of sight as possible. His round trip to Starbucks had been an all-time record for a place that always seemed to live at its own speed. He had gone so fast he hadn't even stolen any essentials—just in and out. The Advil was kicking in; he could walk without the pull of aching. Leaving the tray of coffees on the ground, he went inside and got his folding chair, then dragged it back out. It hurt too much to lift it.

In the cool morning air, perched on the wooden chair that was always on the verge of breaking, he felt his brain was empty, except for one echoing truth: If he was being followed, they would be here soon enough. Maybe they had followed him to Starbucks. Come on, you bastards, he thought. As uncertain as he was that was what he wanted, he didn't see any other choice.

Taking out his switchblade, he rolled it back and forth in his palm. He kept his eyes on the black and silver as he flipped it in his hand, over and over. Occasionally he would swivel and toss it into the tree. The handle would wiggle like a fish tail. The knife edge didn't reflect the light, it captured it. He smiled. He had impressed himself at Ginger's. He practiced a few more underthrows. He nailed almost every time—except for one that bounced off the tree. But he was adding velocity, making the small tree wobble; one throw sent the robins in their nest off in a clatter of chirps and protests.

The coffee was medicinal. If he could pour it directly into his veins, he would. Mind wandering, he started thinking about her red robe. She had looked incredible. Even the pillow crease on her face made him smile. He felt a slight flush rise up his neck as he tried to picture what she looked like without the robe, as in, what kind of underwear did she wear? Lacy. Red. He cringed when he realized how long it had been since he had seen a woman in her underwear.

The knife slipped past his grasp, the blade barely falling between two fingers. He let it lie on the patch of grass next to the asphalt. Who the hell took those muggers out? He didn't think anyone had seen him—from what he could tell, in Camden no one saw anything.

Come to me, he repeated in a quiet inner voice.

All this pain and death for one lousy piece of paper with someone's signature on it.

He pulled out his iPhone and surfed.

He thought of her little dance at the Zumba class— "Pick yourself up…" seemed true beyond words for his life. Fred Astaire and Ginger Rogers? He recalled watching their movies as a kid; but the memories were faded, like the old black-and-white films themselves. Going onto YouTube, he searched for "pick yourself up," recalling that had been the main lyrics of the song she had sung and danced to after he had fallen.

It was nearing noon when Stephen showed up; Alby was just finishing the second Fred and Ginger movie called *The Gay Divorcee*. He paused, clicked off YouTube, and put the phone in his pocket. If Stephen had a special ringtone made for him it would be his crappy muffler.

Stephen walked up, the regular tray with four coffee cups in his hand, and then stopped in his tracks as he came around the tree. "Holy Christ, Alby. Who the hell beat you up?"

He took a cup from the tray. "Thanks. Bar fight. Someone was being less than patriotic."

"Are you kidding me? What's the blood stain on your shirt?" Stephen pointed at his right shoulder; the gauze was leaking. "You're patriotic?" Alby looked at his shoulder and nodded as if this was normal. "Scratch."

"Let me guess. Because of a lousy bar fight, I have to do the hard work—again. And unload all this shit that's been in my truck alone, right? Anyway, doesn't matter—all our jobs were cancelled because of the storm." Stephen was trying so hard not to show his concern, but he gave up. "What the hell happened to you? You never go to bars."

Alby was not giving him an inch. "Yeah, now I know why."

Stephen looked at Alby with a deadpan expression on his face. He bent down slowly, picked up the knife, and tossed it into the dirt between his feet. It bounced on the ground and hit his shoe. "Hey, I need that toe!"

Stephen huffed resentfully and walked away.

Silently, Alby followed a few feet behind Stephen as he got into the loaded truck and started to drive off. He turned momentarily, gave a dirty look at Alby, and then headed the truck back around to the front and onto the street.

Getting rid of Stephen had been his first goal; pissing him off was necessary. Alby knew he had to be alone. If someone was tracking him, then it was he and he alone they would find.

Come and get me, he thought, then realized how stupid that sounded. He wanted it to all go away. One sleeping nightmare had been replaced by a waking one.

Moving the folding chair back a few yards, he turned it so he could see his front door and the narrow driveway that led from the front. See them coming, he thought grimly.

No gun, just a knife. Maybe he had surprise on his side; he began to lay out a plan for when they showed up. They had to be following him; they knew it had to be his crew and they were betting that Alby would lead them to the right member of the threesome. His mind wandered, then he realized that if they came around the corner, he'd have time to run into his room, and escape into the garage. What good would that do? What was he going to do, beat them up with a punching bag?

Maybe he should have taken her bat.

As he sat there, he unconsciously started to throw his knife into the tree harder, with more effort. Focus on that softball-style swing, he thought, nice and easy arc, swing upwards and release. A long swing buried the blade deep into the bark. It took a good yank to pull it out.

Waiting like this was like being in a bad scene in a movie. He tried to breathe deeply as he sat there, waiting. Knowing his idle mind would travel into a thousand dark rooms, he threw the knife into the ground at his feet and took out his iPhone again. Back to YouTube, The Great Distractor.

Again he typed "pick yourself up." The first time, he had found the song and watched the movie *Swing Time*. It was corny but kind of fun. Searching some more, he found an entire collection of Astaire movies. Ten of them. He stared at the tiny screen and started on a different one—the day was warm and the sun was high; the broken chair leg wobbled but he used that to sway slightly to the music. However, Alby made the mistake of leaning to his left a little too much and felt a bolt of pain run up the right side of his body from the scar. His shoulder decided to ping him at the same time to remind him that it hurt, too. He wished his body would just shut up.

Fred suddenly started to sing to Ginger and he leaned forward, cupping the phone like an icon in his palms and bending over to watch and listen. After the movie was over, he re-played one musical number several times—it spoke to him. He had no idea why, but something in it felt sad and romantic all at the same time. Being bad at something, like being romantic, didn't mean he couldn't try.

He sat back as the credits rolled through and smiled; he was beginning to see the charm in the old movie thing. And this one song and dance—"Pick Yourself Up"—really spoke to him.

How strange that he would find himself here, waiting for the Angel of Death and enjoying an old musical. He shook his head—it was like having the ironic twist of his mom's worldview sitting next to him; this was definitely her kind of thinking.

When he got hungry, he went inside to rummage around the small refrigerator. A yogurt. A couple of crackers in a box on the shelf. He had the urge to drive to Starbucks again, grab a tall coffee and a sandwich. True…they were a rip-off, but at least it was good food and close to him. Or he could order via VaxDash, but he didn't want any cars coming in.

Instead, sighing, he sat down and ate what he had found. At dawn, this waiting had seemed inevitable. Now, at midafternoon, he was getting impatient.

As he ate, he kept one ear tuned to the back parking lot. He glanced around the room. The furniture was worn and ragged; the tools were piled on cheap metal shelves. Even the tools themselves were low-quality cheap. There were no windows to look out of—only the inner door and a broken screen door he just couldn't get himself to fix.

What was the difference between this and a jail cell?

Next month was when he was supposed to re-up the lease. Would he even be alive? Not a good thought to have, he mused. But life had made

him a sharp-edged realist, and he knew without a doubt that today might
be his last day on this earth.

Knowing this, though, was not helping matters. As his mind wandered from YouTube distraction to panic, he couldn't help but wonder what a real life would look like—a life where he didn't need to hide in a cave; where he could, maybe, get a real job, a real apartment, go out, have a date.

This shook him to his senses. What right did he have to "normal"? He had gone through too much. Now he was thinking about a damned lease! Last year, when he had signed it, the real estate agent asked if Alby was going to do anything to fix up the place.

"Why bother?" At the time, he hadn't known why he had said that: ignorance, being a contrarian, feeling grumpy—who knew. But now he saw it in a different light: this was his prison. He had no right to change it. He didn't own it…it owned him.

Eyes tired from watching the tiny screen, he put the phone down on the ground—where were the bad guys? This was like some bad *Westworld* episode where everyone was waiting for the showdown. Waiting was its own slow death from unknown hands. Alby went back outside, re-situating the chair so that it faced directly towards where any car would enter from the front.

The sun was nipping the treetops and splitting into random beams. After coming to the end of another Fred and Ginger movie a few minutes ago, *Top Hat* this time, he suddenly realized that he had been staring absently at the robin's nest in the scrawny tree again—watching yet another episode of the sitcom—their comings and goings, the upward and downward chatter of the baby birds, the toils of twigs and worms.

Then his phone rang—Fat Joe. Only because he needed a break from the anxious boredom, he picked it up.

"O'Brien? You answered? You have a goddamned shitload of nerve to not answer my calls."

"Why should I answer? I know what you're going to ask and I have nothing new to tell you."

"I heard one of your crew was murdered at the docks." Alby sat up…and had to stifle a moan of pain as he did so. What was Fat Joe talking about? "Yeah" was all he could come up with in reply.

"Well, with Delarosa gone—"

"Have any idea what happened to them? Who did it?" There was a deep silence like the line had gone dead. Finally, Fat Joe, sounding almost remorseful, said, "No idea. Who knows with you loser contractors." Alby realized that of course Fat Joe knew; he worked for the bank and its mob owners.

"All I do know," Fat Joe had regained his tough guy voice, "is that you better be here with the other two at eight sharp. I'm shorthanded." He paused and spoke in a quiet voice. "If you show up with the other two, I'll give you a bonus."

Alby heard what the man had said, but his mind was so caught up with what he'd just heard about who he figured had to have been Chance that he remained silent for a second. He knew that Lucky was just too smart to get caught. Maybe it had happened when he was fleeing from the liquor store. Who knew. Now, he only briefly wondered, yet again, whether he was being set up. He was so damn tired of this.

"How much?"

"A thousand bucks."

"Okay," and with that Alby clicked off. There was no escaping it. Money was the ultimate bait.

It was nearly seven and now Fat Joe had forced his hand. If he was going to try to make this right, then it meant one last visit to Camden. The obligation of fate called him. If Chance was dead, would Lucky and Darnell even be there?

Waiting all day for nothing made him feel stupid. No one had come for him, no bad guys, hired killers—nothing. Even Stephen hadn't called or come back. The only thing that had happened was the wind picking up, and the sky and clouds getting strange.

Like a toss of the dice, one last visit to Camden—with no reason to gamble they'd be there but he had to try. There was no Rule he could invoke in this situation. Picking up his knife, he got up slowly to move to his truck. Seeing the light changing, starting to elongate the shadows, he thought of the musicals Ginger loved so much and realized that as much as she—or, let's face it, he—wanted the magic of song and dance and those stupid moments, Alby just could not buy it: life was in color, not black-and-white, and color meant unknown options and they all had unknown outcomes.

Would either of the remaining two be so stupid as to show up for work?

When he pulled up to the lot where he'd first picked up the crew, the light was on the edge of disappearing. But there was just enough of it. And he could hardly believe his eyes.

Right there on the corner was Lucky, arms folded, big toothy smile flashing like an evil license plate. Next to him stood two younger guys, both lean and dangerous-looking. They kept averting their eyes, nervously hitching up their way-too-low pants and playing with their hair. How the hell could this be? thought Alby. Chance was dead, only Lucky shows up—where was Darnell? Alby's mind emptied out like sand in an hourglass—this made no sense. Yeah, he had come back with some hope of finding the two of them. But the truth was that he had not expected to see them, especially Lucky. Why would he be here if he was guilty? This made no sense, or maybe there was something he just didn't know.

Alby slowed to a stop, rolled the window down halfway, and decided to play dumb. He spoke to Lucky. "Where's Chance and Darnell?"

"You tell me! Who the hell knows? I looked for them today, nothing. So, I got me two other guys."

"Fat Joe won't like this."

"He won't care. He needs bodies. Sooner we get there, sooner he can fake some papers and get us going. Hey, we get paid Sunday morning, right?" The way Lucky said all of this—Alby felt like he was play-acting, making it up. It had to be Lucky who had the check. No one else was left. There was little doubt in his mind that somehow, Darnell had met the same fate as Chance. So how was he going to get the check back from Lucky?

Instead of answering, he just waved them to the back of the truck. Why would Lucky show up? It made no sense. But Alby's intuition had kicked in—Lucky had it—he was the survivor, the animal. And he wouldn't be going back if he didn't have a plan. Which meant that he might very well have it on him right now.

As he drove to the bank with this new crew in the flatbed of the truck, the sunset clouds were getting that blue-gray tinge that made them look like swollen bladders, the rain ready to burst but the clouds not quite ready to let loose. The wind had quieted down and the air felt tightly wound, the kind of air that made it feel like you couldn't breathe right. He turned on the radio. With his now-undenied fascination with the nor'easter, he'd set it to the all-weather station. The storm had slowed down south of Atlantic City, but in typical nor'easter circling pattern, it would pour twice over Marlton—hitting Cherry Hill around two a.m. —or so they said.

His cell phone rang—the vibration made it flop a little on the seat like a guppy out of water. With his free hand, he grabbed it and fumbled for a second, turning the volume way down as he did.

"Yeah?"

It was Stephen. "Uncle Alby, I'm glad I got you. Was the crew there?"

"Sort of. Why?"

"Chance—just heard on the news he was found dead in the Delaware."

"What?" He made his voice sound surprised.

"They think it happened Wednesday."

"No way. How did he die?" The line went silent; clearly Stephen was reading something. "Not sure. Suspicious cause. In the Delaware River. Investigation ongoing."

"Thanks. Gotta go." As he clicked off, he knew the threads around him were unravelling fast. It was already in the paper. Darnell was nowhere to be found. He had known several stone-cold killers in Iraq and it was clear Lucky was the same breed, except his uniform was a chest of medals made of a mile-long rap sheet.

What about Delarosa and his crew being murdered? That wasn't Lucky. Or Darnell. That was someone from the bank. Lucky and the bank people. All the air around him smelled bad.

He was almost there now. He needed a plan, but his thoughts seemed more in sync with the growing chaos of the wind and trees blowing all around him—and like them, his thoughts were starting to gain in fury. He suspected that Lucky had the check, but he couldn't be sure, and he didn't know who was shadowing him. Basically, he knew shit. That made him the victim, an all-too-familiar role he was getting very, very tired of.

In that second, his thoughts finally went from flight to fight and they cemented there.

True to form, Fat Joe did lose his temper when Alby showed up with two new crew members. He and Lucky stood a good distance from Fat Joe as he huffed and puffed, went into the trailer, came out and waved them all to the building. "Just get dressed; you show them." Lucky briefly gave Alby a look that could only be described as triumphant, but just as quickly, his expression became sullen again as he headed off to the building to get himself and his "buddies" suited up.

Alby turned to face off with Fat Joe: "Delarosa…dead. Chance… dead. Darnell…probably dead." Alby didn't mention the bodies at the schoolyard. "Which means that I probably have a target on my back."

Fat Joe just stared at him, giving nothing. Alby had to decide how much to reveal. He went for it: "I know it's a check; a missing bank check."

Fat Joe's neck got redder, but his eyes and face were blank. "No idea what you're talking about."

"And you know it's my guys, don't you? Don't worry, I've got a plan. Don't worry." Alby had no idea what he was saying. He was actually bullshitting himself.

Still watching Fat Joe, he caught the look on his face that said you *are* a dead man. Alby shuddered inside and took this as his dismissal. He wasn't sure why he had said that about a plan—he had no plan. Truth was, he felt completely lost. He just nodded and left the trailer. Once outside, he went behind the trailer and stood near its main window. He didn't bother to try and look in the window. He just leaned as close to it as he could, ignoring the rising wind that was rushing around him and listened in. He had guessed right—Fat Joe had called someone.

"Lucky is here," he said frantically into the phone. Silence. "Best time to come is near their lunch break around one. The storm? Not sure what it's going to be like then. Yeah, a good cover. What? Yeah, most of 'em will be on the top floor. Yeah, after midnight." Silence.

Alby hurried to his truck. His hand gripped the switchblade handle so hard it made his shoulder ache. With the wind beginning to pick up, he walked back to his truck as fast as his body would let him, climbed in, and headed back to his cave to wait.

At the end of Fat Joe's call, Jagger placed his phone back in his jacket pocket; this was moving at the right pace towards the neat and tidy conclusion he wanted. He complimented himself on having turned it on vibrate to keep it silent. Sitting in the middle of the three stalls of the Marlton Diner's ladies' room was not the place to hear a male say hello.

About forty minutes before, he had pulled the slide lock out of the stall door closest to the bathroom door and enlarged the hole that was left so that he could see when she came in. Before that, he had wasted the day parked on the other side of Route 70, facing the garage, and not understanding why Alby had remained at home. He had seen Stephen come and go. So he had decided to pass the time by starting the process of tying up loose ends. First loose end? Packing. Then taking out the tap dancer, with the finale being at the bank.

But, around seven he had gotten hungry, so he had picked up another Rueben and headed back to his apartment. Just as he had arrived back at the complex, she passed him driving out. Without a thought, he had turned and followed her. She drove to the diner and started her shift. Once he saw which end of the diner she was serving, he had slipped in and sat at the opposite end, near the exit and the bathrooms—that was a gift you didn't pass up, he thought. Eventually she would head to the bathroom and he would simply shoot and rob her. One bullet and done. He'd even wished that he could have placed some blood from Alby nearby, but some things worked out on their own. Once they checked her apartment, with a bloody towel or two from the beating he got, he would be a prime suspect anyway.

But now Fat Joe's call had changed his plan. The dancer would be easy to find after he'd gotten hold of the check.

He got up quickly and opened the stall door, walking out with a confident air. Just then a woman opened the bathroom door and stepped back, startled; Jagger gave her the "innocent/helpless" look and watched her own fear muscles retreat.

"Took the wrong turn, thought it was unisex, sorry," he said as he slipped past her. One turn to the exit and he was back in the parking lot.

As he got into his car, his phone rang again: Kurtz. This annoyed him—why wouldn't the Owners let him remove him? He answered, and of course, Kurtz was a nervous mess; he knew he was the walking dead at this point.

"You've got to go to the bank tonight. I found Lucky and he's meeting me there to hand back the check."

"Why?"

"Why what?"

"Why is he handing over the check?" He could hear Kurtz's breathing get fast and shallow. "Because he called me and tried to bargain with me to pay him to get it back." Kurtz's voice had a pleading tone.

Lucky couldn't move the check, a scenario Jagger had suspected would happen.

"What time are you meeting him?"

"Around one a.m." He was going to have to take out Kurtz, too, and sooner than he thought. He was too impulsive and his fear was too loud—Jagger didn't need to see his face to read it. The Owners had picked a real loser to run this bank; he felt like he was running the Human Resources Department for them.

Clicking off, a familiar sense of satisfaction slid over him; he always felt this near the end of an assignment. This was going to work out better than he had thought. All the bodies would line up neatly under the cover of the storm. And the last stop? Break into her apartment and remove her just for the hell of it. Check in hand, he'd pack and head to the airport to wait for the private jet; hopefully the nor'easter wouldn't cause a problem with that. The plan was very neat. He liked that. And since it would all be done in less than the week he would get that bonus—maybe in money or maybe in time off with pay—those were the only two forms of gratitude they ever showed. "Thank you" was not in their vocabulary. Jagger didn't care. He was a professional, just doing his job. He needed no thanks.

Still, one piece was not in place: Alby. While he had intended to go back to his apartment to eat and pack, Jagger could afford to make a slight alteration to his plans, one that pleased him. The check was where he needed it to be—safely at the bank with Lucky. The urgency was gone. In a few hours, it would be in his hands. Loose ends started with Alby.

Thinking of his list, he had two parts: setting up and shutting down. The shutting down could now begin. After he finished packing, he put on his London Fog raincoat; it had started to rain when he had gotten back to the apartment.

Stephen had called ahead to tell him that he was coming over, despite Alby's protests. Alby complained that he was half-asleep, but in reality, he was just nervously biding his time until he went back to the bank. Even with the intermittent wind punching trees in all directions, Alby could hear the Toyota truck and its bad muffler a mile away. Suddenly, Stephen loomed inside the doorway.

"We gotta talk," Stephen said ominously. "What shit has been going down around here? You've been acting strange for days."

The screen door slammed behind him and then flew open again. Alby was more familiar with the door doing its noisy act, but Stephen jumped at its banging. Still, he stood there, dripping, the wind and the increasing rain blowing into the room.

"Close the damned door. You're ruining my new carpet."

"What happened to Chance?" Stephen, ignoring his request, looked both belligerent and scared as he asked.

The screen door slammed again. Alby turned for a moment and looked around the shoddy, sloppy room—the view that his nephew had taken in every time he had been here—chipped and stained coffee table, binders on the floor, the rickety card table where he ate, clothes that he hadn't packed spilling out of a broken bureau, racks of construction supplies and tools with cleaning supplies and kitchen goods all squeezed into one corner. What a shit life he led. Nothing he didn't already know, but for some reason he now saw it with different eyes.

"Stupid," he said like a non-sequitur. Was he referring to Chance or himself?

"And dead." Stephen shot back.

Alby shook himself to focus on Stephen. "That would count as *really* stupid in my book."

Stephen finally threw his arms up in frustration. "You know something's going on, some bad shit. Everyone around here knew it was a mob bank." Except for me, Alby thought. "Everyone knows they play for keeps. What happened, Uncle Alby? It's eleven at night. You're not going to bed. Where're you going?" He glanced around.

This stopped Alby's flow of verbal redirection and non-answers. Stephen rarely called him "Uncle."

"Gotta go talk to Fat Joe. Alone. You know that. Rule number —"

"Spare me, Alby!" Alby started to get up off the couch, as if to leave. Stephen blocked the doorway. He paused, then spoke each word slowly and deliberately. "Why so late? Where's the knife?"

"What business is that of yours? It's just a knife. I keep it with me. Anyway, it's a kinda hobby."

"Yeah, I guess you don't even notice, do you? That thing you always keep in your pocket? Remember when you moved down here and had to sleep in my room until you found a place." Stephen paused to scan the room with disdain. "Late at night I would hear the slap, slap, slap of that knife opening and closing. You thought I was asleep, but I watched you flipping it and catching it. It took me days before I found that switchblade hidden in your drawer."

Alby looked away, not sure what to say. He didn't like his nephew knowing too much of the dark stuff. "As I said, a hobby, kinda different, I guess...." His voice drifted off at the absurdity of his statement. "Started it in Iraq."

He snorted in disdain. "Iraq. The great black hole you hid in for nearly three years. You have never once told me about your time there."

"Some things an uncle doesn't share with a nephew."

"Christ, I'm twenty-seven! Then, let's not forget about the punching bag. When did that start? I don't ever remember you boxing when I was growing up."

"Helps me sleep," which was half-true.

"Who knows what the hell you do with it." Stephen was starting to sound exasperated.

"Punch it," Alby said matter-of-factly. How could he get Stephen out of here? He was on a rant. "Your grandmother gave it to me!"

"Then you showed us that scar on your ribs the other night. Holy shit, Uncle Alby! That happened in Iraq?"

Alby nodded but remained silent, no longer moving from the couch seat, which was farthest from the doorway. When it came to Iraq, he had nothing to say. He shrugged.

"The design on the knife is Arabic—I took a picture of it with my phone and looked it up. The letters spell 'God is great.'"

"Allahu Akbar," Alby murmured. Then Alby laughed, far too loudly, like a shout laced with a taste of bitters. For some odd reason, it never occurred to him to translate the Arabic. It had just never occurred to him to learn Arabic at all. If there was a God, and as far as Alby had seen there wasn't, why did those words tear his side open?

Stephen looked at Alby. "I know about the bank. The mob have their ways—I went to high school with their kids. Too many people have died since something happened last weekend at the bank." Now Stephen took a step into the room. And then Alby felt like reality shifted when Stephen went on.

"Borrow my gun." Stephen patted his jacket. Alby felt his body clench. The storm outside was getting louder.

"No guns." Alby paused, then asked angrily, "What the hell you are doing with a gun anyway?"

"Let me come with you."

"This is something I can only do alone; anyways I thought you swore off asbestos." Alby tried to lighten the moment and failed.

"We are a team…" Stephen almost pleaded, hating how desperate he sounded and realizing the minute the words left his mouth that it wasn't going to get him anywhere with Alby.

But Alby was getting desperate too. He had to get rid of him, so he faked some anger. "There is no team here. You're my punk-ass nephew. An employee. A shitty one at that. You were right—I was a hypocrite and didn't follow my own Rules. Rule number two: never work with family." He paused. "You're fired."

"That's Rule number seven," Stephen said almost automatically. He stood, silent, looking down. Then he moved over to block the doorway again. Rising slowly from the couch, Alby looked him up and down.

"What the hell are you doing?"

"I'm not sure."

"Well then, get the hell out of my way so I can—you know," and he waved his arm around in the general direction of the door. Stephen realized he had no leverage, so he moved aside and opened the door; as he took a half step outside to grab the flopping screen door, it whipped back and forward like lightning had struck it. It smacked Stephen squarely on his left temple and down he went, crumpled and dazed, straddled the doorway on his knees, one on the gravel and the other on the carpet. The rain flew in like a flood of water mosquitos.

Alby jumped up, but as he went for the door, a gloved hand with a pistol in it hit Stephen like a hammer on the temple; he bent forward as if to fall and screamed.

Before Alby could move, Jagger stepped from behind the screen door, holding the door in one hand like a whip, a gun in the other, aimed at Alby's chest.

"FBI," he said with a smile that wasn't a smile as he now burrowed his gun in the hair of a moaning Stephen.

Stephen could not help himself, "Like hell you are," he said in a daze from his kneeling position.

"Okay, maybe not." He waved the pistol in his hand before it landed with the barrel somewhere in Stephen's hair.

Alby felt his blood freeze; it was that asshole that Ginger had flipped out on at the diner. "What the hell are you doing here?" Alby felt the stitches that held his life together ripping apart; this was like living Ahmed's house scene all over again.

Stephen groaned and swayed unsteadily—again someone he was close to was too close to death. This all had a perplexing sense of logic to it, but it was the logic of the insane and it did not make any sense to Alby. "What the hell is going on here?" he demanded, confused.

"I came to appeal to you. After all, we want the same thing. Just hand it over and we're good."

Stephen's voice was shaky, he tried to sit up but was pushed down by Jagger who now had the gun behind his head. "Ow!"

Neither Jagger nor Alby spoke; they just stared at each other. Eight feet apart, Alby calculated. Too far.

"Hand what over?" And as he asked, Jagger could see that Alby was genuinely confused; this confirmed his suspicions. Alby was a person of shadows, so he'd had to be sure. He was not the one who had the check: Alby had never been a part of it. In fact, Jagger read something else—it was different—he was wrestling with something emotional, something important…love? Jagger had only seen that once, in Rio with that messy family affair. So it was Alby and the tap dancer.

"Aloysius. Really. Do we need to play that game?" Now he stuck the pistol barrel in Stephen's ear, like it was a Q-tip. "The check. The blank check." He paused to study his face.

Stephen groaned, "What the hell is he talking about?" He turned his head sideways as if cracking his neck; a line of red blood was moving down his temple, breaking into small tributaries of a red river as it moved down his cheek. "I think I'm bleeding."

Jagger looked down at Stephen. "Ah, yes, Stephen, Stephen—the erstwhile youth, the struggling artist doing construction to make his mom happy, the only innocent around, right? You can put on quite a performance when you want."

Alby blurted out, "You're an artist? Since when?"

"Since every hour I'm not with you!"

"You any good?"

"Would I be working scut jobs and paving driveways if I was?"

"Explains that screwy girlfriend. She an artist, too?" Alby growled back.

Jagger got a positively gleeful look, like a child who'd stumbled upon an unattended candy store. "How well do you know your nephew, Aloysius?" Alby just stared, trying to figure out what to do. He could not reach for the knife in his boot. The wave of helplessness took him to Baghdad; he tried hard, but he couldn't stop his hands from shaking.

Jagger used his free hand to wave his index finger at Alby. "Tsk, tsk. No reaching for the knife. Scissor, rock, paper. Gun over knife."

How the hell did he know that?, Alby wondered. Then Alby had this feeling like his radar was going off—why was the guy staring at him like that? "Okay, okay..." said Jagger. "You don't have it. That makes the last stop easy."

"I had your number," Stephen muttered.

"Yes, and Uncle Aloysius has his secrets. Working for Bechtel managing and rebuilding a Baghdad power plant, mixing with the locals, a lonely guy who starts having lunch with a guy named Ahmed who has a pretty unwed sister—oh it sounds like some perverse version of *The King and I*!" Jagger caught himself getting too excited—he tried not to focus on his love of old musicals when working. Like a metal Q-tip, he wiggled the gun in Stephen's ear for amusement. "But Stephen The Innocent has a few secrets too —"

Alby felt his mind snap to focus and his hands slowly stopped shaking. He had hurt Stephen. Every Rule went out the window. At that moment, Alby decided he was going to kill this man. Alby had never had that thought before in his entire life, even in the roughest of moments. This guy was a professional killer so the idea of believing he could do it made him even more determined. This man was his.

Of course, if he didn't kill Alby first.

"Stephen, do you have something to tell your beloved uncle? Hiding the truth is a bad thing, especially from family."

"I have no idea what you're talking about, you crazy fuck." Stephen said, not moving his head, every word slow and labored.

"Then let me be the one…." He pulled the gun from his ear, keeping it trained on his head. "Stay on your knees but face forward. I want you to see your uncle." Stephen did so, shuffling a few feet forward out of the doorway on his knees, ripping one knee of his jeans on the sharp door jam. He looked at Alby briefly then looked down again.

The gray man suddenly looked very pleased with himself. "Stephen works for the FBI."

Alby kept every muscle on his face frozen. This guy was getting nothing from him.

"Oh, you're good at this, aren't you? Let's go a little deeper. He is in fact, a part-time informant. Is that true, Stephen?" Stephen also kept his expression frozen but after a long pause he slowly nodded.

Alby couldn't help himself: "The feds? You must be kidding me."

Stephen tried to stand, but the hand on his shoulder and the snub-nosed gun now back in his ear, held him on his knees. Not taking his eyes off the ground, he spoke slowly: "It happened while you were away. These guys came around and asked me to keep an eye out for Arab guys who might cause trouble. Times were tough: they offered good money, no strings." He shrugged. "I did part-time jobs, construction, all types. Met the kind of fly-by-night guys they wanted from the Middle East."

"Did you ever…?"

He nodded and quietly said, "Yeah, a couple of guys. Just called this special number, left a message, and a few days later, they were gone."

"Why the hell would you get involved in something like that? For pocket cash?" Alby shook his head in disgust. This stirred Stephen to try and twist away from the gun. For a second, Alby watched as Stephen turned his head slightly and raised one hand towards his jacket on the side blind to the gray man in the London Fog raincoat. Alby knew what was about to happen but was too slow. Stephen suddenly twisted and tried to pull the gun from his jacket. Jagger had had his full attention on Alby and was caught off guard. But only for a split second. With a fluid, juggler-like motion, Jagger tossed the gun to his left hand and used his right to follow Stephen's hand into his jacket, cup his hand, hand on hand, tight on Stephen's gun.

Stephen jerked his arm back, but Jagger pushed against it and the room snapped in two with a sharp crack of the pistol. Stephen looked shocked. Alby jumped a quick step towards Jagger, but Jagger's pistol was steady, aimed at his stomach.

With a huge, satisfied smile, Jagger stepped a half step back; Stephen's hand and gun were partway out of his jacket, but it and his hand were covered in blood. Stephen's face went pale as he fell forward onto the floor. Jagger reached under Stephen and yanked out the gun; he wiped the blood on Stephen's windbreaker.

"So, here's the deal, Aloysius," Jagger said casually, pocketing Stephen's gun and then nonchalantly wiping a little blood onto Stephen's shirt, as he lay face down on the dirty carpet, writhing slowly in pain. Every one of his groans tore through Alby.

"Stop calling me that damned name." He could see the blood was coming from around Stephen's right collarbone; it was seeping out of his jacket as he lay there.

Jagger ignored him. "Now that I am sure you don't have the check, you're useless to me. I could kill you, but you know, you've been one of the most complex people I have ever dealt with. That means something. You actually challenged me. As much as I want to kill you, it would be unprofessional. You're a rare amateur who knows what you're doing. You're competent. You deserve to live." Alby couldn't believe it; this cold-blooded bastard actually admired him? Jagger prodded Stephen with his foot and rolled him onto his back. Stephen was half-conscious, clutching his upper shoulder. "But I have a plan for you—one that works for everyone. Well, nearly everyone."

Alby nodded, distracted by trying to figure out how fast he could reach and throw his knife.

"Stop thinking about the knife and listen." Alby's head jerked up and he felt a chill along his spine. "As for the check, first the cops will interview you. They will come and give you a very, very hard time. They will think you did it, or at the least, you killed Lucky's crew. Getting out of that mess is your responsibility. I am sure you can do it. Me, I let you live—that's my gift. You may go to jail, but you live. I think that is about as fair as I can get."

"You sure are impressed with yourself," Alby said with a tone that sounded like cracked ice. He was scared but he'd be damned if he was going to show that to this guy. Stephen's moaning was getting him angrier by the second. He just needed to lift his right hand to get to his jacket pocket, but not with that gun aimed at his chest. He would have to take the bet that he could get him with the knife faster than the guy could pull the trigger. And Alby knew fate was against him. This was the guy—the one single guy—who'd done all the killing. That scared him, too. And he was Ginger's neighbor. Suddenly, that thought shifted what had been full-blown fear at what was going to happen to Stephen (and him) into high-gear anger. This was the sonofabitch who was creeping out Ginger, who had kept him alive on the playground—just so he could keep tabs on him.

"I guess Delarosa found that out, too."

Jagger ignored him. "Remember what to tell the cops, Alby, just remember…." As Jagger said it, it didn't take much guesswork to know that once he had the check, this very ruthless sicko would probably come back and kill them all anyway. Including Ginger.

"How do I know your word is good?" But he was gone. Without a word, he had disappeared into the unlit parking lot. It was at that moment that Alby realized the usual dim light over his small lot was out. The killer had probably taken care of that, too.

Alby ran to Stephen. He ripped open his shirt. The wound went through the shoulder; he reached for some rags by the sink and pressed them down on both sides of the wound.

"Those things are filthy," Stephen complained and grimaced.

"Shut up. A bullet will kill you faster than some germs."

"Geez, that hurts." Stephen grimaced again, his lips rippling through a series of movements of pain, but he did not emit a sound. Tough kid, thought Alby absentmindedly. The moment hung on, punctuated by

the broken creaking of the screen door in the blustery wind, half off, half
on, swinging and slapping as the storm built.

"Stephen, what the hell—"

"I knew he wasn't FBI. I was trying to watch your back."

"You're really a snitch?"

Stephen groaned as he tried to press the rags on his shoulder.
"Could you use a word from this century?"

Alby stared at Stephen and all he saw was a mask of pain there.
Then, slowly, a crack appeared, and Stephen smiled. As the smile grew,
he started to laugh, and loudly. Alby surprised himself by laughing too.
Stephen sputtered a moment, laughing had to hurt, but then just laughed
some more. They were both laughing like they had just heard the funniest
joke ever; they were more alike than either of them knew until right that
moment. Then Stephen sputtered and groaned. Alby saw the color drain
out of his face.

"You're just upset I never split the snitch money with you," Stephen
said weakly, as he tried to ignore the pain.

"You have a sick sense of humor."

Stephen coughed. "Family trait."

This caused them to laugh again, but more quietly this time.
Stephen winced as he laughed, the blood now seeping from around the
rags. Alby had to do something—he knew he had to call an ambulance but
knew just as much that nothing was going to go right if he didn't get over
to the bank as fast as possible.

"One more thing —"

"Christ, kid, you're shot. Shut the hell up!"

He shook his head no. "I'm sorry for the other night. She was out
of control and I was a wimp."

"Now you bring that up? Don't worry, I enjoyed spooking her."
Alby lied; it had been a horrifying moment to share that scar with people.
No one had ever seen it but the hospital staff and the Handlers.

Through his pain, Stephen grabbed Alby's arm, almost desperately
trying to speak through the pain. "My phone. A number I have in it…only
one with a 202 area code. Use that number. Call the FBI—he told me his

name was Jagger. They must have some file on him. Christ, he had an FBI badge with him when I first met him—where the hell did that come from?"

Alby's expression grew hard; he didn't want to include the feds in any of this, but now it was unavoidable. The Jagger character—now he had a name—was as efficient a killer as he'd ever seen in Iraq, and some of those mercs were plain old murderers—like the guy who admitted he'd enlisted just to have the license to kill.

"Turn this sonofabitch in. They can get him," Stephen pleaded.

"Sure, good plan," he lied to Stephen as he grabbed a roll of paper towels and exchanged the rags for a fistful of them. For no reason, he noticed that the red of the blood contrasted with the pale floor and white cinder block walls. What strange things the brain registered.

Alby's mind turned to the check. The damned blank check. He might still have time to set this right, though he wasn't sure how. So much of his adult life, he had simmered and stewed in resentment and anger and felt powerless in the face of it, but this was the worst yet. He ran his hand along the knife in his pocket. "I have to go to the bank. This shitstorm has got to be stopped now."

Stephen nodded and tried to sit up; Alby helped prop him up against the wall next to the door. He groaned loudly.

"Sure, sure, but could you do something for me first?"

"What?"

"Call the goddamned ambulance!" Stephen shouted. Alby nodded, called 911 quickly, cut through the questions and just said there was a shooting and gave the address. Then he clicked off and tapped in the 202 number and as he heard someone say, "Hello, hello?" he put the phone on Stephen's good shoulder, next to his ear: The FBI would come, too. He and Stephen exchanged one more look, then his eyes drooped and he passed out. Alby headed back into the room and out through the shower into the garage.

As Alby left the garage, he could hear an ambulance in the distance, hopefully for Stephen. He hated leaving him, but there would be too many questions and he'd be no good to anyone in jail.

Friday: Just Before Midnight

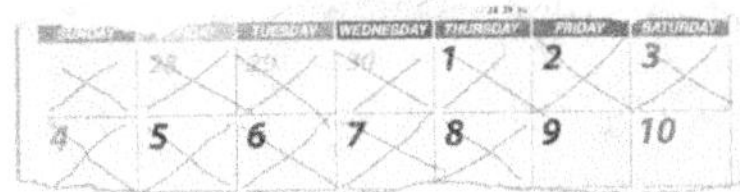

When he got to the bank, the party was full on. The oversized dump trucks, plastic sheets in huge rolls, empty 100-pound metal containers—all the equipment was out; the crews had gone in and the parking lot was empty of cars but full of trucks with closed-lid dumpsters. The wind was teasing the trucks by blowing loose trash and smaller plastic rolls around their wheels.

As he pulled into the parking lot next to the bank, he put on his yellow slicker and got out of the truck. He pushed through the thin line of young fir trees that acted as the back fence to the bank. The wind was starting to make the thin trees kick, whip, and dance like some clumsy chorus line—still not much rain yet but by now it was only a matter of time. Despite what he'd told Stephen, he knew the storm was serious. He'd seen enough nor'easters growing up and done enough house repair work after a few to not take them seriously. He figured the bad weather would help him sneak in.

Getting in the building was not the problem; it was getting a hazmat suit and finding Lucky that was the problem—worse was knowing Jagger was there, too. But he had no choice and waiting outside was not an option. Lucky was in there with the check. His only chance was to find him before Jagger.

Ignoring any pain now, he sprinted across the parking lot, weaving behind cars as he neared the construction trailers. Small branches were dropping all around him.

Whatever he did, he knew it was probably going to cost him his life. In a cool burst of logic, it made sense: you only get a certain number of misses.

Alby saw that Fat Joe's trailer was lit up and decided to check it out. The rain was coming in fits and starts—it felt like someone slapping him firmly in the face, inhaling a breath, and slapping him again.

As he got under the window, he could hear two voices. Fat Joe's was louder. Although he couldn't hear the words, the sentiment was clear; Fat Joe started loud, as he always did, then got real quiet. Then he heard Jagger's voice—that saccharine, deadpan voice. Fat Joe started cursing. Alby sidled back to a small window; he grabbed an empty plastic bucket and stood on it. It was wet and wobbly but he had to see.

Inside the trailer, Jagger was facing Fat Joe. He held one hand, half raised, with all five fingers pointing upwards, like a stop sign at Fat Joe. Fat Joe looked like a deer at a hunting convention. Alby could barely hear them, so he pressed his ear against the wet glass, which was disgusting: "…There's nothing I didn't tell you."

"You idiot. Didn't it occur to you that they might come back?"

"What kind of loser robs a bank and then comes back the next week?"

"As you said… 'Camden.' He's here to meet up with Kurtz." Jagger paused and watched Fat Joe's face. "When they got here—why didn't you call me?"

Before Fat Joe could even get halfway into a shrug and speak, Jagger flipped his stop-sign signal and dug those fingers right into the area under his rib cage, and twisted his hand. Fat Joe screamed and bent double like a card table with its leg kicked out. Jagger pushed him down, stepped back, and threw his leg forward, kicking him in the balls. Fat Joe fell to the floor and lay there, a small, pale, beached whale, moaning and gasping for air. Jagger wiped his hands on his pants pocket as if he'd gotten dirt on them. He stared coldly down at Fat Joe who looked like he would not get up—most likely he'd just get hit again. He rolled onto his back, half-turned to Jagger in a defensive position.

"Get up, you pig. I won't hit you—at least not right now!" Through the window, Alby heard Jagger laugh, and even competing with the building wind and rain, it didn't sound like any laugh Alby had ever heard. It reminded him of his Handlers' laugh, like a person who was half-dead. Unconsciously, he tightened his grip on the knife.

Fat Joe slowly got up, leveraging his weight on his desk. As he straightened up, he wobbled, resembling a drunken Humpty Dumpty.

"We're suiting up and going to find those men." Men? Jagger paused and mused to himself. Animals.

"This isn't part of my job, I don't want any part of it—can't you handle it?" Fat Joe regretted his words the minute they left his mouth. He hefted himself straight up on his desk, trying to put some distance between them.

"Fat Joe, I am going to take that old belt off you, watch your pants fall, and beat you to death with it. That's your choice." Fat Joe looked at the floor and said nothing. "Good. It's not that fun for me…well, that's not entirely true. Get two suits."

"It's not that simple. There's a guard in the lobby where the suits are and inspectors all over the place. The procedures are strict as hell." Fat Joe couldn't stop rubbing his stomach where Jagger's fingers had gone in.

"Fat Joe, you greased their palms with the Owners' money. How stupid do you think I am?" Fat Joe nodded. They left the trailer and Alby stepped off the overturned bucket. It fell over with a clatter. He held his breath and froze. But the wind covered up any sound it made by adding its own clatter.

Once again, he sprinted across the lit parking lot. The light poles were swaying in the wind. Water sprayed on his face. He stopped when he got to the concrete wall next to the entrance. The doors to the lobby were enormous; the long glass floor-to-ceiling led to a massive-looking dou-ble-door into the building. Rows of temporary lockers and a rack of hazmat suits were located behind the guard sitting at the lobby security table. The two men stood at the guard's desk. Alby pressed his ear close to the corner where the glass met the concrete, but it was all muffled. Fat Joe pulled out some documents and gestured at Jagger, who looked innocuous in his beige raincoat. With his suit he resembled a policeman. Alby realized that this man could turn himself into anyone he wanted to, as if he had no real identity at all. He watched as he shook the water off his shoes, ignoring Fat Joe and the guard.

After a few minutes, they all moved past Alby's view. He waited, covering half his face with his hand, trying to avoid the stinging rain in his eyes. Then the guard came back, and eventually the two men emerged in hazmat suits and headed toward the plastic sheet that looked like a giant translucent membrane cutting the lobby in half.

Moving quickly, Alby rounded the corner and entered the lobby. The guard jumped and turned. Alby smiled like they had met before, shook the water off his yellow rain slicker, and walked confidently toward him.

"Hi, my crew is upstairs." The guard stepped forward and crossed his arms. Alby had seen a lot of rent-a-cop night guards in his time; he had even been a night guard himself for a short while back during community college because he hadn't been able to get fix-it work to save his life back then and he needed money. He was 19—a time long before his fiancée, his mom, and Iraq. After six months on the job, he had met most of the local guards as they changed shifts. For several nights, and with the bored obsessions of youth, he had kept his brain busy organizing all the rent-a-cops into categories. This guy in front of him now was an "I'm-a-cop-I-swear" type. His 9-millimeter wasn't hanging in a holster but stuffed in his belt as if he had mistaken southern Jersey for the Wild West.

Alby had seen what a real guard looks like—the merc company guys who wore uniforms but carried no ID; the other private security companies that only hired former SEALs because they knew their stuff. This guy was the back-spit of a guard, in a uniform he was bulging out of, fat and over-confident. If Alby hadn't been so nervous, he would have laughed—the guy even had a piece of food clinging to his unclipped moustache. He looked at the desk and saw an unwrapped sandwich and chips strewn around.

"I'm late. Gotta go!"

"Where's your suit?"

"There, there!" Alby gestured at the rack, a little too quickly. A cocky grin spread on the guard's face as he licked some food off his mustache, his tongue moving like a lizard's.

"Those are extras. Everyone gets theirs in the trailer next door. Why don't you know that?" The guard sounded smug. "Where's your papers?"

Alby slowly walked towards him, arms outstretched. The guard lifted his one arm up, as if warding Alby off. Alby kept walking towards him even as the guard's hand slipped down to his waistband. "I just gotta get up there. I'm late and Fat Joe will kill me."

"You don't want to see him anyway; he's got a bad case of angry going on. With some guy that looks like a cop."

Jagger. Alby was already late.

"You gotta let me in. I am in some bad trouble with Fat Joe," he pleaded.

The guard shook his head no and smiled the self-satisfying smile of a powerless person who believed he held all the cards. What the guard didn't know was that the man in front of him was angry, desperate, and just stupid enough to gamble. As Alby stepped forward, his left leg seemed to give out and he started to fall on one knee. In that moment, he reached into the right side of his work boot. Now the guard took a step forward.

"What's wrong?"

"No…It's okay, I'm —" Unsure how much force to use, Alby just swung his arm up in an fast, arc-like, softball motion, and slammed the metal end of the switchblade into the guard's chin. He fell like a popped balloon. He hit the ground so hard, Alby worried that he'd cracked his skull on the tile floor. When he went to check, he was out, but breathing.

It had been a long time since Alby had hit anyone; one of his secret frustrations about what happened in Baghdad was that he had never even taken a swing at someone—the Handlers being the primo first in the line of a long list of bad people he had met there. He almost felt bad for the guard but he had to smile nonetheless. Enough with the assholes, enough with the low-lifes, con men, scumbags…his brain was racing, he may not know what the hell he was doing, but for the first time, it started to feel right.

Still, as he hurried over to the hazmat lockers, it became crystal clear: this was his last chance to back out. He slowed down. Run away, a voice said as his hand rested on the locker handle. But the voice was distant. Lucky had been playing him for a fool most of the week. Jagger had threatened Ginger. He had shot Stephen. People were dead. For one more moment, Alby paused. But he could not stop seeing that smug smile on the bastard's gray face as he had held Stephen down. Alby banished the voice into its grave.

Taking a deep breath, he slowly and carefully began to put on the hazmat suit. Although he'd only had to wear a suit like this in Iraq once or twice during the power plant work, he hadn't forgotten how to do it. Muscle memory kicked in and he allowed his mind to wander. What hit him first was that this had been the worst week in his life—which was saying something. But what was odd as hell was that it had also been one of the best.

It had been years since had he even thought of the future; but now, he did. And Ginger was in it. The endless nightmares, his mother's death, the deaths in Iraq—it was time to jettison it all—at long last and long overdue. It had become harder to keep it all than to just let it go. It was like looking at his own past in the rearview mirror. Even Iraq.

Leave it behind, Alby, leave it behind.

He could run, but not without her. This was it. Either move forward or not at all.

The moment stretched, but he kept going through the motions, pulling up the final zipper in the front. He paused.

Life paused.

He chose moving forward.

If he survived.

He had the suit halfway on when he pushed it too hard and put a foot through the leg. He started cursing, then paused, and pulled out his iPhone. Quickly he went on YouTube and typed in "putting on hazmat suit." Up came about 100 videos. He watched the one with the most views.

Propping up the phone horizontally on a plastic chair, he grabbed another suit and this time got it right. True, he had to hit replay a dozen times, but it was fast. The hardest part was attaching the heavy respirator canister. It was different than the one he had used in Iraq. This one looked like a giant fire extinguisher—and he had trouble locating the on switch. But it seemed like some people used the tank, and some didn't. Probably cheap old equipment Fat Joe got anyway. Once he had the suit on, he pulled the hazmat helmet over his head. The pumping, whooshing sound from the oxygen tank flooded his ears and his senses. He almost jumped out of the suit, when a sudden gust of air pushed open the glass door—an uprooted bush from a planter outside had knocked against the door and bounced inside onto the floor next to the guard's body. With the roar of the ventilator making him nearly deaf, Alby's imagination filled in the sound of the storm.

It was like being an astronaut with gravity working against you, slow and heavy. He could hear so little, and with that one sense being blocked, the world became almost too visual. To prove it, he glanced outside: the storm was in full blow. Minus all sound, it resembled a full-color silent film—he watched as the plastic silently rippled and made slashing movements like a sail cut loose in the wind, flailing wildly. Branches flew by the lobby window. As an afterthought, Alby slowly walked over to the guard's inert body and dragged him—the fat load of barbecued chicken that he was—away from the entrance and behind the desk in case the glass cracked. He was still out. He'd be safe there.

Before he went to unzip the white wall, he slowly made his way to the gold-lined case where the building tenants' names were listed. The EVP, that was what Fat Joe had said—no name…just a title. And there was only one EVP listed: Joseph Kurtz, EVP, Suite 401. He went up to the first zippered plastic chamber; being translucent, you could just make out that the room ahead and the other beyond that one were empty. He stepped in, zipped it back up, then unzipped the next chamber, repeating the action until he entered the hall of the first floor. He saw the showerheads in each enclosed space. None of those in Iraq. But the videos had shown that too— the suits got covered in the tiny flakes and needed to be rinsed off.

No one was around.

But now instead of a silent world inside the helmet, it was almost too loud to think. The droning sounds of the fans echoing inside the plexiglass were deafening. With the faceplate limiting his view, turning his head constantly was the only way to keep watch for others. The elevators would be out of service and the stairs to the fourth floor were lined with plastic, too. The only exposed areas were the ceilings where the pipes were covered in a hardened foamy substance—stale, white icing filled with poison.

He climbed the stairs slowly. Some men passed him, a few nodding. But everyone was basically isolated in their suits. The rest of the workers would be on the upper two floors. And that thought returned him to the matter at hand. Damned if he knew what had possessed Lucky to come back here; the fact that he'd brought two cronies meant he was desperate. Lucky had a plan. Alby didn't. Worse was the fact that clearly, something was unfolding, but he had no clue what it was, which could be good he realized; there was no expectation of him showing up.

Now *he* was the wild card. That was his only advantage.

As he got near each landing, he slowed down and tried to see if anyone was near the stairs. The doors were open and pinned back behind the plastic sheathing.

He could feel the pressure building up in his ears, from the storm picking up outside most likely. Inside, the ventilators threw the air around, making sounds like moaning ghosts. The whole environment was a flooding of sound, but the sound was only the air, going in and out, in and out. It was like his boxing—the sound jabbed in and out, in and out. His ears ached.

At the fourth floor, he left the stairs and was about to pass a door when he saw a shadow. Quickly, he flattened himself against the wall. A few seconds later, one man came by with a dolly struggling to move a sealed barrel. It was Fat Joe—he knew it was him from the man's height and the waddle in his step.

Heart racing, visor fogging up from his heavy breathing, he entered the floor and made his way down the hall, in the direction from where Fat Joe had come.

Large, open double doors of an executive suite were at the end of the hallway; they were sheathed in plastic with large zippers resembling a Frankenstein-like jagged scar running down the length of the sheet. Behind it, he could make out a smaller chamber that looked like it was wet with dew—probably from people washing their suits off before leaving the room.

With one gloved hand, he gripped and crumpled the plastic and used his other to grip the large zipper, pulling it down very slowly. He could see faint shadows of bodies moving on the other side of the layered translucent sheets. He stepped into the wet chamber. He could see a shower valve on the lower right but didn't touch it.

After one failed attempt to get ahold of the zipper tab on the other side of the chamber, using both of his gloved hands, he finally gripped it. Then he very slowly pulled it down, but only halfway: he wanted to see what was going on before going in. The first thing he noticed was the sound. The noise in this room was even louder. He saw the huge ventilator in the center, with one tube going to the ceiling, the other to the open room, loudly sucking the air clear. Then his eyes scanned the large office space. He saw three people a few yards away, at first all indistinguishable in their white hazmat suits.

But instantly, Alby figured out who one of them was—Lucky was the one near a wall. The visor revealed his dark black skin, sharply contrasted against the white suit. Another black man—probably one of the new workers—stood beside him. The man with his back to Alby and facing Lucky had to be Jagger. As Alby viewed the room, bodies stopped as if in mid-motion. It was then that Alby saw the profile of a gun in Jagger's left hand. Suddenly everyone was in motion again. Lucky yelled something and pointed at Alby. Jagger hesitated, then turned to look, allowing the third guy to throw his full body weight at him.

Jagger almost managed to sidestep his lunge. But the bulky outfit slowed him down. The other man clipped his right shoulder and they both tumbled to the floor. Jagger tried to swivel the gun around. Alby could see the gray electrical tape ripped from the side of his leg. Clever. He'd taped the gun outside his suit.

Without a thought, but with his nerves starting to shake, Alby stepped into the room: the gun went off. The new guy Lucky had brought that night jerked and fell like a fresh fish flopping on a dock; red oozed out onto the white suit like oil rushing from a geyser. Lying prone, Jagger propped himself up on one elbow, looked over, and saw Alby; his gun moved up and over to align with Alby. Alby watched his lips form his name. He was in direct line to a gun barrel and had nowhere to go.

Coming from Jagger's other side, Lucky threw himself on top of him, knocking the weapon out of his hand. They both rolled on the ground and the gun flew across the room, hitting at an angle on the plastic sheet that sloped up the wall—the momentum carried it up, then gravity slid it back to the floor, where Alby was closest to it.

Alby stumbled for the gun as Lucky and Jagger struggled; they looked like giant doughboys with their white suits and clumsy movements. What became clear was that Lucky knew how to move in the suit, while Jagger did not. Lucky managed to wrap his one leg over him in a pincer-like grip and was pounding his face mask with his fist.

Moving within an arm's reach of the gun, but still clumsy in the suit, Alby's boot slipped on the plastic sheet flowing from the walls onto the floor. As his glove grabbed onto the gun, he reached out to push himself up with the other gloved hand, only to rip more of the plastic sheet. Half his body fell into the room behind the plastic curtain.

He caught a glimpse of the exposed dark wood paneling—and saw something other than wood. There it was: a wall safe. A small metal handle jutted out from it; the door was about a foot wide. Alby didn't hesitate; he reached over and grabbed the handle, but he didn't need to turn it. The door had been left unlocked and even slightly open.

This was the check's home.

Struggling back through the plastic, he saw the two men in a wrestling bear hug. Lucky squirreled one of his hands free to disconnect Jagger's respirator from the oxygen tank on his back. Jagger heaved his whole body, bucking Lucky off him, but Lucky scrambled to his feet.

Lucky stood back—his helmet bobbing. Alby knew immediately that he was laughing.

Jagger was twisting and turning, clearly choking.

Suddenly, Jagger spun around, got to his feet, and clamored to pull off his helmet. It came over his head, revealing a sweaty haired gray man gasping like a fish.

Before he could get his breath back, Alby raised the gun and held it on them both. He hated guns, but he hated being dead even more. He held it loosely in the fat glove like he didn't want to grip it too hard. The suit made his finger so fat that only his pinky got around the trigger.

The rush of the air inside his helmet was joined by the rush of pulse and heart: this was it.

"Don't move, either of you!" he yelled over his respirator and waved the gun at both of their bellies. The three of them formed a perfect triangle.

Jagger grabbed a portable respirator off the gas mask in the center of the room and put the piece in his mouth, breathing so heavily he was slightly bent over.

Both men were about four feet away. Feeling a lift on his back heels, Alby knew that if he backed up, he would be on the plastic and would slip. Someone had to make a move and it was not going to be him.

"Don't move," he yelled. Jagger smiled around the metal mouthpiece giving him air. Alby turned very slightly his way to face him and yelled: "You shouldn't have shot my nephew. He died." Alby wasn't sure why had just lied, but it felt right. He was pissed, and it felt good to lie to this bastard.

Jagger yelled but it was slightly garbled by the mouthpiece. "I *should* have killed him. Save you the lie."

How the hell did he know he was lying? Alby pointed the gun at Jagger's chest. "Lucky, give me the check!"

"I don't have it!" he shouted—so why the hell he was smiling?

"Like hell! Give it!"

Jagger looked at Lucky. Even though he was coughing, he had a look of satisfaction on his face, as if he too had known what Alby had guessed: Lucky trusted no one and would never let the check be anywhere but on him.

Lucky unzipped and slowly took off his hood; he coughed but quickly put the mini-ventilator over his mouth. Jagger and Alby watched Lucky intently as he unzipped the front of the suit, reached in, and pulled out the bank cashier's check. Jagger smiled. When Alby got a closer look at it, he saw the tape over the ripped check.

He laughed so loud it fogged his plastic mask. Ripping it had made it worthless. It was no good. All this for a blank, no-good check—it was nothing more than a funny-looking sheet of paper. And this cocky murdering idiot put me here, he thought; he was tempted to shoot Lucky out of spite. But he knew Jagger was the one to worry about.

"I want you to come over here—see that tear? See the safe in the wall? You were going to put it back, weren't you?"

Alby gestured to the wall safe. Lucky hesitated; Alby stepped sideways to open a space for him to get to the wall. They kept their triangular formation; each moved a step left. Jagger slid around so he stood where Lucky had, and Alby stood where Jagger had been.

Lucky hesitated. "Do it!" Alby shouted.

Ever so slowly, Lucky reached past the ripped plastic sheet and slipped the check into the safe.

"Close the door." Lucky did so. "Turn the tumbler." Lucky looked blankly at him. "Turn the tumbler!" he shouted.

Although he was shouting, Alby managed to keep his tone controlled and threatening at the same time. Now he knew why Lucky had returned. "There was no way that would be open unless Kurtz left it that way. Is that what's going on? You return it? He pays you off and everyone's clean? All these dead people, this asshole"—he tilted his head at Jagger.

Lucky laughed like a car backfiring. "Yeah, you so smart. I ain't dead!"

Jagger shouted back: "You're already dead and don't know it."

Then Jagger shrugged at Alby as if to say, what now? Jagger coughed and laughed simultaneously. "You're scared. And you should be." His words were getting clearer, even though he could not take the oxygen mouthpiece out. "I can tell you hate guns. Put it down. Everyone walks"—Jagger glanced at Lucky—"except one."

Alby wasn't sure what was next; he was just trying desperately to hold onto the moment and not lose focus.

"How about I call the cops. Turn all your asses in."

Jagger looked down and shook his head, almost remorseful. Without the helmet, he didn't have to yell but his words sounded clumsy coming out around the mouthpiece. "What an amateur. Here let me show you—" and with that he lunged at Alby, and using his weight, grabbed and pulled his arm and body forward, forcing him off balance. Before Lucky could move, Jagger circled around like a dancer, wrapping and spinning Alby into an almost flamenco-like embrace to where he had his stomach to Alby's back, grabbed his arm, and pointed the gun at Lucky's head and pushed Alby's finger on the trigger. Lucky's visor cracked and turned red.

Alby felt like a showroom dummy being thrown around. With the ventilators going, the pistol sounded like the thunder peal of a storm far away but with a kick that made his wrist ache. He felt himself struggle to push Jagger off him, but Jagger had him pinned back against the plastic and the wall behind it. Things started ripping off the walls and ceiling.

Momentarily turning his gaze away, he looked back at a fallen Lucky, red blood dripping from the open visor onto the white suit and the plastic behind him—like a splash of ketchup on a translucent canvas. Then he felt Jagger's grip around him tighten as they wrestled slowly, awkwardly. With the gun still locked into his hand, Alby twisted and fell into the air ventilator machine, knocking the hose that went from the machine to a hole in the plastic where it shot the asbestos fibers into sealed containers. Alby jerked his arm back, but Jagger was stronger than his smaller frame suggested. He pushed Alby's arm sideways and pulled his finger back again. The gun went off, and this time it hit the sub on the floor, whose lifeless body jerked.

Alby finally yanked his arm away, but as he did so the gun flew from his hand and across the room—Jagger pushed him aside and moved for it. Without even thinking, Alby tugged at the zipper on a small chest pocket on his suit and pulled out his switchblade, opening it as fast as he could just as Jagger was bending to pick up the gun.

Jagger turned and pointed it at Alby's head.

"I just did what we both wanted," he yelled. "Now the check is back. As if nothing happened…." Jagger's face was red with the labored breathing, and the air was getting visibly thicker from the fibers cascading from the broken hose.

Out of nowhere, the sound of someone moving through the plastic chambers rose above the noise. Jagger and Alby both looked at the chamber in surprise and saw someone pulling down the zipper to enter the suite.

It was Fat Joe, still lumpy and dwarfish in his hazmat suit. "I emptied that dead shit out of the barrel—holy crap!" he shouted as he viewed the scene—two dead bodies, blood dripping off the plastic like paint, the hose jerking around like a dancing snake as it is spewed out poisoned air.

Alby knew this was the moment: he knelt on his left knee, rotated the knife handle in his hand, and threw upwards, another softball pitch. Just like he had practiced. Jagger had just turned to face him as it hit him in the chest. He looked down at the handle on his left side below his collarbone just above his heart.

Jagger took a step back, like he was drunk. Surprisingly to Alby, Jagger did not look surprised; he just casually glanced down at the knife wobbling in his chest, as if he were browsing in a store. Then he calmly gripped it and pulled it out. Holding it, he seemed lost as he examined the knife, especially the tip, which was smeared with a mixture of red and silver.

Again without thinking, Alby ran at him and when he got close he pictured the boxing bag and started jabbing—left, right, left, right, left, right, in rapid succession. Jagger fell back and dropped the knife but Alby realized it wasn't enough. He threw himself at him and knocked him down, both landing on top of Lucky's dead body. Alby pounced on his chest, his body completely on top of him. Jagger's hand kept groping for the gun. Fat Joe was shouting, waving his arms like propellers, mouth moving but no sounds coming out. Yet he didn't move. Instead, just stood there, still holding the empty barrel. The rush of sound from the ventilators, the pounding of his pulse in his head cut Alby off from the world around him. Jagger pressed up from beneath him like he had when he had thrown Lucky.

Alby kneeled and pushed Jagger down, pressing one knee on his chest. He saw his knife within reach and grabbed it.

As the oxygen mouthpiece fell out of his mouth onto the ground, Jagger moaned, "God, not a loser like you." He seemed shocked. On his face, Alby now saw an absolutely true expression of stunned surprise.

"God isn't listening. He's got ear plugs for shits like you." With that, he drove the knife deep into the suit, holding him down as he struggled.

Jagger jerked upwards and gasped, his face going pale, his eyes rolling back into his head then closing.

Alby rolled off Jagger, grabbed the large hose flopping around from the air ventilator, and shoved it over Jagger's mouth. He held it there while he struggled and choked.

After what seemed like an hour, but was probably only a minute, Jagger's body stopped jerking.

Alby rolled off Jagger and fell onto the floor on his back. A moment passed. All he could feel was the pulse and throb of air and storm matching his own heart and pulse. He could not tell what had just happened—had he just killed a man? Looking to his side, he saw Jagger's pale face, even grayer than before. It seemed so oddly simple: Jagger wasn't human so it didn't matter. The thought was so cold and rational it surprised him. But he had no time for any more thoughts or one bit of remorse.

But what was he supposed to do now? There were three dead bodies. Two were dripping with blood. The gun was on the floor, not in his hand, and Fat Joe, a loose cannon in all this mess, was looming nearby. Behind the plastic visor, Alby's face was covered in sweat—a rivulet rolled down from his forehead, along the bridge of his nose, to his chin. What would Fat Joe do? Alby wasn't sure he'd beat him to the gun, and the knife was still lodged in Jagger's chest.

Fat Joe smiled so wide and happily you'd have thought he'd won the lottery, his fish-like mouth looking like a happy grouper fish. He clapped his gloved hands together.

"This makes my day," he shouted. "I hated that fuck. I was pretty sure my number was up after tonight anyway." Almost casually, he reached over Alby and picked up Jagger's gun. "Old," he noted as he tossed it from hand to hand. "Classic .45. WWII, I bet."

Alby quickly pulled the switchblade from Jagger. He didn't look at his face. Without thinking, he wiped the blade on his white hazmat suit, leaving a wide brush stroke of bright red. It was an unconscious action. He slipped the folded blade into the pocket and half-zipped it.

"Ever win the Lotto?" Alby, numb, shook his head no. "Yeah, I figured: you don't strike me as the kinda guy good luck finds." He laughed and the sweat in his visor blocked off half his face. "You're gonna get a big break." Fat Joe nodded at the bodies and then the bags. "I thought you were a Grade A asshole and loser." He paused to look at Alby. "Maybe you are!

But not tonight." Fat Joe seemed almost giddy. "This is great, just great," he repeated over and over.

"What—" But Alby couldn't get the words out. The suit felt heavier than ever. He avoided looking at Jagger: he'd never killed anyone and didn't need a reminder. Fat Joe must have caught his look. "Forget him. You just saved more lives than you know. Including mine! And no one can say Fat Joe doesn't pay his debts." Waddling over to the barrel he had carried in, he lifted the lid of the 100-gallon drum and glanced inside. Alby followed his gaze and then jumped: There was blood—the third guy that had been with Lucky. Alby had forgotten about him.

"Yeah, he was on lookout and Jagger took him down." He cleared his throat and the visor filled with fog for a moment. "We load them all...I can fit three more bodies in this drum. We can get this done fast." Fat Joe kicked Jagger again and laughed.

Together, they slowly lifted and squeezed the three bodies into the barrel and sealed it—the dead man's smile on Lucky's face was something he'd never forget; it was like seeing the Devil's son dead as a doornail and happy to go to Hell. The second guy went in pretty easily. Fat Joe used his feet to push and kick Jagger into the drum. He seemed to relish every kick. Now, the drum was so full of bodies, they couldn't even completely tighten it. They had to lean on the lid just to get it in place.

"It's break time, so no one's around; let's take them down the elevator."

"Elevator is turned off."

Fat Joe waved him off and yelled, "Got a key!"

Walking down the hall pushing the dolly with two barrels on it, Alby felt like at any moment it was all going to go wrong, and he was as good as dead.

Fat Joe hit the button for the basement.

As the doors opened to the car garage, Fat Joe waved him around to follow him with his dolly; after a short walk in the garage, they turned to walk up a ramp with a large dump truck parked at the top. Alby almost stumbled as the storm's full rage hit him—rain poured onto his helmet and reverberated around his suit like bouncing marbles. It was disorientating.

Two men in hazmat suits, head gear off, were loading drums on the back. They pounded each lid with a hammer to make sure it was sealed. As the storm whipped around they both looked harassed and anxious. The wind was coming in a series of violent puffs strong enough to knock someone off balance like getting nudged with an elbow. Alby and Fat Joe stood silently and watched the men.

Even in the dark and rain, the two men loading recognized Fat Joe. He took big steps with small legs, and the loose suit only exaggerated his unique waddle. Then he took off his head gear, and they knew for sure it was him.

One wave of the arm, no words.

They lowered the back plate for the barrels to be rolled onto. The men seemed uncomfortable seeing Fat Joe. After all he was the supervisor, not someone who should be doing the work. Hurriedly, they took the barrels from him.

The push-and-pull of the air from the storm and his air tank were giving Alby a headache. The pounding of the rain competed with the ventilator for loudest sound.

"I can't believe that sonofabitch is dead." Fat Joe sounded like someone had given him a winning Lotto ticket.

Alby let out a breath that immediately fogged up his helmet. Hurriedly, he unzipped it and pulled it off. The air swept in, drying the sweat only to have the rain hit him, wiping all thought, feeling, and any doubt away—the storm took hold of his senses. For a moment, he felt dizzy and lightheaded.

Fat Joe's words broke into his distraction. "Guy just enjoyed killing people."

"What now?" Alby didn't want to think about the inherent hypocrisy of Fat Joe's statement, considering the bad things he had probably done for the same bosses.

"That's easy. I am going to tell them they all killed each other and that I put the check back." His face took on the ghostly hue of the parking lot lamp as he looked at Alby. "And you? You need to get the hell out of town. I don't ever want to see or hear from you again. They'll be looking for you, too. No one will like a loose end like you. All that leaves is Kurtz, that bastard."

As they left the dump truck and moved back toward the lobby, the wind seemed to exhale and wither. It was almost silent. Removing the hazmat suit in the rain wasn't easy. Luckily, Alby remembered his switch-blade before he tossed the suit. And he couldn't help but recognize the irony of the fact that what had once nearly killed him had just saved him. He kicked the suit to the curb, now just a fluffy white pile.

Then the air rushed in again, another wave of the storm—wet, hard, pushing at him and goading him. His clothes got soaked. The wind chilled his sweaty skin. He felt ragged but alive, even more beaten-up than before, aching in every bone and especially in his ribs.

And that was just fine.

The hard rain slapped him and told him he was alive, and it was good. He leaned forward to rest his hands on his knees and just breathed.

As he rested, with Fat Joe doing the same, a large black BMW sedan roared into the parking lot. Waves of water splashed. It drove past the lobby doors and stopped in the emergency lane at the loading dock they were at, missing them by a few yards. Fat Joe moved swiftly towards the man who got out, already wet in his overpriced leather jacket, wearing a black ball cap with an Eagles logo. He had a large leather briefcase with him, which he held tightly under his left arm. He looked up and down when he saw Alby and Fat Joe drawing near. He clearly knew Fat Joe.

"I— uh— I...."

"Kurtz, what the hell are you doing here?"

Fat Joe waved his hands as if nothing was wrong and the question had been asked in all innocence. Alby knew exactly what was going on. He followed Fat Joe to the driver's side of the car. As they drew nearer, Kurtz backed up as if he were going to get back in the car. Alby eyed the briefcase: here was Lucky's payoff.

Without thinking, he strode over to the banker and yanked the briefcase from his hand.

Slamming it onto the car hood, he unsnapped it open. The greedy wind immediately clawed its way in and grabbed the contents—money came flying out of the case. The banker grasped at it, practically screaming. With speed that surprised him, Alby snatched a $100 bill out of the air, pushed it into the briefcase, and slammed it shut, putting it down on the ground between him and Fat Joe. The few green bills the wind had grabbed were tossed onto the wet pavement, almost as if in disdain.

"You were going to pay them for returning the check." Alby really hated this guy. This was the jerk who must have started this mess. He reached for his knife. Fat Joe must have seen his move because he cleared his throat rather loudly.

"They didn't know what to do with the check!" Kurtz's tone was pathetic and desperate. "Some guy called me today and said to meet him here at one a.m."

"How much?" asked Fat Joe, but he had his eyes on Alby.

"Ten thousand."

"You're lying," Fat Joe said as he nodded at the briefcase.

"Okay, okay, fifty thousand." Kurtz looked scared to death. Without warning, he reached into his jacket—a lamp in the parking lot revealed his fingers wrapped around the silver handle of a gun. Fat Joe slowly shook his head no. Kurtz stopped. Alby gave him a once-over and spoke. "Go home. The check is in the safe."

"How —? Who the hell are you?"

Fat Joe just dismissed Kurtz with a wave of his hand. "We took care of it. We cleaned up your fucking mess."

Kurtz looked quizzically at Alby then it hit him. "Oh, right. Where is he?" The way he said it, Alby knew he meant Jagger.

Alby and Fat Joe just stared at him.

Alby couldn't resist. "Next time, lock it, would you?!" Just then the skies opened, and the rain pelted down in a painful deluge. Alby felt like nature had decided that enough was enough and was now pissing buckets on them. He didn't care. He felt alive. But the plastic covering the building didn't share his sentiments. The combination of the wind's fury and the rain's weight began to rip sections of it all along the exterior of the building. Everyone on break must have noticed the storm picking up and had come out of the lobby entrance to stand under the overhang and watch.

They saw the plastic ripping too. But then they saw Fat Joe and quickly went back inside.

"They all killed each other," Fat Joe said dismissively, as if it were just plain obvious.

"I'll look like an idiot!" the banker exclaimed, rain dripping down his face and coat. His baseball cap had already been blown off his head. Not the appropriate response, Alby thought sarcastically. It was still hard to believe it was this loser's one stupid mistake that had set all this off. All that fear. All those lives.

Then suddenly there was a flash of brilliant white lightning followed immediately by a roar of thunder and then a huge wrenching sound—like a giant cracking his knuckles five feet away. They all watched as a giant oak limb dropped full square on one of the four trailers. Fat Joe groaned. "Shit!"

Alby looked at this banker, his panic so childish that it was like watching a baby in pantomime, unable to use words but just looking angry and helpless all at once. He had to do it. Gun or no gun. Walking over, he slapped the guy's face so hard he fell back onto the car. "I'm taking the cash as the fee for making this the worst week of my life." The banker looked desperately at Fat Joe, who shrugged and, with a hint of a smile on his lips, said, "Believe me, the guy worked for it." Kurtz, his hands moving up and down, tried to say something—his lips were moving but nothing came out.

Fat Joe slowly lifted his right index finger to his lips and pressed it there: silence. The banker quickly turned to open his car door and get in. "I cannot believe you are doing this to me!"

"You're a stupid person. If I was a killer I'd kill you. Hell, I should do it for what you cost me this week," Alby said. It dawned on him that since his life here in South Jersey was about to end, what he did from now on didn't really matter. This time, he actually pulled out his switchblade and clicked it open. Kurtz screamed and scrambled into his car.

Fat Joe looked over at Alby and laughed wickedly. "You're pretty good with that knife!"

Alby ignored him and put away the knife. As he and Fat Joe watched, Kurtz and his BMW raced off in spite of the rain, maneuvering around empty barrels, now strewn and rolling across the lot like they were part of a driving skills test. Alby picked up the briefcase. It felt heavy. How much paper made it that heavy? Was it really $50,000? It had looked like more. He'd count it later, since he was pretty sure that at least every other word Kurtz said was a lie.

Alby and Fat Joe started walking back to his trailer. "What a fucking mess," Fat Joe moaned as he took in the damage.

By the time they got back inside the trailer, Alby felt like a wet cat, soaked in places he didn't know existed. He didn't even bother with his mask. Fat Joe took some paper towels and sat down, his ass making the spring in the chair squeal. He began to pat his face and hair dry.

Alby put the briefcase on one of the metal tables and opened it. Row upon row of $100 bills. He looked at Fat Joe.

He waved his hand dismissively, like he was pushing a bug aside. "I don't want any. They'd find out. I'd get out of town if I were you. I can cover my part, but you are going to have to deal with either the cops or the feds, or worse, the retired Owners in Florida on your ass. It's only a matter of time one of them gets to you." Alby realized for the hundredth time that week that Fat Joe was just as corrupt and dangerous as the rest of them, but tonight another side was showing its face. He had saved Alby. A part of him wanted to ask why, but he'd learned in Iraq that some questions don't have answers; sometimes people were one way and acted another—it made no sense: and that was that.

"You'll be okay?" he asked.

Fat Joe showed genuine surprise. He grunted. "Didn't know you cared. Yeah, I'm okay. I'm good at alibis. Lots of practice. I am shit glad to see that nasty fucker dead. We did a *lot* of people a favor." Fat Joe looked Alby up and down. "We're clear, right? I paid my debt." Then as a kind of afterthought, he added, "Hope you don't expect to get paid for the job."

This momentarily stopped Alby, but then he laughed quietly, nodding yes; Fat Joe joined in. It was like the air in a balloon that had been threatening to burst had quietly seeped out.

Then as if nothing had changed, Alby answered his question with a grin on his face, putting words to his nod. "Actually, I do."

"You got balls." But Fat Joe opened a worn-out, bulging wallet, and slowly counted out the money. "No crew. Helluva way to make a big profit."

Alby nodded and turned to go, then stopped. He pivoted around and stuck his hand out. "Thanks." Fat Joe took it and they shook in silence. Not many people had taken up handshaking again, even this far through the pandemics.

With that Alby stepped back outside, closing the door carefully so it wouldn't be ripped out of his hands by the wind. He ran to his truck. Once inside, he swung the briefcase on the seat next to him, took a deep breath—then a few dozen more—and just sat there. He jumped when a branch hit his windshield and then slid off.

The "what's next" question rang loud and clear in his head. He knew he had to go back to his place and face the music of the mess he'd left behind, which he was sure now included not just a broken screen door and blood stains but the cops, too, and he paused. Then, oddly, but not really when he thought about it, he heard Ginger's voice singing, "Pick yourself up!" He used his soggy sleeve to wipe off the fogged-up windshield, a river of rain rushing down the outside and blocking his sight. Then another branch hit his windshield, jolting him away from wherever his mind had just been heading. He reached for the key in his pocket and put it in the ignition. The engine turned over and he revved it as if that would shake off the rain. And then he took off. The storm seemed to push him onto the road.

Route 70 was chaos. It was whipped raw and full of debris from broken tree branches and in some places whole parts of their trunks. He exited the road, but as he drove up the service road, planning to enter the back parking lot area, it was hard not to notice the flashing police lights filling the whole space around the one-story building. Glancing at his watch, he saw that it was after two a.m. Stephen would be safe at the hospital. Some of the cops would be there with him, trying to get him to recount what had happened. But thankfully Stephen knew too little about what had really happened; and besides—Alby smiled—Stephen was a good liar.

He drove back out onto 70 and did a loop, coming from the opposite side so he could slip into the parking lot from the main road. Turning off his headlights and going into neutral, he rolled around to the front of the building, going to the farthest end until he faced the garage doors. Getting out, he went to the side door. He took out the key and quietly opened it. The roar of the storm rushed in and pushed its way past him.

From the street, a swinging streetlight cast dancing shadows over the back wall—he headed for the false panel. As he crept through the dark, knowing where the oil spills were, he put his ear to the panel. Muffled voices, at least two. Detectives was his best guess. Must be half-flooded in there with the door wide open.

He moved back and slowly peeled off all his soaked clothes; he knew the garage well enough to find the shelf to put them on to try and dry them. He waited in the dark, nude, thankful it was warm, shivering only slightly but feeling every section of his wet skin. He should have felt colder, but instead he felt alive. It felt familiar and strange at the same time—like the rain pelting him at the bank, it was as if someone had switched his senses on.

His mind was a different story, though. It only felt the familiarity of the pinball part of him, now bouncing from escape plan to turning himself in and then bouncing back again.

At the end of an hour, the voices grew fainter, the screen door slammed, and he heard car engines turn over. They passed by the garage but did not look around any corners and so did not see his truck. Patterned waves of wind and rain retreated to a murmur. Waiting five minutes—he literally counted to sixty, five times—he removed the panel. Reaching over and gathering his still wet clothes off the shelf, he climbed into the tub and pushed the shower curtain aside. All clear.

From the bathroom, he saw the chaos of the next room—chair turned over and crime scene tape everywhere, completely covering the doorway. He averted his eyes from the blood stains on the floor by the door. They had closed the main door, but the rain had already flooded half the room, completely ruining the carpet. He kept coming back to Stephen—no, he knew Stephen was okay. Probably over at Cooper Hospital charming the ladies.

The new Rule number one, he thought with a smile—always work with family; they have your back.

As he got dressed, he put whatever was left into the two duffle bags he'd packed before. Of course they would have gone through them… but, he thought, all to the good since he now could easily see that he had forgotten to pack his mask accessories and sanitizing gear. He noticed his laptop was gone: confiscated. Not much on it anyway. Of the many lessons Iraq had taught him, a very important one was that nothing was secret. If he—they?—were going to start a new life, cash was the most important thing. Taking his knife out, he walked over to the panel in the wall where he had stashed his hazard pay money from Iraq and using the tip, gently eased it away from the wall, once again grateful that the builders of this place had used cheap vertical wood panels on the inner walls of the room. He reached in and pulled out several thick, bound stacks of hundred-dollar bills. He'd put them there when he first arrived for a day just like today. He had forgotten how much he had. No matter. It filled another smaller duffel. Between this and Kurtz's "gift," he and Ginger might have enough to get away and be okay; he would add Kurtz's gift to his bitcoin account for safety.

Alby knew he did not have a lot of time. But he suddenly felt tired—it hit him hard and fast like a storm's gust. It was the kind of tired that starts in your bones and moves out to the rest of the body.

He stepped back through the shower and tossed the two duffle bags through. He went back and got his pillow and a blanket. Climbing back into the garage, he made a bed on the cement near his punching bag.

If he got up early enough he'd be okay. Go to Ginger's and call the Handlers. He glanced at his smartphone to see that it was quarter to three in the morning.

At six a.m. his cell phone rang and danced around on the cement floor by his head. He hadn't realized he'd fallen asleep. Groggily he put it to his ear, "Yeah."

"You were told not to draw any attention to yourself."

His Handlers. They beat him to it; how did they know he was in trouble so soon?

"Couldn't be helped." Like hell he was going to apologize to these assholes.

"Well, now we have to relocate you again. Can't have you showing up in court and the news and some sleeper cell comes for you—and bang! Jersey has so many Muslim sleeper cells they have bowling leagues!" He laughed but Alby didn't. "One more hero we couldn't protect, not the track record we like." Alby found it hard to believe the same guy who had been at his bedside in Baghdad was still his Handler. Alby was tired of being his pet.

"When do I leave?"

"Now."

He knew he had no choice. Starting to wake up, he realized that he had guessed right—his Handlers were handing him—them—the out he needed.

"We will have a car meet you at the Camden Aquarium at nine a.m. No goodbyes to anyone; the cops are looking for you." The man paused; his voice dropped: "You actually took down that guy? Then took the banker's money? Didn't know you had it in you." The Handler sounded impressed. From him, it sounded more like a panther expressing a compliment after being beaten to the prey.

Alby figured it out: Kurtz had turned him in…negotiated a deal with the feds to save himself and his family. A giant red flag went up. For a sniveling scumbag, Kurtz moved fast.

"You don't want to know what happened?"

There was a big sigh on the line, as if the man were speaking to a child. "We know enough. You're lucky we have a deal, or we'd leave you as dinner for any of the half-dozen entities looking for you."

"Can I bring anything?"

The phone went silent. "Hello?"

"Like what?"

"A woman."

"We only allow wives and you are not married."

Alby laughed, "Got you there—just did it the other night."

There was dead silence. The quiet of the Deeply Annoyed, thought Alby with a devilish grin. He was feeling his Irish as his mother used to say. He took the silence as a yes.

"Yes, I appreciate your good wishes. See you at eleven!" he said hurriedly and clicked off. Nine a.m. would never give them—would it be a them…would she come with him—enough time for her to pack and get them there.

He jumped up, brushed himself off, and then smiled, realizing that he had somehow integrated that line from the song into his brain so deeply that he was literally doing it.

He looked out through the window of the garage's side door. The rain had stopped but the parking lot and the main road were filled with deep pools of water and litter; the dawn sky was cast with the brilliant glow of storm-cleaned air. There were no cars to be seen. In spite of the fact that his life was about to be turned upside down—again—he felt good. Even though he'd only slept a few hours, there'd been no nightmares. Yeah, his ribs were aching, his shoulder was throbbing, and his ankle felt sore from the wrestling around, but it was all so minor; he simply couldn't believe that he was still alive. He opened the door and walked over to his truck, filling up his lungs with the early morning air as if he had never inhaled before. Unlocking the passenger side door, he stuffed the bags behind the front seat in the smaller second row of the cab. He started to go around to the driver's side door and then stopped.

The cave. He assessed. Leave no trail, his instincts told him; but his heart sought vengeance: Burn the prison down. For some reason that he could not and did not want to explain, he needed it gone. He got in his truck and moved it onto the side of the road. When he got back into the garage, he took a half-full can of car oil from the shelf and emptied its contents around the inside edges of the garage. He knew that the oil would take a lot longer to build up enough heat and flames, but there was a half-empty gas can sitting on the garage floor in the far back corner. He would have plenty of time to get out the door and in his truck before it erupted into a blowout. He found the matchbox that he kept on one of the shelves, lit a match, and dropped it as he turned and walked out the door, not waiting to watch the ring of fire start to spread. He raced to his waiting truck, ready to pull out onto the service road as fast as he could, and head for the entrance to Route 70.

Then he had a new thought. The cops would know it was arson—they'd even put him at the top of the suspect list—but who cared. They probably already had him down for theft, bank robbery, homicide, and much more. So he lifted his foot a bit off the gas pedal. No sense in getting into an accident now.

As he moved his truck more slowly towards the road, he could see small clouds of smoke coming out from under one of the two bay doors. He slowed even more as he passed them. Then he stopped. Through the glass panes at the top of the door, he could just make out the top of his punching bag hanging from its hook. The fire was mostly on the other side of the room, but it was spreading. The room was almost filled with smoke.

Without hesitating, Alby came to a stop, pulled a bandana out of the glove compartment, tied it around his face to cover his nose and mouth, got out of his truck, and ran for the side door. Taking as deep a breath as he could, he opened it. Smoke poured out. He ran over to the punching bag, put his arms around it in a big bear hug and lifted; then he suddenly worried that his rib scar would pop open. But he kept lifting anyway and unhooked it from the chain. For a second, he stumbled under its weight. But he regained his balance and wobbled out, finally taking in a breath and trying not to cough. He got back to his truck as fast as he could and heaved the bag into the back. He smiled and thought of his mom and drove away without a single look behind him.

Next, the money. He drove by Stephen's, looking for cop cars or an unmarked one. But whatever they might have gone looking for here, they'd either found it or given up and left. He pulled up next to Stephen's truck. Getting out, he walked to Stephen's driver's side fender and reached underneath—where he knew there'd be a spare key.

He went back into his truck, pulled the briefcase off the seat, and opened it. The money was still a little damp. Perfect. He reached under the front passenger side and grabbed a brown bag that he had stuffed there long ago. Gathering up what seemed to be about a third of the case, he put the cash in the bag. Then he closed the briefcase, took a black marker from his glove compartment, and wrote "ENJOY" in all caps on it.

He put the briefcase under the steering wheel on top of the gas pedal. Finally, he thought, I get to be an uncle, not an asshole. Then he paused in mid-congratulations. Well, maybe not—he did get Stephen shot. And the cops would ask him a thousand questions—but Stephen knew how to handle himself. Alby had to keep telling himself: he'll be fine. Maybe his FBI prick friend would help him. He relocked the truck door and put the key back where he had found it.

For the relocation, the Handlers would cover expenses and room and board but not much more. Standing there, he found himself staring at his truck. Ford F-150e. Less than two years old with little mileage and well-maintained. Well, there's no way I can take it…but he had registered it in Stephen's name. He turned around and looked at the punching bag lying in the back. Ginger would have stuff, too. Screw it. Anyway, he happened to like an engine that growled, even if it was saddled by the anemic follow-up of the electric battery.

He drove to the Gatewood Apartments complex. It was quiet. The parking lot was partially flooded. Branches, leaves, even a few yellow trashcans littered the area. There was her green CRV. He walked around to where her apartment was and went to the door. Everything still felt wet from the storm, even him—as if it had soaked him to the point where he couldn't shake the feeling.

This was it.

He rang her doorbell. No response. He waited two minutes, feeling his ribs start to ache, and rang again. Then he knocked. He heard her voice.

"Who the hell is that?" she shouted as she opened the door, holding the bat above her head. "Alby!" Then she just stared, her face registering belief and disbelief at the same time. "Is it done?"

Stepping in the doorway, he nodded. "I'll tell you all of it later. But yeah, somehow this whole mess—" He waved his hand in the air, the sentence hanging there incomplete.

"The check?"

"Back in the safe. Gone."

"As in—we're safe because it's gone?" He nodded, though on second thought he realized it wasn't exactly true. She was wearing a red, midlength robe, this one sheer, with pale silver silk pajamas underneath—how many of these things did she own? How could she afford such expensive stuff? She looked like a movie star from a bygone era. She sniffed. "Geez, what'd you do…Sleep outside? You smell like a dead cat." She sniffed again. "No, a barbecued dead cat. Did someone beat you up? Geez, someone did beat you up! Again!"

He couldn't tell if she was worried, disgusted, or joking. He looked at her more closely—it was all three.

He just smiled at her. She took a step back. They both stared at each other.

"I didn't know you could smile like that," she said slowly. Then she smiled back and pushed her rumpled red hair off her face. "Kind of suits you." Then she caught herself. "Even when you look like crap and smell like a forest fire."

"Thanks." And he decided just to go for it. "Doing anything special today?" He didn't wait for her to answer. "Run away with me."

The words came in rapid fire and hung in the air like brilliant beams of light. He grinned at her, feeling like all his teeth had decided to go on display just to show her how he felt. She turned her head sideways and shook it like she was trying to get water out of her ear. Then she turned back to face him, her eyebrows arched like the wings of sea gulls, as if she was silently asking herself a question. Then they gathered together into a furrow.

"What kind of trouble are you really in?"

"The best kind."

"Really?" she answered with a tinge of skepticism in her voice. "What kind is that?"

"Well…." He paused, weighing his words. "My Handlers are more powerful than the bad guys who are after me. If I leave town, they re-locate me—new city, new name, new life."

"Yeah? What is a 'Handler'?" This time there was no denying the skepticism. "You some kind of criminal?"

It had never occurred to him she would think that, but it made sense. "No, no, I'm actually a hero—no, not really, more a scapegoat, no, more—" She held up her hand for him to stop. He stopped.

"What happened?"

"Later. Can I come in?" She bowed and swung her arm wide, inviting him in.

Once they were both inside, she turned to him again and said, "You really are nuts."

"Ginger—run away with me." He said it quietly this time.

"But we talked about this. I hardly know you… and why are we running away anyway?" she asked, almost absentmindedly, looking still sleepy.

"My Handlers have to hide me somewhere. Like Witness Protection." She nodded as if it was all perfectly normal.

"Oh, boy, I need coffee." She shook her head, almost resigned. "You never stop surprising me." She laughed. "You must have had some helluva night. Do people just like beating you up? This isn't a pattern, is it?"

She paused and smiled, and though it was kind of a weak smile for her, he felt it. His adrenaline was fighting with exhaustion. He sat down on the couch and just let it all out; the entire night as it had happened. When he told her about discovering that the killer was her downstairs neighbor, she shivered visibly and her face went pale, but she remained silent. She sat on a kitchen chair facing him on the couch, her robe slipped off one knee. After he finished about setting the garage on fire, he just stopped. There was silence. She sat there, very still, her head now down. He could see that the one strand of hair in the back was standing out, despite her having run her hands through it. He wanted to brush it back but he knew he couldn't.

"Well, you certainly are thorough…." She said it as if her words made no sense given what he had said.

After what seemed to Alby like years, he heard, "Where are we going?" The words came out very slowly, and she wasn't looking up at him.

Then he exhaled, not realizing that he had been holding his breath for what seemed like years. He felt a smile grow on his face that was wider than the one where his teeth had taken over. "Wherever you want."

"So, what's the deal then?" She still wasn't looking at him.

"You have three hours to pack and then we go meet some official types and they relocate us to another part of the country." She nodded again like it all made sense. He could see she had pursed her lips. She again nodded, shrugged her shoulders, nodded once more, and then, finally, she looked up at him again.

"You're serious."

He rubbed his thumb and middle finger together. "And I have us covered—money will not be a problem wherever we go." She shrugged. "Money is not my issue." What was it with her and money? Now was not the time, he told himself, but he would eventually have to ask.

She sat still, not moving, now only half looking at him.

"I have to go, I have no choice." He paused, pleading for the first time in his life. "And you *have* to go with me."

"Have to?" She repeated his words slowly. He nodded. "Why? Because every law enforcement agency in New Jersey is looking for you?"

"I…." Now he was without words—tell the truth? The whole truth? What was the truth? "I have to go. And I want you to be in my life."

She puckered up her lips, and he could see mischief there. He started to have a good feeling again. "Nah, that's not it," she announced.

He wasn't sure what to say. Then it was suddenly clear: her entering his life had gotten him through the worst week of it. He had to get her to stay in it. So he tried a different tack—one that might ease the way for her to make this choice to go with him. "Ginger, you've moved around a lot, right? What's holding you here?"

"Oh yeah, that's true, but it's not a good enough reason. You're asking me to give this all up—" and she swept her arm across the room, "my life, my job. Just because you have to take off doesn't mean I have to." She was very matter-of-fact about it.

"That love thing." Saying the words was hard—it felt like squeezing a used tube of toothpaste for that last bit.

Suddenly slapping her hands together, she pointed her finger at him, like a cowboy pointing a gun: "Bingo. Boy, are you lucky you found a vagabond to love." He was shaking his head no, but she ignored him. "Okay, I'm in. Anyway, Cherry Hill wasn't panning out." What had he said? It was like a key found the right lock. The relief he felt made him glad that he was still sitting on the couch and he felt a smile tugging at his lips.

He felt so relieved that he even tried for a little humor. "Can we not use the word 'lucky' for a while?" After an annoyed glance, she shrugged and opened the door to the large closet in the living room. He looked in and saw a lot of boxes stacked inside. He realized she'd been waiting for him to come for her. Could his smile get any bigger? "Wow, you know how to stay prepared," he said admiringly. And then he realized that there would be enough room in the back of his truck if this was all she had. But he thought that he'd better not mention his punching bag in case she did have more. He didn't want to make her leave anything that she wanted behind. He just wanted her in the front of his truck, on their way out of here.

She ignored his comment, which surprised him. He was sure she'd react. "Where are we going?" she asked again. He shrugged. "If they're taking requests," she said, "I like hot."

"Hot works for me." He paused and then tried to figure out how to say the next thing. "Uh, one other thing…" his voice faded and he looked down. He didn't know what to say. So instead, he awkwardly pointed at the second finger of his left hand.

"Engaged?" she asked incredulously. When he kept pointing, her eyes got even wider: "Married? Are you nuts?"

He nodded. Now there was a much longer pause. She wouldn't look at him. He started to panic again.

"Hold on," he said. He took out his phone and clicked the number from his six a.m. wake-up call. "—and we want to go someplace warm," he added, finishing up all his demands.

He smiled as the Handler cursed, relented and then clicked off. "Everything is good. We have—" (he glanced at her MGM clock, still on the shelf) "—just a little more than two and a half hours."

"Where we going?"

"Cottonwood, Arizona. He said it's near Sedona. Ever been?"

"Really? It's been a long time." He saw a range of emotions cross her face, but then they resolved into a smile. "Huh. My stepbrother lives near there," she said dismissively, then a little worried, added, "Those crazy Secessionists and Neo-vaxxers are big there. That could be a problem." Wait, he thought, she had never mentioned a sibling. But before he could ask, she changed gears again.

"Hold on! Before we go another inch in this crazy game, a few rules." In response, she must have seen an open expression on his face, so she went on. "I still want to dance." She shook her head, uncombed red waves flopping out in a few more places. "I *need* to dance."

"I'll build you a studio. I just came into some money." Alby had no idea where that idea came from. But still, he lifted the duffel bag. She glanced at it curiously.

"Money…yeah, money…." She looked distracted. "Another time."

She got that determined look that he now had come to know, when her nose got pointy, but cute pointy not sharp pointy. "If we're going to be partners I want someone who can dance."

He didn't hesitate: "Not Zumba." Just saying the word made his tailbone ache.

"No," and then she did a little tap dance in her robe. "Tap. Or waltz."

He rubbed his chin, a little dazed, but he gamely agreed. "Okay." He pictured those black-and-white movies he had watched; those people could dance like they were on clouds.

"You have to promise you will try!" She seemed stern; he couldn't tell if she was serious. He nodded.

"Do I have to sleep with you? We're going away as a married couple and we've never had sex. I'm not so sure about that part. Don't get me wrong, Alby, you're a great kisser, but if you stink in bed, it's a deal breaker."

He smiled. "We don't have to meet them for—well, now it's just under two hours."

"Holy crap you have nerve! Is this whole 'let's-run-away' just an excuse to get me into bed?" She sounded irate but laughed as she said it. Suddenly she stepped forward and kissed him hard. So hard that the cut on his shoulder sang, the scar along his side joined in, and he felt that his whole world had just landed squarely in her arms in this living room at that exact moment. He was so surprised that he could only kiss her back standing stock still, his arms at his sides, helpless, like a mannequin. She pulled back, grabbed his collar with both hands, yanked him an inch towards her and looked him deeply in the eyes.

"What?" he finally asked.

"You're gonna have to work hard to get in my pants. I'm willing to take the leap, but on the sex thing, you have to give me a little time." She started counting off the fingers on her right hand. "And you smell. And you are beat up. And you have a cut on your shoulder. Then there's that outrageous scar on your side…." She smiled but looked confused. Then frowned. Then smiled, fully. "I don't know why, but something about you, Alby O'Brien…" and her voice faded.

"So, you're coming." He said it with finality.

"Let's get out of here." She volleyed back the same finality.

Then in that quixotic way she had about her, the part that both delighted and terrified him, she shook her head as if waking up. "Wait, wait, this is crazy… I must be nuts." It was like a light went on in her head. The light of reason, he thought, desperately trying to believe that he could still convince her. It all had just seemed right to him once he had figured it out. Now the blood rose in his ears. He could feel it flushing his cheeks. He was an idiot, but he couldn't back down now.

"Yeah, it *is* all crazy. I can't explain it right now, but it will all make sense soon." Last night, in the worst moments, she'd been on his mind more than any other person had been in a long time, and in a way that he couldn't explain. He was not going to leave her behind.

"Witness Protection? What did you do?"

"Iraq" was all he said. She pursed her lips. "Sure you weren't a bad guy?" He shook his head.

"Like I said. A good guy. Hero kind of." And in that moment, in a flash of realization, he suddenly knew that his Handlers had been right after all; he had a fleeting image of Ahmed's face as he had lunged at him: there was resolve and certainty that he knew exactly what he was doing. Alby had been set up. "Problem is the crazies want me."

"*This* is crazy." She stopped to think, scrunching up her nose. "Then don't we need new names?"

"Huh? Well, yeah, I guess we do!" She was on the ball.

"I'll take Rogers." She paused and said with self-satisfied joy: "Ginger Rogers." The smile she held was that of a little girl seeing her most fantastical dream come true.

He laughed. "Okay, you got me. I'll be Fred Astaire."

"Ha! I don't think so," she laughed derisively. "Not until you can actually dance do you get the honor of that name. You have to earn it. Fred you can keep. Rogers is the family now."

They laughed together. Then he stopped and looked aghast.

"My name is Fred Rogers? Like the guy who had the kids' show? Are you kidding?"

"Glad we got that settled." Ginger said, and brushed her hand down his sleeve casually, a caress.

"I have to finish packing." So there was more. She glanced at the MGM clock on her shelf of memorabilia. "When's our flight?"

"Uh… we're driving." Feeling like he'd better let it all go, he rushed on. "We meet them at the Camden Aquarium in—" He glanced at her clock. "In—"

"We're driving to Arizona?" There was a pause during which he did not respond or even dare to look at her.

And then miracle of miracles, his phone rang. They were calling back—a good thing because he had to inform them of their new names, which he knew would piss them off, since they probably had already started to "create" their new IDs—but also a bad thing…why were they calling him back? He decided to grab the upper hand while he could.

"Glad you called. We have the names that we want on our IDs. Ginger and Fred Rogers."

There was silence on the other end. But not for long. "Fred Rogers? As in Mr. Rogers? Okay." But he sounded confused. "Smash the phone and throw it away. No traces. Get rid of all personal belongings. This time, you really disappear." And the connection ended. Alby stepped outside Ginger's door, dropped the phone on the ground, and smashed it under his heel. He picked up the pieces and tossed them into the parking lot among the trash of trees' limbs and the puddles.

"Now that felt good. Hate those phones." He looked at her: "Ready to pack the truck?"

"Wait—what about my car?" She seemed genuinely concerned, then like a switch went off: "Who cares. Thing was falling apart."

Then she did a little tap dance—two feet, multiple movements—and said, "When things got tough, you know what Fred and Ginger said?"

He hadn't a clue. Clearly his face said that.

Picking up her iPhone off the table, she tapped a little then held it up as the tinny, 1930s music she'd played in the studio rang out.

As she sang along, she punctuated each line with a tap dance gesture of her feet.

"Nothing's impossible, that I have found.

But when my chin is on the ground. I pick myself up,'" she did a flourish, "Dust myself off...." She did another series of faster taps... "and?" she asked. He was completely bewitched by her. Having spent Friday watching the video clip of this song, her performance was amazingly close to Ginger Rogers' screen version.

"And start all over again!" She did a few more taps, spun once, and drew to a dramatic close, throwing out her arms. "That's called the 'sham.'"

"Sham," he repeated. Then he laughed; he had never seen anything so dumb and cute at the same time in his life. "Pick yourself up?" He sang lightly, happy to see her nod her acceptance, tapping one foot.

"You have a good voice!"

"Dust yourself off?" He placed his right toe on the metal door frame to give it a tapping sound. It rapped. She held out her arms and he took her outstretched hands.

They sang together, "And start all over again!" She seemed sur-

* *(Listen: evenapandemic.com/pickyourselfup)*

prised. "Hey, you can sing!"

As he laughed, he pulled her close; she pushed him away. She pointed her arm straight out towards the bathroom. "I pack. You get cleaned up. Not the red towels!" She repeated slowly with emphasis: "Not the red towels: never, they're mine." He walked over to the bathroom door and turned. She had found a box and was starting to wrap her MGM clock in some towels. She seemed busy but suddenly looked up at him and waved, as if to say, "Hop to it!"

As he went into the bathroom, he heard her yell, "Glad I travel light. But still, thank God, you have a truck with two rows. Where am I going to put my 'The Barkleys of Broadway' picture?" As he turned on the shower, her voice faded. The water fell like slivers piercing his skin—every square inch of his body hurt—and at the same time it felt great, like he had just discovered what a shower was for.

Glancing around, he felt like he had landed on another planet . This was a woman's shower—clean, full of light, lined with products he had no idea did what. As he scrubbed with her lavender soap, he felt a world of scents and sensations seeping in—things that he'd long forgotten or had been cut off from or that he'd never even had. Now it was here. He was leaving the colorless, scentless world behind.

She peeked her head around the bathroom door, "Road trip, Mr. Rogers!"

Alby—Fred—realized that he was in for it now.

He was going to need a whole new set of Rules.

Epilogue
Saturday: Early Morning

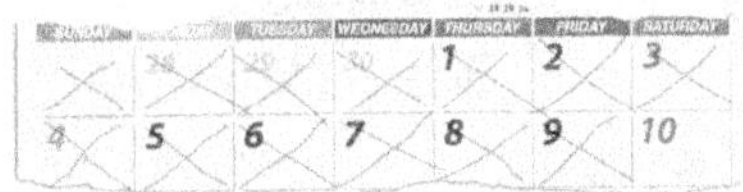

Back at the site, the sun had started to dry the pools of water in the back of a truck that had been abandoned in the storm. Even though the nor'easter wind was gone, one barrel started swaying back and forth. It rocked seemingly of its own power, pushed by a wind all its own. Finally, it fell over and the lid popped off and rolled away. The sounds of gasping and coughing filled the air but there was no one there to hear it. A head burst out of the barrel, followed by the rest of the body. Jagger's breathing sounded like a seal with whooping cough. It was loud and labored, jagged, like pieces of his lung were breaking off—and had there been anyone listening, they probably would have figured that it was causing a lot of pain. For a moment, Jagger just lay there on the floor of the truck bed, on his back, mind blank. Looking down, he saw the blood oozing through the chest area of the hazmat suit and realized his specially tailored gray Kevlar suit had done what it was supposed to do—it had kept the knife from going deep down into his chest. Normally, he would take a moment to appreciate when anything performed as it should. But this was not completely true— the knife had still gone in. He was in deep pain and bleeding.

He didn't feel so happy about himself either. "Amateur." Jagger had won—the check was returned—but failed. Failure was worse than winning. A first. And a loser did it to him. Jagger could barely fathom how such a thing had happened.

He crawled from the barrels to a wall. Propping himself up, he cleared his throat, ignoring the feeling that something was very, very wrong in his lungs, and called The Owners.

"It's done." He could not hold back a sudden hacking cough attack, and during the minute until it subsided there was silence on the other end. Then they spoke: "We thought you were dead. You are now on leave. You were sloppy. Cocky. Go back. Rest. You will hear from us." The connection went dead. He didn't like their answer; *he* could be a target now.

Clearly, Fat Joe had told them the whole story already. As he stared at the parking lot, he saw Fat Joe's gold Lincoln. Struggling to get up, he wobbled his way towards it. He made his way to the car, then pulled himself along the back panel and opened the back door. He slid in, almost collapsing onto the floor padding.

Jagger tried to stay focused. There was no way he would be getting on their private jet after *that* conversation.

The front door opened and Fat Joe hit the seat cushion so hard it almost bumped into Jagger's head. He turned the key in the ignition and gracefully slid the Lincoln out of the parking spot—not a branch had hit it—and started to hum off-key.

"Fat Joe…" Jagger said with just the right level of control to freeze Fat Joe's blood. He hit the brakes, partway into the intersection.

"Jagger?" Fear and surprise ran rampant in his voice. "How the hell are you still alive?"

"You are driving me to Arizona…Phoenix. Once we are there, you're free."

Saturday: 11 a.m.

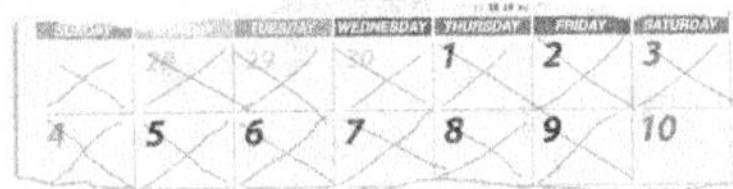

After they had met the Handlers by the Camden Aquarium and had been given their new identities, driver's licenses, Social Security numbers, phones, cash, and instructions, and had endured being basically yelled at for all the trouble he'd caused them, he and Ginger had turned around and robotically walked over to his truck, supposedly to begin their drive to the Benjamin Franklin Bridge, use the Vine Street Expressway since it was the only major artery open, and head west as fast as they could. However, as she was getting in, Ginger glanced back—Alby was just putting the key in the ignition. But that didn't seem to matter to her. She suddenly ducked her head back out the door, jumped back down to the ground, and slammed the door behind her. The next thing he knew, she was stomping over to where the Handlers were still standing by their car.

Alby took a deep breath, then he jumped out. At that point, she was already in the main Handler's face. "Who are you to judge us? You got a lot of balls and if I had my bat I'd whack you one right now!"

Alby was confused—what had he missed? She looked ready to punch the guy. Her face was red, only one shade lighter than her hair. He had seen this in the diner with that crazy Jagger.

"It's none of our business that you only met a week ago and now you're married." But clearly, the guy's sarcastic tone said just the opposite.

"You have any idea the shit he took on back there?" She pointed at Alby but kept her eyes on the Handler. "Didn't he take down something you guys needed taken down? The bank? Mob? Bad guy?"

"We're not in the criminal division, lady. Our focus is protection. Stopping shitstorms."

Ginger slammed her foot down in fury. The two black-suited clichés looked around like no one was there, blithely checking their nails. Then one of them said as if to no one in particular, "Gotta go. Late for church."

And with that, they hopped back into their large electric Chevy Kite—black, of course, she noted—and took off.

Ginger turned to Alby. Her look said it all, conveying both a question and a statement—Alby, you create shitstorms. She'd had it.

"It's a long ride, Alby. A whole lot of open road. You'd have plenty of time to lay it all out. Everything." She waved her left hand like she held a magic wand. " Everything underneath that tortoise shell you're wearing. All out."

Alby fired right back: "Both ways?"

"No," she said instantly, like she had expected his response. "You're the one who dragged me away, and it's up to you to do your best to convince me my instincts about you are right." And there was an "or else" that lingered in her words.

Alby just stood there, silently. He didn't know what to do. She had unloaded a lot in one sentence. But he could see that Ginger was growing impatient. And so he expected her to let him have it even more. But she surprised him. "Yeah, I'll talk, too," she sighed. "Hell, you'll probably clam up so I'll have to. I'll need to speak just to stay awake."

He moved the truck out of the lot towards the Ben Franklin Bridge and the vax screeners. She watched as he looked straight ahead with laser-like focus on the road, also noticing that he was occasionally giving her side glances, which she did not respond to. Was he having regrets? She could tell him to pull over now and she'd be back at her apartment in an hour. But he looked like he was wrestling with himself. So she just remained silent.

Ginger knew crazy—even Stephen's bitch girlfriend wasn't the kind of crazy that she was talking about. But this was getting near it. And yet, it wasn't. She had always had great instincts, and knew that Jersey had been a flat tire experience. It had just taken Alby asking her to leave to make her admit it. The studio owner wanted to cut her hourly rate; the two diners—well, one—since she had been fired from the other—let's say that she now had sympathy for people who worked in the food service. Customers were assholes.

This was not unfamiliar territory. Between her parents at sea and her grandparents in Ohio, she had always felt like she didn't have a home. She almost wondered if she was not meant to ever have a home. Odd turns had happened throughout her life, but they had always worked out. Maybe not the way she thought they would, but she had been lucky. She knew it. After taking her mother's ashes up to that church in Queens that scatters them at sea, or as close to the sea as the New York Bight could get them, she just took her used Honda and just drove, numb. She had already packed her car with everything she wanted and all she'd had to do was that one last thing. Back to the sea, mom, she thought as she crossed the George Washington Bridge.

But the farther she had driven away from the church on the ride back, the more agitated she had become. She had been living in Manhattan, her Brooklyn studio doing well. With the first two waves of Covid, the whole dance studio business and situation went from blessing to bust—and fast. Then from out of nowhere, getting the call from her stepbrother Eddie that Mom had died from the virus; her bad heart made it sudden. Ginger thought she was okay, she had made it this far in the pandemic. Having been there only a few months earlier, as difficult a relationship as she had with her mother, Ginger couldn't shake the guilt: she should have been there, done more, something. It just happened too fast. For a second, she thought of asking her stepbrother if he was vaxxed, but why bother. They had gone this long without talking about it.

Her mother's last wish was using the Neptune Society to scatter her ashes at sea, specifically the Atlantic where she had spent so much of her life.

It all came at Ginger's head at once.

Dropping off her mom's ashes at a church in Queens, meant that for Ginger, it was time to start over. Again. That was her curse and gift: always starting over and being really good at it. Never getting it right. Rinse and repeat. She saw an ad for a dance instructor in Marlton, New Jersey—she had no idea what to expect, but she liked the East Coast.

Now Alby. She looked over at him. She had looked at a lot of men in her 40 years—she recalled having had a boyfriend even as a five-year-old. But Alby was different; he was broken, like many she had known, but yet not. It was like he had needed oxygen or water and was finally getting some.

"76 to…?"

She came back to the firm seat, the growling engine, the movement on the highway, and turned toward him. "Yes, to 276 West for Pittsburgh…." The iPad slipped, but she grabbed it before it hit the floor.

"What?"

"What what?" she retorted.

"You're looking at me weird."

"So?" She had to call him out—what the hell was normal to him? Was there anything normal in what she knew about this Alby? Yeah, he fixed houses. Nothing weird about that. But meanwhile, the week they meet, he fights thieves, a killer, the mob, and he was alive to tell the story. Not so normal.

"So why are you looking at me weird?"

He hadn't been this demanding before. But the answer was simple. "You think all this is normal? We don't even know each other and we're supposedly married?" She shook her head thinking about it. "The government has documents saying you're my husband?" She took a long pause. "Unbelievable."

She didn't want to tell him what she was really thinking about: him.

He kept his eyes on the road.

She switched modes. "276 in about ten minutes. West."

He gave a crisp nod like she had given an order.

The cataloguing, which she had begun after the dance disaster in the parking lot, picked up again. She knew four things for sure about Alby:

He knew right from wrong.
Was tough as hell.
Was broken.
Was a sap. (Momma's boy, she'd bet.)
And she suspected a fifth: he was falling in love with her.

It was a good list. She closed her eyes briefly and one thought flitted through her mind: a partner. She could make this work.

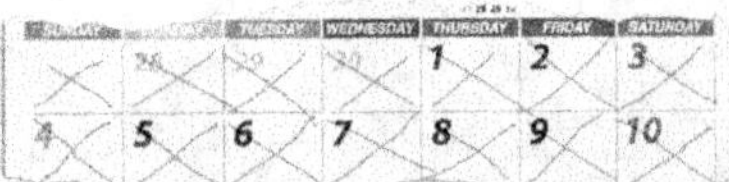